Secrets of Sant'Angelo

Secrets of Sant'Angelo

JEFF SHAPIRO

BERKLEY BOOKS, NEW YORK

THE BERKLEY PUBLISHING GROUP
Published by the Penguin Group
Penguin Group (USA) Inc.
375 Hudson Street, New York, New York 10014, USA
Penguin Group (Canada), 10 Alcorn Avenue, Toronto, Ontario M4V 3B2, Canada
(a division of Pearson Penguin Canada Inc.)
Penguin Books Ltd., 80 Strand, London WC2R 0RL, England
Penguin Group Ireland, 25 St. Stephen's Green, Dublin 2, Ireland
(a division of Penguin Books, Ltd.)
Penguin Group (Australia), 250 Camberwell Road, Camberwell, Victoria 3124, Australia
(a division of Pearson Australia Group Pty. Ltd.)
Penguin Books India Pvt. Ltd., 11 Community Centre, Panchsheel Park, New Delhi—110 017,
India
Penguin Group (NZ), Cnr. Airborne and Rosedale Roads, Albany, Auckland 1310, New
Zealand
(a division of Pearson New Zealand Ltd.)
Penguin Books (South Africa) (Pty.) Ltd., 24 Sturdee Avenue, Rosebank, Johannesburg 2196,
South Africa

Penguin Books Ltd., Registered Offices: 80 Strand, London, WC2R 0RL, England

This book is an original publication of The Berkley Publishing Group

This is a work of fiction. Names, characters, places, and incidents either are the product of the author's imagination or are used fictitiously, and any resemblance to actual persons, living or dead, business establishments, events, or locales is entirely coincidental.

First edition: January 2005

Library of Congress Cataloging-in-Publication Data

Shapiro, Jeff.
  Secrets of Sant'Angelo / Jeff Shapiro.—1st ed.
    p. cm.
  ISBN 0-425-20104-X
1. Tuscany (Italy)—Fiction. 2. City and town life—Fiction. I. Title.

  PS3569.H34119S43   2005
  813'.54—dc22   2004052975

PRINTED IN THE UNITED STATES OF AMERICA

10 9 8 7 6 5 4 3 2 1

An Italian adage states, *Di mamma ce n'è una sola*—As for mothers, you've only got one.

This book is dedicated to mine, Ruth Shapiro, with love.

Acknowledgments

Many heartfelt thanks to Linda Chester and Bob Levine, my agents, and to Leona Nevler, my editor at The Berkley Publishing Group, for their guidance, criticism, and, most of all, for their faith in this book. Working with them reminds me what *good* fortune means. And thanks to Anita Waxman for her amazing talents as matchmaker.

Kyra Ryan, in making suggestions during the preparation of the manuscript, proved herself judicious, intelligent, sensitive, creative. I would continue the list of laudatory adjectives, but Kyra would start to find the language overly descriptive. Thank you, Kyra.

Thanks to Dr. Senatro Izzo from the Department of Earth Sciences at the University of Siena for providing invaluable research material on earthquakes in the province of Siena, and to Dr. Marco Cristofori for the many discussions on sheep maladies. Thanks to my brother, Barry Shapiro, for his insights into some key concepts of Eastern philosophy, and to Francesco Stori for his help with Latin phraseology.

Thanks to Vincenzo Vullo, Antonio Morelli, Giuseppe Baldesi, Silvio Segantini, and Raffaele Puccianti, the musical conductors under whose patient batons I've had the pleasure of singing and playing in amateur choruses and bands. I hope the exasperated conductor in this book makes them smile.

Thanks to friends and family members—Sharon Hallgrimson; Michael Quick; Jerry Epstein; Frank Avruch; my aunt, Ellen Dokton; my uncle, Tom

Dokton; my sister, Suzan Ushman; my brother-in-law, Wayne Ushman; my mother, Ruth Shapiro; my mother-in-law, Luisa Crema—who demonstrated their skills as insightful readers, listeners, and critics while together we talked through puzzles that the writing posed.

Grateful thanks and tears of loss to two much-loved friends, Enzo Cappelli and Ziggy Horowitz.

Thanks to inexhaustible wells of inspiration, Renato Bernini and Giovanni Cappelli. Daily they show how great an adventure human existence can be.

And infinite thanks to the woman who, having read every word of the manuscript some five or six times, let this book become as much a part of her as it is of me. Valeria Indice, my wife. She makes writing, like everything else, an act of love. "... *Ita desiderat anima mea ad te.*"

Faced with a reality which lies beyond opposite concepts, physicists and mystics have to adopt a special way of thinking, where the mind is not fixed in the rigid framework of classical logic, but keeps moving and changing its viewpoint.
—Fritjof Capra, *The Tao of Physics*

Ognuno ha il suo diavolo all'uscio—
Everyone has his own devil at the door.
—Tuscan proverb

Prologue

"*Prendila con filosofia*" is the Tuscan response to just about every worm-devoured fruit in the garden of life. "Take it with philosophy"—philosophy meaning patience, perspective, a pinch of humor. Walk through a Tuscan town during a thunderstorm, complain to a local about the wet weather, and the Tuscan, shrugging, will answer with words that understate the deluge: "Too dry it isn't. That's for sure."

Philosophy takes the edge off everyday mishaps: flat tires, railway strikes, food that burns and sticks to the cooking pot. When love affairs run out of passion, when disappointed dreams die, philosophy eases heartache. To make a Tuscan lose his philosophy, things would have to be bad—very bad for a very long time. One season, half an hour's train ride south of Siena in the small Italian town of Sant'Angelo D'Asso, things turned bad.

In the beginning there was the rain. Too much of it. Rain without pause for all of the autumn months. It waterlogged the grain on the hills and soaked the sheep until their wool stank. The harvest of swollen, tasteless grapes depressed everyone. People picked moldy olives from miserable trees. The year's oil and wine thrilled no tongue.

"A bad year," said Renato Tizzoni, the town Waterworks man, as he leaned back in his chair at the bottega.

Renato's father-in-law, Tonino, owner of the shop, replied with philosophy. "A good year," he said, "it isn't."

Townspeople could not remember the last time they had seen the sun, and its absence left them as glum as if they had lost the affection of an old friend. Destructive as the weather proved to be, however, only the most alarmist would think it had been sent by an evil source.

Then, with the onset of winter, came debilitating influenza. This year's bout killed three old women and one old man, reducing the town's population to one thousand, two hundred and eighty-nine. Sculati the gravedigger preferred drinking grappa to burying the dead. The extra digging made his back ache.

"What can you do?" men and women tutted to each other at the baker's and at Il Piccino's newspaper shop and at the butcher's run by Mauro Giannetti. They swapped an old aphorism, as if folk wisdom had comfort to give. "Fortune is blind," they said, "but misfortune sees us all too clearly."

Mauro the butcher, who had settled into permanent unpleasantness ever since his wife died of clogged arteries five years back, laughed when he heard talk that the influenza had taken four lives. "Could have been worse," he said. "Could have been me." Though no one wished the town butcher dead, few would have minded if misfortune saw fit to remove the sarcastic smirk from Mauro Giannetti's face.

Talk gives birth to more talk. Passing from mouth to mouth, talk of misfortune began, finally, to veer toward the language of ill destiny: *sfortuna, sculo, sfiga, iella, disgrazia, malocchio*. Whatever the word people chose, the meaning was the same: bad luck.

The bad luck infected the town, moving like the influenza. Its early victims were few; then the contagion spread. Soon, everyone had a story to swap.

Tongues fluttered when *sfortuna* came to Signora Porcelli, whose house faced the main street. One gray day, the gray-haired woman squatted, about to sit on her bidet for her morning wash. Her watery eyes focused just in time—thank God!—to see there in the white porcelain basin a scorpion brandish its sharp tail. Pulling up her underclothes, Signora Porcelli quivered to think where it might have stung her. Scorpions, local lore held, were the messengers of worse things to come.

Collecting her courage, she reached for the faucet and released a flood of water to rinse the beast down the drain. For fear that it might crawl back up, she decided to do without her wash. Feeling unclean, she took a bag of stale bread outside to the henhouse in her dead patch of kitchen garden. She smiled when she saw a consoling presence at last—her cat poised to pounce on a mouse foolish enough to venture from the building's basement. "Good kitty," she said. "You kill that mouse." She crumbled the bread and threw handfuls in through the door of the henhouse. Her pretty cat, at least, would protect her from small creatures that might creep in to do her harm. She loved the cat fiercely, the way some people love a child. There had never been a child in Signora Porcelli's long life; neither had there ever been a man. The cat gave her company in bed. When it purred beneath the covers, she hugged it to her heart.

"Good kitty," she said again, then watched helplessly as a falcon swooped from the sky, stabbed its talons into the soft fur of the cat's throat, and flew off with its mewling prey. The mouse turned quickly back to the basement. Signora Porcelli put her hands to her mouth to smother a sob as terrible wide wings carried away her beloved companion.

"Bad luck," old women said in the shops afterward. "Or maybe something worse. Could it be that someone has put us under a curse?"

People resist terror with differing degrees of vigor. There are those who refuse to believe that the problem exists. More impressionable types think about nothing but the problem, until it grows big enough in their minds to block out the rest of the world. Cynics laugh. The nervous by nature start to tremble, the pious to pray.

Thoughts of curses did not capture the imagination of Petula Tizzoni, daughter of the Waterworks man. Daily responsibilities required all her strength. She and Daniele Mangiavacchi had the bar at the train station to run and their six-year-old son, Beniamino, to raise. Petula did not seek to unravel the mysteries of fortune, good or bad. Navigating Daniele's moods kept her busy enough.

Petula's mother, Milena, watched the young couple with growing anxiety. Whenever she spotted a certain look of tension in Petula's eyes—and lately she detected the look a lot—she sought the middle path between saying too much and saying too little. Why, Milena wondered, couldn't her husband, Renato, find a way to speak to Daniele on Petula's behalf?

"And do you think Petula would thank me for interfering?" was Renato's reply. "I'm as worried as you are, but the girl has always been more headstrong than you and me put together. What can we do?" Renato did not look for otherworldly causes for the town's bad luck. He just wanted his daughter to be happy.

By contrast, Marta Sorcini—a widow with gray hair tinted violet as if to beautify the snakes' nest of restless apprehensions that her brain had become—almost welcomed talk of troubles. Secretly she liked the notion that a curse had befallen her. This way she could lie awake beneath her flannel sheets and aim her frantic thoughts against something more than simple loneliness.

The religious-minded in town took the idea of being cursed by bad luck more seriously than others. Convinced that they were God's favorites, they found it logical that the forces of evil would seek them out, too. They mustered prayers for protection. History had largely overlooked Sant'Angelo, the early Christian mystic who had lived in a cave by the river until the Roman pagans made a martyr of him. Seven years ago the Pope, in response to a local plea for intervention, claimed the saint's cave as Church property—stopping the building of the dam that would have eradicated the town. People's gratitude went to the Pope, not to the saint. But now Sant'Angelo, his withered finger preserved in a glass globe in the church, received an unprecedented flurry of prayers to intercede with the Greater Powers.

———

Influenza was bad enough, but the second Sunday in December brought a death so bizarre that everyone became aware of the precariousness of their little lives.

On Sunday morning, Adalpina, the thick-necked wife of the retired streetsweeper, went to pick mushrooms in a small forest that darkened the groin between two soft hills. Rain had ruined just about everything, but at least, Adalpina figured, the damp would make the mushrooms good. A picker since girlhood, Adalpina concentrated like a hunting dog while poking a stick through the dead leaves on the forest floor. Her eyes sighted a growth of golden fungal flesh. A porcino, she was almost sure, and her toothless mouth began to water as she imagined the pastas and soups she would prepare with it. But as she stooped to inspect the mushroom, a young viper fell from a tree branch above and slipped between her jacket collar and her skin. Adalpina's screams frightened the serpent. No viper likes to be trapped inside a screaming woman's clothes. The snake slithered some, then, finding no escape, defended itself with its fangs.

A young and healthy heart, after a viper bite, can usually hold out until the victim reaches a doctor, but Adalpina's heart was neither young nor healthy. Her neighbors did not find her body in the woods until Tuesday.

The population of Sant'Angelo D'Asso now numbered one thousand, two hundred and eighty-eight. Sculati had another grave to dig.

"It happens," men told each other at the bar with a shrug. "Vipers leave their young in the trees, and the little ones have just as much poison as their mammas. Sometimes they fall. Just bad luck if you're underneath when they come down." But, truth be told, no one could recall any similar death.

During Adalpina's funeral, the church air heavy with the mournful smell of carnation wreaths, men and women stared wide-eyed at her coffin, listening to their mortality ticking away like a tightly wound clock. Philosophy be damned. Sant'Angelo D'Asso could not shake its unease. The superstitious had evidence to prove their worst suspicions; even the more rational could not explain fortune's aberrant contortions. Bad luck was upon the town without doubt, and the people dreaded to think when it would strike next.

1

Locking the door to the Sant'Angelo D'Asso pumphouse, Cappelli, the assistant Waterworks man, blinked at the bright sky. Crazy, he thought. This was the fifty-third December he had seen in his life, but a December day as hot as today, never.

After months of rain, an unexpectedly brilliant sun burned the morning. Cappelli sweated inside his clothes. Only the strings of festive lights and tinselly decorations strewn everywhere showed that Christmas was little more than a week away. The air was strangely alive.

But Cappelli was not one to dwell on strangeness, and the talk about bad luck and curses hardly penetrated deeper than the hair around his earholes. Across the pumphouse parking lot Cappelli could see the train tracks and the station. Thinking of the station, he thought of the station's bar. Thinking of the bar, he thought of coffee. *Un caffè*, he decided. Coffee corrected with a nice little drop of liqueur. Not a bad idea.

Music from the radio and the sharp invitation of espresso wafted through the open door of the station bar.

The aroma reaching his nose, Cappelli mumbled a contented sound, as if the coffee were already on his tongue. "Oh, Petula!" He stepped into the bar and blocked the doorway. "Will you make me a coffee?"

Petula looked up from behind the counter. "Signor Cappelli, *ciao!* A coffee right away."

"Corrected with some of that sambuca of yours," Cappelli said. Petula always made him welcome. Ever since she was a little girl she had called him *signor,* though Petula was, officially speaking, the daughter of Cappelli's boss. *Signor* she called him in any case, a nice gesture of courtesy, a sign that she had been raised right.

"Buongiorno," Cappelli said to Daniele, who was busy cleaning the bar with a sponge.

"Good day, is it?" Daniele did not lift his eyes from a crusty food crumb that stuck to the countertop. "Too early to say. We'll see." He attacked the crumb with his thumbnail.

Daniele, Cappelli could tell, was in another of his moods. The young man could light the place with his smile when he had one, but when he was in a mood every part of him went dark. Dark hair, dark eyes, sullen cheeks.

The announcer's voice on the radio introduced the next number: an oldie from when Cappelli was young. Then the sweet-voiced singer glided his way into a song of impossible love.

Cappelli looked away from Daniele and watched Petula. With the practiced movements of someone who has been working in a bar for years, the pretty young woman made his coffee and topped it off with sambuca liqueur.

"On your way somewhere?" She put the coffee before him.

He inhaled the good smell. "And where should I be going?" The first sip almost burned his mouth while his tastebuds soaked in the anise sweetness of the sambuca.

Petula tilted her head in the direction of the train station platform just outside the open door.

"Ah. No. Not taking a train anywhere. I'm working alone today. Your father didn't turn up, so I came to the pumphouse on my own. Not much going on this morning. Gave myself a coffee break." He and Petula exchanged a smile of complicity, both of them knowing well that Cappelli was infinitely creative when it came to thinking up reasons to take a break.

"Babbo didn't come to work? He hasn't got sick, has he? It's hard to believe how many people are laid up in bed."

"He's your father, not mine."

She refilled a sugar shaker while she spoke, her hands always finding something useful to do. "You think my parents tell me everything that goes on in their house?"

"Your dear babbo didn't get sick. It's his sheep who feels like death. Your father was worried. Took the morning off." He sipped more coffee. "Who would stay home from work just to look after some poor beast? Only Renato, *Madonna bona*. Only that father of yours."

"Will you squeeze me some orange juice?" another customer called from down the bar.

"Only my babbo," Petula repeated. "Cares about his sheep like family members." She went to take care of the orange juice order.

The last of his coffee poured down his throat, Cappelli focused his eyes on the bottles behind the bar. Which enticing liquid would enhance, not spoil, the flavor of sambuca on his tongue? Cognac, maybe. Whisky? Grappa? Or maybe more sambuca. Why ruin a good taste?

"Oh!" Cappelli said, to get attention.

Seeing that Petula was busy pressing orange halves into the juicer, Daniele stopped sponging the counter and came to serve. "So, Cappelli?" Daniele said.

"So," was the answer. "So instead of just standing there, how about getting me the refill of what I just had?"

"Coffee with sambuca?"

"*Sì*. Same again. This time without the coffee. Too much coffee hurts the organism, so they say." His hands traced the outline of his middle-aged belly. He raised his eyebrows modestly yet proudly, as if his shape might actually be a reason for pride.

His drink before him, Cappelli swallowed half the glass in one gulp. A small hunger for conversation came over him. "So," he said to Daniele. "How's it going?"

"How's it going?" the young man shot back. "Dangerous question. Ask me how it's going, I might just tell you. It goes the way it goes. Yesterday I was here in the bar working. Today I'm in the bar working. Care to guess where I'll be tomorrow and the day after? One day off for Christmas. That's all we'll get. I'll tell you, with so much work, I've got two balls that are—"

Cappelli laughed. "You're too young to complain about your balls being broken by work. How old are you anyway?"

"Twenty-four."

"Twenty-four! *Madonna sozza!* Twenty-four and you talk as if you've been at it a lifetime." Calling the Madonna filthy had no meaning for Cappelli. Blasphemous syllables came out of his lips as thoughtlessly as sambuca went in, adding, if anything, emphatic punctuation to his speech. "It's only been five years since you took over the bar from your parents—"

"Seven," Daniele interrupted. "Seven years since my father just couldn't wait to pass someone on the highway, could he? Had to bully his way around a car and straight into a truck, same way as he bullied his way through everything. What difference did it make if he killed himself and my mother in the process? Who lost anything but me?"

"—seven years ago," Cappelli continued, refusing to let details stand in the way of the point he was trying to make, "but every day of those seven years you have this beautiful girl here beside you working twice as hard as you while you stand around and stuff the money away. Seven little years of this, and your balls are broken?" He scratched rough stubble on his gray chin. "When I was twenty-four, I had already worked twice as many years as you, and I still haven't stopped, *porca miseria*. Still haven't stopped."

"It's different when you have a kid at home." Daniele was not about to be made ridiculous for complaining. And he suspected rightly that he prodded a sensitive nerve when he mentioned children to a man who had never had any. "When you have a kid—" Daniele snorted manfully. His eyes fixed on Cappelli's glass of sambuca and he drifted away in contemplation. A moment later his mind returned and his face had changed from belligerence to defeat. "When you have a kid, your life isn't yours anymore. You can't just say, 'I want to go somewhere new tomorrow' and *fffftttt*, off you go. You have to say, 'Doesn't matter what I want.' Some days nothing would make me happier than hopping on a train myself and letting it take me wherever it happens to go."

Cappelli saw how young indeed the young man was. "But having a kid repays you in other ways, too, I guess. Doesn't it?"

Daniele lit himself a cigarette. "You think Beniamino notices what we do for him? He's thinking about the presents he wants for Christmas, it is all he thinks about. That's how much he notices us. Little monster."

"All kids are like that." Cappelli finished his sambuca. "I was. Weren't you? Hey. Give me another drop. I have to work outside and it's cold."

"So cold it feels like springtime." Daniele refilled Cappelli's glass.

"Did I hear you calling Beniamino a monster again?" Petula said, approaching Daniele. She cleaned her hands with a towel, wiping away drops of juice from the Sicilian oranges. Sweet liquid, red as blood. "Say it once, and it's funny maybe. Two times it's less funny. Lately you say it too much."

"He likes it when I call him a monster. And can you tell me you never think of him as a monster?"

"Daniele, he's a *child*. He's six years old."

A shadow darkened Daniele's face, the familiar shadow of jealousy. Petula saw this tightening around Daniele's eyes whenever she sided with her son. She tried to tell herself that all men were secretly jealous of their sons, at least a little. In certain moments, though, Daniele's jealous shadow looked as if it might blacken to rage. And who could she talk to about such worries? Her parents would have listened to her years ago, before she got pregnant when she had not yet reached her eighteenth birthday. Back then they—her father especially—would have welcomed any excuse for her and Daniele not to be together. But once her parents learned to live with the idea of their daughter and Daniele becoming a family with little Beniamino, they had slipped, without meaning to, into the attitude of many grandparents. Their message to Petula had become, *Now that the two of you have a child, all we want to hear is good news.*

How could Petula admit to her parents now that, in just the way that particular shadow spread over Daniele's face, more than the occasional doubt darkened her world? At times, Daniele and their life here in the bar appeared as a jailer and cell block must appear to a prisoner, and a longing for her old bedroom in her parents' house pulled her. *I want to go home,* she caught herself thinking when Daniele's surliness became an impenetrable iron door. In those moments, tears pricked her eyes.

"Virgo," said the voice on the radio behind the bar. "A good day for romance. Your months of waiting are over. New love is on its way. Could it be that you'll find your *anima gemella* after all? Libra, be careful of your health. . . ."

"Hear that, Petula?" Daniele winked. "Lucky day for you, my little Virgo. Your twin soul is on its way."

"I'm not looking for a twin soul. But I'd faint in ecstasy if I saw a man with a paint roller come through the door. A fresh coat of color wouldn't hurt these walls, you know." Why could she never tell Daniele the full truth of what she meant? Why did only the least significant fraction of her thoughts become words?

She busied herself filling another sugar shaker.

"Here we go again with the fresh coat of color." He lit a new cigarette and narrowed his eyes while he blew out smoke. "Ask yourself, Petula: Is this a conversation I want to have?"

Of course it wasn't only paint she wanted to talk about. She felt like screaming whenever Daniele cut off discussion this way. Anger smoldering within, she said, "And didn't we have a pact about smoking?" She hated to hear herself nag, but frustration has a way of expressing itself sideways.

"I only promised I wouldn't smoke in front of Beniamino." Daniele took a slow, defiant drag from his cigarette. "You don't see him here now, do you?" Then his eyelids twitched a guilty blink. He drowned the cigarette in the sink and threw the butt away.

Cappelli could not help but notice the tension between Daniele and Petula. It made him nervous, so he interjected a change of subject. "This weather's certainly screwed up, don't you think?"

The couple eyed each other. A small spark, they knew, would be enough to ignite the angry flame again.

"People walking around with no coats," Cappelli went on. "World's gone crazy, I'll tell you that myself. Oh, any more sambuca in the bottle, or are you going to kick me out to get back to work? If your father were here, Petula, I know he'd tell me to get my carcass out of this bar while I'm still walking straight."

"Her father's not here," Daniele said, reaching for the bottle to re-fill Cappelli's glass. "So go ahead and drink as much as you want."

The muscles of Petula's neck went stiff. Why did each of Daniele's remarks aim to provoke her today? She was about to say something when the harsh crackling of the train station loudspeakers overrode all conversation. "In arrival on track one," shrilled the nasal voice of Enzo the stationmaster, "the Northbound."

Departing customers lined up to pay. Petula went to take care of them at the cash register. "We'll talk more later," Petula said to Daniele with a forced smile.

"I can hardly wait." Daniele smiled back.

"Northbound," Enzo repeated. "Track number one."

The noise from the loudspeakers stopped. A moment later, the distant whistle of the approaching train could be heard through the open door to the platform. The radio was back to playing songs thirty years out of date.

With the sound of the train, Cappelli's heart quickened. Hearts always quicken when a train whistle is heard. Human reflex. Couldn't change a reflex if you tried, but why try? Trains mean people coming and people going. Movement in any direction is enough to make a heart beat faster, whether the train whistle heralds the start of a journey to elsewhere or the arrival of a new face.

Cappelli ignored his quickening heart and turned his thoughts to thinking that maybe it was time to switch from sambuca to red wine, seeing as how lunch wasn't many hours away.

When the train came to a stop, passengers boarded: women going to shop in Siena, a couple of teenage students who had slept late and missed their first classes at the high school there. Cappelli went to the

window overlooking the platform. Not much to see. He turned back
to the bar.

"Time for a change," Cappelli said to Petula and Daniele. He indicated the bottle of red wine on the shelf behind the couple.

The conductor blew the all-clear on his silver whistle and, sixty
seconds after it had pulled in, the train pulled out again, signaling its
departure with a big whistle blast. It rumbled up the track into the
countryside farther up, and the station eased back into silence.

Two people entered the bar. Daniele and Petula noticed them at
once, but were too experienced to stand there and stare. Their eyes remained fixed on the unusual pair only for an extra half second. Cappelli noticed Daniele's and Petula's eyes. He set down his wine and
turned to have a look.

The couple put their suitcases beside a table in the center of the
room. The woman was not like the women Cappelli was used to seeing in town, though he could not specify what it was that made her appear extraordinary. Maybe she and the young man with her were
foreigners. But, as the woman sat herself down and asked her companion to order her a chamomile tea, Cappelli noticed that they spoke
Italian. Italian, yes, but the accent was difficult to place. Certainly not
from anywhere around here.

The woman's dark hair was gathered in a tight bun. Her delicate
earrings were of gold. Dark charcoal outlined large dark eyes, making them even larger and darker, yet strangely full of light, as if she
were on the verge of laughter or tears. The mouth, too, was large, the
lushly lipsticked lips moving elaborately, showing clean white teeth
when she spoke with a smile. Her tongue, glimpsed briefly, glistened
wet and pink. The voice that came out was hardly above a whisper.

Cappelli swallowed hard.

When he breathed in, heavy perfume hit his nose, even though he
was standing at the bar and she was seated some ten feet away. He
had not even decided whether he liked the scent when he realized his
body was suddenly feeling things it had not felt for a long time.

Small high-laced boots peeked out from under the gypsy-style
skirts of the woman's long dark dress. On her hands she wore finger-

less gloves of black lace. Only her fingertips, with red polish on the long nails, were uncovered. A *coroncina* of rosary beads wrapped around one wrist. A collar of scraggly fur warmed her long neck. A dark velvet shawl encased her shoulders.

She remained at the table while the man, younger, went to get her tea. Fanning herself, she opened her shawl, revealing the tops of breasts barely contained by the low-cut bodice of the dress. She sat exposed in the train station bar as if trying to seduce the world, yet she had opened her shawl so carelessly, and rewrapped herself now with such nonchalance, that perhaps she was unaware of all she had disclosed.

Cappelli stared. How old was this woman? Who could tell? Certainly not old, but no puppy either. Then there were the breasts. These were the mother of all breasts. Within Cappelli arose the almost overwhelming desire to crawl between the cushioning breasts and lay his head down amid their perfume and warmth.

"More wine," Cappelli said to Daniele.

Daniele's attention was drawn not to the woman but to the young man. He, too, wore a pair of black fingerless gloves. His were of wool. The gloves made the young man look like a peddler, or an artist painting in an unheated garret, or an alms-seeking holy man. Or a pickpocket, Daniele thought, reflexively touching the wallet in the pocket of his jeans.

The young man's hair was long, as Daniele's had been not too many years before. No single feature attracted the eye to him. All the same, eyes tended to observe his face. At least Petula's did. Daniele took note of the way she watched the young man. Watching Petula watching, Daniele felt his stomach harden like a fist.

Petula, once she allowed herself to look again, could not take her gaze off the newcomer. And he looked back, studying her. When this man looked at her, she had the impression he could tell what she had done yesterday and maybe even what she was devising to do tomorrow. His eyes seemed to read the truth inside that she might have preferred to conceal.

Petula found the expression in these eyes unsettling: irresistible, yet not necessarily pleasant. Something in the eyes scared her. The young man's face held, in any case, a charisma. He had not yet said or done anything special. Still, he was as noteworthy as a naked man standing with arms opened wide before a clothed congregation in church.

Petula felt Daniele observing the way she and the young man were looking at each other. It's not what you think, she wanted to tell him. Instead, she forced herself to drop her gaze.

Why, she wondered, was this man traveling with an older woman? Why did his obedience seem so servile?

Cappelli's curiosity embraced only the woman. Why, he wondered, was she wasting her time with a younger man? Where did she come from, with that strange accent? Why had she stepped off the train here? Sant'Angelo D'Asso was hardly a crossroads.

He shook his head. What do I care? Cappelli asked himself abruptly, going back to his wine. A woman and her man get off a train. No business of mine.

But he kept his ears open to their conversation.

Taking the teacup from Daniele at the bar and setting it on the table before the woman, the young man said, "Here, Mamma. Here's your chamomile."

Of course, thought Cappelli and Petula and Daniele, hearing the word *mamma*. She's his mother and he's her son. Cappelli and Petula took this as good news. The world was almost right again. Only Daniele was alarmed, for the young man had suddenly been identified as unattached.

"Aren't you having anything?" the woman said to her son.

The son made a face and sat down. "I do not hunger." His chair scraped the dull linoleum of the floor.

Petula noticed the oddness of the way the young man spoke.

"Drink something," the woman insisted.

"I do not thirst."

"Go on," said the mother. "Get yourself something to keep me company."

The son exhaled audibly, as if duty weighed heavily. "Fine, then," he said. He turned to Petula. "*Un latte caldo.*"

"Hot milk it is," Daniele answered from behind the bar, quick to respond before Petula could take care of the young man's order.

He poured milk into a metal jug and plunged into it the steam nozzle of the espresso machine. Transferring it to a tall glass, he stirred the hot milk with a long spoon, then set the glass on a saucer. "A little *cacao?*" Daniele tilted the chocolate-powder shaker over the glass.

"No. *Grazie.*"

"Whatever you say." Daniele set the chocolate down, carried the milk over to the table, and returned to the bar.

Hot milk on a hot day like today, Cappelli thought as he polished off his glass of red wine. There's no figuring some people. "If you were planning to offer me a refill"—Cappelli held out his empty wineglass to Daniele—"the answer is yes."

The mother tasted her chamomile tea and the son lowered his lip into milk froth. His belly leaning against the bar, Cappelli got to work on yet more wine.

Standing near the bar sink, Petula towel-dried water spots off of wineglasses. Daniele saw how, in between glasses, she stole glances at the young man seated at the table. Once, twice, then again, like a deer stealing quick, wary sips from a spring.

The hardness in Daniele's stomach became pain. Why should his Petula search for something in another man's face? And what was Daniele supposed to do, say nothing while his woman made big eyes to somebody else? It had been a long time since Petula had looked that way at Daniele. All she wanted to do nowadays was nag. Wishing he could touch her, Daniele spoke, instead. "So what exactly is the problem with the color on the walls?"

Petula heard the tension in his voice. She looked at the young man seated at the table, then gave Daniele a *let's not talk about it now* expression.

"We can talk if we want to talk," Daniele said. What kind of a man would he appear to the eyes of anyone watching—and the young man at the table *was* watching—if he let his woman shut him up? "We're talking about paint. What's the big secret?"

"Maybe we should talk about problems in private."

"We have problems, do we? I thought it was only the paint you didn't like."

"It's not just the paint," Petula said.

"What is it then?"

Eyeing the newcomers, Petula said, "Is this really the time?"

The mother and son glanced away from the bar. They sipped from their hot drinks and pretended not to pay attention.

Overcome, suddenly, with futility, Daniele watched Petula wipe a wineglass, doing nothing himself. "My life is a box," he said quietly, not wanting everyone to hear his confession.

"I see." She lowered her voice, too. "And you think I'm the one who has locked you in."

"I didn't say that."

"But you thought it so loudly they could hear across the tracks," she hissed, getting to work on another glass. "Don't you ever think I might feel just as trapped as you? But with a bit of fantasy, you can paint a box and change the inside, and you'd be amazed how much it starts to feel like a home."

"You can't talk about anything except redecorating the damned bar, can you?" he said, his voice loud again. "I hate it when you get your stubborn brain stuck on something."

She groaned in frustration. "I wasn't only talking about the bar," she said, trying to keep her own voice down. But he ignored her.

"It's a station bar," he said. "What difference does the color make?"

"A little imagination, and we could turn it into something new for ourselves," she said, her voice rising with passion as she forgot for a moment the presence of the customers. "We have the money to do it, or we would if you didn't always lock away everything we earn in the stupid wall safe"—with the hand that held the wineglass she pointed to the storage room at the back of the bar—"where the cash just sits and rots."

At the table, the woman squeezed lemon into her chamomile tea. Mother and son were silent.

"It's called a safe because it's safe," Daniele said.

"You got that line from your father, no? He never trusted the bank enough to open an account, so why should you?"

Cappelli, who had devoted a lifetime to avoiding tensions of his own, found that other people's conflicts made his head spin. Or maybe it was the wine. *"Madonna angosciata!"* he said, lowering his empty glass to the bar, his words implying that the couple's turmoil was disagreeable enough to anguish the Madonna herself. "And I always thought you two were happy together! Now I start to believe it when people say bad luck is crushing this town. If even the two of you start to fight like snakes, then what hope is left?"

At the table, the woman and her son had succeeded in making themselves almost invisible. No one saw the way the woman's eyebrows rose briefly at the mention of bad luck.

"Beautiful town you have here," the woman said suddenly. She spoke in that whisper of hers, but it was a whisper that made itself heard.

"Excuse me?" Petula said, not expecting comment of any sort from the pair of quiet travelers.

"Bellissimo, beautiful town," the woman said again. As if by magic, her quiet voice stopped other conversation. She looked out the picture window toward the tracks. "I like it here."

"Then I'm happy for you," Daniele said with a touch of sarcasm.

The woman turned to the bar and smiled. "How many people live here?"

"Not many," said Petula. "A thousand people or so."

"One thousand, two hundred and eighty-eight." Daniele's voice lost its rancor. He became a professional talking to customers, proud of his head for facts.

Petula noticed how the woman's childlike way of speaking seemed to ease everyone's nerves, even hers.

"That's the population for the moment," Daniele continued, "until more people catch the curse and die."

"The curse?" the woman asked.

"*Sì*, if you believe in superstition," Daniele said with what he hoped would appear manly indifference. "Nothing to worry about, signora. Plain bad luck is what I say. It will pass."

"Curses were made to be broken, no?" As the woman smiled, the tip of her pink tongue poked between her teeth. Cappelli noticed. "One thousand, two hundred and eighty-eight," she repeated. "Imagine. Just the right size for a town, don't you think?" She turned her eyes to her son, as if waiting for an answer, but none came.

"Depends on what you're looking for," Daniele said. "People live here quietly. But if you're hoping for big-city excitement, this place will kill you."

"We've had enough of the big cities for a while. Living quietly is what we need."

"Which big cities?" Daniele permitted himself the confidential sort of question that might have sounded intrusive had it not come from the mouth of a barman.

"A town just outside Rome is where we're coming from now. And Naples a few years before. Bari before that. A bit of everywhere really, though Venice is the city of our birth."

The son showed no sign of wanting to join in the conversation. His dark eyes studied the surface of the hot milk.

Cappelli nodded over his wine, without saying anything. Just listening was fine with him. Venice. That would explain the staccato cadence of her speech. Her voice had picked up a few layers of Southern Italian and Roman. No wonder her accent—usually a giveaway for any Italian—was hard to place. Venice. Yes, of course. Venetian underneath it all. Funny people, people from Venice. Tricky to make out. Something different about them. Maybe that watery, misty city of theirs seeped through their skin, right through to their insides, making them as illegible as the currents of the sea. They certainly weren't Tuscans, at any rate. But there was something seductive about Venetians, one had to admit.

"Then Tuscany called to us," the woman continued, "so we knew it was time to leave Rome." While her mouth spoke, her hands, hid-

den inside the fingerless gloves, went into motion, recounting with
fluid elegance a narrative of their own. Perhaps the hands were illus-
trating the same story the mouth was speaking, perhaps not. She said
that they had considered Florence and then Siena, but the prices were
too high. "We looked at a map, didn't we?" The question was addressed to her son. He sat silently, showing no intention to reply, so
the woman carried on. "We looked at a map and noticed the name of
this town. Sant'Angelo D'Asso. I've always wanted to live somewhere with an angel in the name. You told me what *angel* meant, remember?" she said to the young man.

"*Angelos*, in ancient Greek," he said without taking his eyes off the
milk he held in his hands. "It means messenger."

"*Sì*," she said with girlish excitement. "Messenger. What could be
more thrilling than the town of the Sainted Messenger? So we
thought we'd come and have a look. And as we saw the town just before the train reached the station, we knew we had found the right
place to stay." She stopped, as if waiting for her new neighbors to embrace her.

The young man looked at his mother with something Petula
thought might be surprise. He sipped his milk, his eyes surveying the
room across the rim of the glass.

"I guess I've never really wanted to go anywhere else," Petula
added, shooting Daniele a look as if to put to shame the discontent he
had hinted at a moment before.

Daniele grudgingly said, "Has its appeal, I suppose, this place."

"Why should anyone ever want to leave?" the woman picked up
quickly. "Tell me," she said, "would you know how we could find
some rooms to stay in, a little apartment, maybe a house? Would
there be anyone in this lovely town"—the woman smiled again, and
Cappelli watched the lips move wonderfully over white teeth—"anyone looking to rent their house to a mother and her son?" She put her
lace-gloved hand on a wool-gloved hand of the young man.

With his other hand, the son drank his milk.

Must have been the wine in his stomach mixed with the sambuca
already swirling around in his head, Cappelli would later tell himself.

Must have had more alcohol in his blood than even he knew how to handle. Must have been the long-forgotten stirring this woman had created in his belly. Whatever it was, something made him put down his wineglass and open his mouth. "I have a house," he said. And once he had said that much, the words could not be unsaid. "A big house right on the piazza in the center of town. I live in the rooms on the top floor, but right below me there's a whole other apartment that no one's lived in since my grandmother was there when I was a kid. Not too many stairs to climb. Just one flight up from street level. Place is abandoned. Shame, if you think about it." It was a shame indeed, he told himself, trying to believe that he wasn't a fool for being so quick to offer. What harm could come from doing another person a good turn?

"A whole apartment, you said?" The woman's smile projected its full radiance upon him.

"Big, yes, and furnished, with lots more furniture in the basement. Just dirty is all. That's the only problem, *porca maiala.*" He heard himself swear in front of this woman and, for the first time in a long time, wondered if his words had offended delicate ears. In penance he looked away for a second or two. "Years and years of dirt," he went on. "About time, I figure, for someone to give the place a cleaning. I'm a workingman myself, so naturally I don't have the leisure."

"We'd be happy to clean the apartment, if you'd let us stay, wouldn't we?" Again, a question her son left unanswered. "And the rent?"

"The rent?" Cappelli had not thought about this. What should one ask for an apartment these days? And why complicate matters with the taxman or with official permission from the town hall? "Rent we can talk about another time," Cappelli said.

Una mano lava l'altra, people were always saying, no? One hand washes the other. When was the last time he had got involved in washing another hand? When was the last time he had made a decision so quickly? When was the last time, come to think of it, he had made any decision at all?

Petula and Daniele caught each other's eye. *Look at our Cappelli!* was the thought they shared. *Since when has he ever invited a woman to live in his house?* Daniele winked, Petula smiled back, both of them relieved to catch their breath in a moment of truce.

"You can stay there in exchange for cleaning the place up," Cappelli explained to the woman. "Even deal, no? I don't have to do the work myself, and you get a place to stay. People do this kind of trade all the time, don't they?"

"Kind, God-loving people with goodness in their hearts, yes." There was that smile with all that lipstick.

Cappelli was not sure how to feel about being counted among the kind and God-loving and good at heart. A shrug was his only comment.

"One hand washes the other," the woman added.

"Just what I was thinking," Cappelli said. Had she read his mind?

"And the name of the generous man who will have us as his guests?" the mother asked.

"My name?" He came over to the table, his immediate future suddenly appearing soft and perfumed, like the tops of the breasts he glimpsed when he leaned over to shake the woman's glove-covered hand. "Cappelli."

"Pleasure, Signor Cappelli," said the woman.

"Pleasure," he replied, "Signora . . . Signora?"

"My name is Rosa Spina. Rosa Spina Innocenti."

"Signora Rosa Spina," he echoed, asking himself what it meant for a woman to be called Thorn of a Rose. Giddy with wine, Cappelli couldn't resist playing with the name in what he hoped would seem a clever show of charm. "And would you be more Rosa or more Spina?"

She smiled with teeth and lips. "A woman needs to be flower and thorn alike."

Cappelli nodded quietly at the reply, sensing that he had come out the loser in the verbal exchange. He scrunched his forehead for a moment. Words never had been his strong suit. He should have known better than to swap words with anyone, especially with a woman who had lived in cities that he had seen only on television. Her world was bigger than his. Yes, perhaps he should stay away from words. He was, after all, a shy person.

Turning back toward her son, Rosa Spina observed the way he watched Petula behind the bar. She saw the corners of his mouth rise in a smile, but the young woman quickly looked away. The mother sipped her tea.

Cappelli, meanwhile, breathed in Rosa Spina's fragrance. Suddenly a cold doubt came to him and threatened to rob him of his new and happy feelings. "Just you and your son, you say? Will a mister be joining you?"

"There is no mister to join us," said Rosa Spina in her little-girl voice. "Just my son and myself." She paused, as if deciding whether or not to reveal a secret, then said, "But the kind Signor Cappelli wouldn't mind, would he, if the Other One came for a visit?"

The son put down his glass of milk. *"L'Altro?"* he asked his mother incredulously.

"The Other One?" Cappelli echoed.

"L'Altro," said Rosa Spina brightly, her voice as soothing as sunshine. "My other son."

Daniele and Petula both saw that the young man at the table appeared thrown off balance by the mother's words. "Mamma, I don't think L'Altro—" he began.

"But that wouldn't be a problem, would it?" she interrupted.

"No, I suppose." Cappelli wondered why things were becoming complicated. "Where's this other son now?"

"He has other engagements." Rosa Spina smiled. "Still, he might want to spend a little time with us. Who knows?"

"And how old did you say your other son was?" Cappelli didn't relish the idea of some adolescent blasting loud music just downstairs from his own rooms.

"The same age as Emanuele Mosè," the mother said.

"Emmanuel Moses! That's your name?" Cappelli laughed. Interesting names these people have, he thought, this family of Innocents. *"Madonnina!"* he chortled, unable to contain himself. "I'll have half the Bible living downstairs! Talk about a name that carries weight."

Though seated, the young man with the serious eyes gave a not undignified bow.

"And your brother—L'Altro, you say his name is? The Other One? He's the same age as you?"

"My brother and I," said Emanuele Mosè, "are twins."

Petula felt an odd tingle cross her skin. Emanuele Mosè's sensitively drawn face belonged in a fresco, she observed, but the dark intensity of his eyes made her want to keep her distance. Hearing now the mention of a twin, she wondered what the other brother might be like.

Listening and watching, too, Daniele wiped the bar fiercely as Cappelli, with uncustomary gallantness, settled the tab for his two new tenants and for himself, held the door on the way out to take them to see the house, and walked with them into the bright, hot December day.

2

A few days later, Petula opened her son's bedroom window, letting in a rush of fresh cold air. The unseasonable, unnatural heat had passed as quickly as it had come. Petula leaned out to push back the shutters, and the sudden light made her sleepy six-year-old blink.

Enjoying the feel of the December air, Petula kissed Beniamino on the head and said, "Go to the window. Go and look."

He crossed the room with a groggy, disoriented foot-shuffle, but when he saw the world outside, he came awake at once. *"La neve!"* he said. "Snow!"

His joy made her smile. She and Daniele had been fighting too much recently. The boy, absorbing his parents' tensions, had become wary, as if people around him were no longer safe.

"Do I have to go to school?" The schedule had not yet become second nature to Beniamino, who was only in his first year.

"It's Sunday. No school."

His hair poking up from where it had pressed against the pillow, Beniamino would have been happy to run straight outside without so much as putting a bathrobe over his pyjamas.

But first he had to eat something. All through breakfast, Petula watched the boy's excitement. Here she was at twenty-four, often so tired she felt twice her age. Working at the bar, at home, trudging around with Daniele moaning every step of the way. Every now and then, she feared that her entire life would be one uphill marathon of labor. Why, Petula wondered, had her love for Daniele become so much more complicated than her love for their son? And as for passion lately, only fatigue appeared where intimacy should have been.

This morning she watched her little boy eating his cake and hot cocoa while he stared at the snow through the window. His eagerness spread to her, making her anxious to put on boots and gloves and go out to play.

"And this evening," she said to slow Beniamino down. "Here, eat your piece of cake. The snow will still be there in ten minutes. And this evening, we'll go with everybody to the piazza to hear the band play and then we'll watch them light up the Nativity in front of the church."

"Babbo's playing, too?"

"Of course your father's playing. He's in the band, isn't he?"

"Is Gesù Bambino in the manger yet?"

"Not yet. You remember how they do it? They don't put Baby Jesus in his crib until Christmas Eve, and that's not for another five days."

She loved the way her son's eyes went wide when he was listening hard. His lips were wet with cocoa.

Then she saw his expression grow suddenly serious as he looked at the snow through the window and a new thought came to worry him. "Is it too cold for the sheep?" he said.

The sheep, Petula knew, were the four sheep that her own father, Renato, kept in order to make pecorino cheese from their milk. "The sheep will be fine," she reassured him. "They don't even need to put on sweaters. They already have their wool."

The boy's face did not relax. One thought perplexed him still, she could see. He said, "Is Lola's mamma going to die?"

Lola, the pretty lamb whom Beniamino himself had named, had been born to the sheep Renato called Quarta because she always came fourth in the self-appointed milking order of the little flock. How did Beniamino know that Quarta days earlier had fallen victim to an enigmatic malady that neither Renato nor the veterinarian could understand, her illness as indecipherable as any of the other occurrences of bad luck afflicting the town? Without a diagnosis, Renato had told her, repeating the veterinarian's words, there could be no treatment, no cure. Quarta refused food, gave no milk, but stood as rigid as a statue in the stall, staring scared stiff at the empty wall, Renato had said, as if watching the end of the world. Petula could not recall telling Beniamino about Quarta. Maybe the boy had overheard while she spoke with her father on the telephone. Or maybe the boy simply perceived the news by intuition, the way he seemed to perceive everything that went on in the family. Secrets lost their secrecy with Beniamino in the house. "I don't think Quarta will die," Petula said, wanting to speak truthfully yet trying not to frighten her son. "I hope she doesn't."

"What will happen to Lola if she does?"

Petula stroked Beniamino's hair. "Then you'll have to love Lola even more."

She asked herself how it was possible to love a creature as much as she loved her son, more dearly than she loved herself. Maybe Daniele had reason to be jealous of Beniamino.

Beniamino, apparently satisfied by her answer, turned and looked out the window. Breakfast was over, Petula could tell. "You want to go and play?" The boy nodded. "Then let's get you dressed," she said, putting the plates in the sink. "I'll wash the dishes later. It's not every day we get to play in the snow."

In town, holiday eagerness filled the white air. And now, with less than a week to go before Christmas, thick snow lay on the rooftops and the streets. This was no light dusting, but the kind of rare and steady storm that would block the roads for at least a day or two and make time stop.

Fireplaces in houses were stoked. Chimneys puffed, scenting the air with woodsmoke as Petula and Beniamino chased each other through the streets. Mother and son laughed and threw snowballs, Petula's heart feeling lighter than it had for months.

Breathless, they reached the square. The doors to the church were closed, and inside Don Luigi was leading Sunday Mass. The pale stone façade of the church had not changed much in the eight hundred years since it was built. Silence lay as thick as the snow that cushioned the church steps, until a pigeon in the bell tower fluttered snowflakes from its wings and cooed a complaint against the cold.

"See?" Petula said to Beniamino as they came to the Nativity scene. Men of the town had erected a thatch-roofed manger beside the church to house the sacred statues. Maria, Giuseppe, several shepherds, a donkey, and a lovely-eyed cow stood in a semicircle adoring what for now was an empty crib. Above the roof of the manger hung a wooden angel who blew a wooden trumpet and held a wooden banner that announced, GLORIA IN EXCELSIS! Higher above the angel, suspended from wires stretched over the street, the long-tailed comet, its many lightbulbs unlit, awaited illumination. Nuzzi, the town electrician, had done the wiring, Petula thought now. Knowing Nuzzi's reputation for incompetence, she wondered whether he would throw the town into a blackout that evening when he flipped the switch to light up the Nativity.

"That's where Gesù Bambino will go?" Beniamino said, pointing a mittened hand at the empty crib.

"That's where he'll go."

"So where is he now?"

"He hasn't been born yet," Petula said.

Beniamino gave her a skeptical look. "Why don't they put another wall up in the manger to keep the snow out?"

"If they put up another wall, we couldn't see in."

"But Gesù Bambino will get cold."

"He won't get cold," Petula told him. "The donkey and the cow are there to breathe on him to keep him warm. And see? Maria has made his bed ready with lots of nice straw."

Beniamino studied the scene. Then he said, "I know why Gesù Bambino won't get cold. And neither will Giuseppe or Maria or the angel or the shepherds." He smiled at his mother. "Want to know why?"

"Why?"

"Because they're statues, and statues don't get cold!" He laughed.

"Little monster!" Petula laughed back. She bent to make a snow-ball to throw at her son, but he was quicker, splattering her coat with a snowball of his own. "*Sì*, these ones here are statues," Petula said, eager to have the last word, "but think how cold it must have been for the *real* Gesù Bambino to be born without a house."

Beniamino went quiet. He lifted his face and watched the snow fall.

Petula followed his gaze until her eyes, too, traced the paths of the fat flakes that swirled from the sky.

"*Buongiorno*, Petula," she heard.

She lowered her eyes. "Oh," she said, disconcerted to find a young man standing beside her, dressed as dark as a crow against the white snow all around. She had not heard him approach. "*Buongiorno*." She hesitated before saying his name. It was such an odd name, she did not think she could make it sound natural in conversation. Not want-ing to appear rude, however, she pushed herself to say, "*Buongiorno*, Emanuele Mosè."

"I saw you and your son. This is your son, no?"

"*Sì*. This is Beniamino. Beniamino, say *buongiorno*."

Emanuele Mosè held out his right hand. Beniamino looked at the long-haired young man with the unsmiling face. He saw the hand reaching toward him, the hand hidden inside the black fingerless gloves. Beniamino took a step backward.

"Say *buongiorno*, Beniamino," Petula prompted again.

"*Buongiorno*," said Beniamino obediently. Petula could see fear on her son's face.

Emanuele Mosè studied the child in silence. Then he turned to Petula and said, "I saw the two of you playing."

Petula heard his solemnity. She figured he could not be older than she was, yet she found it impossible to imagine him playing, now or ever, the word itself sounding strange from his lips. "*Sì*," she said. "We were playing." Why was it so awkward to speak with him? Why did she have to force herself to talk? "And you?"

"I was walking, getting to know the town."

"And do you like what you've seen?"

He seemed not to understand the question. "I don't know." He stared at her. "But some things here are very beautiful, truth be told." He stared some more.

What does he expect me to say? she asked herself. Is that his idea of a compliment? Everything about this man was alien. Petula could not understand why even a pleasantry coming from his mouth sounded like a curse.

Emanuele Mosè looked at Beniamino for a moment, then looked around the square, taking in the church, the Nativity scene, the houses, the rooftops, the snow. "Well," he said to Petula. "It's cold. I have to help my mother with the fire. I'll see you again, I'm sure."

"See you," Petula said.

Beniamino said nothing.

Emanuele Mosè walked off, letting himself in the front door of Cappelli's house.

When the young man had gone, Beniamino lifted his face to the sky once more. "He looks like a priest," Beniamino said.

"He's just different," Petula said. She kept to herself her feeling of relief that Emanuele Mosè had gone away.

A pigeon flew toward the eaves under the roof of the house next to the church, only to find another pigeon already nestled there. Neither bird wanted to share the niche with the other. They began to fight, two sets of wings swapping furious slaps. The noise they made caught Petula's attention. In their struggle to win a good claw-hold, the birds knocked something loose. Falling, a heavy roof tile hit the corner of a window frame and broke. The biggest fragment ricocheted downward to Beniamino.

Petula screamed his name and yanked him by the wrist.

"Ow!" Beniamino protested. The hand on his wrist felt as strong as a claw.

The jagged shard knifed into the snowy footprint where Beniamino had stood.

"You're hurting me," the child said, pulling away.

"You have to be more careful!" Petula's voice was harsh with terror.

"Careful of what? I wasn't doing anything."

Of course, he was right. The tile could have killed him, she shuddered, and it would have been no one's fault.

Only bad luck.

"Come here," said Petula. She bent down and hugged him tight. Over his shoulder, she looked at the front door to Cappelli's house. Fleetingly, she blamed Emanuele Mosè for the falling tile. Quickly dismissing the thought as irrational, Petula hurried Beniamino down the snowy street to the safety of her grandparents' bottega.

3

Outside the window of Rosa Spina's front room a few hours later, pigeons cooed, then fought. Cappelli sat at the table in the apartment down the stairs from his own. He watched the flames in the fireplace of this house which, until a couple of days ago, had been empty as a cave.

Smoke rose from the flames. Cappelli sniffed himself when Rosa Spina's back was turned. Fireplace odors had permeated his clothes, making him wonder if he smelled like a smoked ham. Maybe I do, he thought. Then Rosa Spina brushed past him, the tops of her breasts as rosy as her cheeks with the exertion of cooking. But *she* doesn't smell like a ham, he thought, not even with all this smoke. She smells like, I don't know. Something I've never smelled before. Something good.

Only a few short days since the arrival of Cappelli's new tenants, and already the woman with the miraculous breasts had turned Cappelli's life inside out like a sock. She had him running upstairs and downstairs, back and forth to the basement to get furniture with that son of hers whom Cappelli could think of only as spooky. A bigger table she said she wanted, and fortunately Cappelli had a big old long table in the basement, though why she needed a table so big to seat only her son and herself Cappelli had no idea. Chairs, too, she wanted, as many as Cappelli could find. What company could she be expecting? She herself got to work scrubbing and sweeping and washing, making everything look like a house instead of the ruins it had been for the last forty years. And today she had invited him for lunch to celebrate the house's feeling lived in again.

Inside the great fireplace now, Rosa Spina bent down low and used a wooden spoon to stir the polenta in a large black cast-iron pot. The yellow corn porridge burped fat bubbles. Rosa Spina lifted her big eyes to Cappelli. Her elaborate lips smiled wide.

Women are funny, Cappelli thought as he tried, perhaps for the first time ever, to make sense of the other half of his species. Look at her. Almost looks like a witch, crouched in her skirts over her pot in the fireplace. You'd think she was cooking little-children stew. But no witch could have breasts as soft-looking as those. And no witch smells spicy and sweet the way she does.

When Rosa Spina decided that the polenta had thickened enough, she said, "Would you mind helping me pour this out? The pot's so heavy." Her giggle was girlish. She handed him a folded dishtowel so that he would not burn himself on the metal handle of the pot.

Was the pot really too much for her to lift? wondered Cappelli. She was no delicate fairy. The arms inside her sleeves looked plump. No matter. Cappelli was happy to show that a workingman like himself could handle a mere cast-iron pot.

He tilted the pot over a wooden cutting board.

Rosa Spina used the spoon to guide the molten flow of the polenta directly onto the board. She asked, "Do you do a lot of cooking?"

"Me? Never."

"Then where do you eat?"

"At the bottega, just about always."

"Well, then. Now I'm even happier you accepted the invitation to come for lunch. You've done so much to help us, and a little home-cooked food never did a man any harm. Don't you think?"

"*Boh.* Never thought about it. I guess you might be right. No harm in it, I suppose." No harm, true, but could he imagine ever feeling at ease in a situation such as this?

Rosa Spina scraped out the last of the polenta from the overturned pot, then spoon-patted the thick yellow mass into a round, even form. "We'll let this cool for just a minute while I check the sauce." She went to the stove and gave the saucepan a stir. "Emanuele Mosè!" she called in the direction of the bedroom. "*Vieni!* The lunch is ready!"

The long-haired, long-faced young man came in and took his seat. He did not have the energetic enthusiasm of many people in their early twenties, neither did he show the mocking arrogance of a young rebel. Instead he gave the impression of inhabiting a foreign dimension, as if his thoughts were not connected to the physical world of kitchen fireplaces and wooden tables and chairs. His preoccupations were elsewhere, and a simple mortal like Cappelli could not begin to guess where that remote realm might be. Emanuele Mosè, seemingly a newcomer to planet Earth, picked up his fork and scrutinized it for a moment, as if he had never before encountered such an object and needed to concentrate hard to discover its function. Evidently he decided he liked the fork because in an instant his brow relaxed, he put the fork back on the table, and, with a sudden smile, handed his mother his plate.

Cappelli asked himself: Why doesn't the kid ever take off those fingerless woolen gloves? What does he have to hide? Does he plan to keep them on even at the table? He can't need them to keep his hands warm, not with the fire making the whole kitchen this hot. Young people are strange, I know, Cappelli thought, but this guy wins the prize.

"Tell me something," Cappelli said to Emanuele Mosè. "Where you come from, do people keep their gloves on at the table?"

Emanuele Mosè looked Cappelli hard in the eyes and said, "No."

Then why don't you take yours off? Cappelli wanted to ask, but the young man's *no* had a tone that did not open the door to further discussion. Cappelli said, "I see," and risked no more questions. He decided that maybe the strange young man had an ugly disease on his hands. Cappelli shifted his attention to the food. He did not want to think about ugly diseases. He certainly did not want to see them.

Using a piece of red string held taut between her two hands, Rosa Spina cut the polenta into slices. She placed a piece on Cappelli's plate, then a piece on Emanuele Mosè's, then her own. The young man raised his eyebrows in surprise, Cappelli noticed, as if he were used to being served first. Rosa Spina spooned on the mushroom sauce.

Cappelli knew from the smell that his mouth was about to become very happy. With the first forkful, the mouth sent word to the stomach that good things were on their way.

During the meal they drank from the bottle of local white wine that Cappelli had brought. "Nothing. The least I could do," Cappelli said chivalrously when Rosa Spina thanked him for his thoughtfulness. The wine was helping Cappelli relax a bit. "Another glass?" he offered when he had worked his way through half the plate of polenta.

"I shouldn't really," Rosa Spina blushed. "But—*ostrega!*—this wine is good." Cappelli enjoyed that *ostrega* of hers, that Venetian expletive that no Tuscan would ever think to say, that dialectal corruption of *ostia*, the holy eucharistic Host. Her way of speaking was one of the many things that made her different from any person he had met before. "Maybe just *un'ombra*. Please."

Cappelli looked confused. *"Un'ombra?"*

"That's what we call a drop where I was born. *Un'ombra*. A shadow."

"A little shadow for Signora Rosa Spina," he said, pouring. He was about to give some to Emanuele Mosè's as well, but the teetotaling young man declined with a gesture of his glove-covered hand.

To hell with him, Cappelli decided and he focused all his thoughts on the mother. How come a woman like this doesn't have a man? he wondered as he watched her tongue lick a drop of wine from her lip. She must have had one once, otherwise where did her son come from?

Church bells rang the hour outside. Rosa Spina turned toward the window to listen, then mused aloud in answer to Cappelli's silent question with the timely intuition of a clairvoyant. "When I was young, I didn't often go to church. The important holidays I went, naturally, Christmas, of course, and Easter, and that was enough for me. But then one evening, when I was still a *fanciulla*, not even of legal age," she said, making Cappelli try to remember the last time he had heard anyone use the biblical-sounding word *fanciulla*, maiden, "the evening of an ordinary day," she went on, "a weekday, I heard a voice."

"A voice?" said Cappelli.

"A faint voice. It called me to the church."

He swallowed wine. "Whose voice was it?"

"It wasn't a human voice." Her hands, never still when she spoke but dancing all the while, made a beckoning motion to illustrate her words. "I entered, just in time for the start of the vespers. I sat surrounded by the widows and the sad and the other people who go to vespers every evening of their lives. And I wondered why I should have been called to go there."

Emanuele Mosè exhaled loudly. Maybe he's eaten too much, Cappelli figured. Or maybe he's heard this story before.

"It wasn't an interesting Mass the priest was leading," Rosa Spina continued. "And just when I started to think I had made a mistake and maybe I should leave, the voice came to me again."

Cappelli did not know what to make of the voice. No nonhuman voice had ever called to him.

"This time the voice was clear inside my head," Rosa Spina said. "Clear and strong. And you know what it said to me?"

Cappelli shook his head.

"It said, 'You shall give birth to a son. And you shall call his name Emanuele Mosè.' Can you believe it?"

Again, Cappelli wagged his head side to side.

"Well, neither could I! I mean—*ostrega!*—yes, I had spent a little time in the company of a man, but nothing much to speak of."

She looked toward her son, but the young man, Cappelli saw, kept his eyes lowered to his plate. Cappelli coughed. "To talk about the company of a man"—he opened a palm in Emanuele Mosè's direction—"with your son listening . . . it's not my business, surely, but I mean, I wonder if this is—"

To Cappelli's surprise, Emanuele Mosè spoke up with a smile on his face. "Most children, Signor Cappelli, listen to fairy tales at bedtime," he said. "Ever since I was a small child, I've listened to the retelling of my mother's life and of my own."

"Fine," Cappelli said, unnerved by the joylessness of the young man's smile, "but I only meant to say that the more intimate details—"

"There's nothing to be embarrassed about," said Rosa Spina, her girlish voice full of reassurance. "I was a virgin, you understand. Practically a virgin."

This was not the sort of mealtime conversation that Cappelli was used to. No one at the bottega ever talks like this woman, Cappelli thought. No one anywhere.

"I certainly had no reason to believe that I could possibly be pregnant," she said. "But the voice that spoke to me inside my head in the church said that I was with child. And sure enough, a week later I discovered that the menstruation did not come to me, and I was pregnant indeed."

Cappelli shifted in his chair. He did not know what to say in reply to woman-words spoken at such close quarters by a woman whose breasts pressed the edge of the table where he sat. "And your parents?" he mumbled before filling his mouth with more wine.

"My mother, you mean. My father had never been there, even when I was a little girl. My poor mother was scandalized. She didn't believe me when I told her about the voice in the church, and she believed even less in my chastity when I told her I was pregnant after all."

"And the man?"

"Which man?"

"The one who . . . you know. The one in whose company you said you spent a little time?" If Cappelli had not known himself better, he would have sworn that he felt the color of embarrassment rise in his cheeks.

"Oh. The man. When I told him that I was carrying a child, he was very quick to say that it was no responsibility of his, because the child couldn't be his. And of course he was right."

Cappelli's head began to spin. With difficulty he swallowed a forkful of polenta.

"And when the time came, almost nine months after I heard the voice's call, I gave birth. And do you know what name I gave to the child who came out of my womb?"

Cappelli looked at Emanuele Mosè then at Rosa Spina. "Emanuele Mosè?" he offered.

"*Bravo!*" said Emanuele Mosè with a wan grin.

"Exactly," said Rosa Spina. "Just as the voice in church had foretold. But that wasn't the end of the unusual things."

"No?" Cappelli could imagine nothing more unusual than what he had already heard. "But wait," he said. "How about your other son? Didn't you mention the other day that you have another?"

For an instant her smile fell. "My other son," she said, losing herself in distant thoughts.

Emanuele Mosè cleared his throat and stared at his mother.

Cappelli saw Rosa Spina's eyes give rapid, nervous blinks. "I'll get to my other son. I promise." Her smiled returned and her eyes refound their light. "But first, you must hear more about Emanuele Mosè. It was three years after his birth, and we had already started to wander. Wander, because once there were too many mouths to feed my mother said it was time for me to go into the world with my offspring alone. So we left Venice and from there we were in the next city for some years, which was Bari, farther down the coast. In any case, one day little Emanuele Mosè was playing on the floor while I was cooking, and he sat there saying a word over and over and over to himself." Her hands wove invisible tapestries in the air. "And do you know what word he was repeating?"

A shrug was as much eloquence as Cappelli could manage.

"*Jerusalem.* That's what he kept saying again and again. *Jerusalem.* So I said to him, 'Emanuele Mosè, why are you saying *Jerusalem, Jerusalem?*' And do you know what he answered? He said, 'Jerusalem is the Mother and the Father and the Son.' That's what my little three-year-old boy said.

"And I had no idea what he meant. Why would a three-year-old say such a thing? It scared me to hear my baby say things I couldn't understand. So after dinner I took him out for a walk through town with me and there I found a church and thought we maybe should go in. I sat in church, not knowing what to think, but little Emanuele Mosè seemed right at home. And I looked up while I was sitting, and there on the wall I saw a fresco of the Holy Family entering Jerusalem. Maria, and Giuseppe, and Gesù as a boy. I understood then what Emanuele Mosè had been talking about, but he was only three years old and I had never taken him into that church before. You see what I mean? He had never seen the fresco, but he knew about it all the same.

"And I became more and more scared. But there was a priest in the church there in Bari, and he saw me crying with my little baby playing by my side. He asked me what was wrong, so I told him. And then I asked him, 'Do you think that it was the Devil who made me hear the voice that told me I was pregnant? Do you think the Devil is talking to Emanuele Mosè now and telling him about Jerusalem? Is it the Devil or the angel of God?' That's what I asked the priest."

"And what did the priest say?" Cappelli had never worried about demonic or angelic beings, and certainly had never cared about any priest's view on any matter. But listening now to this disconcerting story, he figured that priests probably knew as much about devils and angels as he knew about water pipes, and therefore ought to be able to give an expert's view.

Emanuele Mosè spoke up to tell the answer. "The priest said I seemed like a good little boy, not like a child sent by the Devil."

"I'm glad for that," said Cappelli, blowing out air in relief.

"And that's when I told the priest, 'In that case,'" Rosa Spina cut in, "'in that case, if he's not sent by the Devil then he must be sent by God.' Makes sense, don't you think?"

Nothing was making sense to Cappelli.

"So I asked the priest," she continued, "how I should raise a child sent by God. And the priest gave me good advice. 'Don't pressure the boy,' the priest said. 'If things are meant to happen, they will happen on their own, without you pushing.' So I took his advice very seriously and never ever put Emanuele Mosè under pressure to prove to anyone that he was sent by God. Still, it just comes naturally to him."

"For my entire life," Emanuele Mosè articulated slowly, one syllable at a time, "I have lived in obedience to a power greater than my own."

"Obedience?" Cappelli laughed. Looking at the face that had spoken, Cappelli saw a flat expression revealing neither pride nor shame. The eyes that looked back at Cappelli seemed to say, *I state nothing but fact. I could not change fact if I tried.* To Cappelli, everything about the young man appeared a mystery, a closed box. Who could guess what grew inside? Sadness in the eyes was all that Cappelli glimpsed. "But you're young," Cappelli said. "At your age, a little living is important, too, no?"

Emanuele Mosè gave no answer, only the sad look in his eyes.

Rosa Spina reached across the table, taking her son's hand between her own. "Doing good things and helping people wherever we go is what we've *both* always done, is what my son means to say. Isn't it, Emanuele Mosè?"

The young man pulled his hand away and lowered his eyes.

"Doing good is his nature," Rosa Spina went on. "And with good things happening through him, it certainly couldn't be the Devil's work. Don't you think?"

Cappelli waited. He still had one great question: Exactly what kind of good things was she referring to? but he could think of no delicate way to ask. And Rosa Spina's story had finished, apparently, because she had stopped speaking and her dancing hands, with the *coroncina* of rosary beads decorating one wrist, were at rest. Her wide eyes stared at him. Her red lips formed an enchanting smile. Her dark hair, pulled back in a bun, glistened in the firelight. Never in his life had Cappelli heard such a story. He had no notion what it might mean. She expected an answer from him, so stumblingly he opened his mouth and said, "Doing good things for people would seem a good thing to do, I would think. No?"

"*Ma certo!*" Rosa Spina beamed. "But of course! And that is why I wanted you to know about us. Although perhaps you should not tell the other people here in your town. Not everyone is as quick to understand as you. People might get the wrong idea."

"Tell no one?" Cappelli realized that he could not wait to tell his boss that the woman with the body of a goddess claimed to have given birth without the intervention of any man. Renato was the one person on earth who could help him sort out things in his head if ever thinking became a difficult process. But this woman with the good food and soft-looking breasts was asking him to keep a secret, so he promised himself he would try his hardest. "If that's what you want," he said, "you can count on me."

"*Bravo,*" said Rosa Spina.

"*Bravo,*" Emanuele Mosè echoed without enthusiasm.

"Thank you. Thank you from the heart." Rosa Spina put a hand upon her breast. Then, noticing a tiny splodge of polenta that had remained stuck to Cappelli's chin, Rosa Spina took her napkin, leaned across the table, and wiped clean the skin below Cappelli's lower lip.

Never had there been a woman to wipe Cappelli's face as if it belonged to her own body. The only women he had experienced as an adult were the ones he had paid to provide brief, anonymous encounters. This woman's gesture prompted new feelings deep within Cappelli's chest. He did not know what to make of the sensations.

She smiled, seeming to understand his thoughts.

The young man present watched his mother wipe Cappelli's chin, then looked away. "Mamma," Emanuele Mosè said at last, speaking mechanically, sadly, as if duty bound to speak his next words, "I think you should tell our landlord about L'Altro's birth, too."

Cappelli's hair bristled on the back of his neck, though he could not say why.

Rosa Spina looked away from the table. Cappelli followed her eyes until his attention, too, came to rest on a little frame that hung on the wall near the kitchen stove. The black-and-white photo inside the frame showed a young woman—Rosa Spina in her youth, Cappelli recognized—sitting between two identical boys who could not have been more than five or six years old. The photo must have torn once, because yellowing tape connected one little boy to his mother and his twin.

Cappelli wanted to go over and study the photo, but Rosa Spina spoke up suddenly, saying, "I think we've filled Signor Cappelli's ears enough for one lunch, wouldn't you say, Emanuele Mosè?" She arched her brow and gave her son a smile that told him to say no more. "There will be other lunches to talk about other things. Of course I'll tell you all about L'Altro," she said to Cappelli. "Another time. Let's enjoy what we have to eat for our lunch today without talking too much. May I give you more polenta? I think there's still some sauce in the pan," she offered brightly. "And there are other good things to eat. There are cod fillets *alla veneziana*. We're only on the first course!"

Cappelli could find no reason to object.

4

That evening, the evening of the lighting of the Nativity, Don Luigi had the rare pleasure of celebrating Mass before a full church. "In five short days it will be the Eve of Christmas," he said. "Let us transform them into days of reflection and repentance, purification and preparation."

Reading the faces of his congregants through the thick lenses of his glasses, the white-haired priest could see that hardly anyone was listening. His heart fell. The parishioners were eager to be done with the service and go outside to hear the band. Don Luigi was a son of the town himself. The older people in the congregation had known him even before he became a priest, years ago when he was a scrawny, nearsighted loner of a kid who spent more time reading than playing. Maybe they knew him too well, he thought. Had he been a stranger to them, they might have considered him with a little more reverence, at least.

He sermonized on the eternally comforting power of faith. Grim December, and daylight was unbearably short, the world at it darkest. But in biblical times, the priest declared, the bearer of light had come in days equally bleak as these. "'The people that walked in darkness have seen a great light,'" he quoted from the book of Isaiah, "'and they that dwell in the land of the shadow of death, upon them hath the light shined.'"

A thought snaked inside the heads of the few congregants who bothered to listen. "Would it be too much to ask," the prayerful wondered, "for the bearer of light to pay us a visit, too?"

Don Luigi dispensed communion, gave his benediction, and, before officially declaring the Mass finished, said, "My heart is gladdened by the great number of you present this evening, and my gladness would be increased only by seeing a similarly impressive attendance a bit more frequently." He squinted with myopic eyes to see if he had got his point across. The faces he saw through his glasses showed no response. "And who knows?" he added despite himself, hating to stoop to ingratiating methods to reach a crowd. "Renewed faith and regular participation in church functions might prove an effective remedy to the *sfortuna* that everyone has been talking about in recent months."

"*Magari!*" a single nameless voice called back from among the many faces, and that utterance—"If only!"—prompted an uneasy laugh from people tired of bearing one bout of bad luck after another.

"The Mass is ended," Don Luigi sighed. "Go in peace."

Two minutes later the church was empty again.

The band lined up in formation on the steps of the church, facing the throng of spectators who waited in the piazza, ankle-deep in snow. Next to the band stood the manger, the Nativity scene it housed dark in shadow for the moment. The comet above, and the angel, and the GLORIA IN EXCELSIS! message were nearly invisible in the blackness of the night sky.

Huddled in the middle of the saxophone section, Daniele mouthed his reed to keep it moist. "*Madonna*, it's cold!" he said to Petrioli, the musician beside him, the thick vapor of his breath puffing visibly from his lips. The icy air penetrated his epauletted navy blue jacket and dress shirt and fancy trousers with the red stripe down the seams. Cold seeped up through his shiny black shoes. Still, Daniele was in uncharacteristically good spirits. His band uniform never failed to dress him in joy. The brightly polished instruments all around gave him a thrill that daily worries could not tarnish. For Daniele, music was better than life.

"We'll spend the rest of the Christmas holidays in bed with the flu," said Petrioli.

"And if we don't hurry up and start," Daniele laughed, twiddling the keys on his sax, "my fingers will be too frozen to play."

He caught sight of Petula and Beniamino among the people that filled the square, surprised how happy the sight of them made him. He raised his eyebrows in salute.

"See Babbo saying hello to us?" Petula said to Beniamino. "You see him?" She lifted him. Six years old, he was getting heavy.

"There he is!" Beniamino shouted. "*Ciao*, Babbo!"

Daniele raised his eyebrows again, then squared his shoulders in a proud pose to show off his uniform.

Beniamino waved once more, then Petula put him down.

"Are they ever going to start?" said Petula's grandmother, Maria Severina, for Petula and Beniamino stood with a cluster of family amid the hundreds of townspeople.

"This year I don't think so," Renato answered Maria Severina. "This year I think they'll just stand looking pretty in their uniforms for a while without playing a note, then when everyone's had enough, they'll send us all home." Teasing his mother-in-law was delight enough for Renato to heat up the coldest of evenings.

"Who asked you?" Maria Severina grunted back, as stout and tough as a wild boar.

Renato chuckled, about to lay into her some more, when he felt someone pulling on his arm. Turning to see who it was, "Cappelli!" he said.

"Oh, Tizzoni," said Cappelli. "*Ciao*. Listen, I could have stayed upstairs and watched this from my window, but I wanted you to meet— Oh, here she is now. My new tenant. Here she comes." And Cappelli did his best to put on the face of a socially graceful person, though it was not a face that fit easily. "Renato Tizzoni, this is Rosa Spina Innocenti."

"Pleasure." Shaking the woman's hand, Renato felt the lace of her fingerless gloves.

"Pleasure," she replied.

Cappelli said, "And this is her son, uh . . ."

"Emanuele Mosè," the young man introduced himself.

On this hand, too, Renato touched fingerless gloves, these made of wool.

"*Auguri*," Renato offered. "Good wishes."

The young man with the long hair and the face that belonged in a church fresco said, "Likewise."

"My wife, Milena," Renato introduced, "my father-in-law, Tonino, and my mother-in-law, Maria Severina." More handshakes went around the group. Maria Severina could not help but arch an eyebrow as she shook the newcomers' hands. Petula nodded a stiff hello, putting a protective hand on Beniamino's head.

"*Madonna pinguina congelata,* it's chilly!" Cappelli said, making Renato laugh. Cappelli was versatile in his blasphemy. Here in the snow and the rigid cold air, Cappelli's idea of calling the Holy Mother a frozen penguin was inarguably apt.

Emanuele Mosè responded with a pained grimace.

"Finally," Maria Severina said. "I think I see that *imbecille* of a band director taking his place. They're ready to begin."

Baldesi the conductor stood before the band, his back turned to the audience so that he could give his musicians some last-minute coaching. "Play without pushing it," said the quiet, bearlike man who had made a mission of giving a little culture to this small Tuscan town. "Let the music play itself."

A sudden screech of amplifier feedback made everyone in the piazza wince. Standing beside the band, Mayor Morelli blew into a microphone. He smiled widely, and after a long list of bureaucratic thank-yous, introduced the band to enthusiastic applause.

"Maestro Baldesi, please," said Mayor Morelli.

Baldesi's baton came down and the band began.

"God Rest Ye Merry, Gentlemen" and "Joy to the World"—pieces not widely known in Tuscany—prompted little response from the overcoated listeners. "Jingle Bells" drew cheers. Children threw snowballs and ran around the legs of their parents. A percussionist at the back of the band shook a bunch of sleighbells. Beniamino let out a terrific laugh.

"White Christmas" was recognized by everyone old enough to remember Bing Crosby singing it, and the piazza filled now with a collective croon: "La la la la la WHY CHRISMA? La la la la la la LAAA!"

During one of the verses, Daniele had a solo. He had been practicing in the bathroom late at night all week. Petula was relieved to hear his saxophone make it through without squeaking.

Next came "Silent Night." As the well-loved song sounded its last note, Don Luigi moved behind the band. Squinting through the lenses of his glasses, he approached the Nativity scene.

The people clapped. The priest was about to bless the Nativity. Then it would be time for the Christmas lights.

Il Piccino, the midget who ran the newspaper shop, moved toward the front of the crowd so that he could watch everything up close. "Oh, Piccino!" people said as he pushed through the forest of legs. *"Auguri!"*

"Thank you," Il Piccino replied with a polite, dignified nod. *"Auguri* to you, too." He was Jewish, the only non-Christian in town, but never had anyone made him feel unloved. He was happy to participate in the piazza this evening. The celebration of Jesus's birth had for him no connection to his beliefs, yet festivities were festivities. Why miss out?

Up front, Don Luigi took a water shaker from the pocket of his long black cassock. He lowered his head a little to pass beneath the beam of the manger, stepped inside, and blessed the sacred life-sized statues in the name of the *Padre,* and of the *Figlio,* and of the *Spirito Santo.* He shook the water shaker with snaps of his wrist, splashing benediction over the statues of Maria and Giuseppe, the shepherds and the sheep, the donkey and the lovely-eyed cow, and the empty crib that awaited Gesù Bambino's birth.

Stepping back, he nodded a cue to the band conductor. Maestro Baldesi readied the band, then lowered his baton. The tubas and baritone saxophones moaned a low fifth. The droning became richer as trombones, flugel horns, and alto and tenor saxes joined in. People cheered to recognize the song merely from its introductory chord: *"Tu Scendi dalle Stelle,"*—"You Came Down from the Stars"—the only authentically Italian carol in anyone's repertoire.

In came the clarinets and flutes, recalling the whine of the sheep-skin bagpipes that traveling musicians played as they roamed from town to town at Christmastime. As soon as the theme started, the people in the piazza began to sing the first verse about the King of Heaven descending from the stars into a hovel, in cold and frost, trembling.

Petula was aware of Emanuele Mosè's stark figure a few feet away. She felt the odd repulsion again like a jolt. She caught sight of Daniele, looked down at her son, glanced at her parents standing together, and noticed how Cappelli could not take his eyes off Rosa Spina. The air around Petula seemed to crackle as if the connections between people, no longer stable and safe, were shifting polarity.

The first verse completed, the moment for the illumination had come. Don Luigi, a few paces from the Nativity scene, gave a nod to Nuzzi the electrician, who had appeared on the other side of the manger.

The band started the second verse. People sang, their eyes turned upward.

> *You, who are Creator of the world,*
> *Have neither fire nor clothes to warm you.*

Nuzzi nodded to a man beside the switch box at the far end of the piazza. In an instant, strings of white lights sparkled along the main street and all around the piazza. People sang and cheered. The band continued to play. Another nod from Nuzzi, and on came the illuminated word AUGURI, an electrical good wish to the world glittering from the façade of the town hall. More cheers. More applause. Nuzzi nodded again and a spotlight from the church roof threw a brilliant glow on the statue of the angel suspended above the manger. This luminous messenger blew his wooden trumpet and bore the banner exclaiming GLORIA IN EXCELSIS!

The people sang, the horns blared, and the drums pounded now as the song reached its climax.

> *Oh beloved Infant!*
> *How extreme is your poverty!*
> *Your love for us reduced you to this lowly state,*
> *And this makes me love you even more!*

Nuzzi gave a final nod, and, high above the manger, the comet snapped on in dazzling golden radiance, its star-shaped body and streaming tail sending a defiant signal to the darkness. The music could scarcely be heard, though the band blasted in robust *fortissimo*, so loud was the applause.

But then the comet shined too brightly. Cheers turned to gasps. The star became a sun and sputtered audibly, sending out sparks, exploding into flames.

Horrified, the people of Sant'Angelo D'Asso recoiled. The band stopped playing and moved off the steps, pushing into the crowd. Don Luigi trotted to put some distance between himself and the comet that now hissed fiercely, burning away the wire that held it aloft. "*Spegni! Spegni!*" Nuzzi screamed to the man at the switch box. "Turn it off!" No use. The comet glared in full flame.

People scattered, pushing each other, hurrying away from the manger. A moment later the wire broke and the comet became a falling star. It crashed on the trumpet-playing angel and on the banner that said GLORIA IN EXCELSIS!, and these, too, dangled dangerously. The comet plummeted, tumbling down on the manger, setting the straw roof on fire.

Rosa Spina put her hand to her breast. Cappelli whistled softly through his teeth in amazement. Daniele's eyes searched the crowd to make sure Petula and Beniamino were unharmed. Petula clutched Beniamino's wrist to stop him from running toward the danger. In her fearful grip, Beniamino watched the fire, thinking this was possibly the best thing he had ever seen in his life. His grandfather, Renato, was thinking something similar.

"Call the fire department!" someone in the crowd yelled.

"And what do you expect them to do?" laughed Mauro Giannetti the butcher. "The fire station is two towns away. By the time they get here, who knows how far the flames will spread?" People standing within earshot of Mauro expected precisely this sort of cynicism from the man. But he had a point, they had to admit.

Don Luigi's eyeglasses reflected the blaze. Disgusted, he bent down, took two handfuls of snow from the church step, and angrily hurled the frozen water at the flames.

"*La neve!*" screamed a few people who had seen the priest. "Snow!" Following the priest's example, others started to throw snow. The band members put aside their instruments and filled their fists with the stuff. Maestro Baldesi thrust his baton into the back pocket of his trousers and got to work gathering snow. Mayor Morelli, Nuzzi, men from the audience, and women, and children, everyone threw snow.

Renato and Milena joined in, as did Cappelli and Rosa Spina, and Tonino and Maria Severina, and Petula and Beniamino. "Can you believe it?" Daniele said, reaching them in the crowd, and helping, relieved everyone in his family was safe.

Beniamino had a single word to say: "*Fantastico!*"

Suddenly Petula wondered where Emanuele Mosè was. Why wasn't he among the people working to extinguish the flames? Rosa Spina stood nearby, but Emanuele Mosè had disappeared.

It was hard to tell at first whether fire or snow would win. The wires of the dangling angel and the GLORIA IN EXCELSIS! banner burned through, and angel, trumpet, and banner crashed together through the burning straw roof. The manger was not a sturdy structure, merely a flimsy mock-up, and the roof fell to pieces in the impact. But with the fire now at ground level, the crowd were finally able to stomp out the sparkling straw.

People relaxed. "Could have been worse," they said to each other when the flames had died. "Who would ever have imagined such a thing?" They brushed ashes off their coats. Lungs coughed out smoke. On the ground, steaming embers hissed.

Then, just when it seemed things had calmed, someone yelled in horror, "The Madonna!" All turned to behold a sight that sickened the stomach. The sacred statues of the Nativity, surrounded by debris, were soot-flecked and a little charred, but that was nothing a fresh coat of paint could not solve. The Madonna, however, there in adoration beside the empty crib, had lost her head.

Something must have fallen on her. Maybe the angel. Maybe the banner proclaiming GLORIA IN EXCELSIS! Maybe the comet itself.

"Holy Virgin!" Rosa Spina said.

"*Dio boia!*" Renato said, referring to God the Executioner in an expression he saved for moments of great weight.

"*Madonna decapitata!*" Cappelli said. Anyone close enough to hear him had to agree that calling the Virgin Mary beheaded was excruciatingly accurate.

Of course she was only a statue, the rational part of people's brains tried to reason. But this was not a question of reason. The vision of a headless Maria was an image from the kind of nightmare that no townsperson with a snowflake's weight of sensitivity would ever have wanted to dream. The pale plaster insides of the Virgin's severed neck showed like a curse. Old women crossed themselves in the hope that the horrid plague of bad luck sent by some nameless malevolent force had not already infected the town beyond redemption. Little girls and boys stared with wide eyes.

The only thing to do was to try to make the Madonna whole again. People got to work, probing the cinders of the manger, but there was no sign of her head. The toes of shoes kicked aside snow in vain.

Just when the faithful began to think that the mutilated Madonna would remain with them as an unshakable malediction, a voice said, "*Ce l'ho io.*" Eyes turned to the young man who spoke. "I have it," he said.

Stepping out from the crowd, Emanuele Mosè approached the manger. He held a beautiful plaster face in his outstretched hands.

"*Bravo,*" said Don Luigi, coming near to receive the Madonna's head.

Emanuele Mosè said, "Don't worry. I'll take care of it," and he brushed by the priest who, behind his glasses, blinked.

"Young man!" Don Luigi called after him. "Wait." He walked quickly, following Emanuele Mosè, but his black shoes found a patch of ice. Before anyone had time to grab for him, Don Luigi landed badly on the stone steps of his church. His glasses flew from his face, and the bone in his right leg broke loudly enough for people nearby to hear the crack.

The priest's mouth opened in mute agony. A group of people rushed to help, handing him his glasses, urging him not to try to stand.

"But the Madonna!" the priest yelled.

Watching from where she stood, Petula saw the unflinching concentration with which Emanuele Mosè carried the Madonna's head toward the rest of the statue, apparently oblivious to Don Luigi's fall. He approached the beheaded Virgin Mother as if the plaster effigy deserved more pity than did the old priest.

Emanuele Mosè placed the Madonna's head on its neck. "We can glue this later, to make it permanent," he said in soft words audible only to those standing close to him, speaking into the Madonna's face with the tenderness of a family member. "But we can't just leave it balanced here. It will roll off. Here. Let's try this."

The town looked on as some people aided the priest while, only a few paces away, Emanuele Mosè worked to heal the Madonna.

He took off the scarf from his own neck. He tied it around the statue of the Holy Mother so it held her head on, though it appeared as natural as a shawl. "That's better," Emanuele Mosè said to the Virgin Mary. "Wouldn't you say?"

Some men ran to get a car to take Don Luigi to the hospital in Siena. Powerless, the priest held his leg and tried not to scream. His angry eyes met the serene gaze of Emanuele Mosè, who offered a brief nod. Was the gesture intended to communicate compassion or victorious pride? The priest did not know.

Emanuele Mosè, his smile bright, turned and looked down upon the town from the steps of the church. All around him, snow was black with ash. The walls of the manger had burned away, leaving the Holy

Family and shepherds and sheep and donkey and lovely-eyed cow exposed and unprotected. The piazza smelled of sulphurous smoke. "*Auguri*," said Emanuele Mosè to the town before him. "Good wishes."

As if by rote, the people replied, "*Auguri.*"

Glowering at Emanuele Mosè, Daniele wondered just who the hell he thought he was, this mamma's boy who played with sacred dolls before everyone's eyes. Why, Daniele asked himself, should Petula give this guy a second look?

As Petula observed Emanuele Mosè, a thought arose inside her, the same impression that had come when the roof tile nearly struck Beniamino. Though Emanuele Mosè had shoved neither the tile nor the priest, Petula sensed that the young man was dangerous.

Renato went to see if there was anything he could do for the priest. Other men had the situation under control, so Renato stepped back, seeing that too many helpful hands would become a hindrance. Looking at Emanuele Mosè's expression of supreme omnipotence, Renato thought: There's a boy with a problem or two, if you ask me.

Don Luigi, in pain, stared at Emanuele Mosè over the shoulders of the men helping him. Diligently he told himself that detesting a fellow human being was a luxury not permitted to priests. All the same, the dark passion of hatred rose in him, and his heart pumped hard.

Eyeing Emanuele Mosè, Cappelli thought with a chill: And this kid is living in my house.

Marta Sorcini, the violet-haired widow who never had found much relief from her nervous solitude in Don Luigi's Masses, watched Emanuele Mosè in wonderment. Her blinking pink eyes saw how the priest had crumbled like a ruin beside the youth with the serious face. If he can repair the Holy Virgin, Marta thought, imagine what he might do for me.

Generously lit, the butcher's shop displayed the dismembered parts of many animals. Busy calculating her list, Petula did not see Beniamino stare at the row of prosciutti hanging from hooks against the tiled wall behind the counter, each ham an entire leg of pig. Still attached to one prosciutto was a piggishly curlicued tail.

Beniamino's eyes shifted to braces of dead pheasants hanging upside down, plumage shiny still.

Mauro Giannetti, the butcher with burst red capillaries visible beneath the skin of his cheeks, noticed the boy's concentration fixed on the birds. "Do you want to go hunting when you grow up?"

Looking at the brightly feathered dead things that, strangely, retained much of the luster of life, Beniamino said, "No."

Mauro Giannetti laughed as if the child had said something clever, and then returned his attention to the slab of meat he was wrapping in stiff white paper.

Two days after the fire in the manger, three more days until Christmas Eve, the flow of customers had been heavy all day, with everyone eager to buy meat for their feasts.

The glass display counter attracted Beniamino's eye. Petula, too, stood examining all there was to see. There were the cuts of beef—filet, rump, ribs, tongue—and there was pork, and a piglet that had been stuffed with rock salt and roasted whole, its eyelids sewn closed. Near the piglet's snout slept the pink bodies of rabbits whose skin had been peeled off. The rabbits snuggled against a raw leg of lamb.

White plastic tubs held glistening entrails: pig's liver, calf liver, cow's lung, the kidneys of a wild boar. Both Petula and Beniamino studied a vat full of bloodred, mudlike slop. "Bleh," Beniamino said and the two of them made disgusted faces and giggled quietly in the wordless exchange of thoughts understood perfectly, at times, between a mother and her child.

"*Milza,*" Petula said. "Spleen." Then, in a whisper, she echoed her son's sentiment: "Bleh."

"Good idea," said the plump middle-aged woman customer being served. It was Signora Bottoni, whose two sons had moved away from their mother's suffocating attentions as soon as they came of age. "I'll take a little container of the spleen."

Petula caught a whiff of Signora Bottoni's perfume. She smelled of flowers. Tons of flowers, flowers that had died, weighed down by their own smelliness.

Mauro Giannetti took a big spoon, dug deep into the vat of spleen, and slapped a dollop into a small plastic container. "More?" he said.

"More," said Signora Bottoni. A second spoonful plopped into the container. The signora turned to Beniamino. "You like spleen?"

Beniamino made his *bleh* face.

"My boys hated it, too, when they were little, but I gave it to them anyway. Spleen they used to hate, and brains. I used to mix the brains in the blender with fruit juice so they wouldn't notice. They drank it right up. It's good for them, in the end. You should tell your mamma to give you lots of meat to eat."

Inwardly considering the benefits of switching to a vegetarian diet, Petula smiled politely and said, "Sometimes I think that children naturally know what's good for them."

Signora Bottoni twittered a laugh, then asked Mauro for a half kilo of blood sausage, too.

Mauro took the dark sausage from the display case and sharpened his knife. All eyes in the store watched, for there was something irresistible about the butcher's meaty hands in action, the fingernails trimmed with blood.

"Tell me, Signora Bottoni," Mauro said while he worked, "are your boys coming to stay with you over the holidays?" The question was cruel. Everyone in town knew that Signora Bottoni's sons never came to visit.

"My boys?" The muscles around Signora Bottoni's thin lips twitched defensively. "They want to come, naturally," she said. "But with one in Milan and the other in Naples, I told them they shouldn't worry about their old mother. The train is so expensive nowadays."

"Of course it is," said Mauro Giannetti.

"Maybe for Easter I'll go and visit them," said Signora Bottoni, heat rising in her cheeks.

"Of course you will," Mauro said with the smirk that never left his face.

For an instant, the people here—the beefy butcher, the sheep-eyed women, the pork-faced men—appeared brutal in Petula's eyes. Had they been strangers, would she have had any desire to spend time in their company? All at once, her life in this town felt alien to what she might have chosen for herself, if she had ever had the chance to decide.

She thought of Daniele, who would not enjoy Christmas celebrations if they did not include the consumption of especially good prosciutto and freshly killed lamb. Mangiavacchi, she happened to think just now, was his last name after all. Daniele *Mangiavacchi:* Eater of Cows. And if she were to see him now for the first time, she asked herself, would he look like anyone she would want to know?

Trapped by the savage customers in the shop, Petula was sure she could smell the aroma of blood rising from the sausage that yielded to the sharpness of the butcher's knife. She could almost hear the watering of everyone else's mouths. She wanted to go outside, wanted to breathe.

Just then the bell over the door sounded and Cappelli walked in. Petula was so glad to see his familiar face, it was as if he had saved her from the jaws of cannibals.

"*Buonasera a tutti,*" Cappelli said to everyone assembled. "Good evening to all." He looked embarrassed, for he was not accustomed to doing much food shopping, and he reckoned correctly that the eyes of his townspeople watched him in quick understanding that he had

started shopping only because his house was more populated than it
had ever been. Cappelli was not a person who enjoyed being
watched.

"*Buonasera*, Signor Cappelli," Petula said warmly.

"Oh, Petula!" he said, equally pleased to have found a friendly
face.

"Cappelli!" Mauro Giannetti said with his usual leer of sarcasm.
"Isn't this a surprise?" The only butcher in this small town, Mauro
Giannetti knew he could get away with rudeness. "What brings you
here?"

"Thought I'd buy some meat," Cappelli said, talking off his
woolen cap in the heat of the crowd. "Logical place to come, no?"

People laughed and, for Petula, the world became good-natured
again. These were no savage strangers after all; they were the men and
women who had watched her grow up and who now looked on her
child with grandparently affection, however carnivorous their tastes.

Mauro Giannetti handed Signora Bottoni the white plastic bag
made weighty with individually wrapped pieces of flesh and organs.
Upset now, the woman gave him some paper money and poked her
finger through her coin purse for exact change.

"Happy holidays to you," Mauro said with his grin, knowing well
that Signora Bottoni's holidays, without her sons, would be far from
happy.

"Good holidays to everyone," said Signora Bottoni, trying not to
look flustered. She made the bell above the door jangle on her way out.

Mauro turned to Petula and she ordered ground turkey. Poultry,
seeming to have nothing to do with the bleeding parts of mammals
behind the glass counter-front, was less gruesome prey.

The butcher sliced chunks off the large turkey breast and fed the
pieces into the meat grinder.

"Must be nice to have guests in your house," said Marta Sorcini,
the widow who stood beside Cappelli.

Realizing the comment had been aimed at him, Cappelli said,
"Guests? Oh. *Sì*. Nice, I suppose."

"And you certainly picked yourself some interesting guests, I'll say that myself," said Mauro, glancing up from his grinding.

"If you say so." Cappelli did not want his home life laid nude like a bare breast of turkey before everyone in the shop. "They're well behaved. Haven't given me reason to complain." He hoped the conversation would stop there.

"To complain maybe not. But to marvel, I'm sure, they've given you lots of reason." Marta with the violet hair would not be satisfied until the thing had been discussed thoroughly. "I've never seen such a family in this town. Have you seen the way the woman dresses?"

"And for a woman of her age," said Mauro. "Whatever that age might be."

"She looks all right to me," said Cappelli.

"I believe it!" Mauro Giannetti laughed. "Tell us, Cappelli. She always walk around with her dress cut that low, even at home?"

"She lives downstairs." Cappelli's face grew hot. "How would I know what she wears in her house?"

The butcher laughed, his eyes resembling the eyes of a hog. "You mean to say you never go down for a little visit?"

"I mean to say it's my own business whether I go downstairs or not." He hoped he sounded dignified.

"They say her son's a healer," said Marta.

Petula felt a twinge of nausea at hearing this news, as if Marta had said not *healer* but *poisoner*. Sorcerer would have seemed to her a more appropriate profession for Emanuele Mosè.

"You need healing, do you?" Cappelli asked. "And who says he's a healer, anyway?"

"How do I know? It's just what they say." Marta watched strands of turkey meat worm out of the grinder. "Certainly," she said, "they're not people like us. But then, why expect miraculous-type people to be like us?"

"Miraculous?" Mauro shook his head. "Maybe the young man fixed the statue of the Madonna, but it was hardly a miracle. And I don't think the priest was so impressed. Bad break to his leg, I've heard. You just ask Don Luigi what he thinks of that young man with the long face!" he said.

"Maybe the Madonna's head was no miracle." Marta's voice became sharp. Her pale cheeks started to match her violet hair. "But how do you account for his birth? You can't say there wasn't something miraculous in that."

"Right!" Mauro Giannetti guffawed. "A miraculous birth! Is that what they're saying about your houseguests, Cappelli? You have supernatural wonders living downstairs?"

"What do I know?" Cappelli shrugged, but the heart inside his thick chest quickened. Rosa Spina had made him promise to tell no one about the remarkable events surrounding Emanuele Mosè's birth. Faithful to his word, he had not even told Renato. How could it be that other people had heard?

"You may not know, but I'll tell you myself." Marta was thrilled to have a shop full of people attentive to her morsel of news. "They say the mother was a virgin when an angel came to her to say that unto her would be born a son."

Mauro Giannetti, blood running red through the capillaries in his face, said, "If that mother's a virgin, then so am I." He looked at Marta and laughed.

If there was one thing that Marta hated, it was laughter at her expense. She bit her lip and felt her temples throb.

An angel now, is it? wondered Cappelli. I thought it was just a voice from God. And *practically a virgin* is what she said when she told me, if we want to stick to the precise particulars.

"An angel?" Beniamino was intrigued.

Petula was not sure she wanted her child to hear such stories. "Excuse me, but who is going around saying these things?"

"Everyone!" Marta bleated. "I heard it from the baker's wife, and she had heard it from the mother herself."

Why, Cappelli wondered, would Rosa Spina have confided in the baker's wife? Everyone knew that the baker's wife was no more capable of keeping a secret than she was of stopping the smell of hot bread from escaping her shop. Or maybe Rosa Spina, still new to

Sant'Angelo D'Asso and trusting soul that she was, hadn't known it would be better to watch her words around certain people.

"He's a miraculous type all right," said Marta, looking defiantly at Mauro. "That's what everyone's saying. That's what I told the post-mistress when I was cashing my poor husband's pension check, peace to his soul. I told her, 'Don't you wonder about the boy's hands?' Emanuele Mosè's hands, I mean to say. I saw him sitting in his window overlooking the square, and he lifted his hands to rub his eyes. And there were those gloves. Does he ever take them off? They look just like the gloves Padre Pio used to wear. Everyone thought poor Padre Pio was a heretic, but in the end they realized he kept his gloves on because he had the stigmata. It would be messy otherwise." When no one responded, she continued, "Don't be surprised, Cappelli, if I come to one of those prayer meetings I hear he's holding in your house."

"Prayer meetings?"

"Everyone's talking," said Marta. "Individual sessions during the week, group meetings on Sunday evenings."

Cappelli screwed up his face, and Petula saw how uneasy he was to learn that a schedule had been established as if Rosa Spina and her son had set up some sort of clinic in his home. "Wonderful." Cappelli shook his head. "Our very own *santone.*"

"What's a *santone?*" Beniamino asked.

"Someone who's supposed to pull off miracles with a prayer or two," Cappelli answered, "and people come to get prayed over. Though between you and me—" He raised a skeptical eyebrow and shrugged at the boy.

"Other towns have their own *santoni,*" Marta went on. "Why shouldn't we? I think it would be worth visiting your new tenants just to see what's in the gloves. People want to know. People are look-ing for help these days, with all the terrible things happening. But that's not all." The widow paused for effect, looking around her to make people curious about what she might say next. "There's an-other son, too. There's L'Altro."

Petula felt her skin tingle again at the mention of his name. Not a gossiper herself, she usually disregarded other people's small talk. Now, however, she listened intently, despite herself.

"And who is L'Altro?" Mauro Giannetti never missed a chance to put his nose in other people's business. "What's his name? Anything as heavy as the name of that Emanuele Mosè boy?"

"L'Altro," said Marta, wishing that he would lose his tone of mockery when addressing a question to her. "That's his name."

"You're joking!" Mauro Giannetti blurted out. *The Other One? L'Altro?* He's the other son, so they call him the Other One?" He shook his head and mashed more turkey meat into the grinder. "Seems more like an insult than a name, if you ask me. Sounds like something Petula's father would name his sheep."

Cappelli wanted them all to shut up. Why should the family living in his house concern anyone but himself?

"And I say this," Mauro Giannetti went on, "L'Altro is the kind of name you give when you don't know what else to call a son."

"Not at all!" Marta protested with vehemence. "The mother called him L'Altro on purpose. Don't you see? The angel announced the arrival of Emanuele Mosè, so once the mother had given birth to him, she thought she had finished. But no! There was this other one inside her, and the annunciation hadn't said a thing about him! So she asked herself, 'If God sent the first, then who sent this other one?' That's what the mother told the baker's wife, and that's what the baker's wife told me."

She didn't tell *me* that part of the story, thought Cappelli. What else was there that Rosa Spina had forgotten to mention?

"That poor mother." Marta used her palm to smooth down her violet hair. "She and her firstborn have done nothing but good to the Other One, and he's done nothing but bad in return. That's why they locked him up, you know."

"Locked him up?" said the butcher, interested. "As in prison?"

"As in the prison up in Volterra." The woman nodded.

"For what crime?" Cappelli could not help but ask.

"If you don't know, then how could I?" Marta sniffed. "The mother hasn't said what her other son's crime was. Poor dear, she must be too upset. But now it seems they might be letting him out soon, and the poor mother is desperate. She's afraid to have him back in her home, but what can she do? He's her son. Blood is blood. All she can do, she says, is pray."

"*Her* home?" Mauro laughed. "You mean Cappelli's home. Eh, Cappelli? How's it feel to have someone come straight out of prison and into your house?"

Cappelli suddenly noticed how sweaty it was in the shop. He wanted to leave, but he still had his meat to buy. He opened his jacket and wiped his forehead. "So?" he said, wanting to sound as if L'Altro's incarceration were no news to him. "And so what?" He lifted his eyebrows, trying to appear casual and magnanimous. "People coming out of prison have to sleep someplace, too, don't they?"

"Fine," said Mauro. "But I might just put an extra lock on the door of the shop with someone like that coming to town."

"Maybe he's not a thief," said Cappelli, and Petula could see his efforts to hide his distress. "We shouldn't assume he goes around stealing things." He turned to the widow. "Right?"

"He could be a murderer," Marta said.

"A murderer!" Beniamino said.

Petula patted his head, thinking that maybe she should cover his ears. "No one is a murderer," she said.

"He might be," Marta said.

"We don't know that for sure," said Petula.

"Maybe they put him away for unpaid parking tickets," Cappelli said hopefully.

"Or maybe he killed his last landlord," Mauro Giannetti laughed.

"Or maybe," Cappelli said, "he strangled people who laughed too much."

Mauro Giannetti's laughter chilled, but his grin remained.

"Anyway," said Cappelli, wishing he had a nice glass of something to drink, "I don't care what he was. I say *was*, not *is*, because maybe his time away taught him something."

"Another lock is a good idea anyway, I say," said Mauro, scraping the last of the turkey meat from the grinder and onto the paper wrapper. "No one will catch me off guard," he said, punching the price into the scale. "My eyes are too open."

"Mine, too," said the widow.

"Then what's your worry?" Cappelli laughed. "Hey, Petula, you worried?"

"Not me," she said, rising to his defense. "Might bring new life to the town."

"But who's a murderer?" Beniamino asked his mother.

"Nobody," Petula said.

"Then we're not worried," Cappelli said to close the conversation. Inside his hot jacket, however, he was very far from calm.

Mauro put the bundle of ground turkey on the countertop. "What else can I get you?"

Petula ordered lamb for Daniele.

When the plastic bag containing her order hung heavily from her hand, Petula paid, wished the butcher, Cappelli, and the other customers a happy holiday, and left. She was outside with Beniamino when a thought made her stop and re-enter the brightly lit shop.

Cappelli was watching the butcher's knife behead a lifeless chicken for Marta.

"Signor Cappelli?" said Petula. "Remember when I was a girl how you used to spend Christmas with my family?"

"Remember, yes."

"Why did you stop coming?"

Cappelli shrugged. "Who knows? People get older. Habits change. Nice Christmases they were, though."

"Is Signor Cappelli coming to our house for Christmas?" Beniamino asked.

"That's up to him. What do you say, Signor Cappelli? You'd certainly be welcome for the big Christmas lunch."

"Eh!" Cappelli nodded. "Why not?" Then he remembered why not. Rosa Spina had invited him to have lunch on Christmas Day in the downstairs apartment. And he had come here now to buy the meat. For the first time ever, his Christmas plans had become complicated. "I mean," he said, "it's a beautiful idea, having the big lunch together, but my tenants, you know, were thinking of inviting me to eat a little something. And I didn't want to seem rude, so I said yes."

"Christmas lunch with the *santone*," Mauro Giannetti laughed. "Just think! And if fortune smiles on you, the murderer might get out of prison and join you in time for dessert."

"If he really is a murderer," Cappelli said, "I'll send him to your place for coffee."

Petula laughed. "If you have other plans," she said to Cappelli, "that's fine. I just didn't like the thought of your being alone on Christmas."

"Alone? Not this year, no. But let's try to find a moment to see each other, in any case."

"Yes. Let's try to find a little moment."

And she left, leaving Cappelli with an awkward smile on his face.

"You see our Cappelli?" Mauro winked. "Solitary as a monk his whole life, then the next minute he has more invitations than he can handle. Popular man, Cappelli is. Who knows what secret charms he has so that everybody wants to eat with him and live in his house. Eh, Cappelli?"

"Secret charms." Cappelli nodded, not sure he enjoyed the butcher's teasing. Still, there was something flattering in all the invitations he was receiving lately, and he was tickled that people should notice how his company was desired. "Secret charms," he mumbled, wishing he could hide from other people's attention.

When he left the shop, his plastic bag full of meat, he walked up the dark evening street toward his house on the main square. He would ask Rosa Spina whether her other son was really due out of prison. He would ask if, that is, he could find a natural way to bring up the topic. For the moment, nothing seemed natural to him.

His fingers searched for the keys in his pocket. He glanced up as he neared the front door. A light was on in the apartment inhabited by Rosa Spina and Emanuele Mosè. Sure enough, just as Marta had described, the young man could be seen seated at the window, his head bowed as if in prayer. Raised hands covered the face; on the hands were the fingerless gloves. Who knew what mystery those gloves wanted to conceal?

A less than benevolent thought slipped into Cappelli's brain: *If he really has to pray, why do it there at the window in full view of everyone walking through the square?* Cappelli was not one for praying, but he was certain that if the whim to pray ever did come over him, he would not do it in public.

The hands over the face parted. The eyes opened to stare immediately into Cappelli's watching face.

Embarrassed to have been caught looking, Cappelli gave a shy half smile and lowered his eyes to the clump of keys in his hand. His brain hurt from thinking too much without knowing what to think. He put the key in the lock and muttered, "Who knows?" *Why was the kid making his prayers so conspicuous?* he wondered, perplexed. *What business was he advertising up there? He couldn't really be a* santone, *could he? That's all I need. Pilgrims coming to my house and turning the place into a shrine.*

The image of the young man in the window was a softly shadowed picture, but in Cappelli's confused brain it burned like a neon sign that screamed its message into the dark evening: HEALER AT WORK.

6

Midnight Mass was an approximative term in Sant'Angelo D'Asso, for the service actually started shortly after eleven. The crutches that Don Luigi leaned on throughout the service made his armpits sore. Having to stay on his feet so long, he felt his broken leg throb inside its plaster cast. If he got his timing right, the Mass would end in time for Baby Jesus's arrival to coincide with the joyful pealing of the bells at the stroke of twelve. This year, the manger destroyed by the fire, there would be no outdoor Nativity, only Gesù Bambino in his cradle at the altar of the church.

Petula saw the heaviness of Beniamino's drowsy eyelids. She could tell he struggled to stay awake. Candles flickered around the altar. Smoky incense spiced the air. The service proceeded in a slow succession of prayers. Kyrie, Gloria, Credo . . . "Is it almost time?" Beniamino squirmed on the hard pew.

Daniele pointed a finger of warning at his son. "Sit still." He raised his eyebrows when he spoke to let Beniamino know he wasn't joking.

"When will it be time?"

Daniele said, "Sit still and wait."

Beniamino rested his head against Petula and leaned away from his father, shooting him pouty looks.

Petula could read Beniamino's thoughts. He'd been forced to wait for Gesù Bambino to be put in the cradle, even in his little Nativity at home. Now here it was, Christmas Eve, and the cradle in the *presepio* in his bedroom was still empty. All because Daniele had told him that they could not do their procession at home until after the priest put the official Gesù Bambino doll in the cradle.

Petula wondered why Daniele refused to bend. What pleasure could there be in torturing a child? Lately, Daniele seemed to find strange delight in inventing rules for Beniamino to obey.

"How much longer?" A trace of a whine drawled in Beniamino's voice.

"Not too much," Petula said, kissing his head.

"Don't make a mamma's boy of him," Daniele rasped. "He has to learn."

"Exactly what is it he has to learn?" Petula whispered, her own voice becoming tense.

"He can't have everything he wants when he wants it. I can't, so why should he?"

"He's a child."

"It's never too early to learn certain lessons in life," Daniele said. To close the discussion, he folded his arms across his chest, sat back in the pew, and turned his face toward the priest.

More standing up and sitting down. More prayers with Don Luigi's monotone leading the voices of the throng. Petula could see that Beniamino's impatience soon would turn to tears.

"The Mass is ended," Don Luigi said. Finally. "Go in peace. But before we leave the church, we will have the processional to bear Gesù Bambino to his cradle in commemoration of the glorious birth." The priest, his crutches impeding him from carrying Gesù Bambino himself, sent the head altar boy to the sacristy to fetch the sacred doll.

Beniamino stood on the pew, trying to see over the shoulders of the people in front of him. "I can't see."

"Here, *ometto*," Daniele said, picking him up to make him taller. "Can you see now?"

Petula loved the way Daniele called their son *ometto*—little man. Coming from Daniele's lips, the nickname sounded like a sign of camaraderie. She watched Daniele lift their son up into his arms. He was capable of sweetness—Petula knew this—but why did he inevitably poison sweetness with the bitterness of his anger, his frustration, his arbitrary inflexible rules? She knew the answer to her own question. Daniele's father, of course. How could she blame Daniele after the wretched childhood he had endured?

With an entourage of altar boys and girls in tow, Don Luigi hobbled on his crutches toward the cradle, while the head altar boy carried in the statue of the baby whose arms were spread wide as if to rejoice in His own arrival in the mortal world. Just as the priest placed Gesù Bambino in the straw matting of the cradle, the church bells chimed midnight, and long peals of exaltation began.

The congregation crowded to the front, forming eager lines to pass before the holy figurine. Daniele put Beniamino down, letting him wait in line on his own two feet. The lines shuffled forward until at last Beniamino and his parents stood in front of the cradle. Petula put her fingers to her lips, then touched Baby Jesus' toes. Daniele did the same.

"Kiss Gesù Bambino," Daniele instructed.

Beniamino leaned forward and planted his mouth on the doll's feet.

"*Buon natale,*" Petula said, kissing Beniamino's right cheek.

"*Buon natale,*" Daniele said, kissing the left.

"*Buon natale,*" Beniamino said. "Now can we go home?"

"We'll say hello to a few people first," Daniele said.

Beniamino whined.

Petula saw Daniele's finger point at Beniamino's face. "Don't you start," Daniele said.

In the clear, icy air outside, people exchanged greetings on the stone steps of the church. Beniamino received kisses from his grandparents and great-grandparents. The boy seemed happy enough to accept a soft-skinned kiss from Tita Vezzosi, an old woman who had become like a mother to Renato after his parents' death. But Petula saw the boy pull away when Rosa Spina leaned over to give him a kiss with wet-looking lips. "He's a little shy with people he doesn't know well," Petula said to apologize.

"Then we should find a way to get to know each other better," Rosa Spina said in her girlish voice.

"*Buon natale*, Petula," said Emanuele Mosè.

The young man hesitated, as if deciding whether to kiss her cheeks. She had no desire to kiss him. Besides, she sensed Daniele half a step away and she knew he was watching. She put out her hand. "*Buon natale*," she said, shaking Emanuele Mosè's hand in his fingerless glove.

Standing among the well-wishers, Cappelli looked out of place. Rosa Spina had talked him into attending the Mass, though he could not remember the last time he had set foot in church.

"What a beautiful ceremony!" Rosa Spina cooed. "What a perfect town that destiny brought us to! Don't you think so, Emanuele Mosè?"

"*Molto bello*," he said, but his distant voice gave no indication that he believed his own words.

Daniele studied Emanuele Mosè, whose eyes were set on the stars above the piazza. What the hell is he looking at up there? Daniele wondered. The young man seemed to communicate with the secret world of space, as if he alone knew what it meant to be conceived in the heavens and sent to be born among men. I'll bet he's no more of a saint than I am, Daniele said to himself.

Petula, too, noticed the way Emanuele Mosè focused on faraway stars. She wondered if she had hurt his feelings by using a handshake to fend off a kiss. Let him be hurt, she decided. I have enough of other people's feelings to consider.

"I think it would be a marvelous idea," Rosa Spina carried on, "for us to invite our new friends to our apartment to eat a little something with us and warm away this chill. What do you all say?"

Emanuele Mosè kept on staring at invisible galaxies.

Cappelli said, "It's a little late, no?"

"Of course it's late!" Rosa Spina laughed. "But wouldn't a bite of food make everyone's stomach happy before we go to bed?"

Beniamino twisted his body to look up into his parents' faces.

"You promised. You said we could go straight home and make the procession for Gesù Bambino."

"Beniamino's right," Daniele said. A big social event in the apartment of these strange people appealed to him not at all. He certainly did not want to have to sit at a table with Emanuele Mosè. "We *did* promise. You've been waiting long enough, *ometto*, haven't you?"

"*Andiamo!*" Beniamino reached for his parents' hands, as if to drag them. "Let's go home!"

Beniamino's relatives joined in to decline the invitation politely, pointing out that tomorrow would be Christmas morning, and with the presents to open and the meals to cook, they should all get a good night's sleep.

"But of course." Rosa Spina appeared to agree. "Emanuele Mosè? What do you think? Wouldn't it be a beautiful idea if everyone came upstairs?"

"What do I think?" He returned his gaze earthward, looking hard at his mother. "About what?"

Momentarily thrown by the ungraciousness of her son's reply, Rosa Spina refound her equilibrium and said, "It's late, I was saying. And it's cold outside. Which is why we should go upstairs just for a minute and have a little mouthful to make us all sleep better. And how long does it take to eat a bowl of tortellini *in brodo* and drink a nice little shadow of wine?"

"A little shadow of wine?" Cappelli said. He could almost taste it on his tongue. "And a little bowl of tortellini . . ." He was yearning suddenly, craving the appetizing plate Rosa Spina had described. She had a talent for doing that, for making you desire what you wouldn't even have thought about wanting if she hadn't planted the idea. "A drop of broth and a good big glass of wine before going to bed. *Madonna!*" Cappelli felt warmed just thinking about it. "Now that you say it, why not a little mouthful?" He wanted company, though, now that everyone had witnessed him accepting the offer to enter Rosa Spina's apartment this late at night. "You all won't let me eat alone, will you? Come on! She's right, you know. How long can it take? Come up for ten minutes."

A mumble of *Well, if only for ten or fifteen minutes* went around the little group. No getting out now. And it was Christmas Eve. If you couldn't be sociable tonight, then when?

Beniamino let out a despairing cough that was almost a sob.

"A quarter of an hour," Petula consoled. "Then we'll take you home and have the procession to put Gesù Bambino in his cradle in your bedroom, and we'll all go beddies. You've been such a good, grown-up boy. *Dai.* A quarter of an hour more."

"Fine then," said Emanuele Mosè, condescending at last to speak to the human beings around him. He rubbed his gloved hands together. "Mamma has decided for us. If Mamma says we should all go in, let's go in." He spoke without a smile, making no one feel welcome.

He led the way across the piazza, found the key in his pocket, and opened the door for all to enter.

Stepping inside, Cappelli felt like a guest in his own house.

As she took Beniamino by the hand and followed the others up the stairs, Petula felt she was being led into the private world of a family whose secrets she would rather not know.

Everyone noticed the miracle inside. Homey was the only way to describe the apartment that Rosa Spina and Emanuele Mosè had moved into hardly more than a week before. The spiderwebs had been removed, the terracotta tiles of the floor swept and scrubbed, the windows washed. The kitchen had clearly been cooked in. Food was on the shelves, savory smells in the air. Emanuele Mosè went to put fresh logs on the still-hot embers in the fireplace.

The only decoration added in the main room was a little altar placed against the wall and draped in a red tablecloth. On two of its corners there were tall pillar candles, and between the candles stood a row of postcard-sized sacred images and saintly statuettes. On the wall above, there hung a large framed image of a very bloody Jesus at the height of the Passion. His face captured in startlingly intimate close-up, Jesus' eyes yearned heavenward beneath his crown of thorns. Everyone noticed the uncommon goriness of the icon. No one knew what to say.

"We can whitewash the rooms when the weather warms up in the spring," said Rosa Spina, giving a quick tour through the rooms. "There's a lot to do still, but it's like eating an elephant, isn't it? And everybody knows how to eat an elephant."

"How *do* you eat an elephant?" Renato asked.

Rosa Spina's smile showed the tongue tip between the white teeth. "One bite at a time." She opened a door. "This is where I sleep— Signor Cappelli was so kind in bringing up this big wrought-iron bed for me from the basement—and that room there is Emanuele Mosè's. Bathroom's here, and the rest is what you see. The kitchen, this wonderful long table in the eating area, fireplace over there." Then she pointed to the ceiling. "Such a special space, knowing that Signor Cappelli lives right upstairs. He truly is an angel, don't you all think?"

"Cappelli?" laughed Tonino, secretly intrigued by the curves hidden inside the several layers of the woman's shawls. "An angel?"

"Angel my ass," Cappelli said to shirk the embarrassment of attention. "How's the fire going?" he asked, walking away from the circle of people. The logs, already ablaze, sent out woodsmoke as rich as the incense of the church.

The women went to the kitchen to get the food ready; the men all gravitated to the fireplace. Talk was easy and immediate among the women. Words come out on their own when food is prepared.

The men at the fireplace had to force themselves to make chitchat. It shouldn't be so damned difficult, each said to himself. But there was that strange figure sitting in the armchair with his gaunt, unsmiling face, and the serious eyes that watched all, judged, and apparently found the simple company around him lacking. The men busied themselves with the logs and the iron poker, as if keeping a fire alight required the concentrated effort of all of them. They talked about work at the Waterworks Department or at the bottega or at the station bar, but their words were devoid of ease.

In his tiredness, Beniamino bounced back and forth between the world of women and the world of men. The women gave him pieces of cheese to nibble on and told him that he was a good and beautiful boy. When he had enough of their adoration, he went over to watch the flames and sparks in the fireplace and listen to the men talk about grown-up, manly things that he couldn't understand. The women smelled better than the men, Beniamino noticed. Better and more inviting to hug. Still, someday he would turn into one of the men himself.

But no womanly hug, no friendly joke from man to boy, could comfort him now. He wanted to go home. He had had enough of the company of adults.

"Stop running around like a baby," his father scolded. "You're a big boy now, *ometto*. Show everyone that you know how to behave."

"But you said so yourself that we should go home."

Daniele could not let on that he was as eager to get out of there as his son. "Plans changed. We'll be home soon enough. But you don't see me running around like a baby, do you?"

"I don't care what you do." Exhaustion put courage in his words. *"Che m'importa a me?* What do I care what you do?"

"And what do I care how tired you are?" Daniele's voice was a loaded pistol. What would Emanuele Mosè and the other men think if he let his son get away with talking to him like that? "In front of all these people, you call that a way to speak to your father?" Daniele said.

Emanuele Mosè watched but did not say a word.

"Relax, Daniele," Renato intervened. "He's just tired."

"Tired or not," Daniele insisted, speaking only to his son, "you'll show me respect."

"Why should I?" Beniamino found a strange solace in whining insolence. It almost made him forget how close he was to sleep.

"I'll show you why." Daniele wagged his open palm in the air, indicating the slap a single wrong word away. "You know what my father used to say in moments like this? He'd say, *'Mi prude la mano.* I have a hand just itching to be used.'"

"He didn't mean any harm," Tonino said.

"Maybe we can find a place for him to take a nap," Cappelli offered.

From the kitchen, Petula saw the raised hand. "What's happening over there?"

"Nothing," said Daniele. "Beniamino needs to behave himself. That's all."

"I remember," said Renato, stepping in to defuse the danger of the moment, "when Petula was a little girl. The mouth she had on her! She never meant any harm, but when she wanted to she could reason just like a little woman and put even me in my place! Must be a talent that runs in the family."

"And did you hit her?" Beniamino asked.

"Hit her?" The question shocked Renato. "No," he said. "Never. Though sometimes she knew how to make me see red. Your mother, little Beniamino, was an artist at that. But hit her, no."

"What are you doing?" Daniele snarled at his son. He saw his own hand in the air, alert, prepared. He lowered it. "You trying to make everyone think I hit you? You want them to think I'm the same as my father was?"

In Daniele's face, Renato saw angry father and hurt child, two faces melting into one. The question had to be asked. "And do you hit him?"

"Of course not," said Daniele, his shoulders slumping. Heavy fatigue spread through his muscles as anger subsided. He looked over and saw Emanuele Mosè's eyes studying him coldly.

"It's not easy, raising kids," Renato said. "I know. If you ever find yourself losing control, you can come and talk to me."

You'll only side with Petula and Beniamino, Daniele thought. There's no one to take my side. "We'll see," he said, ashamed to have revealed so much of himself in front of these men, Emanuele Mosè especially. He pulled a pack of cigarettes and a lighter from his breast pocket, lit up, and inhaled.

Daniele's tension made the hair on Cappelli's head prickle. Tension, to Cappelli's mind, was one thing to avoid at all costs, even if avoidance meant talking to someone who was an awkward mystery to him. "Nice time of year," he said to Emanuele Mosè. "Christmastime.

People get together. Drink. Eat. Nice time of year, no? You like Christmas?"

With owl-like slowness, Emanuele Mosè's face turned to Cappelli. The outrage in the eyes told Cappelli that his efforts to make tensions pass by changing the subject had failed. "Do I *like* Christmas?" the breathing icon responded. "What is there to *like*? Liking or not has nothing to do with it."

"Yes, but I only meant—" Cappelli wanted to hide, leave, go upstairs to his own house and be alone.

"Liking is for this kind of pasta or that. Like Christmas? Christmas is when the Master of the Universe reduced Himself to become a naked baby born into a place where even the barnyard beasts struggled to keep warm. You ask me if Christmas is something that I *like?*"

Silence. None of the men could think of an adequate rejoinder. Even Renato, usually fast in conversation, was stumped.

This guy's good at sounding like the next Messiah, Daniele thought as he drew on his cigarette, but God help him if he makes a move for Petula.

He had seen Emanuele Mosè trying to decide whether to kiss Petula's cheeks in the piazza when everyone traded greetings. Anger over the thought of the near kiss stuck in Daniele's throat. From his cigarette, he sucked in a hot lungful of smoke.

"Come to the table!" Rosa Spina sang from the kitchen. "Tortellini's ready. Come and take a seat!"

Cappelli blew relieved air out of his lips as everyone took their seats. "Big deal this Emanuele Mosè guy makes of everything," he muttered to himself. "As for me personally, I've always thought Christmas was nice."

Men, women, and Beniamino sat together, tortellini *in brodo* ladled out for everyone, fresh parmigiano sprinkled over every bowl. Mouths blew, then tasted. *"Buono!"* was the verdict pronounced by all.

"You see?" Rosa Spina took a spoonful of hot broth in her mouth, swallowed, and drank a sip of wine. "Who says happiness is hard?

People do such strange things looking for it, but happiness doesn't need much."

Cappelli, his mouth warm with tortellini and broth, drank half a glass of wine in one gulp. His eyes were intent on the woman living in his house.

"Very good tortellini indeed," said Maria Severina. "Made them yourself? Yes, I could tell by the taste. And the broth is good, too, even if I always add a touch of tomato when I make it at the bottega." Maria Severina was incapable of issuing a compliment unqualified by some critique. "Maybe it's because of your Venetian origins that you don't put tomato in the broth. Still, all things considered, this broth isn't too bad."

Tonino held out his nearly empty bowl. "There wouldn't be any more in the pot, would there?"

"Why, of course!" Rosa Spina was quick with the ladle.

Maria Severina aimed a look of recrimination at her husband, as if he had betrayed her by eating too much of another woman's cooking.

Soupy sounds surrounded the table. Every spoon worked away in its respective bowl. Every spoon but one. Emanuele Mosè's lay untouched. His eyes observed the vapors arising from the surface of the broth as they would have examined the ghostly images clouding a soothsayer's crystal ball.

"What's his problem?" Maria Severina said, nudging Rosa Spina. "Doesn't he like the broth?"

"Oh, don't worry." Rosa Spina glanced at her solemn son. "He gets like this. Comes over him. Probably he's praying."

"Praying?" Cappelli said. "Why doesn't he eat a little something first?"

"Because," Rosa Spina explained, "when the prayer comes to him, it's more urgent than anything else around. He's always been good at praying, ever since he was even younger than this sweetness here."

The sweetness in question was Beniamino, who could not tell whether the woman with the little girl's voice really liked him or not. Ignoring her, Beniamino chased a *tortellino* around his bowl with his spoon.

"My son has always had an inclination toward prayer," Rosa Spina went on. "I suppose that's why people come to pray with him, wherever we go."

"While we're on the subject," Renato said, "I've heard people talking about the . . . sessions here. Who comes? What happens?"

Cappelli downed more wine, grateful that his boss had voiced the question he never would have dared ask himself.

"Who comes?" Rosa Spina's dancing hands stroked the air as if plucking strings on an invisible harp. "Anyone who wants, naturally. For the moment not too many. Only four or five on any given evening. But more will come soon. They always do."

"But why did they even come in the first place?" Cappelli joined in, his lower lip glistening with wine.

Rosa Spina smiled. "People just seem to *know*. It's like asking how animals know where to find water in a desert. The soul knows where to look to find what it needs." Her beatific face was framed by open hands in the air, her lustrous eyes seeming to apprehend exactly what Cappelli's soul might need.

Cappelli gave a grunt and drank more wine. "And what"—he licked his wet lips—"do they do when they come?"

"They like to be near Emanuele Mosè's prayers. Sometimes they pray with him. Sometimes they ask him to pray certain prayers, special prayers."

"And what does he do?"

Emanuele Mosè answered. "I do what I can. Nothing less. Nothing more."

"Interesting stuff," Renato said. "I myself have never been much of a church man, but thinking positively to help us out of problems, praying if you like, couldn't be a bad idea."

"You might try praying about your sheep," said Emanuele Mosè.

Renato stiffened to hear that his private difficulties were evidently not private at all. "How do you know about my sheep?"

"How is she?" said Emanuele Mosè, ignoring the question. "Is she healing?"

Renato shook his head, spooked by the young man's apparent omniscience. "The veterinarian can't find anything to heal," he found himself admitting. "But she stands there panicked, is the only way to describe it. Stands there as if death were breathing on her face. She's still alive for now, but how much longer can she last if she doesn't come to her senses?"

"I can come and pray over her, if you'd like."

Renato looked at the somber young man, and his eyes caught the face of the bleeding Jesus in the picture hanging on the wall, the two faces looking eerily akin. "Thank you, but the vet has visited several times. You haven't studied animal medicine, have you? Thank you, but I don't think it would do any good."

"Would it do any bad?"

"I . . . A prayer, bad? No, I would imagine not. But I don't want to trouble you with my problems with the sheep."

"In the next few days, I will come."

The hint of magic surrounding Emanuele Mosè made Renato nervous. But what harm could a visit and a prayer do? "In that case," Renato said, "what can I say? *Grazie.* Don't make a special trip. But if you happen to find yourself near our house, you're always welcome to drop by. Isn't he, Milena?"

Milena was as discomfited as her husband. "Always welcome," she said.

Daniele was pleased to see Petula sneak him a quick smile of conspiracy. At least she's not buying this guy's Savior act, Daniele thought.

Emanuele Mosè fell back into his distant contemplations. A few minutes later, when the guests had nearly finished their food, he raised a hand encased in its fingerless glove and made a small gesture to push away his untouched bowl. "If you will all forgive me, I have to be alone. Good Christmas to all. Good night." He made a point of looking directly at Petula. To her he repeated, "Good night."

She looked at Daniele and saw his displeasure that Emanuele Mosè should speak to her individually. "Good night," she said and quickly lowered her eyes.

"Shame you have to go," Daniele said. "Night night."

Emanuele Mosè entered his bedroom, closing and locking the door behind him.

To fill the uncomfortable emptiness he left behind, his mother said, "Christmas has never been easy for him. He takes it completely to heart. He knows that in the divine birth there must be the seeds of divine death, and it hurts him too much."

Her words, despite her comprehensive motherly smile, did little to dispel the awkwardness. Instead, everyone seemed to feel that a cue had been given for them to go. "*Grazie* for everything," they started to say as they put napkins on the table and rose from their chairs.

"Oh, don't go!" she said. "Won't you have some more? Another drop of wine? Some *vin santo?*" She looked at Beniamino. "Maybe a little piece of spiced cake?"

Thanks all the same, was the general response. It's late. We should rest.

"Then I'll see you all out." She wrapped herself in her outdoor shawl again, accompanying her guests outside to the piazza. "Thank you so much for coming. I want all of you to know that you can come anytime you want. Just ring the doorbell downstairs and I'll be so happy to let you in."

Beniamino perked up when everyone stepped out into the freezing air of the piazza: He could go home and have his procession.

Everyone else was astonished by the abruptness with which Emanuele Mosè had left his guests sitting at the table. Then again, unpredictability seemed an inevitable, intrinsic part of the little family cosmos in which the Innocenti lived. Who could count how many times they had upped and switched cities in their wanderings? Who could predict how long they would remain in Sant'Angelo D'Asso? Daniele hoped not long.

"*Allora, grazie,*" said Renato. "Thank you for the hospitality. Sometime, you must come to our house. Cappelli, no work tomorrow on Christmas Day! Come by if you want, though, to say hello."

Cappelli nodded. This was the first time ever that he had stood outside with a woman saying good night to a group of guests leaving his front door. Despite the son's odd behavior, Cappelli felt that, with time, he might even get used to the role of host.

A round of cheek-kissing good nights ensued. Just then, Petula caught sight of a young man far up the street. "I thought Emanuele Mosè said he wanted to be alone in his room," she said.

Rosa Spina's red lips lost their color, and her luminous eyes, looking past the group of new friends, grew wide. *"Dio mio!"* she said. Everyone turned to see what could possibly cause such alarm.

A lean young man with a canvas sack slung over his shoulder walked up the stone street. Approaching, he passed beneath the light of a streetlamp and his features came into view.

"How did you get out here?" Cappelli said.

"It's not Emanuele Mosè," Rosa Spina whispered.

"Madonna strega!" Cappelli said in a low voice, calling the Virgin Mother a witch. "Talk about similarity! They're as alike as one drop of water to another."

Everyone in the little group in the piazza examined the newcomer. At first glance, Emanuele Mosè and this young man were one flesh. This face appeared painted by the same hand. A closer look, however, and one noticed the differences. The hair on this head was slicked back with gel. The clothes did not look warm enough for the frigid night: black boots, blue jeans, a lightweight leather jacket, no scarf, no gloves. No gloves. This was a night for heavy gloves, yet the hands carrying the canvas sack were bare. It was disconcerting for all to see a creature so like Emanuele Mosè suddenly without the ever-present fingerless gloves. Perhaps it was the lack of gloves that made the difference. Perhaps it was the demeanor in general, the air, the mood, the quality of light that surrounds a body and gives a hint as to the person inside. The young man walking up to everyone now was no celestial being sent from God-knows-where. This brother was a native of earth, at once approachable, physical, beautiful, and disarmingly tragic in some subtle way.

Or that, at any rate, was how he appeared to Petula as he neared the group. Beautiful above all. She remembered her first impression of Emanuele Mosè when he and Rosa Spina had walked into the station bar. Then, too, she had felt drawn in by a young man's extraordinary aspect, but with regard to Emanuele Mosè some warning within had told her to keep her distance. The twin, now only a few steps away, did not have Emanuele Mosè's frightening aura of austerity. He seemed a little menacing, maybe, but not unattractively so. Petula felt her guard drop. He had been in prison, she knew, but he seemed as if he would never wish her harm.

Daniele, as eager as Beniamino to go home, watched the approaching figure. His chest suddenly went hollow, emptied by a pang of loss, an ache far more powerful than any discomfort that the other's twin had ever prompted him to feel. *This* young man, Daniele sensed, was truly capable of taking away everything he thought of as his own.

The man let his canvas sack drop. *"Buonasera,"* he said to all with a nod; then, to Rosa Spina, *"Ciao,* Mamma."

Cappelli was surprised to see Rosa Spina at a loss for words as she stared and said only, *"Ciao."*

Recognizing that his house was about to have one more tenant, Cappelli said, "You must be the Other One. L'Altro."

"L'Altro is what they've called me my whole life." He laughed through smiling teeth.

"Cappelli," Cappelli introduced himself, offering his hand. "Your mother lives in that apartment in my house." He raised his chin in the direction of the windows overhead.

"Good to meet you." One by one, every person in the group said hello.

Petula, unfaithful never once to her Daniele, wondered why meeting this young man should give her pleasurable anxiety so strong.

"I'm happy to see that my mother has made so many new friends." He did not take his eyes off Petula while he spoke.

"Why are you here?" Rosa Spina had refound her tongue.

"They let me out early. Good behavior. Model prisoner, they said."

"How did you find us?"

"Return address on the Christmas card Emanuele Mosè sent. Had to switch trains a couple of times, but I managed to make it here. Why did you move to Tuscany?"

"Wanted to be nearer." Rosa Spina lowered her eyes, as if in embarrassment.

"You don't have to look so ashamed," L'Altro said. "There's certainly no sin in holding a little affection for your son."

"No, I suppose not." Rosa Spina shook her head. "I thought I might visit you."

"But you didn't visit. Not once."

"I thought I might start."

Petula believed she saw sadness behind the smile he gave to his mother. A protective instinct made her want to comfort the young man, though she had no idea what solace she, in her lack of experience, might offer a man who had committed untold crimes and suffered unimaginable punishment.

"Don't worry, Mamma," L'Altro went on. "Now you can see me as much as you want, if Signor Cappelli doesn't mind another person under his roof."

"What difference does it make to me?" Cappelli shrugged. "If it's what your mother wants."

"Then it's up to you, Mamma. What do you say?"

Her face showed no joy. "Could I turn my son away?"

"Invitation accepted," L'Altro said. "I wonder if Emanuele Mosè will mind sharing you. He's had you all to himself for a long time. Or maybe he'll be glad for a break. You're a lot for one son to handle."

"L'Altro," Rosa Spina said with a warning tone, as if telling him not to discuss too many family matters with other people listening.

"And where is my brother?"

"Inside."

"Praying, I suppose?" His grin held just enough sarcasm to make everyone think he had endured his brother's prayers for a lifetime and was still not altogether convinced of their worth.

"He cares about you, you know."

"And I care about him. He might even give me a welcome-back kiss"—everything L'Altro said, he said with a smile—"since no one else wants to give it to me."

"Didn't I kiss you?" Rosa Spina's usually dancing hands were hidden inside her shawl. Amazing how small and befuddled she now appeared in the presence of her other son.

Smiling still, L'Altro slowly shook his head. "No feast. No fatted calf. For the return of this prodigal son, no kiss."

She laughed nervously before the rapt audience. "Come here and kiss your mother." She did not spread her arms to hug him. She stood pillarlike, raising only her face.

He lowered his mouth to kiss first once cheek, then the other. "Merry Christmas, Mamma," he said. "I had hoped that seeing me would be a nice surprise for you. Maybe I should have warned you first." He shrugged. "In any case. I'll go inside, if I may"—he eyed Cappelli, who lifted a welcoming arm toward the front door in reply—"and say hello to my brother. I have a lot to talk about with him. I have a whole new life to begin." He turned to look at the group of people around him. "I will look forward to seeing you all again—"

His eyes were on Petula. Daniele, seeing that she returned the stare, put a proprietorial arm around her shoulder. Petula blushed.

"—and to meeting other people in your town," L'Altro continued, turning away from Petula. "I'm glad to be here. I'm happy to be free."

He took up his canvas sack and went inside.

"It's the door after the first flight of stairs," Cappelli called in after him. "The door after the second flight is mine." Saying this, Cappelli realized that the person who just entered his house had been a prisoner until earlier today. For what crime? Was he a murderer, rapist, arsonist, thief? Cappelli was sure only that he did not have the courage to ask.

Yet another new force was living under Cappelli's roof. It had arrived quietly enough, but who knew if in time this arrival would show itself to be the first chilly breeze that precedes a cataclysmic storm? None of the people in the piazza could foresee if the young man was tempest or sunshine, creature of darkness or creature of light.

But something in Petula had already changed. She and Daniele took Beniamino home to do the family procession to place Gesù Bambino in his crib, her thoughts all the while recalling the familiar features of a brand-new face.

7

"This is Radio Italia," announced the radio on the shelf at the station bar, "wishing happy holidays to one and all."

"Holidays my prick," Daniele said under his breath, lighting a cigarette, feeling as hot and angry as the tobacco leaves that burned red when he inhaled.

Today was the Feast of Santo Stefano, the day after Christmas, and most of the town could dawdle like idiots and savor the nice long pause full only of easy leisure, yet Daniele had to work. One day off for Christmas it had been, then back to the bar to fill orders for customers, make their coffees, wash their cups, pour their drinks, witness their arrivals and departures, as if he had been born to do nothing but serve.

Cigarette between his lips, Daniele opened the small dishwasher behind the bar. Soap-smelling steam came out and almost scalded his hands. "Damn this!" he said, removing the rack of espresso cups, saucers, spoons. Did he ever get to go anywhere? He started to put the dishes away. Did anyone ever serve him the way he had to serve everyone else? He wanted to smash the saucers, but he stacked them instead and their sharp clattering hurt his ears. He snorted out smoke, knowing the bitter answer to his own questions: a great big NO. No, he was not a free man; he was a slave, his master the bar his parents left him, dying when he was only seventeen. Nobody had ever bothered to ask whether Daniele wanted the damned bar or not. And there was his parents' house to keep up. And Petula to look after, and Beniamino. He was already trapped like a man twice his age. The thought set him on fire.

The radio played a trashy American tune from the era when Americans wore polyester and danced in discotheques.

"Vuoi una mano?"

"What?" Daniele had forgotten the human presences around him.

"I said, 'Do you want a hand?'" Petula held a dishtowel. "Thought I'd help you unload the dishwasher."

"You don't think I can handle it on my own?" Just then a toy car crashed into his shoe. "And you"—he pointed a finger at Beniamino, who sat on the ground behind the bar—"if I find your car under my feet once more, I'll break it. You hear me?"

"Come on," Petula said. "It's the Christmas present we got for him. Of course he wants to play with it."

"He shouldn't be back here anyway." Daniele kicked the car back to Beniamino. "The gangway behind the bar is for work, not play. Understand? You don't see me coming into your room and working in the middle of where all your toys are, so you shouldn't bring toys here and play right where I'm trying to work."

"Business is light today," Petula said. "Who do you have to serve right now? The bar is empty. You could take a break and do a little playing yourself, you know."

"Why does he even have to be here?" Daniele said. "Why isn't he with your grandparents at the bottega?"

"No school," Petula said. "It might surprise you, but occasionally he *likes* to spend time with us."

"*Bisnonno* lets me ring things up on the cash register." Beniamino pouted, giving his toy car a shove.

"I'll bet your great-grandfather does." Daniele blew out smoke. "Someday I might let you touch the cash register here, but only when you're ready to come with the right attitude for work, not for playing with your toys and getting in the way."

"One of *those* days, is it?" Petula tossed the dishtowel on the counter. She had given up reminding Daniele of his promise not to smoke in front of their son. She certainly would not remind him now, not when he was like this. "Come on, Beniamino," she said. "Come out from behind the bar. Give your father room to work in." The boy did as he was told. Petula looked at Daniele and shook her head. "We ought to put a sign around your neck when you get this way: 'Danger. Come Near at Your Own Risk.'"

"When I get what way?" Daniele was a pressure-cooker ready to blow. Hearing the rising tension of his own words, he almost began to feel the relief of explosion. "Exactly what way am I, in your opinion? Eh, Petula? Would you care to tell me exactly how I am?"

"No," she said. "It's the day after Christmas, and I have to work, too. But the sun is shining outside, and we're lucky to have Beniamino here with us, so I figure we should try to have a happy day in any case. Why fight?"

"I'm not the one"—he sensed that relief would have to wait— "who's trying to have a fight."

Edgy boxers in a dangerous ring, they went to opposite corners of the bar and pretended to be busy, each in distant silence.

On the floor in front of the bar, Beniamino rolled his car and made engine noises with his lips.

"And don't sit there," Daniele said. "It's dirty."

Obediently, Beniamino changed his position to a squat.

"Virgo," the voice of the radio astrologer said. Petula listened to hear what the stars held for her today. "Venus is in opposition," said the radio. "Intimate upheavals are at hand. People you think you know are not what they appear to be."

You can say that again, Petula thought.

In came a group of young men, construction workers who for weeks now had been redoing a house up near the station and had taken to frequenting the bar daily for coffee breaks, snacks, and lunch.

Petula was glad to see them enter. She had known them forever, these local kids only recently turned grown-up enough to work, not so many years younger than she. They always managed to liven up the sleepy bar. Trying to be big men, they drank beer with their lunch on workdays, and after eating they liked to kick back, smoke their cigarettes, and talk their loud talk. If they flirted with Petula, they meant no harm. They viewed her as an older cousin. In their eyes, she belonged to Daniele. Still, it was fun to playfully push the limits with a pretty girl without having to get too serious.

With time off work for the next week, they would not get back to rebuilding the old farmhouse until after the New Year. They came to the bar out of habit. Where else was there to go?

Daniele was usually glad for their company. Sometimes he would join in their conversations about the soccer matches on TV, and the attentions they paid to Petula gave him the satisfaction that other men noticed what a good choice of woman he had made. Today, though, the boys got on his nerves. He was in no mood to joke around.

"*Ciao*, Daniele!" they called, taking their seats at their usual corner table. Daniele nodded his chin in reply.

"Oh, Petula!" said the guy whose good looks made him the natural ringleader. *Spillo*, everyone called him. Pin. All muscle and no fat on his bones, he was thin as a needle, and his way of joking was to tease people with little sharp remarks. "You're even prettier than usual after a day off. Look how refreshed you seem! Or maybe you didn't get much rest over Christmas, eh? A break from work, some time away from the bar together, and I can imagine the way the two of you spent your Christmas Day!"

Imbeciles, thought Daniele. They don't know what it's like to live with a woman and a child. To their stupid inexperienced brains, living together meant screwing nonstop. Every hour of the day, every room in the house. Daniele knew better.

"But of course!" Petula laughed, coming to their table to take their orders, glad for the chance to joke away the tension that Daniele had left her with. "You're right, of course." She glanced at Beniamino to make sure he wasn't listening. "A child to take care of, relatives to visit, Christmas dinner to cook . . . of course all we could do was jump on each other and spend the entire day in bed! What else could have put such a sparkle in my eye today?"

"If I had spent Christmas with you, dear Petulina," said Spillo, "your eyes would be sparkling for real."

"Know what they say, don't you?" she laughed. "The more people talk about doing it, the less they actually do. And you're the biggest talker in the bar. Now what can I get you all to eat?"

The hell with them, thought Daniele from his post at the dishwasher. Petula's bright behavior, he knew, was good for business. It created a friendly feeling that made people eager to come back. It came to her naturally, because she had been raised hanging around her grandparents' bottega and had learned since she was a toddler how to hold her own with customers. This morning, however, Daniele could not laugh off the fact that his lack of sexual activity over Christmas had become the topic of public conversation. Was there some kind of accusation behind all her joking? Maybe on Christmas morning he should have jumped on her, should have forced himself to find the energy. As it was, though, he had been too grateful for the opportunity to sleep late. And who said Petula couldn't have been the one to jump on him? Why was everything always his fault?

Nothing could soothe him today, not even the sun shining like the beginning of the world in the big outdoors past the picture window, filling the bar with light. Everything anyone said today was an unpleasant mouthful for him to swallow. Nothing went down smooth.

"They all want proscuitto sandwiches," Petula said, returning to the bar with the construction workers' order. "You want to make the sandwiches while I get their beer, or do you want to serve the drinks?"

"What difference does it make? Serve them yourself. I'll do the sandwiches."

"Fine," said Petula buoyantly, determined not to let Daniele drag her down.

She had brought beer to the table in the corner and was working beside Daniele to make the sandwiches when the glass door swung open, letting in a fresh gust of air with a faint tang of tar from the railroad ties along the tracks.

"*Buongiorno,*" said the young man who approached the counter. "*Ciao,* Daniele. *Ciao,* Petula."

"Oh," Daniele said. "*Buongiorno.*" Fantastic, he thought. The ex-con. Well, he can take his meaningful stares at Petula, and he knows what he can do with them.

Petula could hear Daniele's brooding tone. "*Buongiorno,* L'Altro," she said. She was pleased to see him. Why should she pretend otherwise? Daniele's sulkiness tired her. "How are things?"

"Beautiful day like today, hard not to be happy. Wonderful thing it is, *la libertà.*"

Nobody would have the nerve to come out and ask, "So what was it like in prison? What's it like to be out?" In the company of a convict only recently made ex, who would dare allude to the subject even sideways? Yet in walked this man, opening himself like a book, keeping secret not a thing, telling the world straight out that his newly found liberty was a treat. He gave the impression that you could ask him anything you wanted and he would answer without letting the nonsense of common social niceties such as embarrassment get in the way. Something about him made you put aside shame.

"*Buongiorno,*" L'Altro said, looking down to where Beniamino was playing.

Beniamino lifted his eyes. When he saw the face smiling at him, he smiled back. "*Buongiorno.*" This twin Beniamino liked.

L'Altro laughed and mussed the boy's hair.

"On your way to somewhere?" Petula asked.

"I just got here," L'Altro said, "and you want me to leave?"

"I didn't mean that," she laughed. "I meant the bottega in the piazza is so much closer to your mother's house. You came all the way up here to the station, I thought you might be catching a train. Most people stop for a coffee here when they're on their way to somewhere else." She stopped herself and glanced at Daniele, wondering if she was talking too much.

"No train," he said. "I came up to say hello."

"Hello, then," said Petula.

He smiled. "Hello."

Daniele carried on cutting prosciutto with his ham knife.

"Oh!" Spillo called out from his table. L'Altro turned to look. "Which one are you?" Spillo laughed. "You the one they call L'Altro?"

"That's my name."

"Must be a hard name to live with," Spillo taunted. "The Other One. 'No, I wasn't talking to you,' people must tell you all the time. 'I was talking to the Other One.'" The group of construction workers around Spillo chortled gleefully.

L'Altro did not answer. The smile never leaving his face, he stared at the corner table until the laughter stopped. Turning back to the bar, he muttered, "A real wit."

"Don't mind him," Petula said. "That's Spillo's way of making friends."

"Does he have any?"

Petula laughed. "What can I get you? A sandwich?"

"It's good prosciutto," Daniele said. Out came the barman's habit of trying to sell whatever happened to be on hand, even if he would have preferred to fight with the person he had to serve. "It's from pigs killed locally. Truly special."

"I'm sure it is," said L'Altro, "but I've, um, lost the taste for meat."

Petula remembered her own revulsion upon seeing the cuts of dead animal flesh at the butcher's. "For all meat?" she asked.

"Not all," he said, his eyes resting on hers.

Realizing that their words had slipped dangerously close to double meanings, Petula blushed.

Seeing the color rise in her face, L'Altro smiled. "I stay away from red meat mostly," he said, gallantly making conversation chaste once more. "No pig or cow ever did me any harm. I started to feel guilty about eating them in repayment of the favor. Savage, it's all started to seem."

"How about fish?" Daniele said, his long, sharp knife cutting into purple-red ham. "How about chicken or turkey? They ever hurt you? Is it any better to kill them?"

"You're right, of course. If I were really trying to be pure, I wouldn't touch them either. But I'm not in the running for sainthood. So I let myself get away with doing what feels right for now."

"Me, too," Petula said before she had time to think. L'Altro's opinions were uncannily close to her own, but she decided to tone down the enthusiasm in her voice, as if agreeing too much with him constituted overt disloyalty to Daniele. "I mean I know what you mean. I don't feel so bad about eating fish or even poultry. Somehow it doesn't seem as cruel."

"Mammals are the tricky ones." L'Altro nodded. "You have to try a lot harder not to think about what you're eating when you've got mammal flesh on your fork."

"Mammals," Petula repeated. "Yes." Unnervingly, her mind and L'Altro's seemed to follow similar paths.

"Not me," said Daniele. "I like my meat any way it comes." From the cutting board he picked up a stringy piece from the edge of the prosciutto. He stuck it between his teeth and made a point of smiling at L'Altro while chewing the tough rind. "My father used to say he didn't trust any man who didn't have a taste for meat." To punctuate his final words, he smacked Petula on the ass and gave L'Altro a *you get my meaning?* wink.

Daniele had never acted so crudely. Petula, mortified, shot back, "Did he used to say that before or after hitting your mother and you?"

Heat flashed in Daniele's face. "He couldn't have been wrong about everything."

"Who knows?" L'Altro let the challenge pass. "In a year or two, maybe my tastes will change, and then I'll have to rethink everything from scratch."

"Fine, then," said Daniele. "We have other things, too. The pecorino cheese is good."

"A sandwich with the pecorino cheese," L'Altro accepted. "Thanks."

"To drink?"

"I'd love a beer."

"A beer?" Daniele said. "Didn't expect you'd drink beer."

"Why not?"

"Your brother doesn't drink much."

"Emanuele Mosè? I guess he doesn't. But I'm not my brother."

"I'll tell you one thing," said Daniele. "Your brother did a real job on the priest. They say Don Luigi will be in a cast for months."

"*Sì*," L'Altro said. "Emanuele Mosè told me about the unfortunate fall. Bad luck, no?"

"For Don Luigi very bad. But your brother didn't seem to mind." Daniele stared as if waiting for an explanation or justification. None came. "Petula," Daniele ordered, "get him a beer."

L'Altro watched Petula's pretty hand pull on the handle of the draught beer tap. When she gave him the glass, he said, *"Grazie."*

"And another thing I've been wondering about your brother," said Daniele, eyeing the naked hand that took the beer from Petula. "Why doesn't he ever take off those gloves of his?"

"Good question." L'Altro sipped the foam off the beer, then licked his upper lip. "If you want to know, you should ask him yourself."

"Next chance I get," Daniele said, knowing he would never ask Emanuele Mosè. Mystery seemed as important to that one as barefaced frankness to his twin.

To fill the silence that followed, Petula said, "So tell us. Do you like our town?"

"Very much."

"Doesn't seem hopelessly small and provincial?"

"To me, no," said L'Altro. "To you?"

"When I was a girl," said Petula, "there were times when I thought I'd suffocate. Now it feels like a nest. My nest. I don't think I'd ever want to leave."

Daniele shook his head. "It's not the place most people choose to come to unless they were born here. This isn't the Tuscany people want to see. Some tourists stumble in by accident in spring."

"I've come in the winter." L'Altro smiled.

"Then that makes you different from most," Petula put in.

L'Altro took her words as a compliment. "Can't imagine a better place than your town. Only one thing I haven't found here yet."

"Oh yeah?" Daniele said. "And what would that be?"

"A job. I'm hoping that one person here will give an ex-prisoner a chance to prove himself. One person with a little faith. That's what I want to find."

Cutting in half the prosciutto sandwiches he had finished making, Daniele raised his eyebrows with the worldliness of an old working-man. "Town this small, there are as many jobs as there are people willing to work. No extra. It's not as if anyone here is looking to pay someone to do a job that's already filled."

"You wouldn't need another pair of hands at this bar, would you?" L'Altro asked.

Imagining Petula and L'Altro working side by side every day, Daniele clenched his teeth and smiled. "No."

"No harm in asking, I figured."

"You asked," Daniele said. "You got your answer." He walked away and carried the sandwiches to the construction workers in the corner. When he reached their table, he said in a voice loud enough for L'Altro to hear, "How about you all? You looking for another man at your job? Our friend here needs work."

"Construction work is dangerous," Spillo said in an equally loud voice. "Ladders, electric drills, buzz saws."

"I think I could handle it," L'Altro called back.

"Sorry." Spillo smiled. "We're full up."

"We can start asking around," Petula offered.

"Your father, for example," L'Altro said, turning his back to the corner table. "He's in charge of the Waterworks Department, no?"

"Yes, but Cappelli's his assistant, and I'd be surprised if there was enough work to keep a third person busy. My father knows a lot of people, though. I'm sure he'd be happy to ask."

"That would be a big help. Thank you."

Daniele came back to the bar. "What kind of work are you looking for, anyway?"

"What kind of work? That's a bigger question than you'd think." L'Altro's eyes focused on the rim of his beer glass. "I've always watched people, my whole life, you know? You ever watch people? You ever look for some little clue on the outside to see what they're really like inside? I remember once watching the hands of a woman my mother used to know back when we lived in Bari. An embroiderer. Always with a needle and thread in her hands. Interesting part was, after years and years of sewing those little flowers and swirls, her hands got stuck that way. Not really stuck, but her fingers never straightened out entirely. Don't you see? The fingers were always curled as if they were holding a needle and thread, even when they were holding nothing. And then there were her eyes. She'd spent so much time squinting over her stitches that her eyes became next to useless without glasses as thick as this." He held his thumb and forefinger a good quarter of an inch apart. "*Deformazione professionale*, they call it, no? Professional deformation. Force of habit that comes from work. Look around, and you can see it everywhere. The miner whose lungs turn black from breathing coal dust for years. The fishmonger who always stinks of fish, no matter how many showers he takes. The mechanic whose hands go strong and rigid as a wrench. The printer whose skin ends up the color of ink."

"So?" Daniele picked up the knife to cut the pecorino cheese for L'Altro's sandwich. He tried hard not to let his face show his amazement at how this young man had pinpointed Daniele's secret terror that his life might never move beyond the walls of this bar. "So what? Happens to everyone, no? What's the big deal?"

"The big deal is that it's enough to make you stop and think. I mean, you start out life like a green sapling, just like your little son. Cosmic potential through and through, not marked by a single scar. No limits on how high you can grow. Total freedom. Then you get a bit older and you fall into a job, maybe by chance, and before you know what's happened, your infinite possibilities have disappeared. You've become your work. It shapes your body, same way as weather shapes a tree. Not just your body. That's the scary part. Shapes your brain, too. Ever wonder what happens to the brain of the banker who spends his days worrying how much cash is in the vault? Or to the prostitute by the roadside who sees the man in every car as the opposite of affection? Ought to be careful in the job you choose, because one day you'll wake up and find that the person you are has become invisible to the people around, and all they see is the job you do. 'There's the butcher,' people say. Or 'There's the beggar.' 'There's the garbageman.' 'There's the rich man's wife.'"

"Ever wonder," said Daniele, taking L'Altro's words and giving them an unfriendly spin, "what happens inside the head of a guy who does nothing all day but sit around and pray?"

"You're talking about my brother." L'Altro was calm. "Yes. I've wondered too many times to count."

"Or you ever wonder," Daniele went on, feeling he was getting the upper hand in some game too subtle to be named, "what happens to the brain of a guy who spies on the world from the wrong side of prison bars?"

"A lot happens to that brain," L'Altro laughed. "I'll tell you that myself. But don't worry too much about my brain. Right now, I'm just looking for work. Anything honest that'll help my family pay the bills. And I would sure be grateful if you could keep your ears open for any jobs that come along."

How could Daniele stay angry with him? He had a way, L'Altro, of disarming by offering no resistance. If you tried to insult him to his face he seemed to agree, turning the other cheek, making you ashamed for thinking bad things about him in the first place.

"The question remains, though," L'Altro added, as if voicing an afterthought, "of what happens to a young man, full of talent and infinite potential, whose world becomes no bigger than the station bar, always watching other people catch trains to somewhere else."

Suddenly, Daniele wanted to break a bottle and twist the jagged shards into L'Altro's face. His anger was at its boiling point, but he could not hate this person. Instinct told him he was staring at an antagonist, yet, amazingly, he felt he had found a friend. L'Altro had read him and smilingly had reassured him that he was justified in struggling against a life that was becoming cramped.

"Who knows?" Daniele said, not knowing what to say. "Who knows what happens to a guy like that?"

"We'll have to wait and see," said L'Altro, giving Daniele a smile brighter than the picture window full of sun.

Petula watched everything and listened to every word, her breath growing quick. And while L'Altro spoke with Daniele, Petula sensed that he was inviting her to share a secret understanding. A small sideways glance at her was all it took, an infinitesimal instant of eye meeting eye that said he would have wrapped her warmly in a thousand words if only Daniele had not been there.

L'Altro drank his beer and ate the pecorino sandwich that Daniele served him. "Do you like riddles?" he asked Daniele suddenly, though his voice was loud enough for everyone in the bar to hear. "I've got a good one for you. You're walking through the desert when you come to a fork in the road. One road leads to a cool oasis with life-giving springs, the other road to waterless dunes and certain death. At the fork there are twin brothers. One always tells the truth and one always tells lies, though you don't know which twin is which. If you could ask only one brother only one question to find the right road, what question would you ask?"

Daniele looked around. Petula's eyes, he could see, had turned to the corner, the way they did whenever she concentrated on a difficult puzzle. Spillo and the other workers murmured possible answers, trying to calculate a solution. But Daniele was in no mood to strain his brain on any stupid riddle. "I'll think it over," he said to L'Altro. "I'll let you know when I work it out."

"It's a tricky one," L'Altro said. "Take all the time you need." He paid his bill and thanked Petula for the promise to help him find a job. Looking down at Beniamino, he said, "Nice car."

Beniamino smiled and made motor sounds with his lips.

L'Altro glanced at the corner table. "You be careful," he called to Spillo, "on that dangerous construction job of yours." And he left.

"Che tipo!" Spillo announced from his table after the glass door had swung shut. "Strange one, he is!"

"But he's no fool." Daniele was not amused by the workers. To hell with them, he thought. He turned to Petula and said in an even voice, "He's right, you know. *Mi sta stretta questa vita.* This life is getting too tight for me. He's right." The anger inside him had not diminished; it had burned itself into a single white-hot flame. Daniele spoke with the steady intensity of a madman who has found lucidity in delirium.

"Fine," she said. With infinite subtlety, L'Altro had planted a seed inside Petula's brain. She was not ready to say to herself that she wanted L'Altro. Nothing as clear as that. In her mind, however, was the germ of the new notion that it might be possible to spend her life with someone who was not Daniele. Daniele was, after all, only one of the world's many men. Her patience with his lamentations had run out. "The bar is breaking your balls. But it's breaking mine, too." She threw her sponge into the sink. The radio played an old song about a brokenhearted lover who watched his beloved run off with someone else. "It doesn't even feel like *our* bar; doesn't even feel like *yours*. We haven't done a thing to change it since your parents died, and still it feels as if we're working for them." She found liberation in raising her voice, not caring whether Spillo or his workers heard. She had listened for too long. "But what are we supposed to do? We can't give up working. We have to eat. And so does Beniamino. Wouldn't hurt, though, if you'd let me change a few things and make the place ours. I mean, will you look at the color on the walls?" She held out her hands to show the awfulness around her. "So you feel trapped. I understand that. How could I not? You talk about nothing else. But why do you insist on making it look like a prison, too?"

"Here we go again with the damned coat of paint! You're the one who's become a broken record. All you ever talk about is the paint. You think I like the look of cracked paint and chipping plaster?"

"Then why can't we *change* it?" Exasperated, she let her hands fall loudly to her sides. "I keep telling you, all it would take is a little change here and there—"

"A change, you say? Damn! A change is right! But change the paint and the tiles and the furniture and every damned thing, and what do you have? I'll still be nothing but a barman, whether you paint the walls pink or orange or blue. You think I give a fuck for putting up curtains and making the place pretty?" Explosion was coming now. His head came alive.

"Curtains?" Her own fury surprised her. "How dare you think I'm talking about nothing but pretty curtains! Are we speaking two different languages, Daniele? Can't you hear what I'm saying? I'm saying—"

Looking up from his car, Beniamino saw that his parents were fighting. Again. "Vvvvrrr," he said, pushing the car along the floor, pretending that his parents' screams were nothing but the noise of the traffic he had to drive through.

"And when do you ever listen to what I have to say?" Daniele cut Petula off. "You never listen to what's happening inside my head. I always have to keep my thoughts to myself." Dangerous words, *never* and *always*, serving only to stoke a fire when it is already too hot. "You don't begin to understand what's going on in my head."

"Oh!" Spillo said. "You want to keep it down? We're trying to listen to the radio over here."

"You want to listen to the radio?" Daniele reached up to the radio shelf and turned the volume dial to loud until it blared. "Then listen."

"Tell me," Petula shouted. "Tell me what it is that you think I haven't already understood."

"Fine. I'll tell you. I need a break, Petula. I need a change. A pause from it all."

"*Sì*, I know what you mean." She tried to keep her voice steady. She went to the radio and adjusted it to a more reasonable volume. "Sometimes I feel the same—"

"No!" His voice forced itself from vocal cords that felt ready to snap. "Don't tell me you understand! It's different for you. You're free to go anytime you want." He picked up a dishtowel and started drying the stack of espresso saucers even though they were dry. "You have your parents who would be only too willing to take you in. What am I saying, *willing*? They'd be *thrilled*. Nothing would make them happier than if you said you were leaving me." He polished the espresso saucers and smacked them loudly on the stack one by one. "You're free to stay if you want or leave if you want. You can work here with me or walk out the door anytime you choose, and I can't do a thing about it because I'm the one who's stuck here from a quarter to seven every morning to a quarter past nine every night. What else am I supposed to do with my life? Where else am I supposed to go?"

"Who's talking about walking out the door?" Petula said. "Are you trying to break those saucers?"

"I can break them if I want," he said. "They're mine, damn it!"

He lifted the stack of saucers to shift them to the shelf where they belonged. He started to take a step, when the toy car rolled under his shoe. The muscles in his back tightened as he fought to keep his balance. He set the saucers back on the counter and grabbed the car from the floor. "Beniamino!" he shrieked, his voice hysterical. "Where are you?" He saw the boy peering around the bar at the far end of the gangway. "Come here!"

Paralyzed by fear, the boy clutched the corner of the bar.

"I told you to keep this car away from me," Daniele screamed, "but you never listen." He lifted the toy, smashing it hard against the edge of the counter. The car's roof caved in. The plastic windshield broke.

"Hey!" Spillo called out.

"Come here!" Daniele yelled hoarsely.

Silently, Beniamino started to cry.

"Don't you dare cry! I gave you the stupid car and I told you I would break it if you didn't keep it out of my way. Come here now!"

"Daniele—" Petula objected.

"Daniele nothing," he ranted. "He has to learn. No one else teaches him to have any respect. Beniamino, come here!"

Crying, Beniamino walked along the gangway behind the bar and approached his father. "Babbo, I'm sorry," he said.

"Don't give me sorry. You're a monster!" Daniele grabbed the boy by the arms as soon as he was in reach. He squeezed him above the elbows and lifted him to face level. Beniamino's legs dangled above the ground. "Whatever I tell you, you never listen!" Daniele shook him with force.

Beniamino closed his eyes in terror. And suddenly Daniele realized that he wanted to destroy the child.

"Oh!" Spillo called again from the corner table.

Daniele stopped shaking Beniamino, lowered him to the ground, and let go of his arms. Beniamino ran to Petula, who picked him up in a hug.

Full of murderous anger still, Daniele clutched the dozen saucers. With an animal scream that scorched his throat, he hurled the stack toward the ceiling.

Time slowed down. Seconds dilated during the saucers' flight. Daniele wished he could stay in that instant forever. He tingled with the expectation of impact, and at the same time he was warmed by great peace. He had exploded now and could bask in bliss without yet having to pay the inevitable price. Had he been able, he would have liked to curl up on the bar and go to sleep now.

Then came the crash. Saucers clanked on top of the bar and shattered when they hit the floor.

"Oh!" shouted Spillo's gang of workers.

"Oh! Oh! Oh!" shouted Spillo. "What the hell are you doing?"

"Everything's fine," said Petula, kissing the child she hugged tightly. She eyed Daniele the way you watch a rabid dog whose frothy teeth are bared as it prepares to pounce. "Nothing happened."

"Daniele," Spillo said. "Calm, okay? Calm yourself."

"*Vaffanculo.*" Daniele spoke without moving his gaze from Petula's face.

"This is what you're telling me?" Spillo was offended. "I want to make sure that you're not the lunatic you seem to be, and you tell me to go do it up the ass? This is what you say? *Ma cosa c'entro io?* What have I got to do with it if you want break everything you have?"

"Exactly," said Daniele, smiling at Petula still. "You don't come into it. So keep out."

"Fine, then." Spillo bit into his prosciutto sandwich and stood up. He wrapped the remainder of the sandwich in a napkin and put it in his jacket pocket, indicating with a jerk of his chin to the others that they should do the same. "Let's go, guys," he said. "*Andiamo.*"

He led the group over toward the bar. "How much do we owe you?"

"Lunch is on the house today," Daniele said.

"We'll be back tomorrow," said Spillo. "And you'll have calmed down. And you, Petula? You all right? You feel safe if we go?"

"Of course I feel safe," she lied. Her arms trembled as she hugged Beniamino. "What am I supposed to feel, afraid?"

"You sure?" Spillo saw how pale her face had become.

"I'm sure," she said. She wasn't going to let Daniele make a victim of her.

"Tomorrow, then," said Spillo with an unconvinced nod. His group followed him out, leaving Daniele and Petula alone with their son in the sunlit bar.

"Have you gone crazy?" said Petula, anger returning to her voice now that no one else was around. She went into the storage room and came back with a dustpan and broom, without letting go of Beniamino. The boy clung to her, his legs around her waist. "Have you gone mad, or just turned stupid?"

Daniele stood among the fractured saucers. "Don't call me stupid," he said dully. He made no move to help her clean up, but reached for the pack of cigarettes he kept near the cash register, his hands shaking as he lit up.

"Tell me this was an intelligent thing to do." Petula sat Beniamino in a chair by one of the tables in the center of the room, then came close to Daniele and started sweeping around his feet.

"You're not afraid of me?" He exhaled smoke.

"*Vaffanculo*, Daniele."

"If I were my father and you were my mother, it would be you and Beniamino on the ground instead of a few stupid saucers." He took a drag and lifted his eyes to the ceiling. "Maybe you should both walk out the door to protect yourselves."

"What is it with you? Since when am I supposed to leave you? Who said anything about leaving?"

"You could, you know," Daniele said, his voice losing strength, sounding more scared than vicious. "I would, if I were you." His anger had carried him to a dangerous place; turning back seemed impossible. Now he was sad and nostalgic for the woman he thought he had already lost.

"We've always been together. That's not going to change." She nudged his ankle with the broom. "Move your foot. I have to sweep there."

"But it could change, if you want it to." He lifted his foot distractedly, like a horse that shifts its weight while dozing upright. "How do I know? Maybe you feel like a change," he said, probing for reaction. "Maybe you want to be with someone else."

For an instant, Petula fought the desire to agree. "I want to be with someone who's in control of his senses." She looked at Beniamino, sitting alone at the table a safe distance away. The boy's head hung low. His feet dangled beneath the chair. "Usually that's you," Petula went on, lowering her voice so that Beniamino would not hear. She wished he weren't here to witness this argument. She was tempted to tell him to go and play in the storage room, but the protective mother in her wanted to keep him in sight. "Don't you try to tell me what I want. Let me worry about that. You tell me what you want. You act as if you're trying to force me to leave. Is that the change you think you want? Are you crazy enough to think that?"

He took a deep drag from his cigarette, filling his lungs until they burned with satisfying heat. "Maybe you *should* be afraid of me." He blew out a thin line of smoke. "I'm afraid of me. Can't you see it? I'm going out of my fucking head. I'm trapped, and it's making me go out of my head. That guy L'Altro is right. I didn't ask to get stuck in this life. I fell into it. And this is all I'm ever going to be for the rest of my life. What happens to a person who falls into a trap like that? Person goes out of his head, that's what happens. Petula, I need a break. It's too much for me."

"I'll tell you what you need. I hate to say it, but sometimes I think you need to grow up."

"I don't want to grow up into this." He waved his cigarette in a gesture that took in the espresso maker, the tables and chairs, the linoleum floor, the entire bar. "And just how grown up do you think you are? Look at us. We're hardly twenty-four years old. We should be freer than this."

"Free, you say? I tell you what. I had to grow up the minute I gave birth. I can't spend my time asking myself if I'm having enough fun. There's Beniamino to think about."

"Beniamino is all you ever think about. You're like some animal whose only mission in life is to protect her young one."

"He's your young one, too. And you hurt him."

Beniamino sat on his chair, his finger tracing the ring of a water stain on the tabletop.

"Sometimes when I see what you're willing to do for him . . ." Daniele drew on the cigarette. "I don't know," he whispered, trying to keep his words secret from their son. "It's like there's this thing inside me." He tapped his fist against his belly. "Stronger than me, it feels sometimes." He thought of all the times he watched Beniamino climb into bed next to Petula and fall asleep against her body, demanding her love as if he had some kind of automatic right to it. Every time Beniamino demanded, Petula gave. Daniele felt the instinct to grab the child by his throat sometimes and tell him to sleep in his own damned bed. Sometimes he wanted to shake him until the little monster realized he couldn't just insist that Petula give him everything. But Petula gave and gave and gave. Daniele could hardly find the words to explain how furious it made him to see Petula always giving to their son. He said, "I get so mad it scares me sometimes. I don't know what I might do next."

Petula bent down to sweep the pieces of saucer into the dustpan. She tried to be calm, but her hands were trembling. "You scared me," she said quietly. "Is that what you wanted to hear? Well, it's the truth. You scared me. And you scared him. *Ora basta.* Enough now. Enough is enough."

"*Basta,*" he said calmly. "You're right. *Basta.* Enough."

"We ought to get you some help, Daniele. You should talk to someone. My father's a good person to talk to."

"Your father's good for you. You seriously expect him to see things from my point of view?"

"You're out of control." Realizing she had been holding her breath, she slowly released a lungful of air. "You need help."

"What I need," he said, "is a break."

An overwhelming tiredness rose up inside her like a yawn. Why should she fight? If Daniele's head was crumbling, how could she find the strength to sweep up his pieces? Why should she have to struggle that hard? He had become a danger. And hadn't something in L'Altro's eyes suggested to her only a few minutes ago that Daniele was not the only man on earth? The tiredness inside told her that she did not want to argue. Argue to save what? When was the last time she and Daniele had happily made love? Who could say if they were in love anymore? Daniele was right about one thing, however. Her parents would not hesitate to take her in. She could take Beniamino to the safety of her parents' house and she could sleep again in the bedroom of her girlhood. She could wake up without having to wonder about Daniele's mood.

"Maybe—" Petula's mouth was open and words were coming out. For an instant she let them flow as they would, without even knowing whether she had decided to speak or not. "Maybe a little break wouldn't be such a bad idea."

Hairs twitched electrically at the nape of Daniele's neck. He had not expected to hear Petula say such words, ever. Now that they had been pronounced, he, in dreamlike thrilling dread, could do nothing but hold on tight and follow the words' momentum. "When will you move out?"

"What?" Petula, too, was amazed that words could so quickly crystallize into reality and change the configuration of the world. "Nobody says we have to rush."

"Why wait?" Hearing the increasing finality of his own words, Daniele put out his cigarette with unsteady hands. Then, as if to reassure both Petula and himself, he said, "It's only a little break we're talking about here. A time-out, you know? So why wait?"

Petula had no reply.

"I'd move out if I could, but I can't," said Daniele. "I have no place else to go. You and Beniamino could go home right now and pack a suitcase or two. What's the big deal? The two of you take a little holiday at your parents'. You hear that, Beniamino?" Daniele called to his son, his voice unsteady. "You're going to take a holiday."

Beniamino did not look up. His eyes followed his fingertip as it traced the water stain.

"Babbo needs a break," Daniele continued. He closed his eyes and rubbed them with the heel of his hands. "You understand, don't you? Babbo needs a break." He heard only silence from his son. Opening his eyes, he looked at Petula. "Not the end of the world, right?" Everything inside him quivered.

"And work?"

Daniele scratched his head. "I don't know. Nothing to stop us from seeing each other here at work. You could come back to work as soon as tomorrow, if you feel like it."

"This is too strange," she said in disbelief. "You become my boss?" What would it mean to be paid to come here? The notion was as unnatural to Petula as the idea of being given money for looking after her own son.

"I'll be generous. The safe is in the storage room," he said. "You know the combination. You can pay yourself whatever seems fair. I trust you. I could use the help, and you could use the job. Working together doesn't have to stop, no?"

"So what is it that does have to stop?" In these suddenly polite tones, Petula sensed her life slipping over the edge of an abyss.

"I don't know," Daniele sighed. "But you said so yourself. Maybe a break isn't such a bad idea."

Petula bent down again to get the last of the broken saucer pieces.

"Don't worry." Daniele took the broom and dustpan from her hands. "I'll finish the rest. I broke them. I should clean them up. No customers here now, probably won't be more than a few for the rest of the afternoon. I think you should go."

Petula put on her coat, then picked up her handbag from behind the bar and swung the strap over her shoulder. "This is crazy," she said. "Are we doing the right thing?"

"We'll find out, I suppose," he said, trying not to let his voice show how terrified he was. Never, not even after his parents' death, had he felt so orphaned.

He held his arms open. She wrapped her arms around his body

and let herself be held by him. Pulling apart, they kissed on the cheek, acting as if they had never known the taste of each other's mouth.

Daniele went to the table where Beniamino sat. "I'm sorry," he said. Still frightened, the boy did not reply. Daniele bent down and kissed the top of the child's head. "I'll see you soon."

And Petula left, leading Beniamino by the hand. Does this mean Daniele and I are not together any longer? she wondered as she walked into the bright fresh air outside the bar. Is this how separation happens? As quick as this?

She walked in the direction of their house, or Daniele's, already coming up with a mental list of things she should make sure not to leave out of the suitcase. Human ties seemed precarious to her in that moment. People think they build fortified castles of love, when in fact a few minutes of well-aimed words are enough to knock everything down. The awful sense of fragility penetrated her coat like a wintry wind and made her body cold. At the same time, she wondered if this was how L'Altro felt when they opened the prison gates and let him out.

8

The old woman with the violet hair extended her finger to ring the doorbell, but then she stopped. What was she doing? No one had invited her to this house. How could she just ring the doorbell and walk in?

And when asked why she had come, what would she say?

In the darkening piazza, at a chilly five o'clock in the evening, people walked by her on their way to do errands. What would they think if they noticed her hesitating before this door? What gossip about her might spread?

Underneath the perfumed mink coat on her body and the lavender-smelling silk kerchief around her wrinkled neck, beneath the woolen jacket and sweater set, behind the sacks of skin that were now her breasts, inside the cage of ribs that grew brittler every year, her heart—beating still, though she herself sometimes did not know why—her heart began to flutter fast, the way it did at night when she lay sleepless and remembered all she had lost and contemplated the nothingness that awaited her ahead.

Maybe she should walk away. She was still in time. No one had noticed her yet. She could leave, as if she had never come.

Her heart—a mouse chasing freedom round and round the whirring wheel inside its cage—ran so rapidly that her head started to spin. How many times can a heart beat before it stops?

Dizzy panic was not new to Marta. Over the years, it had become a way of life. But the quivering shiver in this moment was different from the customary nightmarish fear of lonely death. The trembling that vibrated in her on the piazza this evening thrilled her, because mixed with her usual terror was unfamiliar hope. Who could say what the young man inside the house might do for her? What if with a word or a touch he gave back some nameless thing that had once been hers but she possessed no more?

She rang the bell. A moment later, the buzz of the electric mechanism replied, opening the front door's latch.

Inside, she found herself at the bottom of a dark stairwell. A door opened at the top of the stairs and loudly the lights clicked on. Rosa Spina was on the landing. She wrapped her black shawl around herself, hiding her cleavage from drafts. Her red mouth glittered in an elaborate smile. "Good evening, signora!" said Rosa Spina as if she had awaited this arrival.

"*Buonasera.*" Marta proceeded carefully up the steep stairs. "I'm sorry for disturbing you at this time of the evening. I just thought—" She did not know what to say. "I thought I might come and, you see, perhaps I thought—"

"Come!" Rosa Spina beckoned with her dancing hands, making clear that explanations were superfluous. "Come, signora, come! But here, let me help you with the steps." She descended and took the old woman by the arm.

"Stairs are terrible for me nowadays," said the woman. "I'm not as young as I once was."

"Of course not, dear signora. Then again, who is?" The perfume spilling from Rosa Spina's breast was spicy and intense. "We're almost there. Only a few more stairs. Careful now. This one is a little higher than the rest."

"If I had to go up another flight, it would be the end of me."

Rosa Spina smiled. "Those other stairs lead up to Signor Cappelli's apartment, but I don't imagine you've come to see him, have you?"

Out of breath on the landing, the woman shook her head.

"I didn't think so. This door here is where we live. Please come in."

Entering, the woman noticed the fresh white piece of card that had been attached beside the door to announce the family name of the occupants.

INNOCENTI

read the handwritten lettering. The old woman, though never would she have admitted to harboring a single superstitious thought in her head, took this name as a good sign: Here lived the Innocents. What did she have to fear?

"Come and sit by the fire," said Rosa Spina, "and when you've had a moment to lose the chill from outside, I'll take your coat. It's Emanuele Mosè you've come to see, no? Well, then, he is busy just now, but in a minute or two I am sure he'll be done."

The woman had not so much as introduced herself; evidently there was no need. She found herself sitting cozily by the fireplace while over there by the window, making no gesture to acknowledge her arrival, Emanuele Mosè sat locked in a concentrated exchange of murmurs with a man whose back was turned to the room.

"You've picked a good time to come," Rosa Spina said. "Earlier this afternoon there were five people here all at once. But in this moment there's only the one gentleman, so I'm sure your wait won't be long. I see you're warming up already. May I take your coat?"

Relieved of her mink, the old woman clasped the strap of her handbag.

"Something to drink in the meantime? A little cup of coffee? Tea? Chamomile? A drop of something else?"

"Thank you, no." The old woman could not recall ever receiving a readier welcome anywhere.

"Thanks, then!" the man near the window said in a suddenly loud voice as he rose from his chair. "If everything goes the way you say it will, there'll be a lot to celebrate. That's for sure."

"You need only believe, and it will happen." Emanuele Mosè spread his hands, the palms of which were hidden by his fingerless black gloves. "Have we not been taught the power of faith? 'If ye have faith as a grain of mustard seed,' it is written, 'ye shall say unto this mountain, Remove hence to yonder place; and it shall remove: and nothing shall be impossible to you.'"

"If only!" said the man. "Let's hope."

The old woman recognized him. He was a farmer who lived a few miles out of town, a simple man with nothing to worry about except his chickens and his pigs, his sunflower fields and his fruit trees, his olive groves and his vines. What could there possibly be in his world worth praying over? What could distress him enough to make him seek this kind of help? The old woman figured that sometimes there was no guessing other people's lives.

"And to thank you?" the man said.

"Don't thank me," said Emanuele Mosè. "Just pray. Pray for me, and I will continue to pray for you."

"Count on that," said the man. "But I'm talking about payment. To tell you the truth, I have to say I'm sorry, but I'm not a person of much wealth. Still—"

"I've never asked for money for doing the Lord's work."

"I have to give you something."

"You don't have to do a thing."

The man had an idea. "You like prosciutto? I have prosciutto from my own pigs. Kill them myself."

"I would never ask—" Emanuele Mosè began.

"You don't have to ask. You just tell me what you like, and I'll take care of the rest. Prosciutto you like, no? And some fresh sausages I can bring you. How about oil? A little olive oil is always a good idea. I'll bring you a big five-liter jug. And some wine, of course. You like wine, don't you?"

"I rarely drink. My mother, however, enjoys the occasional drop of white."

"My red is better," said the man.

"She prefers white."

"Then white it is." Joy animated the man, now that he had found a way to pay his debt of gratitude. He held out his sinewy working hand for Emanuele Mosè to shake.

The youth seemed reluctant to let his gloved hand be touched. He gave in, though, and surrendered his hand to the farmer's enthusiastic grasp.

Obeying some voice of ceremonious protocol inside his brain, the man bowed his head and planted a reverential kiss on the back of Emanuele Mosè's glove, as if performing the necessary duties on a bishop's ring.

"Thank you," said Emanuele Mosè, failing to mask the eagerness with which he took back his hand. "Go in peace. And return whenever you wish."

"*Grazie, grazie,*" said the man, retreating. "*Grazie, grazie.*" Recognizing Marta, the man said to her, "He's a prodigy, this young one. You'll see for yourself, signora!" He nodded to Rosa Spina, then nodded his way out of the apartment.

Rosa Spina smiled at Marta. "Your turn."

"Be comfortable." Emanuele Mosè extended a gloved hand to indicate the chair in front of his own.

The woman looked around. She saw the altar, with the pillar candles and postcard-sized saints and figurines, and the big picture of bleeding Jesus hanging on the wall. She sat.

"Your name?" said Emanuele Mosè.

"Hm?"

"I said, 'Your name?'"

"Oh. Sorcini. Marta Sorcini. Marta is my name."

"Good evening, Marta."

"Good evening." She dared to look him in the eye. The face, solemn as the visage of a painted saint, was studying her own. "I thought I would come. But now that I'm here, I don't know what to tell you. I can't even explain. I hoped—" The flurrying of her heart was unbearable. "Maybe I should leave. Forgive me for disturbing you." She made as if to get up.

"Dearest Marta." Life came into the young man's face, dawning in his eyes. "It was your heart that led you here, no?"

"My heart?" It quickened in her chest to hear its name called. "Yes, I suppose it was."

"Then why do you doubt? Your heart knows what's good for it. You needn't explain."

She put her weight back down on the seat. "Yes, but I should tell you what I've come to find. I would tell you, if I knew."

The nod he gave implied that nothing to him was unknown. "I'll tell you a little thing, Marta. Ever since I was a child, people have come to pray with me. No one has ever told them to come. No one except their own hearts. Why they would come to *me* is as much a mystery to me as it is to them." He smiled modestly. "Their hearts come seeking God, and God has made me into a kind of door for them to pass through so that they may speak directly to Him. *He* knows how to read hearts. *He* is the one who understands. All He has given to me is the eyes with which to see those who want to pass through the door."

"Is that what you see in me?" Marta said. "When you look at me what do you see?"

"What do I see?" He saw the color rise in her cheeks under her makeup, now that she felt observed. He saw the nervous shifting of eyes unsure where to look. Her lips parted, and he listened to the quickness of her breath. He watched the movement of her fingers as she fished for a tissue in the pocket of her twinset cardigan. He read the story written on the lines of her face. People are infinitely legible, he had discovered years ago. Secrecy is an illusion. Everything is visible, if you know how to decipher the signs. The word *widow* came to Emanuele Mosè's mind, as clearly as if it had been tattooed across the woman's cheeks. Another word that occurred to him was *weak-willed*. And *pretentious*. A woman of financial security, he could see, who considered herself a notch above many others in town. "I see a sensitive soul before me," he said.

"Sensitive, you say?" Marta's old mouth began to smile. Her hand gave little pats to preen her violet hair into place. "How perceptive of you! Yes, I'm very, very sensitive. Always have been, even as a little girl, but few people have had the sensitivity to recognize exactly how sensitive I am."

Flattering her was easy. Her vanity became transparent before his eyes. Emanuele Mosè, however, did not mention that. Instead he said, "I see great solitude as well."

"Yes," she said. "Solitude. If you knew how terrible it can be! My poor husband is gone now, and the boys, of course, have grown up and moved off with their wives. Why waste time hoping they might ask me to come and stay with them?"

Emanuele Mosè noticed the puffiness of her red eyelids and the darkness of the eye sockets, the crimson shadows that makeup could not conceal. He said, "Sleep does not come to you easily."

"Not easily at all," Marta said. "I lie at night and listen to myself breathe, wondering if the breathing will stop; then, when I know there's no hope, I get out of bed and straighten things up a little or I make myself some warm milk. But when I come back to bed, it's as useless as before. It's enough to drive you mad!"

"Nothing has been coming easily lately." Emanuele Mosè nodded as if his invisible antenna were picking up the frequency of her misfortune. A furrow of compassion appeared between his eyebrows. "You've had the impression that luck has been working against you, doing its best to take your tranquillity away."

"True, it's true," she said excitedly, "but not only for me. Everything has been going wrong for everyone. Some people take every little thing as a sign, but I'm not a superstitious person myself. Still, I have to say, in my case that is, nothing makes me happy anymore."

"There you are then." He smiled. "This is why you've come."

"I don't understand," she said, blinking. "Why?"

"Tranquillity, happiness, a little good fortune. Sleep. Peace of mind. Joy. These are not bad things to ask. It's all that anyone wants."

"But what can we do? What can *I* do to find what I want?"

"Easy," said Emanuele Mosè. "Pray."

"Pray?"

"We are told, 'Knock, and it shall be opened unto you.' You have come to knock at the door. I will help you pray."

"And what will that do?"

"When I help you pray," he said, "you will feel God's love. From that love, all blessings flow."

As she heard his words, a sweet drowsiness came over her. She wanted to fall into a prayer with him the way her tired body wanted to sleep. But her old companion Panic would not let go of her without a fight. "How can I trust you?" she said. "How can I know you won't take advantage?"

"Where there is love, there is no desire to harm. Why would I harm you? I offer only love. In return, I ask only faith. You must have faith. Otherwise, your disbelief will block the door. God cannot reach you if you put disbelief in the way."

"Yes, but I've heard things, I mean. . . ." She looked around. Seeing Rosa Spina busy filling a pot with water at the kitchen sink, she decided it was safe to speak. "About your family," she whispered. "People talk."

"Ah." Emanuele Mosè gave a small laugh. "My brother. He is what makes you doubt."

"People talk," she repeated. "And naturally I never listen to what people say, not being one for gossip myself, but they say he was in prison."

Emanuele Mosè smiled the indulgent smile of the doctor who reassures the patient that the disease diagnosed isn't so bad after all. "He was in prison, and now he's out. I never hide the truth."

"Is he *here?*" She looked around again. "Is he listening to what we say?"

"Calm yourself," said Emanuele Mosè. "He's out of the house. He's going around town, looking for an honest job."

"But will he try again? To do crimes?" She dared not guess at what those crimes had been. She hoped that Emanuele Mosè would tell her without her asking.

He did not. Instead he said, "L'Altro says that prison changed him. Says he has repented for his former sins. But I don't know. We'll see in time, I suppose." With his eyes he indicated Rosa Spina in the kitchen, and he whispered, "My mother doesn't trust him."

"I see!" This piece of inside confidence thrilled Marta. She could bring it casually into conversation the next time she chatted with other people in a shop. True, she had learned nothing of the nature of the crimes for which L'Altro had been sentenced, but she found delicious mystery in Emanuele Mosè's way of talking without revealing the whole story. Half-truths tease the appetite more spicily than does plain reality. She would strive to give these nibbles of information the same piquant flavor when she passed them on to curious listeners in town.

"Remember, though," said Emanuele Mosè, "that I am not my brother. Between you and me, there is no call for fear."

Marta looked at the young man and saw the bare face of candor looking back. His sensitive eyes had seen her for the sensitive soul that she was. His mouth had spoken nothing but the truth.

"Fine, then," she said. "If you would like to help me pray, if you think it would do some good, that is, then I think we should try."

Emanuele Mosè's smile grew wide. He rose and walked behind the chair on which Marta Sorcini sat. "Here." He took her by the shoulders and readjusted her position so that she faced the wall with the postcard-sized saints and statuettes on the table and the portrait of bleeding Jesus above. "Look at the saints," he said. His hands remained on her shoulders. "As you look, concentrate on their goodness."

Marta raised her hands to feel his fingers. "Your hands?" No longer could she resist the temptation to ask about the secret contained inside those fingerless gloves.

"You have nothing to fear." He moved the hands to hold the sides of her face from behind. His palms were against her neck, the fingers brushing the line of her jaw. "These hands know only peace."

Her question was frustrated, but probing further, Marta knew, would be have been untimely and indelicate. And she was taken by the touch of the gloved hands on her wrinkled, soft skin.

"Look at the face of the Lord," Emanuele Mosè instructed. "Now, with only his image in your sight, close your eyes, seeing still the image of the Lord there on the inside of your lids. See it. Feel the loving good-ness. Feel the peace. Let us each allow our heart to pray the prayer it wants to pray." He stopped.

Silence was not easy for Marta, but unnerving. She had observed the blood-covered Jesus and had closed her eyes as she had been told, and she waited now to feel something she was sure she was sup-posed to feel, though, if the truth be told, she felt nothing.

She was aware only of the glove-covered hands on either side of her neck, not unlike the touch a parent might give a child when di-recting the child's attention toward something beautiful to behold. Marta felt strangely childlike now. What person ever touched her these days? Her husband's touch was long gone. Her boys were dis-tant and untouchable, even on the rare occasions when she sat with them in the same room. They had their wives to do their touching with. The hands on her were the caress she would never get from her sons. The hands on her now did not recoil just because the skin of her neck was old. She saw the face of the Lord inside her eyelids and a young man's hands touched her neck.

Gladly did she receive the touch, and the miracle happened: Marta felt love.

She basked for a minute or so, then the hands patted her with affec-tion and pulled away. "Let yourself have faith," Emanuele Mosè said as he took his seat once more in front of her. "Faith in the power of prayer."

"Something I did feel," she said, suddenly wishing she could stay forever in this house, with the rosemary-scented cooking smells from Rosa Spina's kitchen, with this young man.

"Let yourself have faith."

The glow was so sweet, she had to make sure it would last. "But how will I know? How will I know if the Lord was listening?"

"You will sleep tonight, as a first step."

"What if I can't? What if I lie awake, the way I do every night?"

"If your faith is strong, you will sleep like a child." Emanuele

Mosè stood up, deciding apparently that it was time for this woman to leave. He went to the fireplace and placed logs on the flames.

"I want it to work. Believe me. But what if it doesn't?"

"Then pray some more. Prayer makes all things right. Pray for yourself. Pray for me." He spoke toward the fire, his back turned to Marta. He appeared to her a dark silhouette against the flames. "We are even taught to pray for our enemies. Pray for them, too." With a voice hardly louder than the hiss of the burning logs, he said, "You don't, by the way, have any enemies, Marta, do you?"

"I wouldn't say so." Marta was instantly alarmed by his change in tone. His whisper scared her. The warmth of love she felt began to chill. "No one wishes me harm. They just don't take me seriously. That's all."

"The Lord, too, was mocked. And He told us we will be blessed if we are mocked for His sake."

"Yes, I suppose. Most people think I'm a ridiculous old woman and nothing else."

"Is there anyone in particular who makes you feel this way?"

"No." She reflected. "Or maybe yes," she added. "There's Mauro Giannetti. You know, the butcher."

"I haven't had occasion to buy meat, myself."

"Well, he's just up the road. I was in his shop only the other day, and as always, no matter what I opened my mouth to say, I could see it made him grin, the same as he's been grinning for years. He laughed at me," she admitted with a blush. And Marta recalled how viciously Mauro had teased poor Signora Bottoni about her sons' absence. If he had spoken that way about me and my sons, Marta thought, I would have wanted to die, right there and then. "Mauro Giannetti," she said. "*There's* a man I never liked."

"In that case," said Emanuele Mosè, "if agitation returns and you cannot sleep, say a prayer and ask the Lord to take care of Mauro Giannetti. Pray for him, and all anger will vanish from your heart, leaving only peaceful love." He took her hands in his. "Remember, Marta. If you have faith, you will feel love." As he touched her again, the warmth returned.

"*Sì*," she said. "I will remember. I will have faith."

Rosa Spina appeared, carrying Marta's mink coat.

"Oh. I'll leave your family to have your dinner now," said Marta. "I'll go home and cook a little something for myself. Thank you. I want to thank you a lot. Because while we were praying, something, *something* I felt indeed."

"Go in peace," said Emanuele Mosè. "And return whenever you wish."

"And to thank you?" Marta clutched her handbag. "I saw the man before me promise to bring you prosciutto and oil and wine. I haven't got a farm. We were never farmers. My husband had the insurance office in town. All I have is money. My husband was able to leave me quite a lot."

"Then you have reason to give thanks to God."

"Yes, thank God for that. What I want to say, though, is if I give you some money to thank you, will that be all right?"

"It's not necessary," said Emanuele Mosè. "Yet certainly money is nothing of which we should be ashamed. It is energy made concrete. It gives energy to us and to those with whom we decide to share it."

"Then let me share a little of it with you." Marta opened her wallet and pulled out a banknote. "Here. I won't take no for an answer."

Emanuele Mosè accepted it graciously. "Your intention is what counts," he said. "May God give to you as you have given to my mother and me."

Suddenly Marta realized that she would want God to be less hesitant with her than she had been in her giving. She opened her wallet again and took out another banknote, eager for God to see her generosity.

Emanuele Mosè thanked her with impeccable courtesy, took the money, and handed it to his mother. "Remember, Marta," he said. "Faith."

9

One week into January, a cold morning of steady rain washed away the last of the snow. Outside was no place to be. Farmers found chores to do inside barns and stalls where the bodies of livestock warmed the air. In town, people gathered in the post office, the bank, the school, the barbershop, the beauty parlor, the newspaper store, the bakery, the butcher shop, the fruit and vegetable store, the bar: well-heated rooms where the rain could not penetrate, well-lit places where people could hide from the hostile world that seemed intent on giving them no joy.

Inside the bottega along the main street, Tonino and Maria Severina worked at their usual posts behind the bar. Milena, their daughter, worked in the back kitchen, preparing the food for lunch. Renato, at a table, took his time over a glass of red wine. Normally he did not drink midmornings, but today his internal furnace needed extra fuel. At the table with Renato sat Cappelli, who had a glass of wine in front of him, too. Cappelli, however, swallowed more than the occasional sip. His glass cried out to be refilled often. If anyone asked, Cappelli would explain that his furnace burned fuel fast. Yes, there was work for Renato and Cappelli to do, if they wanted to go looking for it, but work could wait until the skies were not pissing down.

Nuzzi the electrician sat at the next table.

At another table, absorbed, it seemed, in the information the newspaper had to offer, L'Altro sat alone.

"If you want my opinion," said Maria Severina, "they're *coglioni,* both of them."

"Did we request your opinion?" Renato did not want his mother-in-law to start this conversation again. In recent days, this conversation never actually stopped. It was as constant and sense-numbing as the rain. It might wear down to a momentary lull, but a little remark, like the one Maria Severina had just uttered, sufficed to open the flow once more. Renato already did not like the turn this stretch of the conversation was taking. Hearing his daughter, Petula, likened to a testicle struck him as unjust. Willful she could be at times, maddeningly headstrong even, but foolish as a testicle never.

"He's a *coglione* for asking her to leave," Maria Severina continued. "And she's a *coglione* for listening to him. *Un bel paio di coglioni* they make. A nice pair of balls, if you ask me."

Her voice stopped, and Renato hoped she had run out of things to say. Was this the type of thing to talk about in public anyway? Perhaps family matters should stay in the family. True, almost everyone in the bottega was family, even Cappelli. If Cappelli could not be considered family, who could? But there was that young man L'Altro. Not that he, studying his newspaper, seemed to be listening. Not that it would be such a tragedy if he did listen. In Renato's eyes he was an able-minded sort. Yes, he still had the strange feel of the newcomer about him, but that should not be held against him, as far as Renato was concerned. And there was Nuzzi, one table over. Now *there* was a *coglione* if ever one existed. Certainly not a bad person, but he ranked high on the world's list of incapables, no more likely to follow the ins and outs of a family conversation than to wire the town's Christmas lights without setting fire to the Nativity. Come to think of it, thought Renato, maybe he didn't have to worry about who might listen to his mother-in-law.

"And to tell you more—"

Maria Severina had not exhausted her supply of words. Damn!

"—you're a *coglione,* too, for not stopping their stupidity."

"I knew we'd wind up there," Renato said. "We always do. Inevitable. My fault, is it?"

"You're her father."

"And you could at least try to steer her in the right direction!" The sound of Milena's voice drifted in from the kitchen along with the smell of the onions she was sautéeing for the pasta sauce.

The fragrance of the onions in olive oil and the sharp sound of his wife's words reached Renato's senses at the same instant. The smell of onions made him hungry; Milena's tone made him cringe. "She's not a child," Renato called back, his shoulders stiffening. "Her life is her own, no?"

"And you don't care?" Maria Severina scolded. "You sit there and do nothing while she ruins her life and the life of her son?"

"You think I don't care"—he scratched his beard in irritation— "knowing that my daughter cries herself to sleep every night? To say nothing of the boy. . . . You think Milena and I have had a good night's sleep since they came to live with us? You think we don't go crazy between the two of us trying to figure how it will end up? Wonderful New Year we had this year! No festivities for us, no sir. The whole house is in mourning." Renato had always had his doubts about Daniele Mangiavacchi. Seeing how distraught Petula was, though, now that she was living away from Daniele, Renato had to stop and wonder. Could Daniele really be the wrong man for her, when his absence caused her so much grief?

"Certainly," Milena called from the kitchen, "Daniele has to learn to tame the monsters that live inside him, but who doesn't?"

"Petula said he was dangerous," Renato replied, unable to rid from his mind Petula's description of how Daniele had grabbed and shaken their son.

"And you think he'll become safe," Milena said, "if no one helps him? He'll always be Beniamino's father. That will never change."

"So what can change?" Renato said in frustration. "I can't change him. Can you? We look after Beniamino when Petula has her hands full. Anytime she wants to talk, we listen. What else can we do?"

"You should do less listening and more telling," Maria Severina insisted. "Tell her what's right."

"Do I know what's right for my daughter? The decisions have to be her own."

Catching Tonino's eye, Cappelli pointed to his empty glass. Tonino came out from behind the bar, wine bottle in hand.

"I say all along," Tonino commented as he poured the wine, "that it's no surprise really. What do you expect from a couple who never even got married?"

L'Altro looked up. Seeing that everyone had seen him look up, he turned the page of the newspaper and lowered his eyes to the printed words.

Renato shrugged. "In today's world, how many people live together without being married?"

"They have a child," Tonino said.

"How many unmarried people have a child? It's not so strange anymore."

"And you were a *coglione* for not forcing them to get married," said Maria Severina. "You should have forced them the day you found out Petula was pregnant."

"*Force them?* Unfortunately my shotgun was rusty that day. Force them, you say? I'd like to see anyone try to force Petula to do something like getting married. Anyway, doesn't marriage have a lot to do with love and nothing to do with force?"

"*Fammi capire una cosa,*" Cappelli said, emptying half the glass in one mouthful. "Help me understand one thing. They're working together, still, at the station bar?"

Renato said, "Working together, yes."

"How do they do it? I mean, they show up at the bar early in the morning to open it, work side by side all day long, then lock up and go away to their separate homes?"

"That's precisely what they do."

Cappelli squinted, trying to understand. "And is that easy?"

"Easy as pulling your own teeth without anesthesia." Renato lowered his voice, pained to imagine his daughter's suffering. "For Petula, at least."

"So how do they do it?"

"I ask myself the same thing." Renato sipped only enough wine to wet his lips. "All I can come up with is this: What does it mean if you let go of someone but you keep holding on? Maybe it means you don't really want to let go." He sipped again. "Maybe they just need a little time."

The silence that followed lasted for long minutes. The voice that broke it, to everyone's surprise, came from Nuzzi's mouth. "Oh!" he said, as if an idea had snuck up on him from behind. "Oh! Cappelli! Know who I ran into yesterday?"

"How would I know?" Cappelli said.

Typical of Nuzzi, Renato thought. A family was busy torturing itself over a young woman's fate, and Nuzzi had not caught a word. He was the kind of person who made you wonder whether adequate oxygen reached his brain.

"Carla. My cousin Carla. That's who I ran into."

"Fine then," said Cappelli. "But do I care?"

"Did you know Carla was my cousin?"

"If you call her your cousin Carla, I begin to suspect it might be the case."

"You know the Carla I'm talking about," Nuzzi said. "Carla who always cleans your house once a week. Always until now. And clean your house is a pretty way to put it, I say. I've always thought she came to shovel out your stall, the way you live."

"Ah. That Carla." Cappelli put his mouth to his glass, wishing he could hide his whole body inside it. He knew where Nuzzi's comments were heading.

"Is it true what she told me?" Nuzzi went on.

"Depends on what she told you, no?"

"She said," said Nuzzi, "you didn't need her to come and clean anymore because you had another woman to do it for you."

Cappelli drank more. "Is that what she's telling people?"

"Is it true?"

Cappelli guessed correctly that everyone in the bottega was listening, waiting for his reply. He said, "A lie it isn't." Cappelli had spent a lifetime shying away from situations in which his natural social awkwardness might come to light. Why was it that ever since Rosa Spina had turned up, he found himself in one jam after another?

Telling Carla that she would not be cleaning his house anymore had been a prickly task. And now he had to explain the why of it in front of L'Altro and everyone else. Life, thought Cappelli, used to be smoother than this.

"So tell us, Cappelli. Who is this other woman?"

"You tell me something, Nuzzi. What difference does it make to you? Your cousin Carla cleans my house or doesn't clean my house. What do you care?"

"I don't care. She has other houses to clean. Starve to death she won't. But if you have a woman to look after you now"—Nuzzi chuckled—"then this is something for the evening news."

"True!" Tonino joined in. Teasing people was one of life's joys for Tonino. A chance to tease Cappelli was a treat not to be missed. "A woman goes into the den of Cappelli the lone wolf. Must be a brave woman indeed."

"Brave, my prick," said Cappelli. "She's not another woman. She's my, um, tenant." Cappelli eyed L'Altro, who did not stop reading his newspaper.

"I see!" Nuzzi was enjoying himself. When was the last time he had the upper hand in a conversation? He was usually the one to be teased. "A lady tenant in that old house of yours, and suddenly you don't need outside help in keeping the place clean, is that right? But wouldn't you say that this woman coming into your apartment, with your dirty dishes, and your bed, and your underwear lying on the floor, wouldn't you say it's rather intimate, to say the least?"

"Intimate?" Cappelli made a face. "Your cousin came to my house for years. Was that intimate?"

"That was different," said Nuzzi, triumphant. "That was work."

"And so is this," Cappelli tried to explain. "Work, too, so to speak."

"Oh, I understand the whole thing. Your needs are being met, are they, eh, Cappelli, eh? Lady tenant comes up to your place, *bitty-be, bitty-bam*, eh?"

"What *bitty-be, bitty-bam*? It was her idea. Our deal was that she'd only look after the downstairs apartment, but then she said she'd be happy to come up once or twice a week and give me a hand with the washing and the—"

"But of course! You don't need to explain. Payment in kind, is what they call it, no? An exchange of services. And what services, I would imagine, eh?"

Cappelli went quiet. His silence underlined that L'Altro was sitting right there. Everyone had noticed already. Everyone, that is, except for Nuzzi. Cappelli knew that he had no choice but to do something himself to make this rotten embarrassment stop.

"Perhaps," he said at last, "perhaps I should introduce you to the woman's son. Nuzzi, this young man here is L'Altro Innocenti. L'Altro, Nuzzi."

Nuzzi said, "Oh." Too stunned was he to offer his hand.

Instead it was L'Altro who, folding his paper and putting it aside, smiled broadly and leaned over from his table to shake hands. "Pleasure," said L'Altro.

"Pleasure," mumbled Nuzzi, suddenly and painfully enlightened as to the mess he had created for himself. For once he had tried to be the person doing the teasing and not the person teased, and look how things turned out. Life was not fair.

Cappelli was surprised by L'Altro's poise, as was Renato, as was Tonino, as was Maria Severina. Nuzzi had all but called the young man's mother a whore, and L'Altro, with his winning smile, showed himself to be in calm control. They may have locked him away in prison, Cappelli and the others thought, but this guy knows how to take care of himself.

"It's true that my mother offered to clean Signor Cappelli's apartment." L'Altro settled back onto his wooden chair. "Everyone in the family is eager to find ways to pay the debt of gratitude."

"You see?" Cappelli was proud to have L'Altro back him up. "A debt of gratitude, he called it, though of course I tell them not to worry about paying me back." Magnanimity, Cappelli decided, suited him.

"I see," Nuzzi said. "I didn't mean to imply . . . I mean, don't misunderstand what you thought I might have been trying to say before. What I meant to say—"

"No misunderstanding at all." L'Altro smiled. "It's natural for people to wonder about new presences in town, wouldn't you say? Most natural thing in the world."

"Exactly." Nuzzi was thankful that the young man had left him an escape, pointing out the corridor and leading him out of trouble by the hand. "That's what I meant to say."

"Naturally," said L'Altro. "Natural for people to be curious. Natural for them to hesitate before trusting too much. But a bit of trust finds its reward, even with strangers. I've been looking for someone who's willing to trust me. A little job. Honest work."

"Perfect!" Renato broke in. "Looks as if your lucky moment has come."

"In what sense?" Nuzzi looked confused.

"In the sense of *you*. You, Nuzzi, are the perfect person to help out. You can show a little trust, and give L'Altro the job he needs."

"*Io?*"

Renato said, "*Tu.*"

"Yes," chorused Cappelli. "You."

"But I've never worked with an assistant."

"Maybe that's been your problem," said Tonino from behind the bar.

Nuzzi observed everyone's delight in cornering him into taking on the young man. He did not share their glee. "But does he know anything about electricity?"

"The same question," Tonino laughed, "could be asked about you."

"The fire in the Nativity wasn't my fault," Nuzzi protested.

"Of course not," said Cappelli. "And neither is the wiring on the bell at the cemetery that's been going off at crazy hours of the night and scaring the gravedigger out of his mind."

"And neither," said Maria Severina, never one to let pass the opportunity to point out someone else's flaws, "was the bell in the tower you rigged to go off at midnight on New Year's Eve last year, only it rang the whole night and no one could make it stop."

"Didn't happen again this New Year's Eve, did it?" Nuzzi said.

"That's because this year," Maria Severina laughed, "you rang the bell by hand."

"Anyway," said Nuzzi, "it's not true what people say, that Don Luigi's broken leg was my fault."

"Is that what they're saying?" L'Altro said, raising his eyebrows. "I thought everyone blamed my brother for that."

"I'm not saying it was *his* fault," said Nuzzi, "but that doesn't mean it was mine. The priest took a step and there happened to be ice where he set his foot."

"Coincidence," said L'Altro with a nod.

"Coincidence, *sì*, same as these other little mistakes," Nuzzi said, though he knew he had lost irrecoverable ground. "And if coincidences like that can happen to an experienced professional like me, just think what might happen with someone who doesn't know a socket from a plug."

"You have any books on electricity?"

"Books?"

"Books," L'Altro said again.

"I suppose," said Nuzzi. "Somewhere or other, there are the old books that I trained with, when I first learned the trade."

"I'll study." L'Altro smiled. "Learn what there is to learn. I'm a fast learner."

Nuzzi shook his head. "Slow you don't seem. But I don't know. It's the town hall that gives me *my* job, and the town budget being what it is, I can't imagine them giving permission to hire a whole other person."

"Then don't take a whole person," said L'Altro. "Take half. Part-time would be fine."

Nuzzi looked into the young man's face. He seemed bright enough. Too bright, if anything. But Nuzzi had placed himself in a bad position by implying that L'Altro's mother was Cappelli's private whore, and now here was his chance to set things right. Nuzzi could see no way out. "Mornings, I guess. Not afternoons. Most of the work gets done in the morning anyway. You have anything against getting up early?"

L'Altro gave his smile again. "Where I've been, the wake-up call didn't wait 'til dawn. Mornings would be fine."

"Still . . . " Nuzzi scratched his chin. "I'll have a hard time of it, trying to convince the town hall to hire someone that nobody knows. And your prison record's no secret to anyone around here."

"Don't forget," Renato told Nuzzi, "that I'm on the town hall payroll as well. I'd give him a job myself, if I didn't have Cappelli to assist me. I don't see why anyone should object. Seems reasonable enough for you to have an assistant, same as me. They raise any questions at the town hall, you tell them that I'll vouch for L'Altro myself. I like to go on instinct. My instincts about him are good."

Nuzzi looked at all the faces in the bottega. All the faces looked at him. He knew he had lost his battle. Teach him to open his mouth next time he felt the temptation to speak. Make a little conversation was all he had tried to do. His hands dropped loudly to his thighs. "*Boh,*" he exhaled. "What can I say?"

"*Bene!*" said everyone. "*Affare fatto!* Done deal."

L'Altro was still smiling. His grin softened, though, into an expression of thanks, as if the good people here had just given him a precious gift. His face showed a sincerity that no one would have dared question. "*Grazie,*" he said to the people in the room, "for the trust."

Milena leaned against the doorway to the bottega's kitchen. She had heard all the talk. Wiping her hands on her apron, she wanted to call over to L'Altro. I don't care if you're bad or good. Stay away from my daughter, she wanted to say. You leave my Petula alone.

L'Altro had pronounced not a word on the subject of Petula, however. How could Milena chastise him when he hadn't said or done anything to indicate desire for the girl? The voice of intuition spoke loudly in Milena's head, but it was not a voice that she could expect others to heed. Keeping her thoughts to herself, she returned to the kitchen.

Outside the cold rain came down.

10

As the sheep finished their evening feed on the hillside behind his house, Renato felt a touch of the winter sunset's delicate sadness. The sinking sun gave no heat. Its distant radiance implied a bright feast celebrated elsewhere, in a different world far past the horizon; *here* darkness encroached, impatient to make the valley blind.

Quarta, statue stiff, stood beside Renato. She, too, appeared to watch the sun. Her eyes blinked too infrequently, Renato noticed. Something had certainly set out to destroy her, but what? Renato was losing hope.

He turned and saw Beniamino running, chasing after Lola, the youngest sheep, who, if given a choice, would have been happier to stay put and graze. Watching his grandson, Renato laughed. The sadness of the sunset passed.

"Another minute or two," he called to the boy, "and then we'll take the sheep back down to their stall. Aren't you chilly? I am. And I think even the sheep are feeling the cold."

Beniamino carried on making Lola run.

A moment later, "Look who's coming," Renato said, speaking more to himself than to anyone else. He had not expected visitors at this hour, in this place. Yet now in the last scraps of sunlight, he could see a young man climbing the hill. Renato took the backlit figure to be L'Altro. He blinked and, focusing his eyes again, observed the way the young man walked. L'Altro would have jogged up the hill athletically. No, this was Emanuele Mosè who, though mere minutes older than his twin, walked with steps made heavy by the weight of saintly responsibility.

"Buonasera," Renato called out. His voice would have held more spark, he realized, had he been greeting L'Altro. Renato knew which brother he preferred.

"Signor Renato, *buonasera,"* came the reply. *"Buonasera,"* Emanuele Mosè said to Beniamino.

Beniamino stopped running. A smile came to his face when he thought he saw L'Altro approaching. Then, recognizing the young man as the scary priestlike twin he did not like, he lost his smile, turned away, and started chasing Lola some more without returning the *buonasera.*

"He's shy," Renato said by way of apology.

"I've noticed," Emanuele said, watching the boy run.

Unbidden, a line from the Bible came to Renato's mind. *Suffer the little children to come unto me,* Jesus had said, acknowledging the way little ones gravitated eagerly toward the gentle Shepherd of Men. Beniamino, however, showed fearful reluctance in Emanuele Mosè's company. Secretly, Renato felt proud that his grandson should have instincts so akin to his own.

Emanuele Mosè turned to Renato and said, "My brother told me how you spoke up for him, how you helped him get the job as assistant to the electrician."

"If I'm not mistaken, your brother seems anxious to make a new life. Putting in a good word is a small thing to do to give a person a hand."

"No small thing," said Emanuele Mosè with that intensity of his. "You showed faith in him. Faith is never a small thing."

Why, Renato wondered, was this kid so capable of making simple things sound leaden? *"Mah!"* Renato said, keeping his own tone light. "If it does him some good, why not? So tell me, he's started work, no? How's it going?"

"Started a few days ago. He's applying himself as I've never seen him apply himself before. He loves the job."

"Oh. Glad to hear it."

"Let's just hope he doesn't betray the faith you've placed in him," Emanuele Mosè said disapprovingly, as if he were L'Altro's father instead of his twin.

Not trusting Emanuele Mosè, Renato did not want to listen to him speak badly of the other. "My instincts are accurate enough most of the time," Renato said to discourage further comment. "They haven't got me in too much trouble so far." He bent to pick up a small stone, which he then tossed from one hand to the other, back and forth.

"I wanted to thank you," said Emanuele Mosè, "in any case."

"But there's no need." Renato looked around. It would be completely dark in a few minutes. He wanted to go back to his house and find something in the kitchen for Beniamino and himself. Usually sociable, Renato already started to search for a way out of inviting Emanuele Mosè to stay for dinner. Had there been family around, that would have been one thing, but Milena was at her parents' bottega, and Petula was busy at Daniele's bar. Dealing with Emanuele Mosè on his own for an entire evening sounded like hard work. "No need for thanks, really. And that's why you walked all the way out from town, just to thank me? Thank you for your trouble, but really, you shouldn't have."

"That's not why I've come."

"Oh. There's something else? Well, here we are. Tell me."

"Petula," said Emanuele Mosè. "She's here?"

"Ah, Petula! You wanted to see her. Sorry, but she's at work," said Renato, glad to thwart the young man's hopes of seeing his daughter. "And they probably won't be closing up for another couple of hours. I'm afraid your wait might be a little long."

"No, I didn't come to see Petula."

"Ah. Not that either. I thought you—"

"No, I meant to ask if she's here, in that she's living here, in your house with you."

"*Sì*," Renato said, not seeing what the other was getting at. "For a while anyway. She and Beniamino are here with us."

"It must be hard for her."

"Living here? Not that hard, I suppose. She managed it for her whole childhood."

"No, living without her man, I mean."

"Oh. In that sense. Yes, I would say yes. Hard for her, yes."

"She probably needs a friend to talk to," Emanuele Mosè said.

Renato said nothing, but scratched his beard—an unconscious gesture that meant he was not comfortable with what was being said.

"But I can tell she doesn't want to talk with me." Emanuele Mosè bent over to pick up a long stalk of grass with the fingers that poked out of his fingerless gloves. "With my brother maybe, with L'Altro, sì. But not with me." Thoughtfully he stroked the strand of grass.

"Why would you say such a thing?"

"Because it's true. Doesn't matter in any case." He threw away the grass. "But that's not why I've come."

"You like to be mysterious, don't you!" Renato never had been one to relish conversations that said everything except what they meant to say.

"I've come about the sheep."

"The sheep?"

"Don't you remember? I promised to come to pray over the sheep. Here I am."

"Of course! I'd forgotten, to tell you the truth. Christmastime, wasn't it, when you said something about dropping by?"

"I should have come before, but I've been busy, you know, with people requesting prayer at the house. Every evening they want to pray. It's difficult to get away. But this evening I promised myself that I would make the time."

"Really, you didn't have to!" Feeling impatient, Renato flicked away the stone he had been playing with. "Thank you all the same, but to go to all this trouble—"

"How is the sheep?"

"Here she is." Renato held out an arm. "This is Quarta. This is how she is. Rigid as an olive stump."

"May I have a look?"

Just then, Beniamino, running by in pursuit of Lola, slipped on the grass and landed on his bottom with a thud.

"Oh, little one!" Renato called. "Here." He trotted to where the boy sat on the ground. "Let me brush you off. No harm done, see? But I think you should let Lola have her last nibble of grass and we'll head back home in a minute." He turned to Emanuele Mosè. "You want to have a look at Quarta? Thanks, but the veterinarian has already examined her several times, and there's no explaining why she should be in this state."

"How did he examine her?"

"Listened to her heart and lungs. Took blood samples. Checked her stool. Nothing. Still, she's losing weight and perishing day by day. Sometimes she's almost her normal self. Starts to eat a little. Starts to walk. Then something comes over her and she turns into a stone. Maybe she's possessed!" he joked, then caught himself.

Emanuele knelt beside Quarta and patted the wool on her head with his gloved hands. "Might be. All the more reason to pray."

"A possessed sheep? *Dai!* Come on!" Not wanting his grandson to hear talk of this sort, Renato let Beniamino run off to chase Lola some more. "Why would a nasty spirit waste its time possessing a sheep?" The thought seemed funny at first, but Renato disliked the young man's grave tone.

"You said it yourself. Science can find no other cause."

"Listen. I appreciate your desire to help, but even an expert like the vet has given up."

"Had our Lord undergone formal training in orthopedics before he healed the lame? Had he studied ophthalmology before giving sight to the blind?"

Talk of this sort made Renato uneasy. "All right, but there's a difference between Bible stories of what the Lord did and the two of us here trying to find a cure for a sick sheep."

"What difference is there?" He continued patting Quarta. "What the Bible tells is no story; it's the truth. Do you doubt the truth of what the Bible says?"

"I only meant—"

"The Lord accomplished wonders through faith. And he promised us that we, too, can do wondrous things if we have faith enough."

"Fine," Renato said, trying to control the irritation he could hear in his own voice. "But I have to say, this strikes me as a little strange." Renato watched as, in the last light of the day, Emanuele Mosè rubbed his hands on the head of the sheep.

"Nothing strange about it. I simply take the Bible up on its promises. That's all I've done my whole life." Emanuele Mosè held the sheep's head firmly now. He bent over the animal, pressing its face against his chest. He closed his eyes in prayer.

Imitating the visitor at a safe distance, Beniamino grabbed the head of Lola, and held on tight while Lola did everything she could to liberate herself.

"Beniamino!" Renato called out, looking away from Emanuele Mosè. "Leave her in peace!" He knew that he was saying to his grandson what he would have wanted to say to the young man. "Leave her," he said to Beniamino, softening his sharp tone. "It really is time to get them back to the stall."

"*Be-eh-eh-eh-eh-eh!*"

The bleating was sudden and strong. Renato realized with a shock that it was none other than Quarta whose bleat mixed protest with joy. Staring into the increasing darkness, Renato watched as the sheep yanked her head from side to side. Her body appeared animated by jolts of electrical energy. Her fleecy white form bucked. She tried to back away from Emanuele Mosè, but the young man would not let her go.

"Thank you, Lord!" cried Emanuele Mosè. "*Grazie, Signore, grazie!*" He laughed as he resisted Quarta's efforts to tug herself free. "Just a minute, girl. Just a minute more." He held her by the neck with one hand. With the other hand he picked up a clump of gray soil from the ground. He spit on the dirt to moisten it, and worked it between his fingers into malleable mud. He pressed the clay into the wool at a spot just behind the crown of her head, then released her.

She ran off, kicking skittishly. "She always charge around this way?" Emanuele asked Renato.

"She used to, but not since she took ill."

"Then we have reason to thank the Lord. Your sheep is healed."

"I can't believe it." A sickening chill spread over Renato. "What did you do?"

"I did nothing. The Lord did it all."

"*Non ci posso credere,*" Renato repeated, stunned. "I can't believe . . . And if I hadn't seen it with my own eyes—" He shook his head. He watched old Quarta run, giddy as a lamb. He scratched his beard. He looked down at the earth and wondered what healing magic might be hidden in clay. "You see that, Beniamino?" he asked the little boy.

Beniamino nodded, but, too afraid of Emanuele Mosè to speak, said nothing.

Lola ran after Quarta, happy to play with her mother again.

"What can I tell you?" Renato said. "Makes no sense. Never saw a thing like this. The mind searches for reason, but what can I say?"

"What were you expecting?" said Emanuele Mosè. "Thunder? Celestial choirs? The parting of the clouds with a golden beam of light pouring down from on high? Miracles are quiet things. The Lord doesn't need to make the ground tremble every time He intervenes on earth."

"Are we sure this was a miracle?" Renato asked.

"Ask your sheep."

"One thing's for sure," said Renato, watching her run. "Quarta looks fine. Thank you, Emanuele Mosè. What else can I say? Thanks. Tell me what I owe you. I'll pay. We're all very attached to Quarta. It's good to have her back."

"You owe thanks to the Lord alone." Emanuele stood up and brushed dusty earth from his knees.

"A dinner at least I can offer you." *Least I can do,* Renato said to himself. *Considering. Even if he does set me on edge.* "We haven't got much in the fridge, but I'm sure we can find something good to eat."

"My mother and brother will be waiting to have dinner with me.

And I am eager to tell them of my joy in the loving-kindness that the Lord bestowed upon your sheep."

"I see," said Renato, still unable to digest the sort of words that came from Emanuele Mosè's mouth. "Another time, then. I owe you one. On behalf of the sheep and myself, thanks."

"*Arrivederci*," said Emanuele Mosè. He turned down the hillside.

Renato looked out over the evening. In town on the other side of the river, lights glowed from the windows of homes. Streetlamps marked the shape of the roads, the same shape as always, yet everything looked different in Renato's eyes. What had he witnessed a moment ago, a miracle or a sorcerer's spell? Both possibilities, equally unacceptable to his mind, made his skin crawl. He knew only that Emanuele Mosè unsettled him, yet somehow the strange young man had restored Quarta to health—through divinity or devilry, he could not say.

"Is he a magician?" Beniamino asked after the young man disappeared in the darkness of the valley.

"I don't know what he is." Renato shivered. He pulled his coat around his body. "Come on, Beniamino. Help me get the sheep together. I can't understand a thing, but it's time to get ourselves inside."

Later that evening, sleep had just started to ooze into Marta's head from the darkness around her when a bolt of electricity shocked her in the kidneys and made her jump. Wide awake and afraid, she knew that sleep would not be quick to return.

She lay on her back beneath her lavender-scented sheets and blankets, hands folded over her stomach, head in the dead center of her pillow, eyes open. No light ruined the perfect blackness of her bedroom. Shutters and windows, and curtains, too, kept outside the stars and moon and streetlamps' glow. Light, however small, would disturb her, she believed. Air in the room did not move. Marta lay as if inside a box nailed shut. She closed her eyes and tried to let not a single muscle twitch.

Then a thought unnerved her: The position of her body, she realized, was identical to that of a corpse in its tomb. How would she endure it when her time came? Would she suffer impatiently the breathless waiting for eternity to pass?

Agitation accelerated her heart. Scared, she quickly rolled to her side, trying to make her body find again the comfortable curl she used to enjoy when her husband would embrace her from behind.

Pray, she told herself. Pray is what Emanuele Mosè told me to do, and he promised me that peace would come. "Lord send me peace," she prayed silently. But then she wondered if anyone in Heaven had heard her prayer. Emanuele Mosè does not have these problems, she said to herself. He can pray anything he wants whenever he wants, and the Lord's ear is always ready to catch every syllable.

I'll pray some more, she tried to persuade herself. No prayerful thoughts came to mind. In the end she gave up. She was no good at prayer, she recognized, without Emanuele Mosè to direct her. Frustration only added to her nervousness. Her heart fluttered faster than before. Desperate for remedy, she recalled Emanuele Mosè's counsel that she find solace in faith.

Searching for faith, she remembered the feeling of the young man's glove-covered hands on the sides of her face when he prayed with her. Concentrating on the hands that touched her, she sensed the presence of the young man here in her bedroom. She cuddled into her pillow and Emanuele Mosè seemed to materialize like a wizard. As if there in the flesh, he touched her neck and her cheeks. With kisses he smoothed her hair. She felt him slip beneath the covers of the bed and hug her from behind.

Nestling in his pure young arms, the old woman let herself be embraced by love, as if Gesù Cristo himself had climbed down from the cross and had entered her room to blanket her with his body's warmth.

Marta slept.

11

The last day in January, a foggy morning so damp it made bones ache, Marta walked across the piazza. A young man came out the front door of Cappelli's house, and Marta took him for Emanuele Mosè at first. Why did she feel that he had visited her in her room for several nights? Had it been vague fantasy or half-forgotten dream?

But this wasn't Emanuele Mosè, she realized when her eyes saw him better through the fog. This one kept his long hair slicked back with gel. And this one wore no gloves. Must be the ex-convict twin, Marta thought as fear made her heart beat fast, the twin whose own mother doesn't trust him.

L'Altro, however, smiled and introduced himself with gentlemanly manners. "May I give you a hand, signora?" he said, offering his arm. "Look how slippery the street is this morning." Indeed the fog had made the paving stones dangerously slick.

"*Grazie*," Marta said. "But I don't have far to go. I'm only going to the newspaper shop just down the road."

"And that happens to be where I'm going, too," L'Altro said, his proffered arm still waiting.

"Very kind of you," she said unsurely, accepting the arm. When had she ever walked arm in arm with a man who had spent time in jail?

Somehow, thanks to L'Altro's reassuring air, distrust left Marta and she found herself wanting to talk. L'Altro, like his brother, seemed to have an almost hypnotic way to make her forget her wariness and talk despite herself.

By the time they walked together past the fruit vendor and the bakery, Marta thought she had never met a more courteous young man. Thief or murderer he might be, she decided, but at least he was brought up the right way. Besides, the news she had to talk about was too good to keep to herself, and L'Altro seemed a ready listener.

Words came easily. Marta talked and talked along the road toward Il Piccino's shop.

Though his real name was Trieste, everyone called him *Il Piccino:* The Little One. He did not resent the nickname, for he knew it was uttered without malice. He was, after all, a midget; people who referred to him as *Il Piccino* were merely stating fact. No one in Sant'Angelo D'Asso had ever mocked him. In return, he held in his heart a quiet, unexpressed gratitude toward the townspeople here. Many years ago he had arrived from Siena, not that far away. He had been a child during the war. In the end, he was the only person in his family to escape death in the concentration camps. The people of Sant'Angelo D'Asso had accepted him from the start, despite his differences. He had no one to love him for the person he was, but what can you do? Though lonely, he was not the type to complain.

This morning Il Piccino had barely opened his newspaper shop on the main road when his first two customers entered together.

"*Buongiorno,*" said L'Altro.

"*Buongiorno,* Piccino. *Buongiorno,*" said Marta. She was in full flow, talking away to L'Altro and leaving him time only for a polite *Really?* or *You don't say!* when she paused for breath.

"*Buongiorno.*" Il Piccino held out his small arm in a gesture of welcome. "You're up early, the two of you, I must say."

"Well, yes," said Marta. "I was on my way when I saw this young man coming here, too, so we were just having a word. As I was saying," she talked on, "I could hardly believe my own ears when I heard the news. I don't think anyone could. Could you? I mean, who ever heard of such a terrible way to die!"

L'Altro and Il Piccino each caught the eye of the other. A moment of instant comprehension. Not a wink was needed to let them both know they were thinking the same thought, that Marta, once her vocal cords got going, was a force of nature strong enough to make old stone buildings want to cover their ears.

"Ugly death indeed." Il Piccino nodded.

"You've heard about it, then?" said Marta, terrified and thrilled.

"Who hasn't?" said Il Piccino. The death had occurred the morning before, and for the rest of the day people had talked about little else. The town's population had dropped to one thousand, two hundred and eighty-seven. One more grave that Sculati had to dig. Though the news was not altogether fresh, Il Piccino knew that nothing would stop Marta from telling it again.

"They say that when the doctor found him," said Marta, "his hands were clutching at his own throat and his eyes bulged out horribly. His tongue was purple and swollen, and his mouth was opened wide, as if with his last breath he had tried to let out a scream or a laugh. Can you imagine choking to death on a piece of salami? It could have happened to any of us, if you think about it. It's the salami he sold in his own shop, the same salami we all buy, though of course the blame can't really be given to the salami, because none of us have ever choked. And now we don't have a butcher, though I hear his cousin who lives in the country used to be a butcher as well. They say he'll come out of retirement to take over the shop, so at least we won't have to live without meat. Still"—she shook her head while envisioning Mauro's final moments—"choking to death must be the worst torture anyone could ever imagine. He must have been eating too fast, if you ask me. Or maybe he was in such a hurry to stuff his mouth that he didn't take time to peel off the salami's skin. In any case, that's not the part that scares me the most."

"No?" said L'Altro politely.

"No, certainly not! I'm hardly about to start fearing salami at my age. No. The part that scares me the most is that I had talked about Mauro Giannetti just the other day, talked about him with your brother, and now look what's happened! Now poor Giannetti's dead."

"My brother?" L'Altro's voice tightened. "What's my brother got to do with it?" Il Piccino heard the agitation in the young man's words.

"He's got everything to do with it! Don't you see? I went to visit your brother and he prayed over me, praying for God to give me a little peace of mind. And he asked me if I had any enemies. He wanted to find out who was stealing my peace of mind, I'm sure. I see that now. You can see that, too, can't you?"

"One person stealing another person's peace of mind?" L'Altro started to protest. "I would have to wonder if truly that could—"

"So I told him no," Marta continued, not listening, allowing no interruption to her reasoning. "No enemies to speak of. No real enemies, no. But people who laughed at me, yes. That's when I mentioned Mauro Giannetti. Because of all the people I know, he's the one who laughed at me the most. And do you know what your brother said?"

L'Altro shook his head.

"He said I should worry no more about Mauro Giannetti, because the Lord would take care of him. Don't you see? The Lord would take care of Mauro Giannetti, your brother said. Though when I went back to my own house after visiting with your brother, I wasn't thinking of Mauro Giannetti at all. He was the smallest of my thoughts, because I was so anxious about waiting for the peace of mind to come."

"And have you found your peace of mind?" L'Altro asked.

"To the contrary! I've been so worried, wondering if the peace of mind is coming or not, that my heart races in my chest in fear that the peace will never arrive. But your brother told me that faith would give me peace."

"If finding peace were as easy as that," L'Altro began, "then we'd all be floating like white clouds on a summer's day. I think that peace is somehow more—"

"But that's not what your brother told me. Your brother told me it was only a question of faith. And I started to lose my faith, I have to confess, after the first two nights of sleeping less than before. But then I heard about the sheep. Everybody's talking. You've heard, haven't you? Renato Tizzoni's sheep? Miracle is the only word for it, the way your brother healed the sheep. If a poor beast like a sheep has enough faith to be healed, then there must be something very, very wrong with me." She did not mention her sensation that Emanuele Mosè had visited her at night to give her solace. That, surely, was a thought she could share with no one. "And then this happened," she continued. "Mauro Giannetti's terrible death. The Lord took care of him all right, just the way your brother said He would."

L'Altro sighed. "I can see how my brother might give the impression—"

"It's no impression," Marta insisted, "it's proof. If this isn't proof of what faith can do, then I don't know what is. You can tell your brother that I'm coming back to see him one of these evenings. He has to help me work on my faith. I see what *his* faith can do, but my own is—" She shook her head. "Peace is so far away. He has to help me."

L'Altro and Il Piccino looked at each other. What could you say to quiet the torrential outpourings of an agitated old woman?

"Unfortunate thing, Giannetti's death," Il Piccino attempted. With a small hand, he smoothed the child-sized necktie he always wore, tucking the tie neatly inside his suit jacket. In his manners and dress, Il Piccino never left the genteel formality that had characterized the world of his boyhood long ago. "But I don't think the Lord—"

Marta said, "Terrible way for a Christian to die."

"Terrible way for any person to die, Christian or not," said Il Piccino.

Confused, Marta said, "What?" for Il Piccino's remark seemed incongruous.

Immediately Il Piccino regretted his comment. "Nothing," he said. "A small joke I made. Nothing, really."

"A joke?" Marta did not like jokes, especially ones she could not understand. Was Il Piccino laughing at her? She had not come here this morning to be mocked.

"A very small joke, signora," Il Piccino explained. "All that I meant to say—" Il Piccino never had liked this common expression, this unthinking verbal mannerism quick on people's tongues. So many people here were Christian that the automatic assumption seemed obvious to them: Being human implied being Christian. The equation excluded Il Piccino. It always had, ever since he was a boy. And now he had to justify the little remark he had permitted himself, or else Signora Marta might take offense. "That is," he tried again, "you said that choking on salami was a terrible way for a Christian to die. I merely pointed out that choking would be no pleasure even for people not of the Christian faith."

Marta blinked. Then, as the mechanism of reasonable thought began to spin in the aged machinery of her brain, her face softened. "Oh, you know what I meant! It's just a way of saying. Of course I completely forgot that you're different. A Hebrew you are. An Israelite, no?"

"A Jew," Il Piccino said.

"Oh, you know what I mean," said Marta.

"Jewish?" said L'Altro, interested.

"Jewish, yes." Why hadn't he kept his joke to himself? Jewishness had cost him his family. After a lifetime of caution, he should have been more skillful now in keeping quiet.

"How wonderful!" L'Altro said. "I've always admired the Jewish faith."

"Wonderful?" Il Piccino folded his little hands on the countertop and looked up into the eyes of the tall young man. L'Altro's words seemed to express enthusiasm, but the eyes held a look of analytical detachment that put Il Piccino on guard. "Depends on your point of view, I suppose. Wonderful or not, though, that's what I am."

"Even if I've never really understood what a Jew *is*," Marta continued as if she had started the discussion. She had a knack for making every conversation her own.

"Lovely!" said L'Altro, enjoying the situation. "Explain." He looked at Il Piccino. "If you've ever waited for the chance to explain your beliefs, you'll never have a better moment than now."

"Could be." Il Piccino busied himself aligning in orderly stacks the newspapers displayed on the countertop. "Or it could also be that chances to explain my beliefs don't interest me."

"Impossible," smiled L'Altro. "Everyone welcomes the opportunity to let others know what's going on inside his head."

The young man appeared to take the conversation as a game, but Il Piccino could not find the sport in it. "I learned a long time ago," Il Piccino said, his eyes concentrated on the newspapers he was straightening, "that more often than not it's better to resist the temptation to explain oneself thoroughly. Explanations are vain if they're out of place."

"Out of place?" L'Altro said with his light, good-natured laugh. "The signora is curious. She asked. She'd like to know. How could sharing ideas ever be out of place?"

"*Sì.*" Il Piccino hesitated. Did his own awkwardness give delight to the young man? "Yes. Fine. But it's just that, how can we say, an openness to sharing is required. A certain mental flexibility."

"I don't understand." Color became visible in Marta's pale cheeks. "This isn't a complicated subject, is it? I can't stand complicated subjects. They make me anxious."

"Nothing complicated at all." Il Piccino nodded deferentially. "I only meant that people's thoughts after a debate usually remain exactly what they had been before words were spoken. Which is why it's often best to keep silent, and talk about other things instead."

L'Altro said, "A debate, then, is it?"

"Sounds complicated," said Marta.

"No, of course not. I didn't mean that." Il Piccino wanted to escape this talk, but could find no way out. Why did the young man seem intent on forcing him to speak?

"Are you worried," said L'Altro, "that our minds are incapable of being convinced?"

"Not at all." The newspapers tidy now, Il Piccino got to work on the magazines. "That's just the point. I would never try to *convince* anyone. What's to convince? You say you admire the Jewish faith. Then surely you've noticed that our faith has never been one to go and try to recruit anyone."

"That's one of the reasons I admire it." There again was L'Altro's light, reassuring laugh.

"*Bene,* but in the end"—having become spectator to a dialogue she could not follow, Marta had to say something now to take the reins back in her own silver-veined hands—"in the end it will be a religion like any other, no?"

"Of course," said Il Piccino, happy to leave it there. "A religion like any other. And I'm convinced that at the heart of things, all religions worship the same God. It's only a question of which name they use."

"Ah!" Marta was triumphant to be once again in charge of talk that made sense. "You Jews believe in God, too?"

"Certainly." Il Piccino was about to add that his people had caught on to the idea of one God a good twenty-three centuries before Christianity came into being, but he decided that a chauvinistic comment of this sort would do him no good. He contented himself with saying, "If you think about it, your Lord Himself was a Jew. And He believed in God, no?"

"Yes." Marta nodded. "I heard the priest mention that in church, that the Lord was one of you. So I see what you mean. It's the same thing in the end. You believe in God, same as we do."

"We believe in God."

"And you believe in Gesù Cristo."

Silence. Il Piccino tapped a stack of magazines into shape, letting silence answer for him.

"And you believe in Gesù Cristo," Marta said again. "No?"

"That, signora," L'Altro intervened, "is the question that has prompted much of the suffering of the Jewish people for the last two thousand years."

"How do you mean you don't believe in Gesù Cristo? Everybody believes in Gesù Cristo."

"*Ci risiamo,*" said Il Piccino, talking to himself. "Here we go again. You see, signora," he said to Marta, "it's not that we believe, and it's not that we don't believe. It's more that"—he cleared his throat—"the subject doesn't come into it."

"*Non c'entra?*" Marta was confused again. "How can it not come into it?"

"In your church," said Il Piccino, "how often is the name of

Muhammad raised? Or of the Buddha? You see? For those figures, in
your church, it's not a matter of belief or disbelief. It's more that they
don't come into your faith."

If the troubled creasing of Marta's forehead was any indicator,
then Il Piccino's illuminating words had managed to spread no light.
"I don't understand," she said. "What's there to believe in, if not
Gesù Cristo?"

Il Piccino looked at Marta. Then he looked at L'Altro. "*Grazie!*" he
blurted out. "*Grazie infinite!* This is the sharing of ideas that you
wanted to spark off?"

"And what harm is there?" L'Altro laughed, evidently moved to
fondness by the exasperation in Il Piccino's voice. "Here. Let me try
to help you out. I'm no expert, but I've studied some. I had lots of
time for reading where I was. I'll start to explain, and if I say things
wrong, you jump in and correct me."

"*Vediamo un po'*," said Il Piccino, intrigued to hear what one Christian might say to another in describing the Jewish faith. He had read
much himself, though never before had he shared his intellectual curiosity with anyone else. "Let's see. Go ahead."

"Signora," L'Altro began, "you know the Old Testament?"

"That's part of the Bible," Marta said, glad to get hold of something familiar. "Our Bible, in any case. Whether it's part of theirs,
too," she said suspiciously, "I wouldn't know."

"It's *all* of their Bible," said L'Altro. "It's where their Bible begins
and ends. It stops before the New Testament. Before the life of
Cristo."

"No gospels?"

"No gospels."

"But that's the best part! What does their Bible offer, if it doesn't
even mention Cristo?"

"*Prego.*" Il Piccino smiled at L'Altro. "Please continue. You're doing a beautiful job."

L'Altro laughed. "What does the Old Testament offer? How can I
explain? Right. The book of Deuteronomy. Chapter six, verse four.
'Hear, O Israel: the Lord is our God; the Lord is One.' The great reve-

lation of monotheism, springing up in the desert, in the mind of Abraham, two thousand and three hundred years before Christ, equating the mystical four-letter name of God with *Elohim*, a plural noun treated as singular by all verbs."

Marta's pink-rimmed eyes blinked in perfect incomprehension.

"*Elohim*. The Mightinesses," L'Altro continued. "God. The multitudinous Mightinesses of the universe are One. And that, in essence, is it."

"That's it," said Il Piccino, nodding. "Simple as that. He's right, you know. That's what we believe in. 'And you shall love the Lord your God,'" he went on in completion of the quotation, "'with all your heart, with all your soul—'"

"'—and with all your might,'" Marta sang in, recognizing the verse. "But we say those words, too."

Il Piccino said, "They come from the same source."

"But there has to be more than that." Marta was perplexed.

Smiling politely, Il Piccino asked, "Why?"

"Because there *is* more. It's fundamental, no? 'I believe in the Father, and in the Son, and in the Holy Ghost. . . .'"

"Exactly," said L'Altro. "It's a question of the Credo, a question of creed."

"Well, don't they believe in the Credo?"

"We don't have one," said Il Piccino. "Except for what this young man said. 'The Lord is our God. The Lord is One.'" With a short finger he gave a single tap to the countertop as if putting a final period to a complete and conclusive sentence.

"In other words," said L'Altro, "it's the first line of the Credo that we all have in common. '*Credo in unum Deo*. I believe in One God.' That, in a phrase, is the Jewish creed."

"But the rest?" Marta was not a person to let go of things.

"For us there is no rest," said Il Piccino. "The young man put it well. I never really thought of it that way before, but he has a point. Our beliefs start at the same place. For us, though, we finish with our belief in the One God."

"But what about the Trinity?" said Marta, shocked. "What about the virgin birth, and the death on the cross, and the resurrection, and the remission of sins, and the Apostles, and the Church, and the life of the world to come?"

"For us, those things are"—Il Piccino looked for delicate words—"not essential."

"Not essential? But why not?"

Il Piccino could think of no way to explain.

"We might illustrate it this way," L'Altro stepped in. "Years and years ago, when the Jews still had their Temple in Jerusalem, even during the same time that Gesù walked the earth, there was in that Temple, in the most sacred of all places, the Holy of Holies. A tabernacle, of sorts."

"We have the tabernacle in our Church, too."

"Yes. And in ours, what do you find?"

"The Host, no?" Like a girl being drilled in catechism class, Marta was relieved to know the correct answer. "The body of the Lord."

"Precisely," L'Altro praised. "The heart of Christianity. And in the Holy of Holies in the Temple of Old, do you know what was treasured inside as the heart of their religion? I'll tell you what: the Ark containing the scrolls written by Moses. The rest of the room was empty space, filled only, they believed, by the presence of God."

"True," said Il Piccino. "*Vero.*"

"For the Jews, putting anything solid in the empty space would have been sacrilege. Limiting the Infinite to the concrete is something that, to their minds, one must never do. Their religion loves a God who cannot be made concrete, not even in the form of a name. To them, ours must appear a religion in love with the incarnation of things. Statues, icons, the Word Made Flesh. We want all of our concepts to have nice solid shapes." He turned to Il Piccino. "Or tell me if I'm wrong."

Il Piccino studied the young man. He could find no fault in the reasoning. He was not used, however, to spreading religions flat, laying them out as if on the plates of a scale. What did it mean to hear the articulation of concepts that he would not have dared voice? How would those ideas be received now by the ears beneath Marta's violet hair? "In any case," Il Piccino said at last, seeking conciliatory words, "the most important thing to both faiths is love."

"*Questo sì,*" said Marta. "Yes to that. No doubt. But I don't know." Distractedly she looked at the magazines. Her eyes finally found the needlework weekly she had come here to buy. "In the end," she said, paying for the magazine, "I don't know. Poor Jews, is what I say."

"Why poor Jews?" Il Piccino had to laugh.

"What can I say? No Gesù Cristo for you, no Madonna, no saints. Not Christmas even? No. Christmas, Easter, no. Eh." Her thin fingers rubbed together in the air, a gesture that showed the meagerness of the thing discussed. "*Poca roba,*" she said. "Not much stuff. Very little to make a religion about. Poor Jews. You're missing a lot."

"Dear signora," Il Piccino said, "let's each be happy with our own."

"*Mah,*" Marta concluded. "All things considered, I don't know. And you," she said to L'Altro, "tell your brother to expect a visit from me. If he can cure sheep and curse Mauro Giannetti to death, he ought to be able to help me find some rest."

She put her hand on the door, then turned back. Her eyes took in the midget and the courteous ex-convict with his long, gel-slicked hair. Their ideas had proved to be complicated after all, complicated enough to alarm and confuse her. Maybe she should have listened to Emanuele Mosè's words of caution about this twin. For all his good manners, he spoke things that made no sense. And Il Piccino seemed to reason in the same incomprehensible way. Maybe she should not trust him too much either.

A blush of fear reddened Marta's neck. Her heart speeding up until it became a dangerous drumroll, she muttered, "*Buongiorno,*" and left.

When Marta had gone, L'Altro paid for his own newspaper. Handing him his change, Il Piccino said, "You're not a usual young man."

"Thank you, I think."

"The compliment was there, yes. You have a mind that likes to think things for itself. So tell me, now that we're alone. What does your mind tell you about Signora Marta? She looked upset when she left. What do you think of her belief that people choke on salami if your brother prays for it to be so?"

"Her belief is endearing," L'Altro said, "but perhaps she should be careful about what to believe in."

"She believes in your brother." Il Piccino eyed the younger, taller man. "You know, we have a saying in Tuscany. 'Crazy is the sheep who confesses to the wolf.'" Il Piccino watched for reaction in the other face. "You understand?"

"Sweet Signora Marta," L'Altro said. "A little crazy she might be."

Il Piccino was pleased that the young man should have accepted so gracefully this challenge to his brother's integrity. "*Grazie,*" he said. "And good day."

"*Grazie* and *buongiorno* to you," said L'Altro. "I'll look forward to talking some more." Leaving, he let the door swing itself shut.

The fog burned off during the morning. Serving his customers, Il Piccino thought again and again about the odd conversation that had occurred in his shop. *Matta è la pecora che si confessa al lupo,* he thought. Yes, Marta was a crazy sheep indeed. But had Il Piccino become sheep to Emanuele Mosè's twin, enticed by the refreshing candor of L'Altro's discussion? Had he revealed his own mind too much? L'Altro certainly had a knack for encouraging you to say more than you meant to say. In the aftermath, Il Piccino felt as if he had been duped into taking off his suit and necktie and shirt, denuding himself in public. He had shown his beliefs, naked for others to see; now he felt vulnerable and cold.

During quiet moments when there were no customers to serve, Il Piccino stood on tiptoes to clean the shelves and the stacks of magazines with a feather duster. We were only talking to pass the time, he told himself when his doubts became a torment. What harm can come from a friendly exchange of ideas?

12

L ove between female and male. Is it olive tree, sturdy enough to give fruit for centuries? Ephemeral perfumed flower, beautiful as it is brief? Or weed, uninvited yet impossible to kill? The heart in love does not know. It sees the unexpected green shoot, there in the rocky ground where the hidden seed has pushed up its first fresh spear. Incapable of resisting what has already begun, the heart says only, *Let it grow, let it grow.*

Such it is with love, or at least with physical desire sufficiently strong to make itself the indistinguishable twin to love.

It was the kind of icy February morning when early rays of white sunlight cause everything—trees, stones, roads—to shimmer like glass. Petula, still a guest in her parents' house, walked across the bridge on the way to town. "Don't be so gloomy," she said, holding Beniamino by the hand. "You'll see. You and your friends will do wonderful things today at school, and you'll be glad you went. I'm sure."

The boy was unconvinced. The stress of his parents' separation had been showing on him lately. Yes, he was happy enough to live with his grandparents and to play with the sheep every evening on the hillside, but mothers and fathers were supposed to be together, as far as he was concerned, and he was restless for life to be again what it had always been. He had moments of special, quiet brooding when he felt the fear that life would never be right anymore. Seeing his sadness, Petula could not escape wondering if she and Daniele were doing the best thing.

She was surprised this morning to find L'Altro leaning against the town side of the old bridge.

"*Buongiorno*, Petula!" he said. "*Buongiorno*, Beniamino!"

"*Buongiorno*," Petula answered.

Recognizing L'Altro from the station bar, Beniamino said, "*Ciao.*"

"I was beginning to give up hope," L'Altro said, falling in step with them on the road to the stone gate that marked the entrance to town. "I have to be at work soon."

"You were waiting for someone?"

"I was waiting for you."

"And why?" asked Petula.

"And why not?" A few steps later, he said, "I've been waiting for a while. I thought you left the house earlier."

"Usually I do. When I go to open the bar, I let my parents take Beniamino to school." Why did her heart speed up when she was near him? "But today," she continued, keeping her voice calm, "I don't know, I wanted to be with my son. I don't know if we spend enough time together, with work and everything."

"Ah. Then I should leave the two of you alone. Don't want to intrude."

Petula brushed away the strands of hair that the breeze blew in front of her eyes, but she said nothing to indicate that she wanted L'Altro to leave.

"I don't want to go to school," Beniamino said.

Funny how little hesitation the boy showed in L'Altro's company. Emanuele Mosè, she could tell, frightened Beniamino. L'Altro had none of his brother's distant, saintly air. His gel-slicked hair and his vaguely hunted expression made him look like a person you would try to avoid were you to see him on the street at night. All the same, Beniamino showed no fear, but gave instead the instinctive trust he might have offered to a wounded wolf.

"I didn't have much luck at school when I was a boy," L'Altro said. "We moved too many times. Would have been nice, I think, not to be forced to meet new teachers and new kids every few months. What's your teacher like?"

"She's okay. She reads to us."

"Really? What does she read?"

"Stories. Books. There's a big book she's reading to us now. A chapter a day."

"What book is that?"

"Pinocchio."

"Beautiful," L'Altro said. "One of my favorites. You like the book?"

Beniamino nodded.

"And will your teacher read you a chapter today?"

"I think so."

"Then you listen carefully to the teacher while she's reading, and the next time we see each other, you can tell me about the story, no?"

"Sì." Beniamino was smiling now. *"Sì."*

The three of them walked.

"You know . . ." L'Altro looked at Petula. "I have a present for you." From his pocket he pulled a cassette tape. "Here. It's only got one song on it. The rest is empty, but it's the thought that counts," he laughed. "Right?"

She did not take the tape from his hand. What did it mean for a young man to wait for her, then to offer a gift? This was not part of her experience, for her experience until now had been Daniele and Daniele was not one for giving gifts. L'Altro's behavior pushed her to think enticing, unaccustomed thoughts. "Is this a habit of yours? Giving people tapes of music early in the morning, before they've even had time to go to work?"

L'Altro laughed. "Not even close to habit. First time, for me."

"Tell me"—Petula still would not take the cassette—"what's the music?"

"Palestrina. You know him?"

Embarrassed to not recognize the name of the composer, she said, "I have his Greatest Hits album, of course, but I can't say I know him in depth."

L'Altro laughed. "You know the Sistine Chapel in Rome?"

"I've seen pictures."

"That's where he worked. Composer for the Pope in the fifteen hundreds."

"And that's the kind of music you listen to?"

"Didn't used to be. But now it is, yes. You want to hear a story? In prison they have this deal. You know Radio Madonna? The radio of the Church? They have this program on Tuesday nights. Late. It's a program for prison inmates all over the country. The relatives of the inmates call up and give messages, and the prisoners listen. Nice idea, no? I mean, there you are in prison, and over the radio you hear your little kid saying he still loves you and he wishes you a good night, and things like that. Though, to tell the truth, lots of people use it to deliver strange sorts of messages. You know, 'This is Uncle Pasquale calling from Palermo'"—here L'Altro put on a movie-style mafioso voice—"'and I wanted to let my nephew Guido know, if he's listening, that he don't gotta worry about a thing. The family sorted out the problem, and business is going good now.' You see what I mean?"

Petula laughed. It was incredible to be talking so casually with an ex-convict about his experience in prison. Somehow he made everything accessible, within easy reach, even the dealings of sinister figures who played no part in her life. Things held no danger when toyed with by L'Altro's words. Darkness lost its threat. She was wetting her mouth with the liqueur of a different world, and her taste buds started to come alive. "Yes," she answered, feeling important, privileged to be taken into L'Altro's confidence. "I understand."

She was inside the town now, for they had come in through the stone gate. She walked past the shops along the main road of the town that forever had been her universe, and the voice that told her about being in prison was as calm and matter-of-fact as if it were describing yesterday's weather. There was her grandparents' bottega.

She and Beniamino waved in through the window, but kept walking with L'Altro. And there was Il Piccino's newspaper shop. L'Altro and the midget exchanged head nods. Everyone could see her walking with him, she knew. You could not walk with someone new in Sant'-Angelo D'Asso without people taking note. But what did she care? She had separated from Daniele, hadn't she? That was no secret to anyone. Daniele was at the station bar, well past the piazza, past the far end of the main road, past the school and the Waterworks pump-house. There was no chance of Daniele seeing her together with L'Altro. And so what, she told herself, if he did? Separation was his idea. The ache she felt in missing him was his fault. L'Altro clearly did not want to hide from anyone; why should she?

"You were saying?" Petula prompted.

"I was saying?"

"The radio. The music. The tape."

"*Sì*, Radio Madonna. I was saying, there's that program of theirs, and they want to make it possible for every prisoner to listen. So if you're in prison and you don't have a radio, all you need to do is write a letter to Radio Madonna, and they send you a transistor radio for free. So that's what I did. Wrote the letter, and a couple of weeks later, this nice little radio arrived. Became an obsessive listener. Not only to Radio Madonna; to all kinds of things."

Beniamino, not interested in this sort of grown-up talk, kicked a pebble up the road with the toe of his shoe.

"Did you get any messages on the program for the prisoners?" Petula asked. "Did your mother and brother phone in?"

L'Altro gave a smile that held many emotions, but no joy. "Not even once," he said, and shook his head. "But the point is," he went on, "that I happened to hear a different program. A lot more interesting. It was about old music of the Church. And that's when I heard this piece by Palestrina. It was—" He stopped walking, and Petula stopped, too, to hear his words. "How can I tell you? You listen to music in that flat world of the prison, and it's not like listening to music on the outside. Music in there suddenly gives things color and smells. It's like rain after a long, long drought. Music became a drug for me.

This Palestrina was my first dose of transport. Freedom. Love." He paused and put a hand on Beniamino's shoulder. "How about you? Do you like music?"

"Babbo says I can take saxophone lessons when I'm older," Beniamino said, "and play in the band with him."

"Ah. Of course," said L'Altro, pulling his hand away. "Your father plays. Then music probably means the same to him." He looked at Petula. "No?"

"I wouldn't know," she said. "He never told me." She wondered if Daniele had ever talked about anything that mattered to him. Had he ever given words to his thoughts?

"Are you still with me?" L'Altro asked.

"I'm listening," she said. "Music is your drug, you said."

"Yes, but for a moment your mind went to another place, or maybe to another person."

"Do you always trace the path of other people's thoughts?" she said.

"Only when those thoughts are important to me."

She smiled. "Tell me more. Music, you were saying. Palestrina. The tape."

"*Bene.* I did a favor for this guy inside," L'Altro continued, "and he had connections on the outside. So he paid me back by having his people send me a real radio, not just a little transistor, a big radio with a double tape deck. And I got my hands on a tape of that first piece that I had heard. And now"—he held out the cassette to her once again—"I've made you a copy of the song."

She took the tape from his hand now, and said, "*Grazie.* I don't know why you made this copy, for me, I mean. But I'll listen to it."

"And you'll tell me what you think?"

She glanced at Beniamino, who had found another stone to kick. "I'll tell you what I think," she said. She examined the tape and saw the handwritten title. "Sicut Cervus?"

"Latin," L'Altro said. "When you listen, open up the box and read the words inside. I wrote out the Latin along with the translation so you could see what they're singing. Promise me you'll read the words while you listen."

"I'll read them."

"You swear?"

She laughed. "I swear." She had not noticed before the intensity that could flare up behind L'Altro's smile. She liked it. Some people seemed to be all surface; not L'Altro. She put the tape into the pocket of her coat.

When they reached the school, Petula kissed Beniamino and told him to be good and enjoy himself.

"*Ci si rivede*," L'Altro said to the boy. "See you again."

"See you again." Beniamino reached up to give L'Altro a kiss on both cheeks, accepting him as if he were an uncle. "*Ciao.*"

When Beniamino had gone inside, L'Altro said, "Can't remember the last time I got a kiss from a child. Or from anyone, now that I think about it."

Petula's next stop, they both knew, was Daniele's bar. They both understood that it would be best for L'Altro to let her go to work alone.

"Nuzzi will be waiting for me," he said. "We have to change the bulbs in some streetlamps. I better go." Then, "Petula, I want to ask you something. Can I see you tonight? After dinner? Late?"

"I don't know. I shouldn't."

"Why not?"

"I don't know."

"There's nothing to know," he said. "Just come. Ten o'clock, I'll be waiting by the bridge where I was waiting for you just now. Ten o'clock, just come."

"It's cold at night," she said.

"We'll walk to keep ourselves warm. You can tell me what you thought of the tape, if you get a chance to listen first."

"I have to go," Petula said. "Thanks again for the music." She walked in the direction of the station bar.

"Ten o'clock?" he called after her.

Petula stopped, turned, and said, "Ten o'clock."

———

Later that morning, L'Altro worked atop a tall ladder to change a streetlamp bulb. The cold sky was clear. From his vantage point, L'Altro could see the school, the train station, the Waterworks pumphouse, and a hundred yards away, the old house that Spillo and his crew were rebuilding.

"Everything going all right up there?" called Nuzzi from the ground. To steady the ladder at its base, he kept a foot on the lowest rung.

"Fine," said L'Altro. "Absolutely fine."

"I've never liked heights myself," Nuzzi said. "They make my head spin. I avoid ladders when I can. But if you don't have a problem with heights—"

"No problem at all," said L'Altro.

"—then we can do more of the blown bulbs that need changing. There are four others along this street. Then that's enough, I figure. We'll call that a good day's work." The dead bulbs had left this stretch of road without light for months now. Realizing he had confessed his own negligence in not replacing them earlier, Nuzzi tried to readjust his words. "It wasn't easy to change bulbs without an assistant," he said. "Not that the changing itself is so hard, but a ladder takes two men, no? One to climb, and one to hold."

"Absolutely," L'Altro said, without paying attention to Nuzzi's words. Dismantling the streetlamp, he glanced frequently across the distance to Spillo's worksite. Spillo was climbing an old splintery ladder that led to the roof of the house.

L'Altro remembered how, at the station bar, Spillo had mocked his name and had refused him a job. Watching now, he saw that Spillo used only one hand for climbing; the other hand held a bucket full of mortar. He watched as Spillo, nearly reaching the roof, set his foot on a rung. Then he watched the rung split and Spillo fall.

L'Altro did not raise his voice to alert Nuzzi that an accident had happened. He said nothing, only stared.

From this distance, the single sound that L'Altro heard was that of the bucket, not Spillo, hitting the ground. It was not a high enough fall to kill Spillo, L'Altro figured, and he was right. He watched more, and saw Spillo's crew run to where their leader lay. With some help,

Spillo managed to sit up. His face was bloody. By the way one arm hung like a ragdoll's limb, L'Altro thought the collarbone must have snapped. Spillo held his side with his good arm and bent over as if breathing hurt. L'Altro reckoned that some ribs might be broken, too.

L'Altro replaced the streetlamp bulb, then reassembled the covering. I told Spillo he should be careful on the job, L'Altro thought. Construction work is dangerous. Said so himself.

"Right," L'Altro called to Nuzzi after tightening the final screw. "Hold the ladder steady. I'm coming down."

Later examination of Spillo's ladder would suggest that nothing but wood rot had weakened the guilty rung. "No one to blame," Spillo's crew would say to people around town when they recounted the accident. No one's fault. *Sfortuna,* is all. Plain bad luck.

At ten o'clock that evening, Cappelli was in the bathtub when he heard someone knocking at his door. Bathing at this time of night was not his habit. Most evenings he stayed out late at Maria Severina and Tonino's bottega. Today, though, had been an especially back-straining day of pipe laying with Renato in the countryside near town. The frozen ground had made digging with pickax and shovel hell. Cappelli had eaten his dinner at the bottega, had drunk his way toward sleepiness, and then the thought of bathing had come over him. Something enticed him to deviate from his norm of going to bed with a day's work of sweat and dirt still stuck in his pores. Maybe it was the recent unfamiliar cleanliness that shone in his apartment ever since Rosa Spina had started taking care of the place. Whatever. In any case, the thought had come: a hot, soapy bath. Strange idea, he had said to himself, but why not? And now here he was, getting good and waterlogged, feeling weightless while he let his thick arms float upward in the water, his skin already gone wondrously rosy and soft, when someone knocked at his door. *Porca vacca,* he swore to himself. Who would think to come and interrupt me at this hour? He hoped it wasn't a Waterworks emergency. Maybe it was one of the boys from downstairs.

No way was he about to get out of the tub and lose the easing heat his muscles had soaked in from the water. *"Avanti!"* he called. "Door's not locked. Come!"

The front door opened, and a female voice asked, *"Permesso?"*

Madonna nuda! Cappelli thought. The signora is in my apartment, and here I am, naked as a worm.

"Signor Cappelli?" Rosa Spina sang out, searching for him.

"Sì! Sì! In here, signora! I'm in the bath!" The sudsy drowsiness that had seeped into his sleepy head left him in an instant. She wouldn't, Cappelli thought. She wouldn't come into the bathroom while I'm all wet and undefended, would she? He looked over and saw his discarded dirty clothes where he had dumped them in the middle of the room. At least I should wrap a towel around myself, he began to plan. Make myself more presentable. He started to lift his soggy bulk from the water when the bathroom door opened up and Rosa Spina's smiling face appeared.

"May I?" said the elaborate lips, but she did not wait for an answer before coming in.

Cappelli splashed back down in the tub. *"Buonasera,"* he replied, not knowing what to say.

"Sorry for the disturbance." She entered, her arms full of folded laundry. "But I've been doing a little ironing this evening, and L'Altro went out to get a mouthful of fresh air, and Emanuele Mosè fell asleep early after a long day of praying, so I thought I'd bring up your clothes, all nice and clean."

"What disturbance? No disturbance at all." He became aware of his penis drifting toward the surface of the bathwater and wondered if she could see it from where she stood. "Really, this is too kind of you." He was no good at polite pleasantries, but the situation, he sensed, called for graceful words that were not part of his usual repertoire. Across the room he saw the towel hanging on the rack, miles out of reach. "If you wouldn't mind, perhaps you could hand me the towel."

"That towel there?" she said in that charmingly girlish voice of hers. "Absolutely not. I've brought you a clean towel, here among your nice laundered clothes." She placed the stack of clothes on a table in the corner and pulled out the folded towel. It looked marvelously clean. "Still hot from the iron. You'll see. But let me help you first."

"Help me?"

"Help you wash your back." She put the towel on the table and walked toward the tub.

"It's not necessary," Cappelli said.

Rosa Spina held out her hand, smiled with her shiny lipsticked mouth, and said, "Soap?"

She came at him with the unembarrassed assuredness of a hospital nurse. What could he do? She had been cleaning his house for some time now. She had ironed the intimacy of his underpants. Why not let her wash his body as well?

Heart pounding, he gave her the bar of soap.

She reached across him, the softness of her breasts brushing against his wet shoulder, and she opened the hot water faucet. "We'll just make the water good and hot again," she said. She put her hand in, testing the temperature. When it was hot enough, she gave the water a swirl to mix the heat, leaned across him once more to shut off the tap, and said, "There. Now let's soap you up."

Sitting up in the tub, Cappelli hoped his belly would hide his more personal parts. Rosa Spina ran handfuls of water over his shoulders, then, holding the bar of soap firmly in her palm, washed the skin of his back, pressing strongly into his muscles.

Cappelli liked the pressure of her hand as it guided the gliding soap over neck, shoulders, armpits, ribs, and spine. This was something he had seen his mother do for his father, almost too many years ago to remember, but no woman had ever done this for him. He had had his encounters with women, all right. Not many, but enough. Never, though, in his own home. And never had any of the paid women in his experience become associated in his mind with cleanliness, with the heat of water, with the fragrance of soap.

She pushed against an especially sore point in the area of the kidneys. Involuntarily, Cappelli let out a sharp moan.

"Hurts?" said Rosa Spina.

Cappelli wanted to appear stoical, but the pain was strong. "Eh, a little bit, yes. Who knows what there is there? Maybe a little pull from all the digging today."

Rosa Spina let go of the soap and went at the sensitive spot with her naked, soap-slippery hand. "Let's see if we can't make it go away." She worked the flesh with knuckles, fingertips, palm. The pain intensified briefly, then passed. "Better?" she asked.

"*Sì.*" Cappelli moved around to see if the stab would come back, but there was no pain. "Better, yes. A lot better. *C'ha l'arte,*" he said as she took up the bar of soap and passed it over the skin at the back of his waist. "You have the art for making things better."

"Nothing to it," Rosa Spina said. "Your muscles were a little tight. That's all."

"It's not just my back I'm talking about." He became quiet because he was attempting to do something difficult. He wanted to express thoughts that he had not fully thought through. It took effort and concentration to put certain things in words. Most ideas in Cappelli's shampoo-scrubbed head never amounted to more than short-lived, wordless impressions. Making himself plain to Rosa Spina now would force him to crystallize the vapors of thought into solid-bodied phrases. "The whole house, since you got here," he said at last, "it's better. All of it."

"All it needed was a woman's hand."

"A woman's hand. Yes. I don't know. You make the place so clean I don't recognize it. Smells better, too. Every room. And the bed isn't the same place anymore. It always used to seem so . . . " He ran out of words.

"Tell me," she said. "How did your bed used to seem?"

Cappelli thought, then said, "Tired. That's it. Tired. It was always a rumpled, tired bed. Now you put fresh sheets on it, tucked in all tidy. Smells of laundry detergent. It's a different bed, I tell you. Sometimes I even look forward to going there at night."

"Good," she said. "That's how it should be." Her soapy hand passed down to the upper part of his buttocks.

"How things should be, no doubt," he said, trying to keep his voice steady while his attention followed the movements of her hand. "But you know something? I'm not accustomed."

"*Ostrega! Che tristezza!*" she said, her luminous eyes looking him in the face, her hand close to his coccyx. "What sadness! It's a sin not to be accustomed to the pleasures of life, wouldn't you say?" She leaned across him, reached underwater between his feet, and pulled the plug from the drain.

She spread the bath mat by the tub so that Cappelli would not have to put wet feet on the tiled floor. She took the towel from the corner table, unfolded it, and held it open wide. "Hoopah!" she said, as she might have said to her sons when they were little boys. "Time to get you out."

Cappelli touched himself, checking that there was no embarrassing erection. There wasn't, not exactly. Rosa Spina's touches had seemed too innocent to elicit quite that kind of response.

She has already scrubbed me, Cappelli thought. What difference if I stand up in front of her now? Holding the edges of the tub to steady himself, he rose from the water. He watched her eyes the whole time to see if she would steal a glance at anything more private than his face. She was impeccable, taking not even a peek, but smiled a smile that showed white teeth between red lipsticked lips while her wonderful eyes did not flutter from his.

She wrapped him in the towel and gave him a hand to help him step out of the tub. She put her lips against his cheek for a moment. Pulling away, she said, "You are a good man. You don't believe it, but it's true."

Embarrassed, he said, "What can I say?"

"Thank you for the kindness you've extended to my boys and to me." Quickly she stepped away and bent down to pick up the pile of Cappelli's dirty clothes. "These I'll wash for you tomorrow. *Buonanotte,* Signor Cappelli. Sleep well."

Before Cappelli could reply, she was gone, the door to the apartment shutting behind her.

Cappelli stood on the bath mat surrounded by a room full of fragrant steam. Water dripped from his skin. With the towel he started to dry around the tops of his thighs. He could not remember if ever in his life a confusion this overwhelming had got hold of his head.

At a quarter past ten, outside in the icy dampness of the same February night, L'Altro leaned against the town side of the bridge along the road that led out toward the house of Petula's parents. He wondered if he was a fool for standing alone in the cold. How long, he asked himself, before I give up and go home?

A car crossed the bridge. It passed him and drove on.

Fifteen minutes later, when the bell in the clock tower rang the half hour, he heard approaching footsteps on the far side of the river. In the light of streetlamps, Petula appeared over the hump of the old stone bridge. She was breathless and apologetic. "Beniamino wouldn't get to bed," she said. "I couldn't leave until I was sure he was asleep."

"You came," L'Altro said.

"I came."

"Good. Thank you. *Andiamo.*" He made no effort to hide his happiness. "Let's walk."

He offered his arm. After only an instant of hesitation, Petula took it.

13

"Walk where?"

L'Altro turned his face toward the countryside away from town. He appeared to be listening, as if trying to hear birds, but there would be no night birds singing until the winter had passed. Instead, only the cold wind of country darkness blew against him, stirring his long hair. He answered, "We could walk up through town, if you want."

"That's true. We could." She thought of houses and shops closed tight against the night, woodsmoke drifting from chimneys. Only her grandparents' bottega would be open along the main road. The picture window would be bright, the tables occupied by nocturnal drinkers—men, mostly, in no particular hurry to go home to their beds. "My mother's working at the bottega," Petula offered. "We could go and say hello, if we wanted to."

"Certainly," said L'Altro. "If you want."

After a moment's consideration, no decision expressed out loud, they both turned in the other direction, pointing their steps away from town.

They crossed the stone bridge under which the river flowed invisibly in the blackness. L'Altro said, "Nice sound."

"*Bello, sì.*" Petula had walked over the bridge since she was a little girl, the river as inevitable as the sky or the hills. Why should it become beautiful to her only now? L'Altro had a way of making her hear with new ears, see with freshly opened eyes.

They walked on. "Your house," L'Altro commented as they approached.

Petula laughed. "I don't know what to call it these days. My parents' house? Mine? Was mine, for a lifetime. Then I went to live with Daniele. Now Beniamino and I are back here again, since Daniele and I"—how should she define what had happened?—"since Daniele and I decided to take a break."

"Is that what it is? A break?"

"*Boh.*" She shrugged. "Your guess is as good as mine. We'll see in time." Looking at L'Altro, she thought his jacket didn't seem heavy enough to keep him warm. She fought an urge to open her coat and wrap him in a hug.

"What's the problem between you two?" he asked.

"Wish I knew. You know how two people fight then have all the pleasures of making up? Well, we only do the fighting part. One thing's for sure, in any case. I've done an amazing job of turning my little world upside down in an amazingly short time. Since about when your family arrived, by pure chance."

"Is turning a world upside down such a bad thing?"

"Too early to say," she said. "No?"

"Too early to say, yes. Change is scary, but it isn't always bad, I guess."

They looked at the house. Some windows glowed.

L'Altro said, "I've always liked lit-up windows, seen from the outside. You, too?"

"Never thought about it. Yes, looking now, I see what you mean. It's pretty. Yes."

He laughed. "From the window up in the prison in Volterra, you know, I could look out at night and see the windows of people's homes in the valley. I would wonder what their lives were like inside those rooms. And sometimes I would wonder if maybe in some window someone was looking back, wondering about the windows of the prison cells. My cell. Silly, no?" He laughed at himself, embarrassed. "But that's what I used to think. And not just in prison. Even years before. With my mother and brother, we moved so many times, one place then the next, that I guess I've always been looking into lit-up windows from the outside, wondering about other people's lives."

Petula's urge to hug him was strong once again, not to compensate for the thinness of his jacket this time, but to comfort him and make him feel less alone. She put her hands in her pockets instead, and, looking at the house of her girlhood, said, "It would take more imagination for me to pretend I *didn't* know exactly what was happening inside these windows."

"Tell me. What's happening in there, right now?"

"Well, that dark window there is my room. They've put a cot next to my bed so Beniamino can stay close to me. He's in there now, with his eyes closed and his mouth open just a little. His breathing is a soft sound. When he's dreaming, you can see his eyes move."

"This is a lovely part of the picture."

"Best there is," said Petula.

"And the rest?"

"The rest is my father."

"Ah yes. Signor Renato. What will he be doing?"

She found it strange to hear her father's name come out of L'Altro's mouth, but she liked the way he called him *Signor Renato*—respectful yet friendly at the same time. "Usually he's out in the evening, at the bottega, giving my mother a hand. But tonight he stayed in to baby-sit so I could go out."

"Did you tell him where you were going?"

Petula paused, then said, "Yes."

"What did you tell him?"

"I said I was taking a walk with you."

"And what did he say?"

"He told me not to worry about Beniamino."

"No," L'Altro said. "I mean what did he say about the thought of your taking a walk with *me?*"

Petula exhaled slowly. "He likes you, L'Altro—" she began.

"I like him."

"Yes, but what I mean to say is he likes you, but—"

"But?"

She shook her head. "*Merda*. He couldn't stand Daniele, you know, when I was a teenager. But then Beniamino came along, and I insisted on staying with Daniele, and my father, it was as if he forced himself to accept Daniele for my sake. It wasn't easy. Babbo tortured himself to make his brain shift gears in Daniele's favor. And now he doesn't know what to think, as if I'm asking him to put his gears back in reverse."

L'Altro was silent for a moment, then said, "Is that what you're asking him to do?"

"I don't know what I'm asking. I don't know what I want for myself."

After another moment's thought, L'Altro said, "I wouldn't have found a job without your father's help. He's a good man. I don't know how many good men there are in the world."

Unaccustomed to speaking well of her parents, Petula laughed and said, "He could be worse."

L'Altro smiled in the darkness. "Tell me exactly what he's doing now."

"He'll be on the sofa. That's the light in the front room." She pointed. "He's watching television. Or no, if the TV were on, the light would be more blue. Maybe the radio's on instead. Or maybe he's been reading. Whatever. He'll be dozing. Said he and Cappelli worked like slaves today, so he'll already have fallen asleep. Won't move himself off the sofa and into bed, though. That wouldn't feel right to him, putting himself to bed with no one else in the house to look after Beniamino. He'd think he wasn't doing his duty as the castle guard. He'll stay on the sofa, I'd bet, until Mamma or I get home."

"Must be a good thing to have a father," said L'Altro. "Never had one myself."

"You must have one somewhere, even if you've never met him."

"How would I know? My mother says not."

"This would be the immaculate conception story I hear your

mother's been telling around town. Does she really believe it? I mean, do you?"

L'Altro cleared his throat. "Weren't we talking about you?"

"Why not about you?" She wondered why he was anxious to shift the conversation away from himself.

"We're standing in front of your house," he said with a light laugh. "The strange story of my life can wait for another time."

She had so many questions to ask about his family, his crime, his years in prison, but she could see that he wanted to talk about anything except himself. For now, at least. Despite his apparent self-assuredness, L'Altro had a vulnerable quality that Petula found touching. She was afraid of treating him indelicately. "You will tell me?" she asked.

"Give me time. I promise. Another time, though. You haven't told me your mother's reaction," he said, and Petula let him put the conversation back to where he wanted it. "Does your mother know where you were going tonight?"

"*Sì*. She knows."

"And what does she say?"

"What do you want her to say? She feels the same as my father does. But she's a mother. She worries more. She keeps reminding me that I can't only think for myself. I have Beniamino to think about now, and that changes everything."

"Not easy, your situation," he said. "I can see that."

"So tell me," said Petula. "Do you like the little story of what's happening inside those windows there?"

"Very much. Thanks for telling me."

"I think I can see the appeal of window watching," she said, looking some more. "There's a beauty to it, even if it is melancholy." They were standing side by side so closely that the shoulder of her coat brushed his sleeve.

"Beauty, yes," said L'Altro. "But maybe I've done too much watching. Too much watching and not enough doing."

"You don't seem to be one who's short of experience."

"Is that the impression you have? If you knew the truth, you'd be surprised."

"You know," said Petula, "Daniele would go mad if he knew who I was with right now."

"I take it you didn't tell him about our appointment."

"Why hurt him? I think he's already suffering. You should have heard what he said about you this afternoon when the construction workers told us what happened to Spillo. You knew about that, didn't you?"

He hesitated, as if deciding whether or not to speak. Then he said, "I was up a different ladder at the time, but I did see him fall."

"And you didn't do anything to help him?" Reflexively, she moved half a step away. "Maybe Daniele's right. Maybe you are dangerous."

"Is that what Daniele said?" L'Altro chuckled. "I didn't do anything because I saw he had his crew to help him. The situation was under control without my getting involved."

"Daniele thinks you *were* involved." Her voice was suddenly serious. "He says it's too big a coincidence that you threaten Spillo about being careful—"

"Threaten? I didn't threaten. I suggested."

"All right. You *suggested* that Spillo should be careful," said Petula, "and then the ladder he's climbing just happens to break."

"It's generous of Daniele to endow me with magical powers," L'Altro joked. "Sometimes I wish I had them for real."

"No, tell me the truth. Please."

"The truth?" He looked at her face in the darkness. "Truth is, I'm enjoying my walk with you. As simple as that. That's my only thought. And yours?"

"I think I should be careful," she said.

"Tell me what your instincts say. Do they say I would ever want to harm you?"

She considered, then said, "No."

"Good," said L'Altro. "I like that truth best."

He reached out and took her hand in his; she accepted the touch. They continued to walk farther from the town, deeper into the coldness.

When they arrived at the cemetery, they stopped in front of the closed gates. Floating over the dampness, the small flamelike lights that marked the wall tombs burned like the windows of a ghostly, faraway town.

"And here's where the people of Sant'Angelo D'Asso end up," L'Altro said, as if finishing some private conversation of his own. "They spend their few waking years *there*"—he held an arm out in the direction of the town—"and eternity *here*. One side of the river to the other. Not a great journey to accomplish in a lifetime. Funny, isn't it, how little some people move around?"

Petula pulled her hand away from his. Had his words held a subtle criticism aimed, with artful grace, against her? "That's why they call it home," she said. "Is there something wrong with knowing where your home is?"

"Depends on who you are," he said. "I've always thought something. Want to hear? I've always thought there are two types of people."

"Funny," Petula said, a feisty edge audible in her voice. "Listening to people talking in the bar, I've come to the same conclusion."

"Yes?"

"Yes. There are two kinds of people in the world: those who begin discussions by saying, 'There are two types of people in the world,' and those who don't."

He laughed. "If you don't want to hear my little theory, fine."

"I was joking," she softened. "More or less. But go ahead anyway."

He looked into her eyes. "I like that sharper side of you. Glimpsed it there. You have a good mind."

She laughed. "So tell me your theory." She liked the way the corners of his eyes creased when he smiled. She liked the shape of his lips, the whiteness of his teeth.

"Right. This is a little idea hatched in my head from watching the nature programs on television. You like the nature programs?"

"I like the nature programs."

"An interest in common! This is getting better by the minute." He studied the curve of her neck, the soft-looking skin at her throat. "But I was saying. Saw this program once about chimpanzees. Primates, just like us. Most of them stay in the group with the other chimpanzees from the day they're born to the day they die. But every now and then, there's a chimp who gets tired of always foraging the same piece of forest. Something inside him makes him restless and stops him from sleeping at night. So he leaves. Born to wander, he is, and that's what he does. Maybe to meet up with a new group of other chimps after years of traveling, somewhere very distant from his own little group."

"And how does the new group of chimps treat him when he arrives?"

"With distrust, at first, because that's in their nature. They're suspicious of anyone who comes from outside. You follow me?"

"You're saying you're a restless chimp." Petula enjoyed sparring with L'Altro.

"Don't get ahead of me. I'm saying it's the wisdom of nature. It's *genetic*, no? Most chimps are home-lovers who live in fear of change. They want their home insured, and their pension fund guaranteed for their old age. Their genes make them that way, which is a good thing in the animal world, otherwise there would be no lasting connections, and everyone would struggle on his own. But then"—Petula brushed her hair back while she listened and L'Altro noticed the delicate, delectable shape of her ear—"but then there are other, *wilder* genes," he said with a smile, "that make the wanderer need to wander. He *thrives* on change," L'Altro said with emphasis, "so he keeps moving, from one place to the next. And that's a good thing, too."

"*Ah sì?* And why is that?" Laughing, she touched the corner of her mouth with her tongue tip.

"Because he mates wherever he goes. And that's exactly what nature wants."

"Nature wants that?"

"*Sì*," L'Altro said triumphantly. "You know why? Because it freshens up the gene pool."

Petula had to laugh out loud. "Could be," she said. "Strange theory, but who knows? And you would be, of course, the wandering chimp?"

"Of course. It's my nature." Teasingly, he bumped her shoulder with his.

Breathing in, Petula could smell the clean fragrance of L'Altro's skin. "And what kind of chimp do you think I am?"

"That," he said, taking her hand again, "is what science has yet to discover. But the research could be interesting."

His hand was cold. She rubbed it between hers to warm it, then grew serious. *"Che vuoi da me?"* She looked at him in the little light offered by the cemetery lamps. Suddenly she wished Daniele were there to encourage her, console her, give her permission, be her friend. Instead, she knew, she would have to decide and to act on her own. "What do you want from me, L'Altro?" she said.

"What do I want from you?" His repetition of the question was no answer.

"My life is upside down right now," Petula intervened. "I have a son. I don't know if his father and I can call ourselves together anymore, though we work with each other every day. I don't know what I want to happen. What do you expect from me?"

"Why do I have to expect? No expectations. No demands. I just wanted to take a walk. This walk isn't pleasant in itself?"

"You waited for me this morning to give me the music you wanted me to hear. Why?"

"So you've listened?" He smiled.

"That is why we're seeing each other this evening, isn't it?"

"Of course."

"You said you wanted to hear my reactions to the music. Well, I've listened."

"And what did you hear?"

She paused, formulating her impressions into words. "At first I heard only the music. Beautiful, it was, the way the voices wrapped around each other and pushed the whole thing like a cloud, up and up."

L'Altro said, "Yes."

"But it sounded like church music. You said it yourself. Written for the Vatican. Music for the church, with words in Latin."

"From Psalm Forty-two: *Sicut cervus desiderat ad fontes aquarum, ita desiderat anima mea ad te, Deus.*" He spoke the words not with ecclesiastical grandeur but with the whispered passion of poetry.

"Latin," she said. "Latin means nothing to me. But then I read the translation you had written out. 'Like as the deer desireth the water brooks, so longeth my soul after thee, O God.' I listened to the music again, reading the words this time. More than once."

"And what did you hear?"

"Lovely way to think of God, isn't it? Desiring him the way a deer needs fresh water."

"*Molto bello,* yes."

"But it's not just about theology, is it, L'Altro?" She paused. "For you, I mean, is it only a song about God? Is that what you wanted me to hear?"

"You had the right ears to listen," he said. "For me it's not only about God."

"So what is the song about?"

"Did you hear the way the music sounds? Waves of longing. Yearning, wave after wave."

"I heard that, too."

"The way the deer yearns for water," said L'Altro. "The longing of the soul."

They were facing each other in the darkness. Inhaling, Petula liked the light scent of his breath. It reminded her of sweet licorice. She wondered if his mouth tasted like licorice, too. Petula said, "Why did you give the tape to me?"

"I can only tell you the truth. The soul longs. Can't you see?"

"Maybe your soul is longing in the wrong direction. I can't promise to give you what you want."

"And maybe it's not a bad idea," he said, brushing hair away from her face with long, sensitive fingers, "to stop the mind from asking too many questions. Precariousness gives life an appetizing poignancy, don't you think?" His palm rested on her cheek. "Why not follow the soul without fearing the future?"

The young man and young woman standing before the cemetery gates on a dreary February night were so close to kissing, it was as if they had kissed already. Finally they did with their lips what they had been doing in their thoughts. Forgetting the coldness around them, they savored the astonishing warmth that can be shared only between two mouths.

14

O n the landing at the top of the stairs, Marta inhaled the enticing
aromas of what she took to be the evening meal that Rosa Spina
was preparing inside. Onions, celery, and carrots sautéeing in olive
oil, garlic, rosemary, and something strange. A touch of mint perhaps? Focusing again her pink eyes on the family name *Innocenti* by
the door, Marta felt simultaneous emotions rise within: a sense of the
weirdness of the little clan living here, commingled with an expectant
tingle of familiarity. Somehow the enchanted world of Emanuele
Mosè and his family had become *hers*. Here, if nowhere else, she was
welcome. Electric with eager palpitations and a veiled, unexpressed
desire to find her loneliness replaced by love, Marta rang the bell.

She knew the ritual that awaited her: the opening of the door, Rosa
Spina's elaborate lipsticked smile, the welcoming dance of the elo-
quent hands as Marta was bidden to take off her coat, sit down, and
be comfortable until Emanuele Mosè finished praying over some
other seeker of solace. Marta was ushered through these steps in a
dreamlike haze, content to be led. The world, she knew, would explode into exhilarating clarity when she would sit face to face with
him, the one who was no stranger to sorrow, the presence who visited
her between wakefulness and sleep, the young man who offered himself as sounding board for the music of her grief, who would free her
by resonating in time with her troubled vibrations.

"You must help me," she whispered urgently when she sat alone
with Emanuele Mosè before the saintly images of the altar. Rosa

Spina stirred her cooking pots in the kitchen. "My head . . . ," said Marta Sorcini, holding her hands to her temples. Errant strands of violet-tinged hair, straying from the neat set she always tried to lacquer into place, emphasized the disorder that had made its home inside the old skull. "*La testa* is too full of thoughts."

"Dear Marta," said Emanuele Mosè with a voice as soothing as a spring of living water, "what can have agitated you?"

"Agitated, yes!" she affirmed, though while she spoke her head was shaking no. "And *you* know the reason. I can tell that about you, because I'm a sensitive person, too. I can tell that you know my thoughts." The glance of her pink-rimmed eyes flittered over his face in search of answers.

Steadily his dark eyes looked back. He saw the way her head carried on involuntarily in its sideways negative wagging. The habitual tic, he knew, would be unconscious on her part. Emanuele Mosè was adept at deciphering the body's secret language. Marta was waiting for him to tell her what was on her mind. An annoying little game. Why couldn't she be forthright? Marta was one of those people, he clearly saw, who do not say straightaway what they intend. Instead the Martas of the world come at every subject sideways, slanting their way into discussions, always self-conscious and vain enough to worry about the impression their appearance might make. Tiresome they were, people like Marta, but not difficult to deal with. Sideways minds were easy for him to steer, for they had no strong direction of their own.

"You haven't slept," he said at last.

"Not for more than two minutes at a time," she agreed, wagging her head more. *Unless I feel your presence come to comfort me,* she thought but did not say.

"Tell me, then," he coaxed, "what thoughts are stealing your tranquillity."

"But you know already! Why didn't you tell me you had the power to kill with your prayers?"

"Calm, dear Marta. Calm. Kill? You say kill?"

"Perhaps Signora Marta would like some tea," Rosa Spina called from the stove.

"Hm?" Marta jerked her head in confusion. She had not expected to hear a voice from the open kitchen.

"Some tea," Rosa Spina repeated, "to calm the signora."

"Oooh, I couldn't, but thank you," said Marta, looking over her shoulder toward Rosa Spina. "My stomach is all closed up with the nerves."

"No need for nerves," Rosa Spina said with a wide smile. "No one has killed anyone."

Marta realized that Rosa Spina, from behind her steaming pots, could hear every word spoken in the apartment. Marta did not mind. If anything, the presence of another pair of sympathetic ears increased the intimacy of conversation, making her feel embraced by family while she spoke. "Someone was killed indeed," she said, turning back to Emanuele Mosè. The physical strain of twisting to speak to Rosa Spina hurt her neck.

"And who would that be?" said Emanuele Mosè.

"The butcher, of course. Mauro Giannetti, who was always mocking me. You asked me if I had any enemies—remember?—anyone who might want to wish me harm, and Mauro Giannetti was the only person who came to mind, and now he's dead, choked to death with his mouth frozen open in a horrible laugh, and you mean to tell me there's no connection?"

"My son does only good in people's lives," Rosa Spina said from the kitchen. "Doing harm would be against his nature."

"I suggested that in your prayers you left Mauro Giannetti in God's hands," Emanuele Mosè said with a gentle tone. "That was my advice, if you think back."

"And God's hands choked the last breath out of him! Why didn't you tell me your prayers were so strong? To say nothing of the miracle of the sheep over at Renato Tizzoni's place. Everyone's talking, you know."

"Credit," Emanuele Mosè said modestly, "should be given to the Lord, not to the simple servant who prayed to Him. But why do you seem so frantic? If, as you say, there is no one to mock you anymore, then you should be sleeping like a lamb."

"But what lamb! It's worse than before! Every time I get into bed and settle myself under the blankets and close my eyes, just as I start to doze, a chill comes to me. Sharp, like an electric shock. As if someone is stabbing me with a cold finger here, at the small of my back. Wakes me up with a jump. You should feel how my heart races! And it's that way the entire night, every time I almost drop off. Shock, shock, shock! The finger points, poking me in the back. And the mind starts whirring with the thoughts faster than before, so fast I'm in danger of being swept away if I don't hold on tight. To calm myself"—she ventured a quick glance in his eyes before looking away—"I think of you."

Emanuele Mosè smiled.

Marta cleared her throat. "Anyone else, I know, would say I was losing my grip, but I can see you're sensitive people here"—she tilted her head in Rosa Spina's direction to include her as well—"with powerful, powerful love and powerful, powerful prayers."

With measured slowness, Emanuele Mosè reached his gloved hands across the table, took her arthritic fingers in his miracle-working palms, and held her firmly.

Already Marta could feel the love. Her fingertips touched the wool of his fingerless gloves. Had her nerve endings been younger and more sensitive, she might have tried to divine the mystery that the gloves concealed. She felt blessed, in any case, to be permitted contact so intimate with the unrevealed.

He rose slightly from his seat, leaned toward the woman, and gave Marta's forehead the kiss she had dreamed of. He sat back down while brief elation washed over her. "We should concentrate," he said, "on the touch that shocks you out of sleep. Whose touch do you think it could be?"

"No one's. What do you mean whose touch? I'm alone in bed at night. I thought you understood that."

"Why insist on a literal reading of the world, Marta? The Lord Himself reprimanded Thomas for believing only in those things which were visible to the eye. Do you want to be guilty of the same sin of doubting what the heart understands but the eye cannot see?"

Emanuele Mosè paused, trying to decide on the best course to chart for this conversation. He hesitated, because discussions of invisible forces always sapped him. Looking quickly toward the kitchen, he saw his mother nodding, pushing him to go on. Emanuele Mosè sighed, then spoke. "Tell me, Marta. Listen to that whisper inside yourself. Tell me who comes to you at night to take away your sleep."

"But how would I know?"

"Don't resist, Marta." He squeezed her fingers encouragingly. "Fear obstructs the way. Don't be afraid of the truth."

"Which truth?"

"The truth you already know. Let's think out loud together, Marta. Whose touch is it that wants to steal your peace?"

Marta's eyelids blinked more quickly. Her gaze passed over the saintly icons on the little table against the wall, resting for a moment on the image of bleeding Jesus in the picture frame. She said, "I don't understand."

"The touch that wakes you, does it come from inside of you, or is it a touch from outside?"

"It feels like a touch from someone else, not from me. But how could that be? I'm alone." She did not, would not speak of the touch she had felt from him, at night.

"In the visible world, alone, yes. But in the spiritual world, are you really alone?"

"What are you saying?" Her voice shook.

"I'm not saying anything," said Emanuele Mosè. "The Lord tells me the questions to ask. That is my gift. Questions. The answers are yours, if you let yourself listen inwardly."

"But I've never thought about things like this before. I've always been happy to live in the world with all my nice things around me. To think of invisible beings touching me—it isn't Christian."

"Calm, Marta," he soothed. He saw his mother smile to him from the kitchen. "There's nothing new here," he said. "Nothing could be more Christian. It's part of the Credo itself. Doesn't the Creed that people recite at every Mass speak of all things *visible* and *invisible*? We shouldn't be afraid of the invisible worlds, but we should learn not to give them power over our lives."

"But does Don Luigi know that this is what he's making us say in church? I've never heard him talk about things like this."

"Of course Don Luigi knows. Remember, though, that priests have a long tradition of keeping the most powerful secrets to themselves."

Marta reflected. There was an indisputable logic to the young man's words. She was chilly with fear, but he was here, too, holding her hands, loving her, offering himself as a lifesaving buoy in the perilous sea where without his help she might drown. "Are you saying that someone from a different world is coming to upset me, making me as upset as I've been since I can't remember when? Someone visits me from beyond the tomb?"

"Beyond the tomb?" Emanuele Mosè tried not to let annoyance show on his face. He shot a look at his mother, who raised her eyebrows and made a flowing *go on* motion with her hands.

"But who would curse me from the other side of the tomb? Mauro Giannetti? You're not saying he touches me in my sleep as a vendetta because I told you he was an enemy of mine—you're not saying he has cursed me, are you?"

"It's not for me to say," said Emanuele Mosè with judicious caution.

"Well, if not Mauro Giannetti, then who? My poor dead husband? He wouldn't want to curse me, would he? Why should he want to do such a thing? I made him happy, didn't I?"

"It's not always easy to explain the source when we feel cursed. But we needn't necessarily search beyond the tomb. Sometimes the fount of our afflictions is very present, right here in our everyday world, if only we have the courage to look."

"Someone living is cursing me?" Her anxiety increased. "Someone I know?" She put a hand to her bosom, checking for danger signs of her heart about to burst. "Someone here in town? Who?"

"I'm not a fortune-teller. I don't pretend to know anything that you don't know yourself. I can only help you discover the answers contained in the heart beating now so fast inside your chest."

"Beating fast, yes," she said. "Takes my breath away. But tell me, please. I have to know. Who would want to prod me in the night? Who would want to do me so much harm?"

The time was right, Emanuele Mosè could see, to speak. The skin of Marta's face had grown especially pale inside its frame of violet hair. Her heart probably could not endure the stress of waiting much more. Emanuele Mosè knew that he had to speak, and knew, too, what he was supposed to say. But his throat tightened and refused to pronounce the words.

"Emanuele Mosè?" Rosa Spina prompted from the kitchen.

The young man stared at his mother mutely.

"Tell me," Marta urged. "If you know who is harming me, please tell me."

"Tell the signora," Rosa Spina said.

Emanuele Mosè shook his head.

"You must excuse my son." Rosa Spina stirred a pot with her large spoon, then gave the spoon a rap on the pot's edge to make it come clean of sauce. The rap was stronger than necessary, implying impatience. Marta, absorbed in her own fears, did not notice the gesture. Emanuele Mosè, however, saw his mother's irritation. "Doing the Lord's work can be difficult at times," said Rosa Spina, "especially when the Lord asks us to be severe. Emanuele Mosè has the nature of a lamb. Severity does not come to him easily."

"Tell me, please," Marta said again, unable to understand what terrible truth it was that made the young man afraid to speak.

"Emanuele Mosè has come to know," Rosa Spina said, answering for her son with her girlish voice, "that you frequent the newspaper shop of that Jew."

"That Jew?" Marta's expression showed her confusion. "Ah!" she said, understanding at last. "Il Piccino! The Little One! Il Piccino, sì." Never, in the many years of her recollection, had anyone in town referred to the owner of the newspaper shop as *that Jew*. "I buy a magazine at his shop from time to time, yes. Used to buy the needlework magazine every week, until a few years back. But with these fingers? What needlework can I do now? Still, the occasional magazine is a little treat I give myself. And *La Famiglia Cristiana* is a favorite," she said, hoping to appear pious in Emanuele Mosè's eyes because of the impeccable moral quality of the periodical she read, "or an embroidery magazine, just to keep my eye in, or sometimes one of those other papers about the lives of the television stars. I know it's trivial reading, but a little indulgence every now and then never hurt, no?"

Emanuele Mosè sighed. His mother had launched the conversation, and he, though unwilling, could do nothing now but continue it. "The question is not what you buy," he said without a smile, "but where you buy it."

"But everyone in town buys from Il Piccino's shop. We always have. Il Piccino is one of us, even if he is a quiet little man. We've all felt affectionate toward him since he came here after the war, poor soul."

Emanuele Mosè let out a humorless laugh. "Incredible! Hardly more than a month since my family and I have been here, and already so many people have come to talk with me, come to pray. The stories I've heard people tell! Falcons swooping up cats, vipers appearing out of season, men and women dying unexpected terrible deaths. *Sfiga*, people call it. Bad luck. And nobody seems to know why. Groups gather here for prayer meetings, people coming one by one, all with mysterious unease in their hearts"—he tilted his head toward Marta, his eyes indicating the heart in her bosom—"men and women desperate to discover what the source of their unrest might be." He let go of Marta's hands suddenly, as if he did not want to be contaminated by some hidden sin of hers. "And everyone, you say, does daily business with a Jew. Incredible, don't you think?"

"But what does Il Piccino have to do with anyone's troubles? I'm sure he has troubles of his own, no? Why shouldn't we buy newspapers from his shop?"

Emanuele Mosè's eyes showed his pain at having to explain. "Imagine," he said, his eyes shutting tight, "the person you've loved most in your life. No, don't tell me who. Doesn't matter. Husband? Or father perhaps. Even your mother. Think of your love for that person. Think of their infinite love for you." He was silent until he heard Marta exhale a wistful sigh. "Yes, Marta, yes. Feel that person's love.

Now, Marta, think. Think how you would feel if someone else should come along and take the one life you love more than your own." His eyes opened and looked hard into hers. "Someone comes and destroys your loved one, though your loved one never has done this other any harm. Your loved one is without sin, without stain, yet this other comes and beats the person you love until your beloved bleeds. Spits upon and whips your beloved, then puts your cherished one to death in the most merciless of ways, driving nails through the beloved hands and feet, hammering hard, nailing the precious body to rough, splintery wood, leaving it to die slowly in more pain than your body or mine has ever known. Can you imagine that, Marta? Can you imagine that?"

Her blanched face showed that in her head she saw the image that Emanuele Mosè had painted with his words.

"Now imagine, Marta, that the assassin of your beloved should happen to set up shop in the town where you live. Look inside yourself for the honest answer, my dear Marta: Would you be in a hurry to make the shopkeeper rich by giving him your business? Would you rush to smile at him and make him your friend?"

Marta's eyes looked bleakly at Emanuele Mosè's face.

The young man raised a hand, its palm bandaged by the fingerless glove. The hand pointed to the framed picture of the agonized Jesus on the wall. The eyes, however, would not release Marta from their accusing stare. "There, Marta, is the Beloved. Now is the moment to put your faith to the test. Is your love for any person on earth greater than the love you should feel for Him?"

"No. For certain. No."

"Then behold the Beloved, Marta. Behold your Lord. Look how they broke His body. Look how they made Him bleed."

"But it's terrible," she said, tears of emotion overspilling the pinkened rims.

"Terrible, sì. Terrible, sì. Do you know how many hours I've spent contemplating this image? I've studied its details, trying to bring myself closer to His pain. I've sat before it for full nights without sleeping, until my own body began to partake in the sacred suffering of that other flesh. I love that image, Marta, because it invites me to bleed with Him. It reminds me that I must never forget."

"But Il Piccino—" Marta could bear to look at the icon no more. Her eyes fluttered, searching for something less horrible to rest upon. "Are you telling me that I love the Lord less if I buy magazines from Il Piccino's shop?"

"I tell you nothing. But you must ask your own heart whether or not it wishes to return to that store."

"The store," Rosa Spina called from the kitchen, "of that Jew."

"But what about *perdono*? Forgiveness exists for everyone, I've always heard. Don Luigi has said so in sermons thousands of times. Isn't there forgiveness for the Jews?"

"Of course! There is forgiveness for everyone, so loving is our Lord. But be careful in your reasoning. Remember that pardon exists for *they who ask*. Knock, says the Lord, and it shall be opened. But how can the door open to those who do not wish to come in?"

"I don't understand," Marta said.

"My son is asking you," Rosa Spina said, peeling potatoes with a small sharp knife, "to question yourself about the Jewish midget behind his countertop, Signora Marta. Has he ever repented? Has he ever acknowledged his guilt?"

"I see." Marta nodded, her own conscience feeling heavy. Thinking some more, she looked at Emanuele Mosè and said, "But your brother buys newspapers from Il Piccino, too. I saw him in the shop just the other day."

"My brother—" Emanuele Mosè started.

"My other son," Rosa Spina said amid the smells of good cooking in the kitchen, "my other is no example to be followed." Her smile turned sad, and she shook her head. "In the prison where they locked him up, there were nonbelievers, and Muslims, and people of every sort. He had no choice but to become ecumenical in his tastes. If you gave him the opportunity, my other son would point out the likable side of the Devil himself."

"He seems like such a nice young man, though."

"Indeed," said Emanuele Mosè. "My brother is very good at *seeming.*"

"But there in the shop he was chatting with Il Piccino about how much there was to be admired in the religion of the Jews."

"Is that what they were saying?" Emanuele raised an eyebrow and stared at Marta in such a way as to make her feel she had committed a crime. "And you participated in a disquisition of this kind?"

"Listened more than participated," Marta pointed out, trying to sidestep an encroaching sense of guilt.

"And did the Jew make mention of his need for forgiveness?" Rosa Spina asked. "Or did he deny the divinity of the Lord, the way his people have been denying for the past two thousand years?"

Thinking hard, Marta could not exactly recall. The conversation in the newspaper shop had been too complicated, too different from the gossipy exchanges of small talk that usually filled her days. She was sure, though, that she had learned a fresh piece of information from listening to L'Altro and Il Piccino talk. It had been news to her that Jews appeared contented enough to have a religion that did not include Gesù Cristo. No Gesù Cristo, L'Altro and Il Piccino said, and no saints, and no Madonna either. She could not remember now which mouth in the newspaper shop had uttered these notions, but yes, she remembered her own reply.

"I told them," said Marta, pleased to be able to report something about which she finally could feel not guilty but proud, "that to my mind it was sad to have religion without Gesù."

"You did well," praised Rosa Spina, "in saying to the Jew a thing that most Christians would not have had the courage to utter."

Emanuele Mosè looked at his mother. Watching him, Marta could detect only fatigue and sadness in his expression. He folded his gloved hands and closed his eyes. He had tired himself, Marta figured, by engaging in talk about ugly things that would not exist in the world if only everyone loved the Lord as much as he did.

Marta could tell that her privileged moment of intimate dialogue with the holy youth was about to end. "*In somma,*" she said, "so in short, you're telling me that God is punishing me because I buy magazines from a Jew. Or are you telling me that Il Piccino has put the Evil Eye on me? Or is it someone from beyond the tomb who has put the Evil Eye on me? My husband maybe? Or Mauro Giannetti? Or maybe someone else? So much was said. I feel confused."

"In short," Emanuele Mosè said with saintly patience, "you must tell me. When the finger touches your spine, making you jump with fright in the night, do you feel cursed?"

"*Certo!*" she cried. "Of course! Who wouldn't feel cursed?"

"Exactly. You *feel* cursed. That is all that matters. Who has done the cursing is of no importance."

"But I want to know who's cursing me. Won't you tell me?"

Emanuele Mosè rubbed his exhausted eyes. "I'm not a fortune-teller, I say again." He shook his head. "And I'm not one of those charlatans who do their tricks with magic salts."

"Magic salts?" The idea appealed to Marta. Her problems might disappear with ease, she knew, if she could go home with some potion as a cure.

"You don't know about the magic salts?" said Emanuele Mosè. "There are specious healers doing their trickery in more places than you'd imagine. You go to one of them and say you have a problem. They give you an envelope of magic salts that have been prayed over, so they tell you. They promise that if you go home and mix the salts with water, the magic will remove the Evil Eye from your house, making it vanish, just as the salts vanish in the water. So what do you do? You take the salts home, stir them up with water, watch them disappear, and you feel relieved. Until a week or so later when you look at the water and notice the white powder sitting there at the bottom of the glass. You telephone your healer, who warns you that the reappearance of the powder is a very bad sign. It means a curse has indeed been placed upon you, a curse to which there is no simple remedy. Therefore you must pay the healer—great sums of money, too—and the healer will start an endless series of voodoo rites and incantations, the only result of which will be to make your wallet lighter."

"But the magic salts?"

"There is nothing magic about the salts, Marta," Emanuele Mosè said, masking his impatience. "Sodium chloride. Table salt. Leave salt in water for a week, and it will *always* reappear on the bottom of the glass. Curse or no curse."

"Terrible people these charlatans, taking advantage of other people like that."

"Terrible indeed," said Emanuele Mosè.

"And I have to say, I wonder about the intelligence of the people who let themselves be tricked. But, as they say, *Mal voluto non è mai troppo*," Marta quoted the popular saying. "An evil that's asked for is never more than what's deserved."

"We should be more charitable toward the poor souls who go searching to meet some genuine need. Still, Marta, if that's what you want of me, we can pretend to give you magic salts. Mamma!" he called to the kitchen. "Have we got a little pouch to put some salt in?"

"Of course." Rosa Spina smiled. "If that's what the signora wants."

Emanuele Mosè looked back at Marta. "Is that what you want?"

"Absolutely not!"

"Absolutely not is correct, dear Marta. And notice, please, that I have not told you that you have been cursed. You told me, no? You told me about the finger that pokes you and takes away your peace. Now, as a remedy, I offer you no voodoo spells or witchcraft, but humble Christian prayer. Lots of prayer, for it will take much praying, Marta, to wash you from the stain that the hand smears on you night by night. We will pray together when you come here, and I will keep you constantly in my prayers even when I pray alone. And have I requested money in exchange for prayer?"

"True," she said. "You've never asked."

"Because I pray for reasons of love, dear Marta. Not lucre. Love."

"Still," she said, "I would be in the wrong if I did not thank you with a gift of gratitude." She reached for her handbag and opened her purse. "How much should I give your mother on my way out?"

"You could give all the wealth you have in the world," he said, opening his gloved hands in benediction, "or you could give nothing. My prayers for you would not change. Be assured of that. We might remember, though, that God gives us money not for us to hoard in the bank, where the energy sits and dissipates. You decide, Marta, how much fuel, how much power is to be spent in freeing you from the nightly touch of the hand."

Peering into her wallet, Marta realized that it did not contain nearly enough. "There's hardly anything here," she said dejectedly. Then she brightened. "And if I come back tomorrow evening? I could go to the bank in the morning and have them prepare a check."

"Tomorrow evening is fine," said Emanuele Mosè. "Any evening when you feel the need to pray. Alone or with the group."

"But cashing a check can be difficult," Rosa Spina said with a smile from behind her pots. "My son and I prefer not to spend our time waiting on line at the bank. It's draining, having to mingle with the darker, materialistic side of the world, don't you think?"

"Then I'll go to the bank and withdraw cash. *Tanta energia* I'll give you both," she said, her hopefulness making her fresher and more vital already. "So much energy!"

"You are a dear person, dear Marta. Be sure to leave enough in the bank for your other, less spiritual, needs." Emanuele Mosè nodded toward the kitchen, and Rosa Spina came to show the old woman out. "Go with my blessing. We've talked so much this evening; tomorrow evening, we'll devote more time to our prayers."

"I just have one little question," Marta said as Rosa Spina took her arm to lead her toward the door. "Where can I buy my magazines now? They do give me a little comfort after all."

Rosa Spina stopped, turned toward the front room, and said, "Emanuele Mosè, answer the signora's question."

Seeing the insistence in his mother's eyes, Emanuele Mosè reluctantly replied. "Dear Marta," he said, his voice hardly more audible than a whisper, "if the tempting desire to buy a magazine should come upon you tomorrow"—he pointed to the bleeding Jesus on the wall behind his back—"remember our Lord."

When Marta had gone, Rosa Spina approached her son's chair from behind and placed her hands on his shoulders. "You did well to remind the signora of the Lord's suffering."

"Why did you have to set her against the man in the newspaper shop?"

Rosa Spina stroked the young man's long hair. "I know it upsets you to warn one person against another. I hate it as much as you do. But we are humble soldiers in the Lord's command. We can do nothing but obey His orders. Trust me, my son. We are doing right." Her voice was as soft as a lullaby. *"You're* a good boy, not like L'Altro, eh?" She smiled. "Besides, think how great our guilt would be if we left the signora unprotected against the curse of that Christ-killer."

She leaned over and kissed his cheek. His skin, like stone, was cold beneath her lips.

15

The stones that made up the town of Sant'Angelo D'Asso—and what is a town, after all, but a collection of stones?—were not troubled by the miserable weather this one night a week into February. Long sufferance comes easily to stones. These in particular had first been unearthed by human hands when the Etruscans cleared the wooded hills and transformed the landscape into a blanket of pastures and fields. Then the Romans came to make their temples, houses, taverns, bridges, and roads, crafting the stones into geometric order. A handful of centuries of Roman rigor had to pass before gravity's tug won out and the stones could nestle again in the earth. Most of the stones then lay in peace. Some were assembled into crude homes for crude peasants. The more perfect were chosen by human hands to make the Christian church; the rest left undisturbed, picked up and tossed aside occasionally when they became irksome obstacles to farmers' plows. Not until the 1200s would the bulk of the stones be uplifted again, this time to shape a town. With the exception of the little stone tabernacle that Renato and other townspeople put up at the mouth of the saint's grotto by the river to commemorate the Pope's intervention to stop a dam that would have flooded the entire valley, the architecture of Sant'Angelo D'Asso had hardly changed since the times of the medieval masons.

The stones had resounded to rounds of wedding bells and funeral knells, had housed the birth and death, the love and loneliness, the greed and hope, the sensuality and sterility, the joy and indifference, the strength and frailty, the humor and grief of little human lives. So why should they be bothered if this one night in February the clouds poured out rain as if to drown the stones themselves? The stones knew they would outlive their present masters.

Tonight, the human members of Sant'Angelo D'Asso did what people have done in every century: They searched for ways to feel less alone.

The building that contained Daniele's apartment was not an old stone house, neither did it stand inside the fortified walls that marked the boundaries of the center. It had been constructed of cement in the 1930s just past the town walls, up toward the railway station. Like other products of Fascist design, the apartment block emphasized function over beauty. Daniele was inside his apartment this February night. Alone. Though the windows were airy enough and the ceilings high enough, the rooms were boxlike in their rectangularity, the linoleum on the floor too brown, the pipes snaking up the bathroom and kitchen walls too exposed. The place had never felt like a home. It was, however, the only house in which Daniele had ever lived, and, in the years since Petula had come to live with him, she had accomplished miracles in giving the rooms a welcoming atmosphere. With Petula gone now, and Beniamino, too, the house had taken on the sadness it had held when inhabited by Daniele's quick-fisted father and whimpering mother. The Fascist form of the apartment reinforced the message Daniele's father had tried to beat into his son: *Don't fuck with the people in charge.*

Tonight Daniele sat at the kitchen table. Cold white light came from the circular fluorescent lamp overhead. Though shaped like a halo, the lamp gave off a cold radiance in no way heavenly. How many times had Petula asked him to buy a warmer light? Petula had a point. The industrial-style glow was depressing. Made no difference now, though. Too late. He puffed on his cigarette, then stubbed out the butt.

Spread on the table were the pages of musical scores. With the house this silent and empty, why not spend the evening practicing his saxophone for the band?

He played through a medley of themes from Verdi's *Rigoletto*. The piece would be a showstopper at the next concert, but the band had to learn it first. It was far from ready, and rehearsal the other night had been a disaster. Baldesi the conductor, after explaining for the fifth time the rhythmic changes throughout the piece, had started to run out of patience. He had whacked his baton against his music stand and screamed at the woodwinds. "How can you keep in tempo if you don't watch me?"

"How can we watch you," answered Petrioli, a clarinettist who never let anyone's tantrum perturb his own enjoyment of the world, "if we're reading the notes almost for the first time?"

"Real musicians," the conductor said, closing his eyes as if intently imagining the band he wished he had before him, "know how to watch the baton and read the notes in the same moment."

Daniele was happy to be at the rehearsals two evenings a week, even when the conductor was in a mood. Rehearsals got him out of the lonely house.

At the kitchen table now, Daniele practiced his part in the planned program. More often than not, the saxes huffed away at backup harmonies. That was the problem with playing sax in a band: You almost never got to shine.

Following the score, Daniele segued from "La donna è mobile" into "Tutte le feste al tempio." He hit a clunker and the dissonance ricocheted off the kitchen walls. Practicing at home had been no pleasure when his parents were alive, for his father was always telling him to *fare silenzio* and threatening to break the saxophone over the young musician's head. Things were better when Petula was in the house. She would get excited and clap her hands when a line came out especially well, which made him feel like the reincarnation of John Coltrane. Beniamino could be a pest, always grabbing at the sax and pleading, "Can I try?" Thinking now about Beniamino's pestering, Daniele laughed to himself. There was something flattering in a kid's way of wanting to do what his father did.

No applause for Daniele this evening, and no childish demands for a turn. Only Daniele's notes—not all of them right—and the echoes of himself.

In the thick of "Bella figlia dell'amore," his playing began to make no sense at all. The notes weren't hard; it was the damned changes of rhythm that made him lose the beat. Why did Verdi have to switch tempo so frequently? Just when you settled into the comfortable oom-pah-pah of 3/4 time, you found yourself suddenly coping with bars of 4/4. And then, when you made your peace with the swing of dotted notes, triplets came at you out of nowhere.

Sucking excess spit out of his reed, Daniele squinted to understand the metrical mess. It was no use.

"*Ma vaffanculo,*" Daniele said, hoping that Verdi could hear him, wherever he was. If Daniele was having this many problems, then the rest of the saxes would be struggling even more, for Daniele was one of the best. Let the conductor try to sort it out at the next rehearsal.

Daniele pushed the pages of music away. Sitting in white fluorescent light, he heard rain rush down hard outside. He considered putting his sax away, but it was still too early to lie down in front of the television. Besides, something inside had not expressed itself yet. As he lit another cigarette, an urge rose. Though he had next to no experience with it, he wanted to play jazz.

Daniele had always treasured a secret fantasy. In this imaginary picture, it was hot summer and he was seated by the open window of his big-city apartment. Perhaps it was New York. Perhaps his leg was out the window, his foot resting on the fire escape. He wore loose trousers and a white tank top visible beneath his unbuttoned, untucked white cotton shirt. Daniele, sexy in his solitude, was blowing into his sax and out came haunting, gritty, soulful notes. Was it a picture he had seen in a movie once, or did it come from a TV ad? No matter. Even if the image lacked originality, it was precious to Daniele. People passing beneath his window would hear his improvised runs. They would stop to listen and would whisper to each other, "That man's an *artist*. Don't know what hurt him so bad, but listen to the way it makes him play."

And who knew? In an open window across the road, couldn't there be a slim-waisted young woman, touched with unblushing urgency by his sound?

Gershwin, Daniele remembered at the kitchen table. The band had played a medley from *Porgy and Bess* a couple of years back.

He was about to go looking for the music, when he decided it would be better if he could play it by heart. He tooted his sax, searching for the right note to start on. Once he had found it, he let "Summertime" slide its way out.

The sliding was, in truth, more scratch than slide. In any case, he remembered most of the notes, and the lines he couldn't remember he mastered by ear after some trial and error. Finishing up that number, he asked himself if there were any other good songs from the medley the band had played. "Oh, this one," he said out loud, having got used to the notion by now that when you live alone you can say your thoughts in full voice and there will be no one to look at you as if you're crazy. Moistening the mouthpiece, he began "Bess, You Is My Woman Now."

After the first line of melody, Daniele could not remember what came next. "That's all right," he thought while his lungs continued to blow. "I'll improvise the rest." To launch himself into a riff, he leaned his body forward and blew with heartfelt force. His brain had no idea of what notes to play, but he waited all the same for the music to soar.

Each rhythmless squeak he played was worse than the note that preceded it. "*Vaffanculo,*" he reiterated, this time not to Giuseppe Verdi but to himself.

How much he hated himself, how unbearable did he find his own company. Reincarnation of John Coltrane, my prick. I'm a mediocre saxophone player in a small town's marching band, he told himself. There was no sexy music hidden within, bursting to express itself. Inside was emptiness.

He had resented Petula and Beniamino because, to his mind, they had limited him. Certainly they made him laugh and did nice things for him, but, through no fault of theirs, of course, they had their needs, their ever present needs for a house, for food, for clothes.

Petula worked hard for her share. But her very presence was in itself a request. It was woman and child who kept him trapped, stopping him from hopping a train, sax in hand, to look for his big-city windowframe with its fire escape. Suffocating, he had grown angry. With anger had come fear. He had already come too close to destroying Benimiano when he had seized the boy behind the bar. So, yes, thinking it through again, he had done what was best for everyone. Though the way he felt tonight, despicable in his loneliness and mediocrity, his life improved not in the least now that he had his freedom, he could see nothing good in having sent away the two people he was sure he loved. And for more than a month now, he had only been making things worse whenever Petula at work asked him how things were going for him. "I'm better alone," he lied to her, and he had repeated the lie so many times that she no longer bothered to ask.

"*Vaffanculo*," Daniele said aloud to himself. "Idiot and nothing else. *Vaffanculo*."

He would have telephoned a friend, had he had one. The guys in the band were friendly enough, but Daniele knew no one with whom he could risk talking about real problems. The kids with whom he used to waste afternoons and evenings hanging around along the *corso* had moved away once school finished. Pippo Alboretti had got a job up in Volterra. Marco Giusti was earning big money in Florence, and Ghigo Petrocelli had moved to Rome. Only Daniele had stayed behind, stuck where he had always been because he had no talent for doing anything else.

Daniele noticed that his cheeks were wet. He was crying. Angrily he wiped his eyes with his palms. The tears would not be stopped. His body fell into spasmodic sobs.

He cried for many minutes, then his shaking was blocked by a terrible thought. Never in his life had he been alone while crying. Someone—his mother when his father used to punch him, Petula the night his parents died—someone had always been present to witness his tears. Crying, he thought, is meant to be done in company. It asks for something, just as a cat does when it purrs. But tonight there was no one to ask for anything.

The magnitude of his pain scared him.

He knew only that everything inside him hurt. Why had the story of his life become a series of hurts? His father, God knew, had hurt him. He loved Petula, of course. He knew she loved him. But did he know how to be loved without causing hurt in return? And what was there to love in him, anyhow? Why did love signify pain? He dreaded himself. He loved Beniamino so much it hurt, though he rarely managed to show his love. The kid was a drop of water that had poured out from his own well. Yet what if someday he damaged his son?

He had nothing in life but a wall safe full of money. What good did that do him or anyone else? He would have been happy to spend all of it in exchange for only a little joy, but years of living with his father's tightfistedness had paralyzed his own power to put his money to use.

The emptiness inside Daniele ached more than any hunger he had ever known. Tears blurred his vision again. He wiped his eyes, wishing he could wipe away the question that arose in his mind. Can you be in so much pain, he wondered, that you simply break? Something inside him, he could tell, was breaking now.

He removed the mouthpiece from his saxophone and put the instrument away in its case. Sitting back down on the kitchen chair, he lit a cigarette and sent smoke rings to hover over his head.

The same night, within the fortified walls of the town, Cappelli readjusted his position in the hot soapy water of the bathtub so that he could wash between his legs. Certainly, he had to admit, taking a bath was a lot more interesting the night Rosa Spina walked in and scrubbed his back. Magical that woman was. She brought a sense of occasion to everything, even to a bath.

He spoke out loud to his belly while he soaped it. "Strange," he said. "Look at you. You're fat enough, but still you're hungry. I should have put something solid into you before coming home. That was my mistake." Indeed, it was well past dinnertime, yet Cappelli had eaten nothing. Drunk a good deal, but eaten no food. *Errore,* he told himself, smelling the alcoholic fumes of his own breath and watching his pinkened bulk roll whalelike in the tub. The movement of the bathwater made his head dizzily swirl. Big *errore.*

"Why didn't we get you something to eat?" he asked his belly now. "We were sitting right there in the bottega. Everyone else forking away at their pasta." He knew the answer. A dreamlike hope had come to him at the bottega. He had imagined that maybe, with Rosa Spina in the house, he would come home to his own table and find a tasty dinner all laid out.

He soaped between his legs again, felt his head spin with all the strong liquid in his stomach, and laughed. He was getting waterlogged as a prune in his bathtub, drunk and alone. *Coglione,* he called himself. *Imbecille.* What dinner on the table! She scrubbed your back for you once. End of story. Don't go kidding yourself or getting any strange ideas in your head.

He started to rise from the tub when from downstairs he heard an unmistakable sound: *CLO-clo-clo-clo-clo-clo-CLO!*

How could this be? he wondered. A hen? Downstairs in Signora Rosa Spina's apartment? A hen?

He heard the clucking again. No doubt about it. A hen was inside his building.

We'll have to see what this means, he decided as he got dressed in clean things from the pile of beautifully ironed clothes that Rosa Spina had placed on his chest of drawers. And there it was: the excuse he had been looking for to invite himself downstairs.

"Come in! Come in!" Rosa Spina said, opening the door after Cappelli knocked. "I'm just doing some little jobs, but if you don't mind watching me work, your company is always a pleasure."

"Don't want to disturb you," he said, following her inside, "but I was sure I heard a chicken. You know, a hen."

"*Ah sì!*" she said with the childlike delight that emanated from her like an appetizing perfume. "Poor thing, I couldn't leave her out in the rain on a night like this, no? We set her up in this box on top of the fridge. See? I put some straw in to make it comfortable."

"But where does she live?" Cappelli watched the stroking motions of Rosa Spina's hand while she patted the shiny-feathered hen. The *coroncina*, the string of rosary beads, was wrapped three or four times around her wrist, bracelet-fashion. On her, this improvised jewelry was as titillating as a set of little bells tinkling around a gypsy's ankle. Enviously, Cappelli wished her beautiful hand would pat him instead of the bird.

"Just outside the bathroom window. On the roof of the little shed that's in the garden down below. Can't bear to think of her alone in this winter weather."

"There's a hen living on the roof of the shed?"

"Only since this morning, of course. She arrived this morning. A gift from one of the people who come for prayers. That lovely older man who lives in that nice old house up past the school. You know who I mean."

"Pellegrini?" *Lovely* was no adjective that Cappelli would ever have chosen to describe the toothless old farmer who had less brains than the chickens he kept and half their pleasantness. "Pellegrini comes to pray? *Here?*" Thinking of that horrid other man giving presents to Rosa Spina, Cappelli felt for the first time in his life the knife-edge of jealousy.

Rosa Spina gave that elaborate smile of hers. "You should come yourself to one of the meetings," she said, "and see what happens when the people pray."

"Right!" Cappelli blurted. "*Contaci!* Count on it! Me, at a prayer meeting? I don't even go to Mass in church. Imagine me coming to the special kinds of things that you all do here." It was then, once his drink-slowed brain let his eyes concentrate on the things before them, that he noticed what was spread out on the table. "Look at this," he said. "Rolling pasta, are you?" Indeed, what at first glance appeared to be a golden tablecloth was none other than an immense sheet of dough rolled thin. "And you roll it right on the table? No board beneath?"

"No board. But if you look, there's my old white tablecloth under the dough so it doesn't stick to the wood."

"*Sì*," said Cappelli. "*Sì*. You make me remember that I used to have a grandmother once. She used to do it precisely the same way. Right here on this same table."

"The good things never change. But you must tell me about your grandmother, Signor Cappelli, and about yourself as a little, little boy."

"What's to tell? She was old and I was young, and now I'm almost as old as she was."

Rosa Spina laughed. "What did you call your nonna?"

"What do you think? I called her Nonna."

"And what did she call you?"

"When she wasn't calling me little monster, or beast, or mischief maker, she called me by my name."

"Which is?"

"Which is my name." He shrugged. "What do you want?"

"I want to know your name. You can't expect me to believe that your grandmother called you Signor Cappelli."

"People call me Cappelli and that's enough. My grandmother, naturally, was different. But it doesn't matter."

"Maybe everyone calls you Cappelli because no one knows your name."

"And why do you want to know?" His first name had caused him a lifetime of embarrassment. Nothing would make him tell this woman now. Being laughed at by her would hurt too much.

"Wouldn't it be a wonderful thing for you to have a person who knows your real name?" Her lips did not close completely when she finished speaking, and Cappelli lost himself for a moment studying the delicate entrance to the secret cavern of her mouth, to all the world that was inside her.

"Call me little monster or beast, and you won't be far from the mark," he said. She made him feel strange, as if she took his clothes off and put him outside under the rain. To change the subject he said, "It's a lot of pasta that you've rolled out."

"When Signor Pellegrini gave us the chicken, he also brought a basketful of eggs." She let pass the subject of Cappelli's name. Cappelli was relieved, but the mention of Pellegrini gave him no pleasure. "Such beautiful eggs," Rosa Spina said. "I had to make something. But how terrible I am, Signor Cappelli! I haven't offered you anything to drink!"

"Drink? I'm already floating, I've had so much to drink. On an empty stomach, too."

"But this is no good! *Ostrega!* We must set this right at once. Empty stomach all evening? No, no, no, no, no. We'll put some water on to boil and cut you some tagliatelle, lovely and fresh."

"Me alone? What about you?" He glanced around, but saw no signs of anyone else. "You and your family?"

"Had our dinner. I was making the pasta for tomorrow. But no matter. There will always be more eggs, now that we have our own hen. I'll put the water on."

Cappelli enjoyed watching her move around the kitchen, the way her skirts swirled, the way her shawl opened occasionally to give glimpses of her breasts—those breasts on which he wanted to lay his head. Watching her move was like watching someone dance. Her perfume spiced the air while smoke from the fireplace made the atmosphere wintry and warm. From its box atop the fridge the hen went *clo-clo-clo.* "Don't want to trouble you," Cappelli said.

"What does it take? Only a little patience to let the water boil, and it will be done. You can help me cut the pasta. Here." She took a bowl of flour from the countertop. "Help me sprinkle this over the dough so it won't stick when we roll it up."

Cappelli inspected his hands: They were still bathtub clean. He followed her example, taking fingerfuls of flour and smoothing it onto the yolk-yellow dough. Watching the sensitive way in which her hands caressed the surface, he tried not to be clumsy himself. "Good job you did of rolling it," he said. "Not a hole. Not one."

She used the back of her hand to push a strand of hair from her forehead. Her eyes, unobstructed, smiled into his. "Each person has his art," she said. "No?"

Cappelli nodded. "And cooking must be yours."

Smiling again, she said, "I have more than one."

He was mesmerized by her hands as they picked up a knife to cut away the edges of the dough, putting aside the thicker parts, as Rosa Spina explained, to be cut up later as noodles for soup. The hands rolled the dough into a great sausage-shaped spiral, then, taking up the knife again, carefully sliced the roll to make the tagliatelle strips. "Do like this," she said, showing him how to disentangle the tagliatelle so that they would air-dry for a final few minutes before she put them to boil in the pot. "And while we wait," she said, "we can have a little glass of wine."

"If I drink again this evening . . ." Cappelli said, and he made a gesture to show how befuddled his head would be.

"Just a little shadow in the glass," she said, pouring, "to keep me company."

"Your sons?"

"Don't worry about my sons. L'Altro went out. Emanuele Mosè went to bed early. He has a lot of praying to do. People have given him so many prayer requests. Don't worry about the boys. They'll leave us in peace."

"A little drop then," Cappelli said. Rosa Spina had already put the glass in his hands.

The wine did in fact befuddle Cappelli's head, yet the sensation was not unpleasant. Anything but. He hovered as if in a dream while Rosa Spina drained the boiled pasta, spooned over it some fresh tomato sauce from a little pot, grated a generous snowstorm of cheese on top, and set the steaming plate in front of Cappelli's eager face.

He ate and drank, then ate and drank some more. All the while Rosa Spina talked. He hardly followed what she said, but he became drunk on the music of her voice. Her hands danced their enigmatic dance, as if they sought to sculpt the air, and Cappelli was bewitched by the woman who sipped from her glass nearly as frequently as he swallowed from his. Reality was still warm and fuzzy-edged when he noticed that the pasta was gone and the woman was crying about some memory of something; he could not catch the exact reason. At a dreamlike distance from himself, he heard his voice make consoling sounds to her, not unlike the comfortable mutterings of the hen on top of the fridge. And he was too swept up in warm weariness to be surprised in any kind of abrupt way—for everything flowed so gracefully into everything else—when she responded to his cooings of reassurance with a kiss on the lips. The kiss became deep, until Cappelli felt his whole consciousness slip into oblivious wonder inside the warmth of her mouth.

Surprised he was, however—astonished, shocked—when his brain woke up enough a little later to notice that it had just exploded in physical ecstasy, bone-shaking as a sob, and that she lay by his side in his bed. How had they got upstairs to his rooms? Had he done something for which he should be repenting? Could he be sure that these things were real, the woman beside him and the various pleasures she had given him, pleasures which, now that he had caught up with the ghosts of their recollection, had been extraordinarily sweet? His brain kept on riding the ocean groundswells of too much drink, but unhappy was one thing he could not say he was. Unhappy, no. That, if nothing else, was for sure.

And she was talking still. Now the melody of her words had become a concentrated solo, like a violin singing alone. His hand was on her naked breast, and gently, while she spoke, her hand stroked his, the *coroncina* of rosary beads around her wrist the only clothing she wore. She spoke into the darkness of the room around them both. "I don't know what to do with the thoughts," she said, her voice no louder than a whisper, "when the years of my life collapse, one inside the other, until they're all present, all at once. Like an artichoke, each layer succulent and good to chew on, but the tip of each leaf so sharp that it hurts. You see, don't you?" Cappelli had no idea what she was saying. He knew only that something she usually held inside was coming out now. "The places I've lived in or run away from are always with me," she said, "and so are the people I've let inside my heart. When I lie in bed alone and think about one place, I get lost, and can't be sure where I am *now*. Is this what God has written as my destiny? is what I ask myself. Is this how He wants my sons and me to live forever?"

"*Certo,*" said Cappelli, hearing how fluidly blurry his words were. "A life with a certain movement to it." He tried to respond to the only part that he could understand of what she said. "You never thought of staying in one place and making your life there?" By the sound of his own voice, Cappelli could tell he was falling asleep, losing consciousness fast, too fast, probably, to make sense of any reply that Rosa Spina might give. He was terrified by the newness of all this. Women were occasional encounters for Cappelli with months if not years between one encounter and the next, and he was not used to letting himself erupt in ecstasy with a woman whom he had not paid to tolerate his brief bliss. What did this woman expect from him now, she whose words wove a lacework far more complicated than he could unravel? Never before had he made love in his own bed, and never, come to think of it, had he ever done what he so unavoidably was about to do now: fall asleep with a woman in his arms.

Questions whirled in his head like vapors of wine, and he knew only that her hair smelled good when he pushed his nose into it and that his hand on her breast had found its perfect place in the universe. His last thought before his mind switched off altogether was that she was the most wonderful armful he had ever held.

People who are in love describe the experience as similar to that of being drunk. For Cappelli the inverse appeared true: In his wine-scented dreams, he began to believe he had fallen in love.

On a dark hilltop above the storm-drenched town of Sant'Angelo D'Asso, Petula pulled in among a group of olive trees, shut off the headlights and the engine, and cranked up on the handbrake. "We're alone," she said. "Incredible, no?" Then her smile disappeared. Her fingers traced the steering wheel. "I think my father understood everything when I asked to borrow the car. My mother understood *for sure*. She asked me if I knew what I was doing. I didn't have a good answer."

"Petula," said L'Altro, "what we're doing is no sin."

"Who said anything about sin? My parents don't want me to get hurt."

"But they gave you the car anyway."

"*Sì*, they gave me the car, but I could tell it was against their instincts. Twenty-four-year-old daughter wants to use the car to go out with a guy at night—"

"They didn't say no."

"How could they? I'm a mother. My child is six. They can't pretend I'm a little girl anymore."

Was it sadness he heard in her voice? Nostalgia? Regret? To comfort her, he said, "My mother made a comment when I said I was going out tonight. She stared at me for a long time, then she told me it probably wasn't my fault if I was tempted to do a little living outside my own head for a change."

"And is that where you do most of your living?" Petula said with a smile.

"Probably. Too much, *sì.*"

"Don't be embarrassed," said Petula. "You don't have to blush."

"How can you see in this dark?"

"I can hear you blushing."

He laughed. "Nothing to blush about, I suppose. This is no sin."

"But what sin? L'Altro, why do you keep talking about sin?"

"My brother, you know, Emanuele Mosè. His whole life he's planned on saving himself. His purity. I don't understand why. Maybe he thinks it's what God expects of him. Maybe he's the last of the great twisted romantics, and thinks he should only give his body when he's one hundred percent certain he's found a love that will last forever. Maybe he's just scared to jump in and swim. I don't know. I don't think he knows either. But even he is beginning to have doubts about himself lately, for all his holiness. He wonders if it's a good idea after all to keep so much"—L'Altro's hand searched the dark cold air in the car, trying to grasp the right word—"distance."

"Your brother, I can imagine torturing himself that much. But you've had more experience."

"I've been locked away from the world. No women in my wing of the prison."

"But before prison, I meant."

"Before? I was barely old enough for them to prosecute me as an adult when they put me inside."

"L'Altro, why did they sentence you? What was your crime?" There. She had asked at last.

He opened his mouth to speak, then stopped. "I want to tell you." He shook his head. "But I can't. Nothing would make me happier than telling you everything. Please believe me. My mother made me promise to tell no one."

"Do you always do what your mother says?"

He laughed sadly. "I promised," he said. "Maybe someday I can tell you. Does it have to be now? Can't you feel safe with me, even without knowing my crime?"

Petula asked herself what she was feeling. If her heart was beating fast, it was not for fear of danger. "I think I'm safe enough," she said. "But will you tell me something else? Whatever your crime was, were you the only guilty one in your family?"

"Try looking at my family from the police's point of view," said L'Altro, leaning back in his seat with his knee against the glove compartment. "My mother, when she wants, can appear like the Virgin Mary's saintlier sister. My brother looks like the Lamb of God returned to the world, and me, one quick glance is all it takes to tell you that I was born a black sheep. Beh-eh-eh!"

"Sometimes," she said, "I wonder if you went to prison for things your mother and brother did. I can't imagine you committing any crime."

"In my family it doesn't make much sense to go searching for individual guilt. Or innocence."

She stared at him, then asked, "If I ask you something, will you tell me the truth?"

"I'll try."

"People are wondering whether their bad luck got better or worse since your mother and brother arrived. Would you tell me if your family has come to harm the people here?"

After a long pause, L'Altro said, "If that were the truth, do you think my conscience would let me sit here with you now?" More silence. "But listen. I'm not forcing you to do anything. You can trust me or not. Your choice."

"I trust you more than I trust anyone else in your family. You're the only one who has a regular job. And you're the only one who seems to want to tell the truth."

Her hand reached out to find his face. She touched his cheek, then leaned in to kiss his mouth, enjoying his slightly licorice taste. What had Daniele's kisses tasted like, she wondered, back when they used to kiss with passion? Coffee, now that she thought about it. First coffee of the morning. Exciting. Delicious. Warm.

L'Altro pulled away. "Are you sure of what we're doing?"

"I'm too nervous to be sure of anything. But I'm trying not to think too much."

They kissed again, and Petula forced herself to push memory away and concentrate only on the mouth that hers touched now.

Between kisses, L'Altro said, "It's exactly like a theory of mine."

"Oh, God! Another theory!"

"No, no. You'll like this one. It's the theory of attraction and repulsion. Take two bodies—"

"I'm starting to like it."

"People who don't know each other, I mean. Like when you're looking for a seat on the train. There's an empty seat next to this person over here and another seat next to that other person over there. Which seat do you choose? All a question of attraction or repulsion. Animal signals."

"I can't believe it. We're back with the chimpanzees again."

He laughed. "It's a kind of gravity. One body naturally wants to fall into another body. But with some other bodies, you naturally want to move away. That's what makes your decision for you on the train."

Listening, Petula liked his humor and his playful way of analyzing a subject. They were traits that set him apart, gave him an almost princely air despite his decidedly unaristocratic birth. His peculiar perspective seemed to keep his head just that bit above the human sea in which everyone else struggled to swim.

"Since the first minute I saw you, Petula," he said in a suddenly tender voice, "I've wanted to fall closer and closer."

"Not a bad theory," said Petula, touched by his words. "Here," she said, reaching down to the seat release beneath him. The backrest fell until it was nearly horizontal. She leaned over and kissed him more intensely than before.

"You have a wonderful mouth," he said, pulling away once more. "It's so—how can I say?—active."

"You like my mouth? My mouth likes you." Her hand found its way inside his shirt. Her fingertips brushed the skin of his belly.

"Petula, when I said I liked your mouth, I wasn't trying to imply that you had to—"

"No one is making either of us do anything. Don't be embarrassed."

"Do I seem embarrassed?"

"I think I can hear you blushing again." She was astonished by the sudden impression that she might know more about physical love than he. "You're strange. Most of the time you seem to be the one who is in control."

"Are you always this willful?"

"I'm pushing myself," she said, then withdrew her touch. L'Altro heard her sniff. In the shadows of the car interior, he saw her fighting off tears. "I know who I am with Daniele," she said. "I'm the same person I've always been. With you, I start to feel like a woman I don't know yet. I'm looking for courage, but I'm scared."

He touched her cheek. Recognizing her vulnerability, L'Altro put aside his own and felt in control again. "You're not worried about doing the wrong thing with me?"

"I don't know if I should be ashamed or what. Then again, as you say, this is no sin."

"Now I can hear *you* blushing."

"Listen to me, L'Altro. I'm on my own. Daniele left me, or asked me to leave, anyway. Every time I try to talk to him about it, he tells me he's better without me." She sniffed again. "Damn!" she said, hitting the steering wheel in anger at herself as she tried to hold back tears. "I don't know if he'll change his mind. I don't know if I'll change mine. But in the meantime, it could be that I should do some of the living that maybe I haven't done enough of either. Is there anyone who says we shouldn't do what we both want to do?"

"No one," he said. "No one at all." After a long silence, he said, "I can think of nothing, no one more beautiful than you."

She soaked in his words, then, drying her eyes, said, "Let's stop talking, no? I like listening, but I might lose my courage if we talk too much more." She moved in the darkness, crossing from her side of the car to his, until she straddled him, face to face.

"'Like as the deer desireth the water brooks, so longeth my soul after thee,'" he said to her.

"The music you gave me." She smiled, moved by the softness of his voice, for it reminded her of what yearnings they both, in their not much experienced ways, were groping to fulfill. "The longing of the soul," Petula said. The thirst within her belonged as much to the spirit as to the body.

L'Altro pulled off his sweater and she helped him unbutton his shirt. Then together they unbuttoned hers.

Touching her, breathing in her perfume, tasting her, L'Altro said, "God made this too wonderful to be a sin. I think this is what God wants, too."

"What was that other theory of yours?" Petula said. "Two bodies want to fall into each other. Let's see how far they can fall."

By the time Petula clothed her body once more and turned the key to restart the car, the rain had stopped. The clouds drifted away, leaving only a full moon to shine coldly in the sky like a ball of white ice.

Agitated beneath the old-fashioned, lavender-scented flannel sheets of her bed, Marta slept fitfully. Her breathing was jerky. The hair around her face was a tangled spider's web. Her eyes, thinly covered by paper-skinned lids, twitched in a dream.

She saw Mauro Giannetti's face in its final grimace. His head lolled toward her, and from out of his choking throat came a rattling laugh. She tried to run but her old legs could not carry her fast enough. She came to the open tomb of her husband, who, however accommodating and reassuring he might have been in life, always at pains to acquiesce to her ever-jagged nervous demands, offered her no solace now. The bluish skin of his cheeks collapsed in a frown. His eyes watched her with unfamiliar archness. "Protect me!" she cried to him. "Haven't you always loved me?" He did nothing but stare. Was he simply unmoved by her torment or was he cursing her now in repayment for the unhappiness she had inflicted upon him during his years of life?

She curled in bed to hide, yet from under the bed she heard the voice of Il Piccino muttering unintelligible words. Language of the Jews, she figured. Was he uttering a prayer or a curse? "There is no Lamb of God," he said, his mumbo jumbo becoming distinct. "Your priests have lied. You worship paintings and idols. Pagans you are! The Lord is displeased." And out from under the bed came the arm of the minute man, his stubby finger pointing in furious accusation. Il Piccino prodded her in the back, in the sensitive point near her kidneys.

Marta jumped awake. Then drowsiness like a drug overcame her before she could calm the fluttering terror in her chest. She sank back down unwillingly into the inferno of her dreams. Centipedes writhed inside her nightgown. She feared her heart would stop, then Emanuele Mosè came to her, floating in an aura of honey-hued light. One arm was extended to comfort her, caress her troubled head. The other hand was open, glove-covered palm up. "Give," he said, "so that I may give to you. My faith will free you, but you must give."

She had already given thousands, sufficient money, she knew, to leave her husband speechless had he been alive. But clearly she had not yet given enough. What value did worldly wealth contain if it did not serve to ease the soul? Emanuele Mosè's glow began to touch her and gradually warmed away the chills of fear. Her muscles relaxed.

In a moment of half consciousness, Marta promised herself that tomorrow morning she would return to the bank to withdraw more money.

Under her bed she thought she heard Il Piccino snicker.

Il Piccino, in his bed, slept well. Why should he not? Yes, he had noticed a certain scarcity of customers in the last week or so. That Marta Sorcini woman, for example, had not come to buy her magazines. Maybe she was not well, he figured. There was, after all, a bad head cold going around. And the cold must be responsible, too, for the other regulars who had not made their appearance in the doorway of his shop. As long as the autumn's fierce influenza didn't return, there was really nothing to worry about. Next week, he was sure, business would pick up again. Why not sleep undisturbed?

Not half as canny as some in town had begun to think him, he did not foresee the coming plague.

Spillo's broken ribs and collarbone never stopped aching, not even while he slept. In nightmares, he felt the ladder rung give way beneath his foot. The muscles of his back clenched in vertiginous fear as he fell into emptiness again and again.

Don Luigi rolled over. How, he wondered, could a broken leg take so long to heal? Last time he had complained, the doctor smiled patronizingly as if relishing the chance to sermonize to a man of God. "Old bones," said the doctor in a comment that was of no comfort to the priest, "need more time to mend."

Don Luigi feared that lack of sleep would drive him mad. Keeping his leg elevated on a pillow did not help, yet if he took it off the pillow it started to throb. He stared into the blackness with nothing to do but think his dark thoughts, and when he did drift off, his thoughts became darker dreams.

The Lord, he told himself tonight, is trying to teach me compassion for those poor people who live forever in pain, physical or moral. How do they cope?

He remembered the Romans had broken the legs of crucified bodies to hasten the precious oblivion of death.

Maybe Hell is like this, he thought. They break one of your legs when you enter the Afterlife, then they leave you to try to get a good night's sleep with a bone that never heals.

In a nightmare, he saw Emanuele Mosè laying hands—glove-hidden hands—on his leg, but the miracle backfired and the pain sharpened. Don Luigi shuddered. This boy is the beast who everyone says is tempting my congregants away from the Mother Church. In the dream he saw the other brother, L'Altro, watching him with eyes full of grief. Then the young man cried out as his hands were nailed to a cross. Enduring unspeakable tribulations himself, this youth looked upon Don Luigi's discomfort with an empathetic gaze.

Waking to bone-sore lucidity, Don Luigi contemplated the enigma of the two brothers. They were pieces in a puzzle, the ultimate shape of which he could not comprehend. I'll have to discover what they're about. Talk to them maybe. One or the other. Perhaps both. Is it not my duty as shepherd of my flock to square off face-to-face with the enemy that wishes to lead the sheep astray?

And as for the mother of the boys . . .

Alone, as always, in his bed, Don Luigi was sucked by exhaustion into brief minutes of restless rest, with Rosa Spina's pretty white teeth and red lipsticked mouth glittering moistly, sinfully before his mind's eye. She was dressed like a harlot in his dreams, save for the pious *coroncina* of rosary beads entwined around her wrist.

Milena lay awake, worrying about the child of her child. She loved Beniamino limitlessly. Tonight, however, she felt no joy. What joy could there be in observing the change in the boy? Endowed with the sensitivity shared by all children, he was a walking antenna, subtly attuned to every tension between his parents. Lies as to the inevitability of their becoming a couple again did not work, and no longer did the boy accept vaguely optimistic answers to his constant question, "When can we go home?" He had taken to worrying about things. Small things. Strange, symbolic things. The shadow beside the wardrobe, the space between his mattress and the wall. Nightly his sleep was violated by scary dreams, unspeakable fears. Milena would gladly have suffered physical agony herself as price for the boy's happiness. But with a grandparent's powerlessness she could do nothing but watch, trying never to say the wrong thing.

Tonight Beniamino had screamed in his sleep. A moment later he had appeared at the foot of Renato and Milena's bed, his face full of tears. *"Mamma dov'è?"* he sniffled.

"Your mamma's out," Renato mumbled, trying to shake the sleep from his voice. "She'll be back soon."

"I'm scared in my bed," Beniamino said.

"Poor little one!" said Milena. "You had a bad dream? Here. Let's do a little something. Your Nonno Renato has to rest so he can get up early and work tomorrow. But why don't we go back to your bed, you and I, and I'll lie down beside you? Would you like that?"

Wiping his nose, Beniamino said, *"Sì."*

In his bed, his grandmother's warm body under the blankets with him, the boy told her about the snakes he insisted he had not simply dreamed but had actually seen. He talked away. Little by little, he was soothed in the special sense of perfect love that a grandmother gives. With the tip of his tongue he tasted the tears that rolled down to his lip. When the skin of his cheeks felt stiff with the drying saltiness, he said, "Does Babbo cry sometimes?"

"Your father? I don't know. I imagine so."

"You've never seen him cry?"

Searching for a reply, Milena kissed the boy's head. *Your father deserves any tears that come to him now,* she wanted to say. And she thought about what she would have said to Daniele, had he been here to witness this scene. *Do you see your son?* she would have said. *Do you see how even in his own sadness he worries about yours?*

Afraid to say too much to the child or too little, Milena spoke the truth, or the part of the truth that she hoped might help. "I remember one of the times I saw your father cry. It was the most beautiful crying I've ever seen."

"Beautiful? Wasn't he sad?"

"He was crying a lot, but not because he was sad." She stroked his face while she whispered. "He was crying on the day you were born, little Beniamino. He was crying when he came out of the delivery room in the hospital and told Nonno Renato and me that you had come into the world. I wish you could have seen it, my Beniamino. Beautiful, beautiful crying. He loves you so much." She kissed his hair. "And your mamma loves you. And your Nonno Renato. And me."

Inside herself, Milena wondered what Petula was busy doing in the car she had borrowed. "And your great-grandmother, Maria Severina." She smoothed his hair with the palm of her hand. "And your great-grandfather, Tonino . . ." The boy's eyes closed in sleep as his grandmother, listing the people who loved him, whispered on, to make the world around him happy and good.

16

With great effort Petula arrived punctually the next morning to help Daniele open the bar. She could not hide, though, the weariness on her face. Making espresso and cappuccino for the first customers before they caught their trains to Siena, Petula struggled to keep her lips closed, covering her yawns.

Solitude was reshaping Daniele, filing down his jagged temper. He faced the world defenseless and sore this morning, as if undergoing a slow operation without medicine to numb his pain.

He watched Petula with new eyes while she expertly handled the knobs and nozzles of the espresso machine. He could see that she, too, was different from what she had always been. Usually she asked questions about how he was managing on his own, and he knew he could get away with playing the indifferent one. Just once, he was sure, just once was all it would take, answering her questions just once with some little line like, "House is pretty empty. Feel like coming back?" and she would, if he wished, return. How could she not? Each of them had always been the other's only love. Today, however, she was the one with doors shut to keep him out. She went about her work without looking at him. Not once. No questions. No approaches. Nothing. Only the occasional yawn. Her thoughts evidently had nothing to do with him.

"*Stai bene?*" he asked when they crisscrossed each other on the gangway behind the bar while filling customers' orders. "You all right?"

"I'm fine" was all he got back. She walked away, showing no eagerness to pursue this or any conversation.

Then came the breakfast-time arrival of the construction workers. "Look who's risen from the dead," Daniele said when he saw Spillo. "Back among the living?"

Spillo's arm was in a sling. One side of his face, not yet fully healed, was more scab than skin. Under his shirt, white tape held his ribs in place. "I bounce back. See what a tough nut Spillo is? Takes more than a couple of broken bones to put me out of commission." He jerked his head at his fellow workers. "Cappuccino good for you all, too?"

Cappuccino they all wanted.

"A round of cappuccino," Spillo ordered. "And bring over a plate of those pastries of yours."

"Coming up," said Daniele. "You're not going back to work yet, are you?"

"I've been laid up for so many days, I figured I'd go crazy if I didn't get a little fresh air. I won't do any work myself. But I want to take a look at the site and keep my eye on this pack." He looked around at his crew. "Have to set an example for the men, no?"

Ever since his fall, a strange superstition had grown in Spillo, a suspicion that, in a way he could not explain, L'Altro was connected to his mishap. He walked a wide circle around L'Altro, avoiding him anywhere he went. Today, though, he wanted to appear fearless and not think about L'Altro at all. Catching sight of Petula, he switched on as much of a grin as his bruised face would allow. "*Madonna*, don't you look beautiful this morning!" he flirted, eager to prove to anyone listening that his injuries had not diminished his virile appeal.

"Glad to see you're still breathing," Petula said with a smile. "But shouldn't you still be in bed?"

"Bed, she says!" He sat down at the corner table. His loud voice carried across the bar. "Sorry, *cara*, but you'll have to wait until I'm in one piece before I can give you the kind of bed that you're talking about. I appreciate the offer, in any case."

Petula smothered a yawn with her hand.

"Sleepy, are we?" Spillo laughed. "I thought I saw something different about you today. Usually you're so bright and fresh in the morning, but today, just look at those big, watery eyes. Seeing a girl with this sleepy air makes you want to curl up under the covers and get all nice and warm, no? A girl yawning like this, you can tell she has bed on her mind. Wouldn't you say, Daniele? Eh, Daniele? What do you say?"

"I didn't quite catch your order," Daniele answered, mashing coffee into the espresso maker. "How much rat poison did you say you wanted in your cappuccino? One spoon or two?"

Spillo spoke without losing his lopsided grin. "You shouldn't joke too much. Nice piece of woman is our Petula. And if you're idiot enough to let her out of your hands, you can't blame others like me for trying. One of these days, a person will come and show her what real happiness is. What do you say, Petula? How about you and I get together when my bones are back together?"

"Why not?" said Petula with a voice so sweet, Spillo might almost have taken her smile to be sincere. "I hear the doctors are accomplishing miracles these days. Try a brain transplant, and we might talk about the subject again."

Daniele laughed. At least he and Petula were still on the same side. He hoped to exchange a quick wink with her, but she looked away and did not give him the satisfaction of letting his eyes meet hers. "Listen, Spillo," he said, walking over to the corner table with a tray of cappuccino cups and pastries. "The next time you plan to go up a ladder, you let me know. I want to be there to give you a shove."

Spillo smiled. "Strong words for a man who can't keep his woman."

"Tell me something," Daniele said. "*Non ti bastano i cazzi tua?* Your business isn't enough for you, so you have to put your nose in everybody else's?"

"What do you imagine?" Spillo grinned on. "A town this small, and you think everyody's nose isn't already in your business? You ball things up with your lady, it's public news. You're lucky I have no personal interest in coming between the two of you. You're good guys. But if I were to expose my full charm to Petula . . . "

"This is all I need," Petula said, drying her hands on a dishtowel behind the bar. "People exposing themselves in the middle of the bar."

Spillo, Daniele knew, was all bluster. Would Petula ever demean herself by falling for a man like that? Never. But Petula's interest might already be ignited by a different young man.

Daniele was pleased to see Spillo and his boys finish their breakfasts and leave.

A lull in the bar's traffic came after the first throng of workmen and passengers had gone on their way. Petula picked up a broom to sweep away the first few hours' worth of pastry crumbs and discarded paper napkins. Perfect moment, Daniele thought, for her to tell me what's on her mind. No one around.

But Petula's eyes never lifted from the floor she swept. Not trying to punish Daniele with her silence, she merely could not imagine what to say. She struggled still with the urge to treat him like an intimate friend or brother and tell him everything about L'Altro. But Daniele was not her brother, and his interest would be anything but dispassionate. What could she do but seal herself in silence?

"I'm going to the storage room for a minute," Daniele said. "To get out a new prosciutto to cut up." He waited for a reaction. None came. "Old one's almost finished." More silence. "We'll need it to make the sandwiches for lunch."

Petula stopped the broom only long enough to let out an exasperated sigh. "And what am I supposed to say before you go to the storeroom? *Buon viaggio?*"

"That's better than nothing. '*Buon viaggio,*' she tells me. Thanks, Petula. I'll send you a postcard."

Daniele growled to himself on his way to the storeroom, but he was half-relieved. Sarcasm counted as dialogue, at least. Even a good fight, should one blow up, would wound less than silence.

In the storage room, he took down a prosciutto from a hook beside the wall safe. He looked at the safe and, thanks to a lifetime of habit, checked that it was closed: It was. Holding the heavy prosciutto, he looked around. He liked the storage room. It held the familiar reassurances of olive jars, stacks of water bottles, baskets of yeast-fragrant bread from the bakery, vats of sun-dried tomatoes and artichoke hearts, whole rounds of pecorino cheese, entire prosciutto hams. A sound mingled with the fragrances and reached Daniele's senses subtly. It took Daniele a moment to realize that the sound was music, lines of melody seeping in from out front.

"What's that?" he said, returning to the bar with the prosciutto in his arms.

"Hm?"

"The music. Sounds like a church in here."

"Anything wrong with me putting on a tape?"

"That's what the stereo's for." He set the prosciutto on the work counter behind the bar. "But this stuff?" Daniele listened. Sacred music was not his usual. Still, he could not help but hear the beauty of the four human voices that overlapped in layers, intricate and delicate as the feathers of a bird's wing. "I'm waiting for a flock of nuns and priests to come running through if we play music like this in here," he said.

"Well, I like it."

"But what is it?"

"'Sicut Cervus' by Palestrina. Palestrina the composer."

"I know who Palestrina is," Daniele lied. "And since when do you listen to Palestrina?"

"Since for a while now."

"*Ah sì?* And where did you get this tape from?"

"From a friend." What else could she say? She herself did not know what to feel about the young man with whom she had made love.

"I understand," he said, not understanding. "A friend." This was unbearable. The word *friend* was simple enough, but he could not decipher the significance of the way it had come from Petula's mouth now. Never before had Petula's meanings been for him a code. Was she keeping a secret? Her aloofness made him ache.

Daniele listened more. *"Sicut cervus desiderat ad fontes aquarum,"* sang the singers in contrapuntal perfection.

"What are they saying?" he said.

"How would I know?" Petula's turn to lie. Why cause gratuitous pain? "It's Latin."

Incomprehensible as the words might be, the music itself spoke clearly of the longing of the soul. His fingers lightly tapping time on the hard rind of the ham, Daniele started to love the music, yet he was upset to respond to the love the notes conveyed because he knew that the music given to Petula had not come from him. He asked, "So who gave it to you?"

"I told you. A friend."

That word again. How could such a common word become so tremendous? "*Sì*. But which friend?"

She hesitated for a long time, shoving chairs aside to sweep beneath tables, then said. "L'Altro." Petula felt she was risking something great by speaking the name in front of Daniele, as if now, by naming one man in the presence of the other, she were betraying one of them, though she was not certain which one. To make the name seem harmless, she added, "You know. One of Rosa Spina's sons."

"Sure. L'Altro. I know. But I didn't know he was your friend."

"Friend," she said with a shrug intended to appear casual, sweeping dirt into a neat pile in the center of the floor. "We speak sometimes."

"He gave you this tape."

"So what? He heard the song on the radio in prison. He wanted me to listen to it. That's all."

"I can imagine," said Daniele. "A guy comes out of prison and picks a woman he can share his music with."

She swept the pile of dirt into the dustpan.

He forced himself to articulate the question, the answer to which he did not want to hear. "Has he kissed you yet?" Daniele surprised himself by the delicacy of his question, when the image he visualized of Petula and L'Altro's possible activities was cruder by far.

"What's it matter to you?"

"What's it matter to me? It matters."

"I don't see why. You keep telling me you're better off alone. Where does that leave me?"

"So he's kissed you."

She emptied the dustpan in the garbage can and put away the broom. *"Non ti rispondo,"* she said, and busied herself sponging down the tabletops.

"What do you mean you won't answer me?"

"You heard. *Non ti rispondo.* I won't answer you."

"Then that's an answer."

"No. It's the opposite of an answer."

"So why no answer?"

"Because," she said. "Why? Because. Because the answer could be yes or it could be no. Does it matter if I answer yes or no now?" She heard the flustered tone of her own voice. "Separation was your idea, Daniele. This is what you wanted. Best answer I can give you is to tell you that the question is not yours to ask. It's not your place."

"Not my place to ask if you're with another man?"

"Right. Not your place. And don't make me hurt you by talking about this anymore. It kills me to hurt you." She looked at him and tears rose in her eyes. "I don't want to talk about this at all. I want to get back to work."

"Why are you so upset? Tell me."

She heard the gentleness of his voice and wished she could respond. Instead she said, "Daniele, don't ask."

He came out from behind the bar, approached her, put a hand on her wrist to stop her sponging, leaned forward before she could protest, and tried to kiss her mouth.

Her lips stayed closed against him. She pulled away and glared. "Daniele, don't."

Daniele saw what he took to be frightening iciness in her eyes. "Petula, I want to talk."

"Talk to someone else." She freed her wrist from his hand and continued wiping a table with the sponge. Truth be told, her heart was anything but icy. She wanted to return Daniele's kiss so much she could cry, but he had hurt her. If she gave in now, wouldn't that make her weak? And what about L'Altro? What did she want to happen with him? She missed Daniele's kisses, but they had become infrequent long ago, well before Daniele had asked her to move out. Wiping crumbs from the tabletop into her hand, she hated herself for feeling this confused. She squeezed the sponge hard to make her hand stop shaking.

Daniele stared at her and wondered when his Petula had become so hard. He had intimate knowledge of her body's every soft place; now her bones appeared to be made of steel.

He disciplined himself to behave with caution. A word out of place, he knew, would ruin forever his chances of softening her again. "I'm sorry," he said.

Petula looked at the tabletop. She shook her head and said, "Forget it."

Perhaps it was a mercy that a customer walked in. Conversation had to stop. It would take time, Daniele knew, for conversation to become normal again.

Petula removed the tape from the stereo, switching on a light-rock radio station instead.

"Palestrina," Daniele muttered while he put the coffee grounds for the customer's espresso in the machine. Problem is, he told himself, she's right. The distance between them was of his own creation. "Palestrina." He put the spoon on the saucer beside the coffee cup.

For the rest of the day, with Petula speaking to him only words pertaining to the business at hand in the bar, Daniele heard the notes of Palestrina in his head, perfect music that repeated itself relentlessly until its beauty became pain.

17

One side of Sant'Angelo D'Asso's main street could not see the other for the morning fog. Any person who looked out a shop-front window perceived only gray-white, until passersby came close enough to materialize visibly from the cloud.

Il Piccino laid the morning editions on the countertop, then wiped his hands on a rag to remove black ink from his short, chapped fingers. Feeling the beginnings of a cold, he sniffed, and his nostrils filled with the smell of newsprint. He glanced out the window in search of customers, but there was only fog to flatten its pale, feature-less face against the glass. Streetlamps had been left on late this morning in the hope that they might assist sight; they did nothing but make the fog a shade brighter and, consequently, even more impene-trable. Alone in his store, Il Piccino sneezed.

Where was everybody? Il Piccino could not exactly say that no-body had come in—Renato Tizzoni had dropped by to get a paper, as had Don Luigi the priest, and L'Altro—yet the impression remained that many of his regulars, usually punctual, were absent. And not just this morning. Yesterday, the day before, even the day before that, busi-ness had been thin.

But what thin! he told himself. Couldn't be. Must be the miserable weather making people reluctant to leave their homes. So why worry? He had a nice sweet *sfogliatina* breakfast pastry melting inside his belly along with the hot milky coffee he had taken at the bottega. Why ruin his digestion with outlandish fears that his business should spoil from one day to the next? Silly, he told himself, giving his nose a vigorous blow. Leave a mind on its own and it starts to think crazy ideas. He stuffed his handkerchief back into his trouser pocket and shook his head at his own preposterousness.

And look. Wasn't that a customer he could see in the fog now? Wasn't that old Signora Fiore shuffling in her tiny-stepped way toward the door? And here was another ancient regular, Signora Porcelli, who approached with quicker stride and started up conversation just before Signora Fiore could reach the door handle.

Well, Il Piccino said to himself as he watched from behind the counter, if I know these two gossipy dears—and I'm certain I do—they'll be out there swapping medical complaints for a good few minutes, then they'll be in to chat some more. And if they remember why they had come here in the first place, they might even buy a magazine or two.

He could see the two old mouths speak to each other on the far side of the windowpane, but he could not hear a word. He took his handkerchief from his pocket once more and thought he would have to blow again. Or perhaps a sneeze was on its way.

"*Aspetti*, signora! Wait!" Signora Porcelli rushed to Signora Fiore and seized the older woman by the forearm. "Signora, what are you doing?"

"Who's that?" Signora Fiore could not understand the interruption of her progress. The fog through which she had navigated from her own doorstep to this shopfront was not very different from the fog that had settled years ago inside her head. "Who's there? Ah!" she said, recognizing the woman who grabbed her arm. "*Buongiorno* to you, signora. You made my heart jump. Can't see past the tip of my nose this morning. And this dampness does nothing good for the bones. Getting out of bed this morning, I could tell, you see, I said to myself—"

"It's a good thing I caught up with you. You were about to go inside the newspaper shop, or am I mistaken?"

"The newspaper shop? Of course I was going in. But what am I saying? *Am* going in. And you, too, no? Today isn't Sunday, is it? No,

I don't think so." She peered through the windowpane. She could not see the midget who observed her from within, but she did make out the glow of the store's lights. "Look, the lights are on," she said. "So yes, I'm sure it's open. Chilly out here, don't you think?" With an old hand she tucked her scarf into the collar of her coat. "Let's go in where it's sure to be warmer."

"Go into the shop of the Jew? Imagine!" said Signora Porcelli, as if entering the shop where she had been buying her magazines for the last forty years were suddenly an idea too ludicrous to mention in right-minded discussion. "Don't tell me you haven't heard, signora. Everyone's talking."

"Heard what?" Signora Fiore had always found Signora Porcelli to be a woman who leaned toward the frantic; today her conversation was simply impossible to follow. "And which Jew?"

"Il Piccino, naturally. The midget. He's the Jew."

"You mean he's converted lately?"

"What converted? He's always been a Jew."

Signora Fiore squinted toward the windowpane, vainly searching for the human face inside. "Now that you say it," she said, "I think you could be right. Since forever he's a Jew. Yes, I think I remember hearing that once. *E allora?*" She blinked toward Signora Porcelli's face. "So what?"

"How can you say 'So what?' You really haven't heard?" Signora Porcelli felt a flutter of pure pleasure at being the first to tell news to someone else. She licked her lips hungrily, the way a glutton savors the anticipatory salivation before tucking into a rich tableful. "I was sure everyone had heard. And I, of course, am not the best person to explain such things. *M'intendo poco della religione.* I'm certainly no expert in questions of religion, if the truth be told. *Però—*" And that single *però*, a mere "however," entitled her to thrust into a lengthy account of how she had heard it directly from none other than the mouth of Marta Sorcini herself that the most likely explanation for all of poor Marta's recent nervousness could be traced back to no less than a curse cursed upon her very probably by Il Piccino the Jew—of all people!—and that Marta was undoubtedly not alone in being cursed by the malevolent midget, and that according to Emanuele Mosè, the wonder-working young man living over there in Cappelli's house, poor Marta had brought the curse upon herself by frequenting the Jew's shop, thereby causing grievous offense to the Lord, who had been killed in the first place, if you think about it, by the Jews.

Signora Fiore could not see her way clearly through the quickly uttered account. What curse? she wanted to know. Nervousness, she said, was nothing for Marta Sorcini. And why should Il Piccino want to curse anyone anyway, whether he was Jewish or not? And why should the Lord suddenly decide that buying newspapers from Il Piccino was not a good idea, when everyone had been buying from him for years?

Signora Porcelli replied that she would sooner die than have the arrogance to try to interpret the Holy Lord's motivations for doing whatever He wanted to do whenever He wanted to do it, but as for the curse cursed upon poor Marta—and not only Marta, there was no denying that everyone for months now had been noticing the abundance of bad luck inundating the town like an overflooding river, and who then, if not the Jew, was the source of all the bad luck?

"Bad luck," said Signora Fiore, "you mean like the falcon a few months back that stole the rabbit from someone's garden only a day before the rabbit was supposed to go into the cooking pot?"

"Wasn't a rabbit," said Signora Porcelli. "It was a cat."

"I heard it was a rabbit."

"It doesn't matter what you heard, Signora Fiore. Fact is fact. It was a cat."

"Could be." Signora Fiore shook her head doubtfully. "Or maybe you're wrong."

"What are you saying, wrong? It was my cat, signora. Do you hear me? *My cat.*"

"In that case, you should know," the elder woman relented. "I suppose."

"Suppose all you want, but I saw it with my own eyes. And it wasn't about to go into the cooking pot, it was about to catch a mouse. My poor pretty little cat!" She bit her lower lip and shook her head, the pain of loss still fresh. "Most horrible thing I ever saw, the sight of that flying monster carrying my cat away, and I wish I could forget, but I know I never will."

"Imagine," Signora Fiore bleated sympathetically. "Poor cat. Poor you, signora. Poor you."

"And now that I think about it . . ." Signora Porcelli's eyes grew large as revelation hit her hard. "*Sì!* Now that I think about it, yes! Why didn't I think before? He had wanted my cat." With a turn of her chin, she indicated the midget shopkeeper on the other side of the window-pane. "*He.* Only a week or so before, he had been telling me about the mice that nibbled sometimes on the corners of the magazines at night, and I told him he needed a good mouse-hunting cat like mine, and he said he would be willing to buy the cat from me if it would help him get rid of the mice, but I told him I needed the cat for my own cellar. So that's why— Don't you see? Makes the hairs on my arms stand up at attention just thinking about it. Makes sense, no? I said he couldn't have my cat, and doesn't it seem too strange to be coincidence that the very next week a falcon should come and steal my cat?"

"You're not saying Il Piccino sent the bird, are you?"

"Ooh, it makes me tremble, just to think," said Signora Porcelli, starting to scare herself.

A man walked out of the fog. It was Grezzi who, though not as old as the two women, was far from young. One more year of work, he had been promising himself for several years, and he would retire from his shoe repair shop. Grezzi was an unwashed man. He smoked short fat cigars without pause all day, and full ashtrays surrounded his wrinkled bed at night. He coughed whenever he laughed. The smell of cigar smoke followed him everywhere. His leathery fingers were tinged nicotine yellow; the edges of his nails were shoe polish black. He cherished a theory that you could tell a lot about people by the way they wore out their shoes. He never managed to elaborate the theory in words, yet he liked to let on that he, as caretaker to the town's footwear, knew the intimate truth of the lives of everyone from the banker to the garbageman's wife. Grezzi himself had had a wife once, much younger than he, and she had given him a son, but she left after not too long, desperate enough to abandon even her only child. Everyone at the time knew why, yet not many people repeated the whole story. "The way he treated her, poor woman! Shouldn't happen to a dog," people would say, and express their conviction that she had done well in leaving him, less well in leaving a boy in the hands of that brutal man. Then people would change the subject, respecting some centuries-old code that some things were better left undiscussed. Real atrocities do not make for good gossip when half-truths and suspicions are more satisfying by far.

Signora Porcelli did not like Grezzi much, and neither did Signora Fiore. Perhaps no one in town did. They accepted him as an unavoidable fact, in any case, and did not often talk about him behind his back. What news was there to say? Whatever his past sins may have been, his years of lonely living with his son were punishment enough. Besides, he had a certain magical art for restoring shoes to their pristine shine, and he saved people from having to buy a new pair every time a heel gave out or a sole wore thin.

"Signora." He nodded to Signora Porcelli; and "Signora," he greeted Signora Fiore as he walked toward the door of the newspaper shop.

"Ah, Grezzi. It's you." Signora Porcelli nodded back. "You're not going in *there*, are you?" Even though she was no particular friend to Grezzi, she knew it was her citizen's duty to warn the man of the malignant curses he might bring on himself if he set foot inside the midget's shop. "Of course, I'm no expert when it comes to religion," she began, "*però . . .*" And her mouth got to work again on her explication of the array of curses that the Jewish shopkeeper had cursed upon various people. While speaking, she noticed that her recounting came out even better now than it had before. The story had made a home among her lips and teeth and tongue. She liked its feel in her mouth.

The story worked, she noticed, for Grezzi's expression darkened. He puffed on his cigar and coughed out the smoke. "Explains a lot of things," he said. "Lots of things going bad these last few months, and that foul little half-a-jerk-off is the reason why. Excuse the word, ladies, but when a thing has to be said it has to be said. Jew, you say?" Judiciously he studied his saliva-slippery cigar. "The more you think about it, the more sense it makes. Not fashionable in the world of today to say it out loud, but Mussolini—say what you will about his faults—knew what he was doing when he put the Jews in their place. Il Duce wasn't all bad, you know. Wasn't all bad at all. And now that we're talking about Jews in their place, am I right in remembering— *Sì!* I am right!"

"Right about what?" Signora Porcelli could not resist new insight.

"*Sì, sì, sì.* The *presepio.* The Nativity. In the piazza this very Christmas past. Hardly more than a month and a half ago. *Sì!* The flaming comet, the fire it caused in the manger, you remember? The decapitated Madonna."

"Remember?" said Signora Porcelli. "Who could forget?"

"True, true. Very true." Grezzi coughed. "And isn't it also true that *he* was in the crowd of us people watching?"

"He?" Signora Fiore never had been quick to catch other people's points.

"The Jew," said Grezzi.

"You know, you're right," said Signora Porcelli. "But what was he doing there if his religion—can you believe it? it's what Marta and everyone is saying about the faith of those Jews—doesn't even recognize the Mother of the Lord? I'm sure I saw him in the crowd, too. And then the Blessed Nativity turned into the flames of Hell. If that's not the hand of Evil at work, then I don't know what is."

"But I heard Nuzzi had wired the comet badly," said Signora Fiore, still slow to see what was evident to the others.

"No good running from the truth," Signora Porcelli scolded. "Evil might be worked through poor wretched agents like Nuzzi, but that doesn't mean all the blame is his, poor incompetent. He didn't know that his clumsiness was being manipulated to do the work of the Evil One."

"You're not saying Il Piccino is the Evil One!" Signora Fiore had only come to buy a newspaper this morning. The terrifying prospect of Satanic presences in her town was more than she could hurry to accept.

"Can you tell me he's a normal Christian?" Grezzi put in. "*Altro che.* Anything but. Why, just look at the man!"

———

It was then that Il Piccino, standing behind his counter, saw the three people turn their faces to the window and look at him. Owls, they seemed to be before the white backdrop of the fog, with their round eyes staring and their mouths shut like wordless beaks.

Unsure as to why regular customers should behave so oddly, Il Piccino nodded his head, smiled at them, and articulated a friendly *buongiorno,* slowly, so that they could read his lips.

There was no accounting for their reaction: With a simultaneous movement, all three turned and walked away.

"I'm not sure," said Signora Fiore, starting toward the piazza. "Curses? Evil One? I've always thought of him as a good little man."

"Then you go back and buy your newspaper," challenged Signora Porcelli.

"I said I wasn't sure." Signora Fiore shook her head. "That doesn't mean I want to risk it."

As the trio retreated into the fog, they saw another woman approach the shop. *"Buongiorno,"* Signora Porcelli saluted.

"Buongiorno," Tita Vezzosi said back.

"You're not going in *there,* are you?"

"Why shouldn't I?"

"You mean you haven't heard?" Signora Porcelli warmed to another opportunity to recount her story.

A woman of sense, Tita Vezzosi had no time for rumor spreading. She had loved her husband, Aristodemo, for fifty years and had held him through his death. She had finished raising Renato Tizzoni after he had been orphaned. Alone now, she worked her olive grove and made wine from the grapes of her own vineyard. She hoed her vegetable garden by hand. Trouble to her was a frost that threatened the olive trees or a parasite that attacked the vines. In her view, minutes were too precious to be wasted on gossip. "If you mean," she answered Signora Porcelli, "have I heard what I think you're going to say, then I will tell you. Yes, I've heard. No, I don't believe any part of it. And yes, I'm going to keep buying my newspapers from this man's shop."

The fog rang with the ping of the bell over the shop door as Tita Vezzosi walked in.

"Always a stubborn woman, that one," tutted Signora Porcelli in the blind cloud that covered the street. Across her own chest she piously drew the sign of the cross. "We can only pray that she doesn't wake up to find herself the victim of some terrible curse."

Signora Porcelli, Signora Fiore, and Grezzi walked in their separate directions, each wondering where they would buy their papers from now on.

That night, hours after the shops had closed and everyone had gone to bed, the thin transparent window separating Il Piccino's little world from the rest of the town shuddered in the cold wind that blew up the *corso*. The wind rocked the streetlamps angrily and tested the fastness of doors. When for a moment the loud wind stopped, there was no noise.

Then too much sound came all at once when, thrown by a nameless hand, a rock smashed the taut windowpane of Il Piccino's shop, shattering the glass into a thousand spears that crashed on the stones of the street and inside on the tiles of the shop floor.

The violence of the sound made several people stir from their sleep in houses nearby. A light or two went on as the few waking tried to understand, but no further sound was heard, so sleepy eyelids closed again soon.

The wind blew into the newspaper shop during the remaining hours of darkness, strong intrusive gusts deranging what had been piles stacked with care. On the floor, among the scraps of paper and glass, lay a message that would wait until morning to make its meaning understood. The message was a symbol painted in yellow upon the fist-sized rock that had been thrown.

There was nothing equivocal in the message that lay on the floor of Il Piccino's shop. The hand that had painted and delivered the Star of David on the rock had done so with the opposite of love.

18

"*D*io *mio!*" Walking toward his shop in the predawn light of the streetlamps, Il Piccino saw the violated windowpane. Must have been the wind, he tried to reason, yet since when does the wind break glass? Maybe a pigeon lost its bearings and had an unfortunate crash. A thief? But what's to steal?

One fear after another twisted in Il Piccino's stomach as he turned the key in the lock and switched on the lights.

Crunching over broken glass, pushing his way through the papers that the wind had blown here and there, he went to the cash register: nothing missing.

Then he saw the rock. *Non è possible,* he said to himself, staring at the imprecise lines and corners of the crudely drawn six-pointed star. Who today could do this thing? And why? What is there, some old political movement trying to resurrect itself from the tomb? Is there a crazy person loose in town? Or could it really be that so many people have it in for me? Business has been a little slow lately, but *this?* Since when do people care whether I'm Jewish or not? Since when should they decide to come and break my balls?

Remembering his recent conversation with Marta and L'Altro, he did not know whom to blame or how to comprehend such violence. Surely Signora Marta was no vandal, and that L'Altro? Too intelligent for an action this brutal. Or at least so he would seem. One thing was clear: Il Piccino had revealed his beliefs, and now this had happened. How could that be mere coincidence?

Il Piccino went to the closet in back. With broom and dustpan he started to clean up, his thoughts as fractured and jagged as the glass on the floor.

Other early risers in town could not help but notice the ugly gap in the shopwindows along the main street. "What happened here?" they asked, poking their faces in.

"Perhaps you could tell me," Il Piccino answered, brush in hand, dark doubts about everyone already taking root in his brain. "I don't understand a thing. Maybe you do?"

A crowd gathered, for no one could recall an incident of similar violence, not since the war ended long ago.

The *comandante* of the police came with three officers to take a report. One young *carabiniere* busied himself with a camera that had a bright flash, taking shots from every angle. Another dusted the guilty rock for fingerprints, but there were none to be found. "Nothing," said the officer to his commander. "Sorry, sir."

"Grave mistake," the *comandante* scolded Il Piccino, "to have swept up the evidence before we got here."

"Grave mistake my ass," replied the little man, desperation making his good manners grow thin. "With all respect. What difference does it make, sweeping or not?"

Serious and imperious, the *comandante* was secretly thrilled by the occurrence. When was the last time this town had offered him a real crime to solve? Unraveling this case, he knew, would be impossible with no fingerprints and no clues except for the rock itself. Oh, he would take statements from Il Piccino and from the owners of neighboring houses. No one, he was sure, would have seen anything. Nonetheless, he would have an excuse to conduct a lengthy investigation and he would have a crucial place in people's conversations for the next few weeks. If nothing else, the cumbersome procedures involved would make for good hands-on training for the lower officers in his charge.

Il Piccino, from his lowly vantage point, studied the black leather gloves of the *comandante*. Then the black leather shoes. And the black leather belt. Buttons on the crisp dark uniform glinted like the metal of a weapon. High on the head, the hat showed the pride that comes with power. Il Piccino looked out the broken window at the curious faces that looked in. The mouths had already set to gossiping, offering theories about the who, the how, the why. Il Piccino had not felt so alone for many years. He wished he could faint, and fall unconsciously away from everyone. Their voices became to him a noise without sense. What did he think of these people? What did they think of him?

Then others came, friends—could he let himself think of them still as such?—friends who crossed the threshold and started to help.

Renato Tizzoni, on his way to the Waterworks, stepped in. He took in the scene and said, *"Dio boia!"* It seemed appropriate here to refer to God as the Executioner, for Il Piccino's eyes showed the shocked bewilderment of some little beast facing its own sacrifice.

"Madonna rana benedetta!" cried Cappelli, stepping in behind Renato, his boss. There was nothing especially timely in Cappelli's likening of the Holy Virgin to a blessed frog. All the same, the astonishment expressed in the music of the outburst provided an oddly fitting comment on the moment.

Milena came, too, on her way to help her parents open the bottega a few doors up. "Poor Piccino," she said.

The couple who ran the fruit store in the piazza came in, and so did Nuzzi and L'Altro. "This can't be," L'Altro said, and everyone in the shop saw his face lose its color. Shock paralyzed him for a moment. Even Il Piccino, seeing the young man's stricken expression, could not doubt his good intentions. "How could anyone do this?" L'Altro said, his arms hanging at his sides.

"Nobody touch anything," the *comandante* ordered. No one obeyed.

"And leave everything in this mess?" said Cappelli.

"The sooner we get this shop back in order," said Renato, "the sooner Il Piccino can get his business running again."

"He has a point," said a police officer to the *comandante.*

"Who asked you for an opinion?" the *comandante* snapped.

"By the way"—Renato looked among the papers scattered over the countertop and found a newspaper still intact—"this is exactly what I was coming here to buy." He took a coin from his pocket and placed it beside the cash register.

"Lucky day for me, too," said L'Altro, regaining his composure. He took money from his pocket and put it next to Renato's coin. "There's that magazine I've wanted all week. Glad it's not sold out."

"*Permesso?*" said Milena, asking Il Piccino's permission as she took the dustpan and broom from his hands. "You men are good at cleaning, but somehow things never get clean enough when the work is left to you."

"But you have to go and open the bottega," Il Piccino protested, brushing dust off his trouser leg.

"The bottega can wait."

In fewer minutes than Il Piccino would have imagined possible, the floor was swept, the newspapers were folded and piled up in neat stacks, and boards were hammered over the windowframe to keep the inside in and the outside out, while plans were made to order a new pane of glass. The sun was rising only now, yet already today Il Piccino had had cause to feel more varied emotions than he had felt since he could not remember when. Seeing the eagerness with which people helped him, he did not know what to think, so he let himself be led by the direction of their goodwill. The cruelty of the rock had toppled his sense of balance in the world; now, with people quick to make things right, he felt as if in falling he had been caught by unexpected arms. Could he let himself trust?

"I inform you all," said the *comandante*, getting no backup, not even from his own officers, "that you are interfering with a police matter."

Nobody wasted a word of reply.

19

The fight for territory between pieces of land was nothing new. Who could be surprised, therefore, when one slab of planet gave its neighbor a *move over* shove?

A stretch of forest on the old volcano of Monte Amiata lurched at the earthquake's epicenter. Seismic waves raced out in concentric rings, primary waves expanding fast at four miles per second, slower secondary waves at two and a half miles per second. Slower still but stronger, surface waves made the ground ripple and roll, like a gigantic carpet held at the corners and snapped into shape.

The ranks of waves weakened by the time they descended from the mountain, crossed the Val d'Orcia, and climbed the hills toward Sant'Angelo D'Asso. Destructive power dissipated as the waves traveled the more than thirty miles to the town. All the same, the approaching vibrations held enough violence to give the valley of the River Asso a good shake.

At the town cemetery, the arrival of the shock waves rattled bones inside their coffins.

On the hillside behind Renato's house, the four grazing sheep felt the earth hum beneath their hooves. Panicking, Lola ran here and there, looking for some piece of ground that did not move. Quarta, ever with a taste for the dramatic, listened for what she took to be Death's advance.

When the vibrations crossed the river, the old stone bridge buzzed but held firm. The town walls bounced as the waves climbed toward the central piazza. In the houses, plates danced in the china cupboards and hanging lamps started to swing. At the bottega, bottles trembled. Coffee cups rattled in their saucers. *"Madonna bona!"* Tonino swore in unison with his customers and he held tight to the bar.

"This is all we needed," Maria Severina said, grasping a table when her stout body began to vibrate. "An earthquake to top off our troubles."

The waves rolled under the paving stones of the piazza and reached the church. Inside, the building rumbled as if the organ were stuck playing its lowest note. The faithful clutched the backs of pews. Don Luigi had just finished giving out the eucharist and was maneuvering with difficulty to carry the communion plate back to the altar while supporting himself on his crutches. In a niche beside the altar, an ancient glass globe held the town's most sacred relic: the right index finger of the patron saint, Sant'Angelo. The priest had nearly reached the altar when, feeling the floor quake beneath his feet, he glimpsed a nauseating sight. The trembling of the church made the sainted globe stutter toward the edge of the niche. The bones and blackened skin of Sant'Angelo's finger seemed to come to life and wag in admonition.

Moving as fast as he could, the lame priest wished he had more hands. He tried to set the communion plate on the altar, balance himself on his crutches, and grab for the hopping finger before it smashed to the floor.

The communion plate made it safely to the altar. Don Luigi, however, fell. The seismic waves moved on and the glass globe with the finger froze in dead equilibrium, still inside its niche. Don Luigi collided with the ground. He howled in pain.

Congregants rushing to help him discovered that the plaster cast around his broken leg had cracked open. Plans were made swiftly while the priest held his leg and moaned. A car would take him to Siena to have his leg reset. Someone had the presence of mind to push the glass globe securely into the depths of the niche.

——

"We've survived this, too," said townspeople, relieved that the tremor had caused no serious damage. A few broken vases, some fallen picture frames and chipped plaster cornices, but no loss of property or human life. In the earthquake's aftermath, however, came a devastating sense of dread. Terra firma had proved itself not solid at all but sickeningly mobile. If people could not rely on the earth to hold still, then what could they trust?

The eyewitnesses to Don Luigi's misfortune harbored a more monstrous fear. Not nature, they sensed, but a cruel intentional force had invaded the holy territory of the church. Their town had become a cosmic battlefield. Victorious, for the moment, Wickedness had made none less than the priest its victim. "Evil is upon Sant'Angelo D'Asso," the pious congregants said to each other. God and the Devil, they believed, were wrestling with each other, competing for control of the town's fate, and the earth had trembled with the force of their struggle.

The more superstitious read the priest's fall as proof of his weakness. If Don Luigi is a general in God's army, they thought, then the powers of Goodness don't stand a chance. Eager to follow a mightier leader, several congregants deemed Emanuele Mosè a more virile combatant against demonic onslaughts.

So it was that the earthquake drew to the magnetic young healer a handful of fresh followers. New visitors knocked on the door of the Innocenti family, ready to offer cash in exchange for hope.

20

I must have been very bad in a previous life, the band conductor said to himself as the liquid harmonies of Verdi's "Caro Nome" curdled to cacophony. Yes, I must have been nastier than a snake. And the payment for my sins is now. Here, boxed in by the moldy plaster of the auditorium walls, here, on this podium where I must stand forever in front of this band that makes little music and too much noise.

Baldesi wanted to scream. His screams would not have clashed with the sounds coming from his musicians. Restraining himself, he tapped his baton on the music stand until they stopped. "Flutes," he said in as gentle a voice as he could manage, "if I ask you to play softly, why do you take it to mean that I want you to blow yourselves blue in the face? Maybe I explained it badly. When I say the notes should be soft, I mean soft. The contrary of loud. We're trying to make music, no? Listen to the lightness of the phrase: *nya-ta-duh-duh-duh-duh-DYA-A-A, nya-ta-duh-duh-duh-duh-DYAH.* But don't play softly because I've asked you. Do it because Giuseppe Verdi has asked you. See? He went through all the trouble of writing *piano* here. *Piano,* please. *Piano.* Softly. Even better, go ahead and pencil in two *p*'s, not just one. Play *pianissimo,* if you can. Three *p*'s and I would be ecstatic. It might sound less as if you were whistling to get the pigs back in their stalls."

The reference to whistling for pigs got a laugh out of the band.

He tapped on the music stand until he had the musicians' attention once more. "Now listen. If we want to have this *Rigoletto* medley ready for the Easter concert—and Easter isn't that far away—we'll have to get our heads inside the music. *Mi raccomando*, everyone. Don't forget. Play not just with your fingers and lungs, but with your heads, too. And this time, *per favore*, let's try to give Verdi the *piano* that he's asked us for. *Un soffio* it should be here. A little breath as light as the breeze. One, two, three . . ."

"Excuse me," interrupted a pimply teenaged girl among the clarinets. "Where are we taking it from?"

The conductor sighed. "Same place we've been taking it from for the past five minutes."

"And where would that be?" asked the bass drum player, the oldest band member. Which did this grandfather have less of, the conductor wondered: hairs beneath his cap or teeth in his mouth?

"What difference does it make whether you know where we are or not?" said Baldesi, fighting hard not to lose the smile that stiffened on his lips. "In this piece, there's no bass drum. You don't play."

"I play when I feel like playing," the octogenarian protested, "whenever I think the music needs a good strong beat. *Foom! Foom!*"

More laughter from all quarters, and Baldesi could feel the reins of this ungovernable beast of a band slipping from his grip. "Listen to me, Signor Foom-Foom. There's your error, right there. You shouldn't have to decide when you feel like playing. The music in front of you tells you when to play and when to stay quiet. In this piece, for example, do you see any notes for the bass drum? None. See? None. That means, 'Don't play.'"

The old musician was unconvinced. He smiled, closed his eyes, and shrugged. "You know I can't read music."

"You don't have to read music to play the bass drum. All you have to do is count. And there's nothing to count in this piece because you don't play."

"Counting was easy when I was young," the bass drummer began, and the conductor knew that a sentence starting this way would have a long road to travel before it reached its end.

Stopping the old man's speech from shifting into gear, Baldesi tapped for attention with his baton. "'Caro Nome,'" he said. "Once more. From the top. And one, two, three . . ."

Huffing with the other saxophones, Daniele kept losing his place. Strange, because he was usually alert, so much so that the other players in his section were accustomed to taking cues not from Baldesi but from him. When he put the sax to his mouth and took a deep breath in, the others knew it was time to play.

Tonight, though, the sounds that glided and squeaked and boomed and moaned inside the old auditorium had nothing to do with the separate piece of music that played like an obsession inside Daniele's skull. Why is it that some tunes are slow to enter your ear and impress themselves on memory, while for others one quick listen is enough to fix the notes inside your anatomy and make the melody an everlasting part of you? Daniele had heard "Sicut Cervus" only once, when he had caught Petula listening to the tape given to her by L'Altro. He could not understand the Latin words. One word, though, he did catch: *desiderat*. He knew the word spoke of longing, and everything in the music—the crystalline simplicity of the theme, the subtle intricacy of the counterpoint, the sensuous overlapping of voices—told of yearning for love beyond the ordinary, love that reached toward the sublime. What man could have written such notes?

Sicut cervus desiderat ad fontes aquarum . . . The rising line of melody soared unrelentingly in his head. It had become for him the song of pure desire; it had become Petula's song. He had seen enough movies in his life to know that the heroine got a signature theme of her own. This had happened now for the woman inside his thoughts. He could not envision her without hearing what he had come to name "Song of Petula."

Despite the music's sunlike radiance, it resonated in him with a tragic kind of depth. Tragic, because he knew that the music to her connoted another, not Daniele himself. It had been given to her, no doubt, as an expression of the longing that pulsated inside that other heart. How did she hear the phrases? Had they become another man's theme in her head? Tragic, because Daniele had turned into the eavesdropper, the spy, the uninvited watcher at the window to her desires, and he could not deny that he was the one to have exiled himself from her.

At the bar this morning he looked at her while she served the customers. He studied her through what he imagined to be other men's eyes. She was more beautiful than he had ever noticed. Her hands, her eyes, the curve of her hips. Had he ever told her that he found her lovely? How could he tell her now? Fear had made him seek distance: fear of inadequacy, fear of his frustration, fear of harming Petula and Beniamino in his own rage. Daniele said nothing in the bar this morning. He tried to look away, but neither he nor the radio playing in the bar could silence the music in his head.

Desiderat. He ached with the beauty of the piece, equal in his mind to Petula's beauty. Whom could he blame but himself if that beauty was no longer his to cherish?

He thought about the way she recoiled the other day when he had tried to give her a kiss. A simple kiss! What an innocent offer it had been, when Daniele would have preferred to pull down the shutter over the front door, close up for an hour or so, and make love, right there and then. But Petula had not wanted even the kiss. "Daniele, don't," she had said, sponging away at the tabletops as if the tables deserved her attention and he did not.

Or could it be, Daniele thought, that Petula had refused him because returning his kiss would have meant betraying the son of a whore who gave her the tape?

And two, and three, and four. Daniele lifted the saxophone to his lips and drew in a big breath to get him through the long phrase ahead. The other musicians in the section followed his lead.

After the rehearsal, Daniele was in no hurry to dismantle his saxophone. He watched the others leave one by one as he dawdled, wiping the spit out of each piece, then putting it carefully away in the case. He wanted a word with the conductor without other listening ears.

"Daniele," said Baldesi when they were alone. "What do you think of the Verdi medley? Think we'll have it ready in time for Easter?"

"Nice music," Daniele said. "Not too hard to play."

"Or at least it wouldn't be too hard," said Baldesi, taking a handkerchief from his pocket to mop his forehead, "if we concentrated a bit. Even you were screwing up this evening. That's not like you."

Daniele looked away. "Sorry." He waved a hand in front of his face to illustrate the confusion that had clouded his thinking throughout the rehearsal.

"Head too full of thoughts? You look distracted, Daniele. What's on your mind?"

Should Daniele speak? He was not in the habit of swapping anything more than friendly banter with this man, twenty years his senior. He was not in the habit of opening himself past small talk with anyone. Anyone except Petula. "It's nothing," Daniele said. "It will pass."

"So tell me."

"Tell you what?"

"What you waited for everyone to leave so that you could tell me."

"Nothing important." He was embarrassed. "A question really. But it's a stupid thing."

"*Coraggio,*" the conductor encouraged. "Ask."

"No, I was just wondering, you ever heard of a composer named Palestrina?"

"Ever heard of him!" Baldesi laughed. "*Sì.* I've heard the name."

"And you ever hear of a song he wrote? *Sicut* something?"

"'Sicut Cervus.' Motet for four voices. You know it?"

"Heard it recently. You know the melody?"

"Let me see," said Baldesi, remembering. "*La, la si la, mi la so do do re do, la re do re mi do.* Something like that."

"That's the one. Stays in your head, no?"

"Stays in your head, yes. And you were wondering—what?"

"Nothing," said Daniele. "Just wanted to know what you thought of it."

"Masterpiece of Renaissance counterpoint. One of the finest works the Western World has ever produced. But you tell me. What do you think of it?"

Daniele lowered his eyes. *"Bello da morì."*

The conductor had not expected this. Who would have imagined that this kid, this barman, would listen to a piece written for the Vatican in the sixteenth century and deem it "so beautiful you could die"? Baldesi's usual postrehearsal weariness lifted a little. The effort of prodding amateurs to make music seemed lighter in this moment, for he was reminded that there was something nearly noble in the endeavor. "If you want," he said, "I can get the sheet music for you."

"And what would I do with the music?" Daniele laughed. "It's for the voice. You think I screw up on the sax, you should hear me try to sing."

"As I say," the conductor repeated, "if you want."

Daniele started shaking his head, then he said, "I wouldn't mind taking a look. I want to see what the notes look like, the way they wrap around each other. I can't picture what kind of notes could make those sounds."

"Wrap around each other." The conductor smiled. "That's exactly what they do. Fine, then. I have to go to the library in the next couple of days anyway. I'll search out the piece. I can give you a photocopy next rehearsal. Sound good?"

"Grazie."

"Anything else?"

"Nothing," said Daniele. "That was all."

"Listen." The conductor was no fool. Besides, he had heard comments in town about disruptions in Daniele's life. "Everything going okay for you?"

"Everything's fine." Daniele picked up his saxophone case and headed for the door. *"Grazie mille.* See you soon. Good night." As if he had exposed too much of himself, suddenly he was in a rush to leave.

Walking home through the sleeping town, Daniele listened to Palestrina in his head for the thousandth time.

21

G REZZI'S SHOE REPAIR, Rosa Spina read from the sign over the door. The name promised nothing good. *Grezzi* meant coarse people. Opening the door, Rosa Spina hoped that the owner would not be crude like his name.

As soon as she entered the cramped, tiny shop, Rosa Spina wanted to leave. The February morning air out on the street was crisp and bright. Inside, the smell of Grezzi's cigar smoke nauseated her. *"Buongiorno,"* she said courteously, placing her high-laced boots on the counter.

Grezzi, behind the workbench, puffed on his cigar with thick wet lips. *"Buongiorno* to you," he said, drawing out the last word with a leering inflection. He narrowed his eyes to study his new client while blowing out a stream of sour smoke. "What can I do for you?"

Rosa Spina showed him the boot on the countertop. "The heel broke off. I was hoping you could glue it on."

"But certainly," Grezzi said, rising from his workbench and approaching the counter. Coughing, he picked up the boot and forced a fat hand inside. "You'd be amazed," he said, starting to expound on his favorite theory, "what you can tell about people from their shoes." He examined the boot as if it were a body part.

Rosa Spina did not see why, to glue the heel, he had to put his hand inside. And she did not like the idea that this unclean man might explore any of her secrets by pawing her footwear. "All it requires is a little glue," she said in her girlish voice. "If you sell the glue in tubes, I'm sure I could do it myself."

"But no!" he said. "I'll take care of the repair." His eyes shifted from the shoe, homing in on Rosa Spina's breasts instead. She pulled her shawl more tightly around her body to hide her cleavage. "You must be," he said, "Cappelli's tenant."

"*Sì,*" she said. "Signor Cappelli is kind enough to let us stay in his house."

"I'm sure he is," Grezzi said, smiling with his cigar between his teeth. "So you're the mother of the twins everyone's talking about. One works with Nuzzi, no? And the other I've seen sitting in the window up at Cappelli's."

"That's right," Rosa Spina said. "Do you sell glue in tubes?"

"It can't be easy for a woman to raise two boys on her own," Grezzi said, ignoring her request.

"The Lord provides."

"And so does Cappelli, I'll bet."

"Signor Cappelli is a good, good soul."

"Cappelli?" Grezzi laughed, phlegm rattling in his throat. "I would imagine." Peering over the counter, he looked at all of her, from the tips of her shoes to the crown of her head. "I have a son of my own, you know," he said. "I know how difficult it is. Ever since his sow of a mother walked out, I have to finish raising him myself. Children don't give much satisfaction nowadays, do they? They've forgotten what it means to obey. Twenty-one he is. Me, I can't wait until he finds a job and goes to live on his own."

"Oh," she said, "I'm still happy to have my boys under the one roof with me."

"Mothers are like that, I suppose. All the same, three mouths to feed"—he stared at her lips—"that's a lot of responsibility for one woman. I'll tell you what," he said, saliva glistening, "I don't have a big house to offer in return for services. No extra rooms at my place for you and your boys. But you ever feel like paying me a little visit and doing for me what I'm sure you do to keep Cappelli smiling, I'll repay the favor with cash."

Rosa Spina's cheeks reddened. "You have misunderstood my arrangement with Signor Cappelli," she said with dignity. "You have misunderstood, too, the person that I am."

She reached for the boots on the countertop, but Grezzi's fat fingers, stained black with shoe polish, seized her wrists. "I have eyes," he said. "I don't misunderstand."

Rosa Spina yanked her hands away. Grezzi held her boots hostage. He was angered now. He did not like to be refused. "You're an odd group, you and your family," he said. "At least the one son who works with Nuzzi knows how to labor. But that other kid of yours—" Grezzi shook his head. "Only point in his favor, from what I hear, is that he appreciates the importance of putting Jews in their place. Still, you won't see me coming to those prayer meetings people talk about. It's not normal for a boy to waste his life praying every day. A little activity with the female half of the human race is what he needs, I'll tell you that myself. Or maybe he isn't normal. Is that your son's problem? Isn't he a normal boy?"

With great speed, Rosa Spina snatched her boots away. Her body and her shoes free from his grasp, she took a step backward in the direction of the door. "You may misunderstand Signor Cappelli and you may misunderstand me. But no one speaks against my son," she said, fury in her voice. "The Lord will teach you the meaning of a parent's care for a child."

"Keep your gypsy curses to yourself," Grezzi laughed, puffing on his cigar. "You need cash and your shoes still need repair."

"I'll repair the shoes myself," she said. "Your problems won't be so easy to fix." She flung the door open and walked quickly into the fresh air outside.

Grezzi went back to his workbench. "Stupid whore," he said to himself, picking a fleck of tobacco off his tongue.

That evening Grezzi closed the shop early. Not a single customer had come in after Rosa Spina. Why waste the final hours of daylight with nothing to do? Locking up, Grezzi went home, put on his tall rubber boots, got his rifle and his son, and headed for the woods. Evening mist filled the valley early, but there was time for an hour of hunting before total darkness came. Dusk was good for hunting. Technicalities like licenses, legal seasons, and registered hunting squads did not interest Grezzi. Any animal foolish enough to appear in his gunsight deserved to end up as stew. A hare, a pheasant, he might even kill a boar.

Grezzi and his son walked separately through the dense undergrowth of the woods, where there was more dimness than light, reckoning that two pairs of eyes would have better luck in spotting prey if they searched independently. Grezzi's son had to bend almost double to pass through a tangle of pines. Grezzi himself, smoking a cigar, followed a fern-clogged path between oaks. The forest reeked of rotting leaves. Dampness made everything drip: trees, sharp-thorned bushes, moss-slippery rocks.

He heard a noise, a movement, and Grezzi was sure a wild boar had woken in its hiding place among the dead leaves and branches behind a thicket. He pointed his gun into the mist and shot. Approaching the carcass, he discovered that the animal he had killed was not a boar but his own child.

Occasionally life presents certain forms of agony that make further living appear impossible. When he had finished hugging his dead son, Grezzi sat on the ground, took off his own hunting boot and sock, and used his big toe to pull the rifle's trigger.

Other hunters would not find the bodies until the following weekend. Not much of Grezzi's head remained after the shot, but the position of the two corpses would allow the hunters to reconstruct the sequence of the deaths. Bad luck, would be the verdict townspeople would give in judgment of the incident. Two more deaths, two more graves for Sculati to dig, a double funeral for Don Luigi to perform. The local population fell to one thousand, two hundred and eighty-five.

Nobody would ever know that the final words to ring in memory through Grezzi's brain before he pulled the trigger were those spoken to him by a beautiful lipsticked mouth.

22

One clear gusty Sunday evening in early March, the bell in the church tower chimed six o'clock. Don Luigi pulled the rope of a smaller bell, summoning his congregation to evening Mass.

At the same moment, a prayer meeting was to begin in Emanuele Mosè's front room.

Out in the piazza, two impromptu processions approached at odd angles, crisscrossing, as wary of each other as battalions from unallied states.

The churchgoers were the bigger band, though they hardly amounted to more than fifty. Mostly widows, they were, and a widower or two, these pew-sitters and kneelers whose tongues had been mumbling the same remembered prayers for years, out of habit, out of the thirst for a drop of divine grace. Perhaps to escape loneliness, they wanted contact with the comforting familiar presence of Don Luigi, or maybe with God.

The other group—some twenty-five in number—was smaller but more ardent. Here were the people sure they had discovered new truth. God was on their side, they believed, because they alone had the perception to recognize the Lord's earthly mouthpiece in the person of Emanuele Mosè. They found in the house of the serious-faced young man an intense, hypnotic spirituality far more electrifying than anything the unchanging words of church liturgy could provide.

The two groups passed each other in the piazza, exchanging unfriendly looks. Such a rift would have been unimaginable only a few months earlier, back before Rosa Spina and her two sons arrived. Who would have guessed how easily factions could grow up, giving rise in turn to rivalry and distrust?

The churchgoers, eyeing the disciples of Emanuele Mosè, saw them as the mindless inductees of a cult, bewitched into adherence to something mysterious and dark. "I hear," whispered a widow whose thin white hair formed around her head a halo of unruly wisps, "that the mother drugs their tea."

"Imagine!" breathed another widow more than ninety years old. "That would explain a lot. Poor disgraced ones! Pray for them is all we can do. And maybe light a candle as well."

Emanuele Mosè's two dozen devotees, for their part, looked with disdain at the churchgoers, judging them as unenlightened creatures of stale routine.

Marta Sorcini, with Signora Porcelli by her side, walked in the ranks of the disciples. Marta did not look any of the churchgoers in the eye, and thereby avoided the necessity of exchanging so much as a *buonasera*. Her heart beat dangerously fast inside her mink coat. She hated to be surrounded by folk not of a like mind. She could not stand the pious *buonismo* of the churchgoers, that smiling self-righteousness of theirs. And to think, she thought, these goody-goodies still give their business to that evil little Jew.

The breaking of Il Piccino's window had catalyzed conviction on both sides. The followers of Emanuele Mosè came together, united in boycott, outraged that anyone should put money in the coffers of a nonbeliever whose people had earned eternal guilt by killing the Lord. The churchgoers, though unsure of the particulars, were pretty certain that it was no longer Vatican policy to bear a grudge. "The Pope pardoned the Jews not too long ago, didn't he?" they said to each other, and they carried on buying their newspapers from the shop that had always had their business.

Il Piccino—poor Piccino!—was far from peaceful. His heart had shattered into as many pieces as had the glass of his windowpane. Once fractured so thoroughly, can a heart ever be whole?

The new window had been ordered but had not arrived yet. This evening, wooden boards covered the shopfront, an ugly reminder of an uglier deed. The bell in the tower welcomed the churchgoers to their prayers while Emanuele Mosè's throng rang the doorbell at the house on the piazza and waited for Rosa Spina to let them in.

"Nel nome del Padre, del Figlio, e dello Spirito Santo," Don Luigi intoned.

His faithful made the sign of the cross and said, "Amen."

The priest's leg wore its new plaster cast. Though the leg had not broken again in the earthquake, the doctor said the second fall would retard the healing. However much Don Luigi despised superstition, every twinge from his sore bones made him wish his fortune might improve.

"The Lord be with you," said Don Luigi.

"And also with you," replied the congregation.

"Brothers and sisters, before we celebrate the Holy Mass, let us recognize our sins." A customary moment of silence followed, and the Mass was set in motion, its canonical path made plain by centuries of steady steps.

Emanuele Mosè stood with his back to the image of bleeding Jesus on the wall and the postcards and statuettes of the saints on the table. The ordering of the ceremony was his, and the people who had been coming for weeks knew by now how things would proceed. It being Sunday evening, this was the once-a-week chance for all the souls that put their faith in the extraordinary young man to combine their prayers as a group. Emanuele Mosè would speak first, offering his views on some theme that, uncannily, always happened to be on the minds of everyone present.

"Dearest spirits," he started, "we are met just as the first Christians were wont to meet. We are few. There"—with a hand in its fingerless glove, he pointed to the wall in the direction of the church—"they are many. They have amassed in a stone temple. We, instead"—he looked toward the kitchen where, from the fragrant steam of her cooking pots, Rosa Spina proffered a red lipsticked smile to all—"we are hud-dled in a humble home. The inevitable question that screams for re-ply is this: Which gathering is crowned by the favor of the Lord?"

From its box atop the fridge, the hen exclaimed, "*Clo-clo-clo?*"

History, Emanuele Mosè went on to illustrate, was rife with in-stances of the institutional corruption of God's word. Had not the Children of Israel been the Chosen People at first? But they forfeited their right to call themselves so when, thanks to their pharisaical bu-reaucracy, they loved the letter of the law more than the law's spirit. Was that not why God, seeking in his boundless compassion to renew the spirit, sent his only begotten Son, the Man despised and rejected, the Man of sorrows, acquainted with grief?

While Emanuele Mosè spoke, a sadness was visible on his face, a sadness so bleak that only the utterly unfeeling would not have been moved.

He recounted the story of how the Man, in repayment for His love, was crucified by the purported administrators of God's justice.

Then, after waiting for the horror of his recounting to sink in, Emanuele Mosè began again in a quieter voice. He asked his group to observe how in history's cyclical course the same awful drama was played out again and again. A church was founded on the teachings of the Rebel Divine. How long before bishops and cardinals substi-tuted the Pharisees of old?

The same tragic drama, he said with a sad smile, was happening today in their very town. The lovers of the institutional church still hold the power, he said, but God's favor remains with the blessed few—"with they who see with open eyes," he said. Extending his gloved hands to embrace the group, he said, "God's favor remains with *you.*"

"*Sì.*" His flock nodded. "*È vero.* It's true."

He himself, he pointed out, had no power but was a humble ves-sel of God's love. Had they not seen for themselves how, through this mortal conduit, God channeled His magnificent healing strength? Had they not heard how, through the young man's prayers, life had been restored to a sheep on that hillside over there?

He raised both of his gloved hands toward the window to indicate the hillside in question. The effect was supreme. Emanuele Mosè's eyes appeared incandescent with supernatural light.

"Now ask yourselves. How does that church"—he motioned with his head—"the church to which God sends earthquakes as punishment, how does that church regard *me?*"

Those at Mass felt the dampness of the air around their old bodies, the hardness of the creaky wooden pews beneath their bottoms, and the emptiness in their stomachs: Dinnertime approached. They had only to sit through the homily, then take communion, murmur the closing prayers, and be on their way. Not much longer now, they told themselves in answer to the grumbling of hungry bellies, if, that is, the priest doesn't get long-winded.

Leaning on his crutches at the head of the church, Don Luigi looked into the eyes of his aging flock and asked himself why. Why bother to sermonize? Why not just say *buon appetito* and let them go home? Isn't that what they want?

Protocol, however, called for a few words. Don Luigi made bets with himself as to how many minutes of sermon it would take before he saw heads nod in naps.

"Did you see what a beautiful day it was today?" he started.

"Come no? Sì!" replied a few of the more enthusiastic listeners. "Beautiful day, yes!"

Good trick to begin with an interactive question, he congratulated himself. Might keep them awake. "A day like the one we had today makes us think of spring. When we think of spring we think of Easter. And when we think of Easter, we must first think of Lent. Ash Wednesday is just around the corner. What is Lent, if not a time of preparation in which we make ourselves ready to relive the resurrection of our Lord, the annual rebirth of life itself?" There. He could see it: the first pair of weary eyes starting to close.

"This evening, however"—he spoke more loudly, hoping to rouse everyone with his tone—"in preparation for the preparation, we

might say, I want you to think for a moment not of our Lord, not of
the true Christ about to be crucified only to rise forth from the dead.
No. I want to open your eyes to that which is false."

He had succeeded in touching their curiosity, if nothing else, for he
could see that some listeners were anxious to hear his next words.

"'And Jesus answered and said unto them, "Take heed that no
man deceive you. For many shall come in My Name, saying, 'I am
Christ,' and shall deceive many."'' So we read in the twenty-fourth
chapter of the Book of Matthew, and these are the words I ask you to
contemplate this evening. 'Take heed,' the Lord says to us—to *us*—
'for many shall come in My Name, saying, "I am Christ," and they
shall deceive many.' Deceive. Lead astray."

Don Luigi smiled and pushed the glasses back up the bridge of his
nose. "I could talk to you about the Apocalypse." Smiling more, he
continued. "But I'll spare you gory quotations from the book of Revelation. I do not intend to speak about the Beast, or about the stigma
upon the right hand—the mark of the Beast—or about the false
prophet of the Beast. I want to talk to you—no, to ask you—about a
homier species of false Christ. I'm not referring to the End of Days;
I'm talking about *now.*"

He mentioned no names, but posed a series of questions. How are
we to discern between the true Anointed One of God and the falsi-
fiers who come in His name? How can people of good sense tell when
they are losing their senses?

In every era, he noted, false prophets have appeared to tempt
Christians away from the Church, charismatic charlatans who, endowed with no scruples but much charm, have shown themselves
capable of recruiting a following among the misguided. "We should
neither criticize nor judge our brethren when we see them stumble
from the Path. To the contrary; we must call to them with the voice of
love and await their return with arms"—he opened his arms as wide
as the crutches would allow—"ready to re-embrace. We should pray
that soon they might rebuild the foundation of their faith on true and
solid ground." He glanced sideways at the mummified finger of the
saint in its glass globe. It remained still.

He spoke and was gratified that not too many heads drooped in slumber. He was soberly aware, at the same time, of the futility of his words. The souls in real peril, he knew, were not these present, but those in attendance at the coven in that other house on the piazza. Inwardly he chastised himself while his mouth carried on making words, for he knew it was cowardly of him to speak within the safety of his own church. If he had any conviction, he prodded himself, he would have to confront his beastly adversary eye to eye.

In Rosa Spina's apartment, just downstairs from Cappelli's rooms, Emanuele Mosè gazed at his followers and awaited their individual requests.

He did not look directly at Marta. He had a slight headache this evening and did not feel up to handling the nerve-wracked woman with the violet-tinged hair. Peripherally, though, he kept an eye on her, hoping she would stay quiet. He could see her shaking her head tremblingly as if in negative reply to some question in her perpetual argument with herself, the tiny flywheels inside her skull whizzing ceaselessly of their own momentum.

But I can't ignore her, Emanuele Mosè reminded himself. She's already given a good chunk of her savings, as Rosa Spina frequently pointed out. No, mustn't let Marta feel unloved.

He conceded her a compassionate smile, then closed his eyes and nodded, as if to communicate to her, "You need not even ask. My prayers are with you already, dear one, as they are always." And this was precisely the message that Marta received from the gesture, for she smiled back and, mercifully, held her silence. Relieved, Emanuele Mosè looked away.

His attention came to rest on another woman. Could well be her turn this evening, Emanuele Mosè thought while his now expressionless face looked into hers. She's a volcano ready to blow.

Genoveffa was her name. Her appearance revealed a fearsome force. She ran a pig farm not far from town. The rank odor of pigsties permeated her clothes. Her payments to Emanuele Mosè and his family were usually in the form of salami, sausages, and hams from the animals that she had nurtured and slaughtered herself. Her husband, everyone knew, was of no help. He had drunk and smoked himself to a grossly premature stroke. He lived in his wheelchair now, limp-limbed and wordless as a fallen scarecrow. Genoveffa had not reached fifty yet, but her uncombed fox-colored hair had turned mostly gray and the teeth still clinging to her gums were few. Her eyes, however, were alight with vivid animal passion, and Emanuele Mosè was not certain that the relief she craved from him was altogether spiritual in nature.

Genoveffa looked searchingly at the young man's immobile face. Then she noticed that one of his eyebrows rose a little. A request it seemed to her. A prompt. She interpreted the meaning of the eyebrow's movement. *Are you going to do something,* it seemed to say to her, *or not?*

Suddenly, with such violence that the hen jumped in its roost on the fridge, Genoveffa exploded in screaming sobs and hurled herself on the floor in front of Emanuele Mosè's feet.

Rosa Spina looked up from her cooking pots in the kitchen. Hardly surprised, she kept stirring with her big wooden spoon.

The guests, however, were horrified. "*Che c'è?*" Signora Porcelli asked. "What is it? Are you all right, signora? Are you not feeling well?" Everyone stood from their chairs to get a better view.

Genoveffa's eyes rolled wildly. "It's inside me!" she managed to spurt out between shrieks.

Emanuele Mosè stood above her, steadfast as the statue of a saint. "Tell us," he said.

"It's inside me! It's inside me again!"

"What is inside you?" His voice betrayed no fear.

"*Il demonio!*" she gurgled. Inside her open maw, her crimson tongue writhed like a fat earthworm cut in half. Saliva trickled from the flabbiness of her lips. "The demon again!" she screamed, her blood-engorged face contorting hideously.

"Again, you say?" Emanuele Mosè asked.

"He's been inside me before and now he's inside me again!" The palms of her hands were planted flat against the floor as were the soles of her shoes. The middle of her body bounced in paroxysm. The bucking of her hips pushed her skirt up her thighs, well past her knees.

"How long has this presence been inside this woman?" Emanuele Mosè interrogated the others.

"Never seen it before," murmured Marta. "But she's always been a bit peculiar."

"You mean your village priest has done nothing to unmask a hidden demon?"

"Don Luigi wouldn't know a demon if it bit him in the balls," spewed Genoveffa with remarkable lucidity for a woman so brutally possessed.

"Then there is no choice," said Emanuele Mosè. He knelt beside the woman whose hips thrust upward in feverish *accellerando.* "I'll have to do it myself."

She trembled visibly when she saw that he spread his glove-covered hands a few inches over her body. "You mean to touch me with *those?*" She brayed raucously, as if something malevolent inside her had commandeered her larynx and throat, utilizing them for its own wicked ends. "You intend to touch me with those hands?"

"No fear, sister. No fear."

"Help me!" she cried out, this time with a voice that seemed her own. "Please!" She reached up and grabbed his hand and squeezed his palm to her breast. "Feel how fast my poor heart beats. Help me, *ti prego!* I beg you!"

Emanuele Mosè's composure disappeared for a moment. He was touching, after all, the abundant breast of a woman more than twice his age. People present in the room would later swear, in their recounting of the incident, that they saw him blush.

He looked toward the kitchen. His mother smiled back. Her head gave two little nods, urging him on. *Vai!* was the wordless message of the minute movements seen only by her son, for all other eyes were concentrated on the placement of the young hand on the older breast. *Go on,* Rosa Spina seemed to urge silently. *You can't stop now.*

Shaken yet obedient, Emanuele Mosè continued the service he was providing the woman on the floor. He removed his hand from her breast, however, and with both hands took firm hold of her savage-haired head. She grew rigid under his touch. Her gums pressed together and her lips parted in a grotesque grin.

"*Fuori!*" Emanuele Mosè ordered, looking hard into her eyes. "Out! Demon, I cast you out! In the name of the Father, and of the Son, and of the Holy Ghost!"

Her back arching, Genoveffa squealed like a sow giving birth. Then she collapsed.

"*Madonnina!*" said several people in the group, seeing that the woman's fit had passed as swiftly as it had come upon her. Her breathing steadied while she lay on the floor now, conscious still, but empty of all strength, tranquil as the sea when, by miracle, the tempest has passed.

Exhausted, Emanuele Mosè let his chin fall to his chest.

Refinding his energy, he stood and helped Genoveffa to her feet.

"Maybe the signora would like a nice cup of tea?" Rosa Spina, walking from the kitchen, had the steaming drink ready in her hands.

"*Grazie,*" said Genoveffa, smoothing her skirt back down over her knees. She accepted the cup and saucer. "A little tea, yes, please."

The astonished people who had watched this liberation relaxed when they saw her seated once more on her chair.

Sitting down in her own chair, Marta was, for once, speechless. Never had she witnessed such a scene. Never in church. Never in her worst dreams. Never. The heart in Marta's fragile chest could not keep pace with the terrible speed of her agitated thoughts. Was it possible that Genoveffa had truly been possessed? Had it been only the feeling of spring in the air that made her so frisky, or had it been a demon indeed? Well, why not? She always had been a strange one, that Genoveffa. *Something* inside her had often made her seem more ferocious than even the most aggressive of hogs. And maybe that dark demon, finding itself face-to-face with the sunlike brilliancy of Emanuele Mosè's unquestionable faith, had been forced to abandon its hiding place.

Which entity was it, though, who grabbed Emanuele Mosè's hand and squashed it onto Genoveffa's breast? Genoveffa or the demon within? How would Marta ever explain that enigma when retelling the story in the days to come? That was one thing for certain, that Marta would recount the incident to anyone with half an ear to listen. A story like this was too good to keep to herself. But I'll say this, she already knew she would say. He didn't take advantage of the situation, the way other young men might have. He was a perfect gentleman through it all. That's what I'll tell people because it's true. A perfect gentleman, even in the middle of casting out demons. No impure act on his part. He even seemed in a hurry to take his hand off the woman. Untouched by temptation he is. Incapable of sin.

The thoughts of the other disciples in the room were no different from those in Marta's head. Misgivings about Genoveffa's integrity might prove longer-lasting than the demon itself, but Emanuele Mosè emerged from the crisis with angelic splendor. He had performed a miracle before the eyes of his followers, and *that* was beyond doubt.

"The Mass is ended," announced Don Luigi. "Go in peace." He paused before leaving the altar. He was tired, wearied by the difficulty of the present moment in the life of his congregation. At the same time, he observed that the faces in front of him were those that he had seen in this church for too many years to count. "*Buonasera* to everyone," he added, hoping his voice sounded more like that of a friend than that of a priest.

"*Buonasera* to you, Don Luigi," a few parishioners answered back.

"And *buon appetito*," he wished them before hobbling on his crutches to the sacristy.

The exorcism seemed to have put a natural end to the disciples' prayer requests this evening. No one knew how to ask for help without appearing frivolous by comparison.

Emanuele Mosè wasted little time in closing the meeting, thanking the Lord for His limitless healing might, and nodding then to the people that it was time for them to leave.

The group members got their coats and, on their way out, demonstrated special generosity in the offerings they stuffed into Rosa Spina's hands. "I'll make a little withdrawal in the bank tomorrow morning," said Marta, leaving, "then I'll be back in the evening with a gift for your family."

"Not necessary," said Rosa Spina, "but your freely given contribution will be much appreciated, as always."

"Tomorrow," Genoveffa said, "I'll come by with a prosciutto for you all. The whole ham." She glanced at Emanuele Mosè. "No, make that two. Two hams and some of the special pigs' feet that I cook up myself."

"The Lord will love you for your kindness." Rosa Spina smiled, guiding Genoveffa and the other disciples to the door.

When the people had gone, Rosa Spina returned to the kitchen. "Everything's cooked," she said to her son. She stirred, then laid the wooden spoon on the counter. "You were very good this evening. Managed to satisfy everybody, *especially* that woman what's-her-name. She certainly enjoyed herself, I'll tell you that."

"It was obscene," said Emanuele Mosè. "She was shameless. She wanted her needs met, right there in front of everyone."

Rosa Spina raised her eyebrows. "The others will talk about the miracle for the rest of their lives."

"Miracle," Emanuele Mosè said darkly. "I didn't want to touch her." He looked at his glove-covered palms. "She forced me. It was obscene."

"Don't be so uncharitable," his mother said with lovely and irresistible lightness. "Who are we to pick and choose among the little jobs assigned to us in doing the Lord's work? And how can you be so sure," she said with the mystifying tone he had heard since childhood, "that you *didn't* cast a demon out?" Her beatific smile left no room for reply. "Come here."

He did as he was told.

She reached up on tiptoes and gave him a long kiss on the cheek.

Then with her thumb she wiped off the lipstick left on his skin. "Wash your hands," she said. "It's time to eat."

Out in the piazza the two flocks crossed paths once again, every head more convinced than ever of the wrongness of the other point of view.

High above the streetlamps of the piazza, the moon was serene. It had been, after all, a beautiful day.

23

B efore the prayer meeting had finished in the downstairs rooms, Cappelli heard the noise. The hysterical shrieking from below clashed with his tranquil mood, for Cappelli, soaping himself, was busy concentrating on the gentle sound of bathwater lapping against the sides of the tub. He had been bathing a lot in the last few weeks, finding pleasure in the sensation of floating among the suds. Bodily cleanliness seemed in keeping with other recent discoveries: the bliss of fresh sheets and crisply ironed clothes. There was another reason, too, for his frequent visits to the tub. Truth was, though never would he have admitted it, he wanted to look and smell nice for Rosa Spina. Shaving had become an almost daily habit. And though he had not gone so far as to have Domenico the barber devise a new arrangement for his gray hair—he had always looked like an alarmed porcupine, so why change now?—he did shampoo regularly during his baths, for Rosa Spina had mentioned once that she liked the smell of his hair after he washed it. Almost everything he did these days was done, albeit unconsciously, to make Rosa Spina want to be with him in the privacy of his bed.

He had heard someplace that soldiers after war were visited by flashbacks—scenes of fear and horror relived infinitely in the mind. Cappelli, too, had memories of images and sensations that stole the spotlight of his attention, but his were of pleasure, not of dread. He would be digging a ditch, fixing a pipe, anything—for thinking about her made every job lighter—and he would taste her miraculous breasts on his lips, see her nakedness embellished only by the *coron-*

cina of rosary beads around her wrist, touch the softness of her skin with his fingertips, feel the unspeakable liquid heat that warmed him like bathwater when part of his body was inside hers.

He had been drifting in the tub now, his mind as light as opalescent soap bubbles, when he heard the hollers from downstairs.

A woman screaming. Definitely a woman. He shook shampoo out of his ears and listened. *"Madonna scrofa!"* he mumbled. Didn't sound like Rosa Spina's voice. Had it been hers, he would have run to her aid. But no, this voice belonged to another female, a woman who, by the sound of things, was more animal than human. Sounded like a sow giving birth, Cappelli judged, and not an easy birth at that.

The she-pig's shrieks were followed by the upset squalling of the hen that Rosa Spina kept. Downstairs, Cappelli thought, is starting to sound like a farmyard.

And what am I supposed to do if people down there are screaming? he asked himself. Nothing. Rosa Spina and her two sons can handle it. What goes on during their meetings is something I don't want to know.

They must have twenty, twenty-five people packed into the rooms down there, he figured, estimating the number of people he had seen enter beneath his window before he took his bath. And I've heard people say that, though payments are never requested, donations are always welcome. Twenty-five people who donate—what? A fiver each? Some people probably a lot more. But even five a head times twenty-five is a hundred and twenty-five each week. Times four weeks is five hundred a month. Plus what people donate one by one when they visit on weekdays. Plus what that son L'Altro earns for working half-time with Nuzzi. *Certo,* he calculated. Money comes to that family. But what do I care? It's their business. I'm content without rent from them. Poor, though, they're not.

Hearing the screams from the lower story, Cappelli knew it would not be a good moment to go downstairs to find out if dinner were on offer this evening. Certainly no time to nose out whether or not Rosa Spina had intentions of paying a nocturnal visit to his bed.

He did not want to spend the next hours alone in his rooms waiting for the answer. He pulled the plug in the bathtub, reached for the towel, and decided to go out and get himself a little grappa until he could be more sure that dinnertime had come.

Walking down the stairs, he heard mumblings. Emanuele Mosè's voice, probably. Cappelli did not listen to that which he did not want to hear.

Outside, he walked in moonlight along the main road toward the bottega. Before he reached his destination, he ran into none other than his boss. Renato was not alone, but walked hand in hand with Beniamino.

"I was just going for a little drop before dinner," Cappelli explained. "Want to keep me company?"

Renato shook his head. "We've been indoors all day long, haven't we, Beniamino? And that's why I was given the job of taking the little one out for a mouthful of fresh air. We intend to walk from one end of the *corso* to the other, back and forth, for as many times as it takes to give this one some exercise and wear him out a bit. Otherwise he'll never get off to sleep tonight."

"Got to get to sleep," Cappelli said, trying to make conversation with the child. "Tomorrow's Monday, no? And I guess you have school to go to, right?"

The boy nodded.

"Then you want a good night's sleep before school." He stopped and heard the silence. Making conversation with a child, he discovered, was a thing that looked easy until you tried doing it yourself. "You like school? What do you do there?" He was fishing for an interested response. Maybe that was what you had to do: fish until you got a bite. He wasn't sure that he was using the right bait. Why did grown-ups always end up asking children about school?

"Teacher reads to us," Beniamino said.

"Oh yeah?" Cappelli cheered to have gotten a nibble. "What's she reading to you now?"

"*Pinocchio.*"

"Beautiful! *Pinocchio*. I think my teacher read that one to us when we were in school. That's the one about the little boy who wishes he could become a puppet, right?"

Beniamino laughed. "No. He's a puppet who wants to become a little boy."

"Right," Cappelli said. "I never was any good at school." He knew he was not coming off as the world's most educated person, but at least he had made the kid laugh. "So tonight you want to rest up good so your teacher can read you *Pinocchio* tomorrow. Need your sleep. Getting to sleep's no problem for me. Never has been. Truth be told, I love to sleep. If your grandfather here could convince the town government to pay me to sleep all day, I'd give them more than their money's worth, *Madonna dormigliona!*"

"Oh, Cappelli!" Renato exclaimed. "This is the way you teach the boy to curse?"

"What curse? Calling the Madonna a good sleeper isn't too bad, is it?"

Renato laughed, for only Cappelli could blaspheme with sinless innocence. "Beniamino, too," he said, "Beniamino was always a good sleeper. But lately—" He made a face. "Nightmares almost every night, eh, Beniamino? Then he lies awake for hours."

"No kidding? Why?"

"Too much going on in his head. I suppose he has a lot to think about these days. Don't you, Beniamino?"

Cappelli looked perplexed. "He's too young to worry."

"Oh," said Renato, "he's old enough for family things to worry him. Wouldn't you say, Beniamino? I can't blame him for having a head full of thoughts. A little nervousness is natural, given the situation."

Beniamino nodded, and his eyes studied the hand, big and grandfatherly, that held his.

Cappelli did not know what to say. He could not get used to Renato's way of talking to the boy. Renato spoke as if Beniamino were a little adult, a full person capable of openly discussing life's difficulties. Almost nothing was barred, Cappelli knew, in the talks between Renato and Beniamino, and Renato's ear was open whenever the boy wanted to reason things through aloud. No one had ever spoken to Cappelli that way when he was a kid, that was for sure. And now he felt just terrible, seeing a child suffering because of problems between his parents. Cappelli would have been the first to wave a magic wand to make everything okay for the boy, but he was one magic wand shy of having any. He felt inadequate and embarrassed to hear the boy's torments discussed with frankness when he could do nothing to help. Retreating from conversation, Cappelli said, "I'll let you two get on with your walk, then. I'll go and have myself that little drink."

"And you?" Renato asked. "You have a good day off today? You get to relax a bit?"

"The usual." Cappelli shrugged. "When we're not at work, I don't know what to do with myself."

They were walking by the window of the toy store. When Beniamino stopped to stare at the toys on display, Renato felt free to talk with Cappelli about grown-up matters. "How are things going," he asked, "between you and the woman in your house?"

"Signora Rosa Spina? What do you mean how are things going? Why do you ask?"

"Asking, that's all. Anything happening between you and her?"

Cappelli looked at Renato, then looked at the boy, whose concentration zeroed in on a train set. He said, "And would it be so strange if something were to happen between her and me?"

"Strange?" Renato smiled. "New, maybe. Big change for you. But strange? I don't see why."

"Good." Unexpected emotion came up quickly inside Cappelli, perhaps for the simple reason that someone he trusted wanted to know what was going on in his head. He was tempted to say that the woman had become the sun that burned bright in the dim world of his thoughts. Instead, he said, "And would it seem so strange if I said that I'm thinking maybe of the possibility of asking her to marry me?"

Renato's eyebrows rose high above wide eyes. "Serious as that, is it? Oh, Cappelli, this is a change indeed. In a way I'm not surprised. I thought you've seemed different lately. I've been trying to under-stand what it meant. That there's a woman in your life, this makes sense now. But marriage? Surprised I guess I am." He smiled and stopped talking, for he did not want to say a wrong word in what might prove to be a vulnerable moment in Cappelli's history. "I'm glad— How can I put this? I'm glad she makes you feel this way. Marriage . . . *È roba!* Serious stuff. But I think, understand me"—he put a hand on Cappelli's sleeve—"I think you should remember that if you ask her, then it means exactly what you just said."

"I don't follow."

"I mean you should remember that you would be *asking.*"

"I'd be asking," Cappelli said, missing the point. "Of course. Meaning?"

"Meaning when you ask, then the other person gives you an answer. Her answer could be yes, or it could be no."

"Why would she say no? You think she wouldn't want to marry me? Why wouldn't she?" Cappelli could not decide whether to feel offended or not.

"No reason for her to say no. She'd be a lucky woman if she said yes. I'm only saying that when you ask, you should be ready to get back either answer."

Cappelli perceived that the other man was trying to protect him from something, but until this moment he had not imagined that hurt might be possible. Did he need protection? "You don't think I should ask," he said.

"I think that you should do what your heart wants you to do." With a knuckle, Renato smoothed his beard at the corners of his mouth. "If you want to ask, ask. But keep in mind that her heart might, on the other hand . . . Who knows what's in her heart? Ask. You'll find out."

The color left Cappelli's cheeks. His hair, like quills, tingled on his scalp. "Or it couldn't be, could it, that you might have some interest in me not asking?"

"Me? Interest?"

"A beautiful woman like that, who could blame you?" Yes, Cappelli thought, stabbed by jealousy. He wants her for himself. "You have eyes. When your eyes see what they see, your brain"—with his hand he made a gesture next to his head to illustrate the workings of mental mechanisms—"starts to think its thoughts."

"Oh, Cappelli! What are you saying?" Renato raised his voice, making Beniamino look up from the toy store window. "You like that train set?" Renato said to distract him. "Maybe for your next birthday." Excited by the possibility that the train might someday be his, Beniamino returned his gaze to the store window with new concentration. Renato whispered to Cappelli, eager to finish the conversation. "My brain thinks its thoughts, *sì,*" he said too softly for Beniamino to hear, "but it thinks them about my wife."

"About Milena, without doubt," Cappelli whispered back, feeling he had discovered a scoundrel inside his boss's clothes. "But you're still a man, and man isn't made of wood." Cappelli's eyes grew large, partly in anger, partly in pain, as if he had been betrayed for real.

"Oh, Cappelli," Renato whispered. "Calm yourself. There are two reasons I would never take that kind of interest in your friend Rosa Spina. The first is that Milena would castrate me in my sleep."

"And the second?" Cappelli's eyes blinked while he tried to decide whether to forgive Renato.

"The second is that I care about you too much to ever do you a nasty trick like that."

"You care about me?" His anger abated. The pain of imagined betrayal, however, was slower to subside.

"*Sì,* Cappelli. About you." And there's a third reason, Renato thought. Rosa Spina, for all her exotic loveliness, did not look like a person Renato could ever trust. This reason, though, he kept to himself, for Cappelli, he knew, would not believe him and would only take offense on Rosa Spina's behalf.

"Fine then," whispered Cappelli, momentarily mollified. Realizing he had risked alienating his friend, he mumbled, "*Scusami.* This woman has upset everything inside me. You understand?"

"It's nothing," Renato said, putting a hand on Cappelli's shoulder. "Don't worry."

"*Bene,*" Cappelli said, now in a louder voice because he would be saying nothing not fit for Beniamino's ears. "I think I'll go and get that little drop of grappa. But what little drop! I need a double. My brain is starting to ache. I didn't think I had anything to worry about. Now I wonder if *I'll* be able to sleep tonight. Listen, if I don't see you at the bottega later on, I'll see you at work tomorrow." He took a step toward the toy store window and put his hand on Beniamino's head. "And you, *sogni d'oro* when you go to bed, all right? Golden dreams."

"*A dopo,*" Renato said.

"Until later," Cappelli echoed back. He trotted toward the door of the bottega, where the comfort of grappa awaited him.

Behind his shoulders, the square started filling. Mass now over, people came down the stone steps of the church. Other people were coming out the front door of Cappelli's house, but he did not turn to look.

As for asking Rosa Spina to be his bride, Cappelli did not know what to think. Just when he had aimed his courage in the direction of proposing, along came Renato to tell him that Rosa Spina might reject him.

The more Cappelli thought, the less he liked the cloud of doubt that Renato had placed in front of his sun-bright love for Rosa Spina. Almost completely, he believed Renato's denial of any personal interest in keeping Rosa Spina unattached, but now that the thought had arisen of another man having designs on her, Cappelli feared losing something that had become precious to him.

Why hadn't Renato simply congratulated him on his marriage plans and left it at that? Why didn't Renato wish for him the same happiness he had with his Milena?

He should have spoken up and told Renato to keep his cloudy comments to himself. Maybe that was exactly what he would tell Renato tomorrow. Maybe not. Cappelli no longer had any certainty about what to say or not. Now that doubt had bitten into his body, all tranquillity was lost. Maybe he would ask Rosa Spina to marry him as soon as he got home this evening. Or maybe he would wait until there could be no chance of a no from her beautiful lips.

Thinking hurt. The conversation with Renato had left a bitter aftertaste. He wanted grappa instead.

24

Hugging Beniamino to stop him from falling, Petula clung to the uppermost branches while the wind tried to uproot the tree. L'Altro sat on a nearby branch, his perfect balance undisturbed by the way the tree heaved. He smiled and said, "I am the wind. Why are you afraid? Come to me." Daniele leaned a ladder against the tall trunk and climbed to reach Petula. Crying, he screamed her name. He came close and kissed her lips. L'Altro became a snake that slithered between the branches, then coiled, stabbed its head toward Daniele, and pushed the ladder away. The wind increased. Dangerously, Petula leaned over and saw Daniele's broken body on the ground. When he looked up at her, she saw in his sad eyes that he had no one to help him, but that he pitied himself immensely. L'Altro became a hawk. He walked toward her, his talons digging into the bark of her branch. Afraid of the bird, Beniamino pressed his face into Petula's breast. "The wind is good," said L'Altro, opening his wings. "We need it to fly."

Suddenly furious, Petula thought, *Damn them both. How dare they? How do they presume? The tree is mine.* She kissed Beniamino's head while she set out to climb higher. The tree lurched sideways and started to topple.

Petula's heart pounded as she fell into wakefulness. She looked out the window and saw the first gray light of a chilly, rainy day. Ash Wednesday today, she remembered. She was surprised by a powerful need to go to church with Beniamino to get the boy and herself blessed. Unable to sleep again, she lay in bed and tried to make sense of her thoughts while waiting for the day to begin. Her fear from the dream would not leave her; neither would her rage. But the jolt of anger was not unpleasant. She felt awake, alive, open. She thought back to how Daniele had tried to kiss her in the bar. She thought of making love with L'Altro. Lent brought penitence, but she could feel no remorse. Was she sinning or setting herself free? Who could say what new direction her life might find during the season of rebirth?

After giving Beniamino his breakfast and getting him ready, she walked with him toward town, with one hand holding a big umbrella over herself and the boy. She saw L'Altro waiting on the far side of the bridge. His jacket was soaked. His long hair dripped, stuck to his head like moss on a wet rock.

"*Ciao*," Beniamino laughed. He had never before seen a grown-up who did not care about getting wet.

"*Ciao*, Beniamino!" The enthusiasm in L'Altro's voice implied that Beniamino was one of the young man's most favorite people in the whole wide world.

"No umbrella?" Petula called, crossing the bridge.

"It's only water." His earth-loving grin gave him the air of a madman or a saint.

"Come under," said Petula. "You'll catch cold. You're wet as a sponge." She held the umbrella high enough to make room.

Most men are quick to take control of any object at hand: umbrella or car or television remote control. L'Altro, this morning, did not. Was it lack of gentlemanly manners or adherence to the more modern code of chivalry, according to which the man should never make the woman feel that she is incapable of managing things herself? Perhaps L'Altro was reluctant to touch her hand on the umbrella handle in front of Beniamino. Whatever the reason, Petula had to smile, for there was something amusing in L'Altro's boyish way of letting himself enjoy her protection. Still, she could not lose the tension of her dream.

The three of them walked together. Anyone who had not known the people under the umbrella would have assumed them to be a close and happy family.

"I was hoping I'd catch your mother taking you to school today," L'Altro said to Beniamino. Apparently he noticed Petula's tension and seemed to think it safer to speak to her through her son. "I thought I'd keep you both company for a little piece of the road."

"We're going to church first," Beniamino said. "Mamma says it's Ash Wednesday and Don Luigi has to bless our heads."

"A blessing you'd call it?"

"Mamma says Don Luigi sprinkles your head with ashes and then says the blessing."

L'Altro stared at Petula. "'Remember, Man: Dust thou art, and unto dust shalt thou return,'" he muttered so that Beniamino could not hear. "That's what your mamma calls a blessing?"

"Something like that," Petula answered. With her eyes, she told L'Altro not to push the point in front of the child. The priest would say the words in Latin. What difference did it make if Beniamino didn't know their meaning?

"Well, what a coincidence!" said L'Altro. "Want to know where I'm going? I was just on my way to get my head blessed, too."

Petula said, "I didn't take you for a churchgoer."

"I could say the same about you. But maybe we both feel that a prayer wouldn't be out of place."

"I bet your brother's not going," said Petula.

"Emanuele Mosè? In church? No. He's too busy being the Messiah to pay his respects to the competition."

"You don't hold back when you talk about your brother, do you?"

"I'm just trying to tell the truth, though not many people are willing to listen." He looked down at Beniamino and said, "So tell me. What treats are waiting for you at school today? Your teacher still reading *Pinocchio* to you all? Remember when you told me about that?"

Beniamino nodded. "And today we find out what happens with Mangiafoco."

"Ah, Mangiafoco!" said L'Altro. "*Fantastico!* One of the best parts of the book. Great name for the puppetmaster, no? Mangiafoco, the Fire-Eater. And do you like Mangiafoco, Beniamino?"

"Like him? He's *terribile*."

"*Terribile*? Why do you say that?"

"Yesterday the teacher read us that Mangiafoco wanted to roast a ram for his dinner, but he didn't have enough wood for the fire, so he wanted to use the puppets as firewood. And he's about to burn Pinocchio's friend, Harlequin, only we didn't find out what happens because the teacher ran out of time. 'Grab Harlequin,' Mangiafoco ordered the wooden soldiers." Beniamino put on an ogrelike voice. "'Tie him up and toss him on the fire! I want my ram roasted well.' That's when the teacher had to stop."

"I see," said L'Altro. "So what do you think? Will Mangiafoco go ahead and kill Harlequin or not?"

"I don't know." Beniamino shrugged. "I'll find out today. I can tell you tomorrow, if you want."

"But I already know what happens to Harlequin," said L'Altro. "I remember it clearly. I've read lots and lots of books, but I've reread *Pinocchio* more than any of the others. It's never easy, trying to become real."

"You sound as if you recognize yourself in the story," said Petula.

"Probably so," L'Altro said. "I keep trying as hard as I can to be real."

Beniamino picked up the words that interested him most. "You know what happens to Harlequin? Tell me."

"Don't want to ruin the surprise. But you might get a clue, even now, if you really start to think about Mangiafoco as a character. How's he seem to you?"

"I told you! *Terribile*. He's a monster."

"Monster? But don't you remember what happens when he thinks about tender things?"

"Yes, but—"

"What does he do when he thinks about tender things?"

"He starts to sneeze."

"*Bravo*, Beniamino. He starts to sneeze. Maybe he doesn't know how to cry, so he sneezes. And does this sound like something a monster would do?"

Beniamino went silent. Petula looked down at the top of his head. She loved Beniamino whenever he went silent this way. A word came to her mind now, as it always did in similar moments. *Capino.* That Little Head. Beniamino in his silence, she knew, was trying to decipher the world. Petula could almost hear his fresh young brain at work.

They were walking through the ancient stone gate into town. Beniamino's quiet deliberations evidently had come to a verdict. "Then I think," Beniamino said, "that Mangiafoco won't kill Harlequin."

"And why do you think that?"

"If he sneezes because he can't cry when he thinks tender things, then he isn't a bad enough monster to kill Harlequin. I'm right, no?"

"You'll find out today, Beniamino. I won't tell you the answer. I'm not that easy to corrupt. But right or wrong, you did a good piece of reasoning in your head. *Bravissimo!*"

Petula looked at L'Altro. There was something rare in this moment. L'Altro certainly knew how to talk to a child. Was there anyone he couldn't talk to? Had Daniele ever managed to put himself so much in tune with the boy? The rain was punishing the stone street with chilling drops, yet three people walked together beneath the safe dome of the umbrella.

Seeming to read her mind, L'Altro put his hand upon the hand of hers that grasped the umbrella. The gesture would have passed unnoticed by anyone walking along the street. What could have been more innocent than for two grown-ups to share the duty of holding an umbrella over the head of the child that walked between them? Petula noticed, however, and her heart pounded. With or without the pretext of the umbrella, this was the first time she had walked along the main road of her town holding hands with a man who was not Daniele. A reflex made her wrist muscles twitch. For an instant she tried to pull away. What if Beniamino were to raise his eyes and see their hands joined above him? What would happen then?

"You used your head well," L'Altro praised the child, squeezing Petula's hand to hold it still. "And keep using your head when you lis-

ten to the rest of the story today about Pinocchio's adventure with Mangiafoco. I'll let you in on a secret. I'll share with you one of my favorite
thoughts, and, by pure coincidence, it's a thought that the book *Pinocchio* taught me. It's this: Always look for the good in people who seem
only bad, and don't be too quick to trust people who seem only good.
Keep that in mind as your teacher reads you the rest of the book."

Beniamino went silent again, then surprised Petula by uttering un-
foreseen words. *"Allora sarà vero anche per il mio babbo."*

"What?" said L'Altro.

"Then the same is true for my dad," Beniamino repeated.

Hearing her son speak of Daniele, Petula insisted now and pulled
her hand away, leaving L'Altro to hold the umbrella on his own.

"What do you mean?" L'Altro was off balance.

"He's not only bad."

L'Altro had not wanted the conversation to go this way. He had
been enjoying holding Petula's hand beneath the umbrella. Daniele
the Cow-Eater was the bottommost name on the list of people whom
he would have wanted to consider just then. The discussion had
slipped from L'Altro's control. For lack of anything better to say, he
said, *"Sì,* Beniamino. I'm sure you're right. If it's true at all, then it
would have to be true of your father, too. He can't be only bad." His
voice held no enthusiasm. "And it's natural, I suppose, for boys to
feel loyal to their fathers. . . ." L'Altro did not finish the sentence because he did not know where he wanted it to go. The sentiment was
not one that he had ever experienced. There had never been a father
to whom he could have been loyal. There had been Rosa Spina. Only.
Always. Since forever.

They were getting close to the piazza. Petula said, "I think you
should stop and buy a newspaper."

"But aren't we going to the church?"

"Beniamino and I are going to the church."

"I'm coming, too."

"Fine. But buy yourself a newspaper first. We shouldn't walk into
the church together." Her tone was as tense as if they had been fighting, though not a single unkind word had been said.

"We've walked together before."

"If I'm on my own with you, let people think what they want. But it's different when there's my son."

They stopped before the door to Il Piccino's shop.

In a softer voice, Petula said, "Keep the umbrella. The church is just there. Don't get wet."

"I was wet before you came along." He put the umbrella in her hand. "Listen. Everything's all right, isn't it? We'll see each other again, no?"

"Don't start thinking paranoid things. You say you watch nature programs. You should understand."

"Understand what?"

"That I'm a mother lion," she said. She saw the injured way he was staring at her. She saw the eyelids blink defensively. She was startled by how quickly L'Altro could appear fragile in her eyes. "Don't go worrying. Of course we'll see each other again. There's no problem. Really. Things just take time."

"Then no rush," he said, grateful for reassurance. The conversation was no longer unfriendly. He regained his equilibrium. "Tomorrow night?" he said with a grin. "No rush, of course. But what do you say? Tomorrow night?"

She smiled and lowered her eyes. "Tomorrow night."

"I think I'll check out what's in today's paper," said L'Altro. He wanted everything to be smooth with Petula. Looking down at Beniamino, he knew that everything was not smooth with the boy, who clearly had declared himself to be on his father's side. Unaccustomedly stuck for words, L'Altro could think of nothing to say to win back the child's favor. He patted Beniamino on the head, but the boy pulled away. "*Bene,*" said L'Altro to make light of the rejection. "I'll catch up with you both in the house of the Lord."

25

In the bottega the next morning, Il Piccino sat, eyeing the sweet pastry on his plate and milky coffee in his cup. The atmosphere indoors smelled deliciously rich, as if the air itself could be savored on the tongue.

Il Piccino poured sugar into his coffee, then, transfixed, noticed how the sugar formed a little floating island which, melting, became transparent before it sank. His nearly microscopic concentration revealed the extreme beauty of sugar as it dissolved, so beautiful that it pained him. Why had he never noticed before? Why did the world behave this way, showing its viciousness one minute, then disclosing its tear-inducing tender beauty the next?

The other people at the table saw Il Piccino lose himself in his cup of coffee. Nobody knew what to say. Sadness was difficult to witness, especially sadness of this quiet kind. Il Piccino was still a fresh wound, and no one was sure what touch would not increase his suffering.

There were other reasons, too, for discomfort around the table. L'Altro, sitting with Renato on his right and Cappelli on his left, glanced at Renato and thought: I wonder if this man knows that I've been sleeping with his daughter. Cappelli, for his part, did not dare look at L'Altro directly. He sat there thinking: I wonder what this kid would say if he found out that I've been sleeping with his mother. If she marries me, will that make him my son?

Cappelli was reluctant to speak again with Renato about Rosa

Spina. He did not want to hear Renato repeat the notion that Rosa Spina might reject him. The whole question confused his brain. He would have to resolve it, he knew, alone.

Nuzzi, also sitting at the table, thought of nothing in particular.

"Tonino!" Cappelli called suddenly to Milena's father behind the bar. "An extra drop of sambuca in my next coffee!" A nice little dose of alcohol would not make matters better but certainly could do no harm.

It was the arrival of the priest that changed the tone around the table. Entering, Don Luigi spotted the men and said, *"Buongiorno."*

"Buongiorno, Don Luigi. *Buongiorno."* They found him a chair and helped him settle in, leaning his crutches against the wall and getting an extra chair to prop up his broken leg.

Removing his hat, he stared at Il Piccino and saw the bleakness of the man's face. He took off his thick glasses, cleaned them with his handkerchief, and put them on again. "I'm glad to see you back in circulation. Glad to see you taking coffee again here at this bottega. Content, too, to hear that the more sane among your clients have not abandoned their patronage of your shop. All the same"—he searched for words—"it's my duty, I feel, I believe, my duty, that is, to apologize once again. That is to say, I'm sorry. Believe me, how sorry I am."

Il Piccino's eyes lifted from the coffee. "You were hardly the one to throw the rock."

"I personally, no. But how can I say?" With a long finger he adjusted the glasses on the bridge of his nose. "Nothing new, in any of this. Even our church has done its share—"

"Perhaps Don Luigi is referring to the Inquisition?" L'Altro prompted. "Or maybe to the foundation of the ghetto in Venice in 1516. Or to the ghettos in Florence and Siena in the 1560s. Or maybe Don Luigi meant the burning of the bodies of ten Jews in Siena, right in the Piazza del Campo, in 1799, hardly two hundred years ago."

The priest cleared his throat. "A history expert, eh?"

"History books are there for everyone to read," L'Altro said without a smile.

"Regrettably, the sons of the Church—my own beloved Mother

Church—have been all too quick to make a sacrifice of the Jews," said Don Luigi. "It's true."

"But why look so far back?" L'Altro continued. "The twentieth century abounds in hatred. Facism, Mussolini's racial laws, the last war—"

Don Luigi lifted a hand to interrupt L'Altro. "I don't think we need to remind our friend here of *that* experience." He turned his gaze to Il Piccino. "You lived through that yourself, didn't you?"

Il Piccino nodded.

The priest looked hard at the little man. "In short, *chiedo scusa,* I'm sorry that, with something happening like what happened to your store, some people have not learned a thing."

Cappelli dried his sambuca-drenched lips on the back of his hand. "*Madonna bona!* Excuse me for the language, Don Luigi, but *Madonna bona!* Burning bodies in the square! Tell me something. I know I don't know much about Christians or Jews or what the difference between them is if there is one, but tell me something: Why?"

The priest smiled. "Why the violence? Why the blood? *Bella domanda.* Good question, Cappelli. If I knew the answer, they'd make me the next Pope."

"Or perhaps the question's not so complex, really," L'Altro suggested. Strands of hair fell tormentedly around his face, giving the impression that his head was full of difficult thoughts. "Simpler than it seems."

"Simple you say?" Don Luigi squinted through his glasses to study the young man who imagined he knew it all. "Do you intend to offer solutions as simplistic and venomous as the advice I understand your brother is spreading around town? I was pleased to see you in church yesterday morning for the Ash Wednesday blessing, but your brother? Never seen him cross the threshold of the church. Not once. Yet he considers himself authorized to give counsel in matters of faith."

"My brother only gives voice to what people already think."

"And you, of course, are different from your brother, I imagine. So tell us, O young sage, what's your answer then? Why this hatred between the children of God?"

"Law of the Excluded Middle." L'Altro's face did not show the satisfaction of the only schoolboy to know the answer to an apparently insoluble problem put to the class. He seemed instead downcast, as if forced to be the mouthpiece of some tragic truth.

"A student of Aristotelian logic, are you?"

L'Altro hesitated, then lowered his head. "In prison, I read all sorts of things."

Watching, Renato wondered whether the young man was pretending to be humble or whether his embarrassment about his time in prison was genuine. No clear boundary divided L'Altro's seriousness from his playfulness, both traits endowing him with particular charm. Renato understood why Petula wanted to spend time with this young man, but he was afraid to think exactly what they did in their moments together.

"Care to let the rest of us know what you're talking about?" said Renato.

L'Altro raised his eyes with a look that everyone present took to be sincerely deferential. "I'm sure Don Luigi is far better equipped to explain a concept of this sort."

"No, please," said the priest with a small smile of challenge. "I'm sure we would all be curious to hear you explain yourself."

"Should I go ahead?" A smile appeared on L'Altro's face as well. *"Vado?"*

"Prego," said the priest. *"Vai."*

"Well," the young man began, "in its simplest form, the Law of the Excluded Middle states that something is either A or not-A; there is no third."

"Ah," said Renato. "With that explanation, I now see everything. Clear as mud."

Nuzzi the electrician laughed, refreshed to find someone else as confused as himself. He had a hard enough time telling the difference between a ground wire and a live cable.

"You catch a word of that, A and not-A?" Renato asked Cappelli.

Cappelli nodded and whistled through his teeth. "Sure. *Proprio.* I just know I could do with another little drop. Mouth feels suddenly dry." He raised his coffee cup toward Tonino behind the bar.

"You understand?" Renato asked Il Piccino.

"To tell the truth, no." Il Piccino's curiosity was aroused, even though the conversation so far seemed to make no sense. He liked the taste of the words that L'Altro had spoken, for they held the flavor of the geometry proofs that used to whet the appetite of the mind years ago in school. If nothing else, Il Piccino enjoyed the distraction from his anguish. He said, "My private studies appear to have overlooked this concept. A and not-A. Meaning?"

"Meaning," L'Altro went on, "that nothing can both have a certain property and not have it." He rapped his knuckles on the table. "What's this? Tell me. Table, yes or no? The answer must be like a light switch: on or off. Yes or no. There is no in-between."

"Table, yes," said Cappelli while Tonino poured more sambuca into his cup. "Even I can arrive at that. Of course it's a table. If not, what?"

"*Bravo*, Signor Cappelli," said L'Altro. "Law of the Excluded Middle. A or not-A. No third way. You've just applied the law. Here comes a trickier question." He knocked on the table again. "Solid or not? Feels solid, but any physicist would tell us it's really ninety-nine point nine nine nine nine nine nine nine percent empty space. There's the ultimate truth for you, and the truth is ambiguous to the core. To say nothing of murkier human judgments! A man and a woman fight: Who is in the right? If we can't find a single truth in answer to that simple question, God help us when we start to dabble in the salvation or damnation of souls!"

"Yes," said the priest with some impatience, "but the relevance?"

"To what?" L'Altro tilted his head as if nothing further remained to be elucidated.

"To why someone would paint a Star of David on a rock and use it to smash up Signor Trieste's store," reminded the priest.

"But that's evident, no?" said L'Altro. "A or not-A. That principle stands as the cornerstone of the Western world. Western philosophy is built on it, and Western science, Western religion, the whole of Western thought. And whether they want to admit it or not, Jews and Christians are hopelessly Western through and through, clinging to the Law of the Excluded Middle everywhere you look. We like our dualisms neat and tidy: good or evil, body or soul, life or death, human or divine, God or Devil, sex as sacrament or sex as sin. No middle ground." His words, like a thrilling piece of music, grew louder and faster, for he could not contain his own excitement in playing with an axiom that lay at the explosive epicenter of myriad other ideas. "The middle would make way for messy concepts like paradox, and ambiguity, and contradiction, and opposites that coexist in one and the same thing. No, no, no. Avoid contradiction at all costs we do. Allow contradiction, and the world we have constructed would collapse. That's why we're all so stubborn. The Jew and the Christian are no different from each other here, Westerners to the end."

"And the relevance?" the priest said again.

"Ah. The relevance." He knocked on the table once more. "Solid table, yes or no? Same question as regards the Lord. Jesus Christ: human incarnation of God Almighty, yes or no? The Jew says a stubborn no, but the Christian won't relent until everyone accepts his own stubborn yes. How's that for mental rigidity? 'No one can have God as Father,' as San Cipriano said, 'unless he has the Church as Mother.' Still, the Jews refuse to budge. There sits the headstrong Jew"—he pointed toward Il Piccino—"who says no to Divine Incarnation yet claims to be in God's good graces all the same. That's a position that no dogma-loving Christian can bear. They can't both be right. That would be A and not-A together. Result? Rock through the window."

Il Piccino, not entirely comfortable with being pointed at as *the headstrong Jew*, shifted in his chair. "Perhaps," he said. "But in the end, I don't know. My first temptation, the other morning when I saw what happened to the shop, was to leave. Run. Move away. But move where? If I can't handle the problem here, why should it be easier elsewhere? I'll tell you something. I was a child during the war. I hid when they rounded up my family and the other Jews in Siena to take them off to the camps. But it was Christians, different Christians, Christians that loved God in their way, who helped me hide out for the rest of the war and kept me safe. Christians in this town later on let me make a new life. So how can I think Christians bad?"

Don Luigi smiled at Il Piccino, then turned his gaze to L'Altro. "Yours," said the priest to the young man, "is a piece of logical argumentation not without interest. And I must say, your mind is not without particular capabilities, if developed properly. A shame it is that the university was not part of your—how shall we say?—education. You've read widely, I can see that. But perhaps your studies have been without clear direction."

"I'm the first to admit to being a magpie without method," L'Altro said. "I pick up twigs and scraps where I can."

"Nothing wrong with curiosity," the priest continued, "but this little syllogism of yours leaves me . . ." He spread his hands, then let them drop to his lap. "Hopelessly Western, you say?"

"The Eastern mind," said L'Altro, "rejects our sacred Law of the Excluded Middle. The East doesn't hide from more complex truth. 'Is this a table?' asks the East. And it answers, 'It is a table. It is not a table. It is neither. It is both.' To the Eastern perspective, opposites do not contradict each other but are different aspects of Oneness."

"Of course," said Don Luigi, pushing his glasses back up his nose. "Now I see. Your time away gave you opportunity to delve into Eastern mysticism as well. Perfect place for it, prison, to play with the yin and the yang—oh, I've done reading myself—the rejection of dualism, for the white contains the black and the black contains the white, just as good contains evil and evil contains good." His smile was calm. "Comfortable place, the prison must be, to find solace in such ideas. Convenient, no? But tell me, my boy, is it gratifying in the end to study without conviction, putting Eastern philosophy on one plate of the balance and your own native faith on the other, as if they had equal weight? Seems a pretty cold faith to warm you up at night. And your conclusions after your research? Are you of the East or the West?"

"I was born in Venice, don't forget"—L'Altro grinned—"the meeting place of East and West. I am neither. I am both."

"You do the Church an injustice," said the priest without losing his smile. "You say we run from contradiction? *Anzi.* We embrace paradoxes, I'll tell you that myself. Immaculate conception and virgin birth. There's paradox for you, no? The unity of the Trinity. There's another. And the Lord Himself: man and God in one. You can't tell me that we go looking only for simple, one-sided truth."

L'Altro laughed, as if the priest were slow to understand. "But dogma is the death of curiosity. Dogma claims to be the only truth. If a truth says to you, 'I am part of the truth,' then maybe it should be listened to. If it says, 'I am the only truth,' then we should fear that truth because it is a liar. Dogma orders the mind to back away. Just when the brain starts to probe, dogma blocks the doorway and says, 'Go no further. Everything past this is a mystery. Useless to try to think any more.' And with that, dogma slams the door."

"Mystery," Don Luigi echoed. "But divine paradox *is* a mystery. You have a better way to put it? To you *mystery* is a cowardly word?"

"It is the mark of intellectual castration," L'Altro said with a flat voice.

"To me," said the priest, "it's the most wondrous and beautiful word that exists."

"*Bravo*," said Il Piccino.

"Thank you," said the priest, bowing like a victorious gladiator.

"I remember once," Il Piccino said, "I heard a wonderful commentary on the story of Eden—"

"Marvelous story!" said L'Altro. "A world of meaning if you don't get stuck on the literal. See it as metaphor and it holds infinitely beautiful truths. Take it as history and it becomes a lie."

"As I was saying," Il Piccino went on, gently shirking interruption, "this commentary discussed an old question, the presence of the serpent in the garden. Why should a perfect place contain such a destructive animal? Because that's life, says the commentary. Every life is an Eden. Every Eden ends in exile. That's why for us Jews the story of Eden is not a tale of Original Sin. The serpent was no Devil. He can't be reduced to simple evil. He was like a catalyst in chemistry. He was *inevitable*. He was the agent of Change, and change comes to every life."

"The question of Original Sin," began Don Luigi, "is perhaps too prickly to be dismissed so—"

"Where would the Church be," L'Altro laughed, "without its cherished dogma of Original Sin? Without that mythic stain, what would there be to save us from?"

"My point," said Il Piccino, "is that according to this commentary, the serpent was A and not-A, to use your words." He smiled at L'Altro. "And another paradox," the little man continued, caught up in the excitement of uttering ideas that he rarely felt safe to voice. "My favorite one, this is. I remember my father—peace to his soul—before they took him and the family away. He told me something when I was too young to understand, but I've never stopped thinking about it, and it's helped me always. It was a thing that a great rabbi—can't remember which—once said. 'Go through life,' said the rabbi, 'with two slips of paper, one in each pocket. On one piece of paper should be written I *am nothing but dust and ashes*—"

"Exactly," Don Luigi intervened, relieved to have found a point on which he could easily agree with Il Piccino. "The very phrase I recite while sprinkling the heads with ashes on Ash Wednesday. Straight from the Old Testament. Book of Genesis, chapter three: *'Memento, Homo: te esse pulvis et in pulverem reverterebis.* Remember, Man: Dust thou art, and unto dust shalt thou return.'"

"*Sì,*" Il Piccino continued patiently, "but that is only half of the equation. One piece of paper in one pocket, as the great rabbi said, should say *I am nothing but dust and ashes,* but on the other slip in the other pocket should be written the words *For my sake was the world created.* Both, you see, are true. Either truth on its own becomes a half-truth. The fuller truth is a magnificent contradiction. 'I am nothing but dust and ashes.' 'For my sake was the world created.'" He put his hands on his hip pockets. "If you walk with both thoughts in mind, you can't wander far from the good path."

"*Bello questo,*" said the priest.

"Very beautiful, yes," said L'Altro. "And that's why I always look forward to my visits to your shop," he told the midget. "I could always see that inside that head was an intricate, subtle mind."

A quiet smile rose on Il Piccino's face. Never before had he dared reveal his mind as fully as he had done just now. Usually he limited himself instead to politeness when making pleasant small talk with his customers, and his own passion for reading he kept a secret. But he had opened himself to the men at the table this morning. Astonishingly, they seemed to approve of the man living inside the small body. Il Piccino could not help but smile.

Everyone at the table saw the smile, and everyone, even the priest, knew that L'Altro, like a gifted doctor with a nose for finding the proper remedy, despite the apparent eccentricity of his approach, had helped Il Piccino feel less besieged.

"I tell you one thing," Renato put in, "I can't remember the last time this bottega was home to a conversation like this. Eh, Milena?" he said to his wife behind the bar. This was what talking should be. Not the usual litany of medical complaints.

"Food for the brain," Milena admitted with reluctance, for she had been listening from the start. She could not deny L'Altro's virtuoso dexterity with clever words and notions, but she could not share her husband's enthusiasm. She did not trust the young man. How could she be kindly disposed to someone who toyed with her daughter's life? Food for the brain indeed, she thought, but maybe it's poisonous.

"I wouldn't know if it's good talk or not," said Milena's mother, Maria Severina, wielding a mop in her hands. "I try not to eavesdrop on other people's nonsense. But look what the bunch of you have done to the floor! You tracked in dirt." With her mop she made the men move their feet.

"*Certo*," said Tonino from the bar. "Interesting stuff, I guess, for people who have time to read."

Just then, the door to the bottega opened and Marta stepped in. As she walked toward the bar, her head tried to remember the few grocery items she wished to buy. Her pink-rimmed eyes saw no face in particular. "*Buongiorno*," she said to the room in general.

She was surprised by the specific voices that replied, for she received "*Buongiorno*" from Renato and Cappelli, "*Buongiorno, signora*" from Milena, Tonino, and Maria Severina behind the bar and from Nuzzi, Il Piccino, and Don Luigi at the table, and "*Buongiorno, Signora Marta*" from L'Altro.

She took a minute to connect the voices with the faces of the people who had addressed her, identifying them one by one. "Oh!" she exclaimed, then stuttered *"Buongiorno"* again. She stared at the table, amazed to see who was sitting with whom. There was that Jew. The nerve he had, she thought, to mingle with respectable citizens! And there was L'Altro, evidently at ease to sit so close to the Jew. Marta had been sucked into trusting this twin once in Il Piccino's shop, that time when they talked about the evil midget's Christless religion. Thank heavens she had had no dealings with this other ever since, but had stuck loyally to the company of the miraculous healer, Emanuele Mosè. But why was the priest sitting so casually in the midst of this coven? At the prayer meeting, Emanuele Mosè had implied that Don Luigi and his church, for all their piousness, were not on God's side. She would never have expected, though, to see a man of the cloth collude unabashedly with the Jew. As for Renato Tizzoni, he always had been too much of a liberal-minded dreamer for his own good. Why were these men here together? Was this bottega their meeting place?

A feeling of panic gripped Marta, as if she had stumbled unwittingly into a nest of enemy spies. She wanted to flee, but how could she run away without losing face?

"What can I get for you?" Tonino said.

Marta did not know what to say. She remembered the items she had come for. "A box of bouillon cubes," she muttered. "A packet of sugar, and some clothes-pegs."

Tonino went to get the items from the shelves. No one seemed to notice her alarm. She kept her ears alert to hear what scraps of the men's wicked discussion she might pick up, but their talk seemed to have finished.

Nuzzi rose from his chair. "It's time for us to get to work," he said to L'Altro.

"Us, too," said Renato to Cappelli.

"Just as well," Cappelli replied. "My head was beginning to swirl from all this talk. And I don't want to start to ask myself about the forces that are living under my roof. You hear the way the kid speaks?"

L'Altro laughed.

Il Piccino finished his coffee. "I think," he said, getting down from his chair, "I ought to get back to my shop and see what customers come in today. My thanks to you." He nodded at them. "To you all." He nodded courteously to Marta on his way out.

She twittered a nervous laugh in response.

After Il Piccino had left, the men helped Don Luigi to his feet. Leaning on his crutches, he stood before L'Altro. "I've enjoyed our talk," he said. "And I realize that there's another talk I should have, one that I've put off for far too long. I believe you know which person I have in mind."

"*Ah sì?*" L'Altro lost his smile. "I can't imagine who."

The priest gave a joyless grin. "I'll expect your brother this evening. In church. Right after Mass. That should give him time to finish with his—what shall I call the people who pay their evening visits to your brother's salon? Disciples? Customers? Clients?"

"Never know what to call them myself," said L'Altro, eyeing Marta and giving her a smile. "In any case, they are people who find exactly that which they seek."

"And what is your brother seeking? Money?"

"You should ask him yourself."

"I intend to. But you seem a decent enough young man, though a bit misguided. Maybe prison taught you a little something."

"We can all repent for our sins and change the course of our lives, no?"

"Indeed," said Don Luigi. "As far as I can see, you're the only member of your family whose income is the fruit of legitimate work. But tell me something about your brother. It is people's life's savings that he wants, no?"

How little Don Luigi understands of what it means to truly serve the Lord! thought Marta.

"I have to be sincere," said L'Altro. "Emanuele Mosè never asks. People simply give. But I will say this. He does know how to steer people's credibility. He's skillful with gesture. He's an artist with words."

Snake! thought Marta. Listen to how evil shuns goodness. I must tell Emanuele Mosè what a traitor his brother is.

Don Luigi said, "I'd like to hear some of his words myself."

L'Altro paused. "I'm not sure he'll accept your invitation. Spending time in church is not his style."

"And why not? If he's half as holy as some people claim he is, he should feel right at home in the Temple of the Lord. And he should welcome the chance to share his ideas with me. If they have any foundation in truth, he might even succeed in converting me to his following. Unless, of course"—he glanced at Renato and Cappelli and Nuzzi, then smiled at L'Altro—"unless he has something to hide."

L'Altro recognized that Don Luigi had issued a challenge and had done so in the presence of witnesses, in the presence of Marta, one of Emanuele Mosè's most devoted followers. Were Emanuele Mosè not to accept, word would spread through town that he was afraid to meet the priest face-to-face. "I'll tell him," said L'Altro uneasily. "But I take no responsibility for his choice. The decision is his."

"This evening after Mass." Don Luigi nodded. "Tell your brother I'll be waiting." He put on his hat. With a *buongiorno* to all, and with the aid of his crutches, he left.

"One thing, though." Renato put a hand on L'Altro's arm. "No theory from logic can convince me that taking a rock to smash the window of that poor man is anything but bad. No room for not bad. Just bad. But your conversation got me thinking. The words about pairs of opposites. Funny, if you think about it, when everyone in town is trying to work out which of you—between you and that saint of a brother of yours—is to be trusted. Funny those reflections should come from you, no?"

L'Altro smiled. "Let they who have ears hear."

"People are taking sides." Renato gave L'Altro's arm a pat. "Clear," he said, "which side my faith is on."

From behind the bar Milena watched her husband touch the arm of the attractive young man. Be careful, Renato, she thought. Don't trust too much.

Marta paid for her groceries and could not wait to leave. That evening, she would have much to report to Emanuele Mosè.

26

"That priest is cunning," said Rosa Spina late that afternoon, her words sounding with the bell-like innocence of a little girl's voice. "You don't have a choice. You have to go."

Emanuele Mosè hated having to do anything that he did not want to do. He did not want to have to enter the church later this evening and defend himself in the face of Don Luigi's interrogation. He did not want to have to do what he was busy doing now, which was rubbing his mother's feet.

Rosa Spina lay on her mattress. She had woken from her afternoon nap. As required by daily ritual since he was a small boy, Emanuele Mosè sat on the bottom edge of the bed. Rosa Spina liked to have her feet rubbed when her nap was over. She said the little massage cleared her head and helped her return to daylight in the gentlest of ways. When it was time for the foot rub, her toes would nudge aside the sheets and blankets at the bottom corner. That was the cue for Emanuele Mosè to take his post. Once he was seated, she would put her bare feet in his lap.

"And what am I supposed to tell the priest?" he asked. His thumbs worked to ease tension from the center of her right sole. When he was a boy he had to take a nap in the afternoons as well. Always by her side. He did not have time or desire to nap now. Thank God he had convinced her several years back that he no longer needed a daytime rest. Consequently he was free to do what he wanted until she woke, and then duty brought him to her feet. In moments like this, her feet, small and baby-soft, were warm from their sleep under the covers.

"I don't see why you're so worried," Rosa Spina soothed. She shut her eyes, savoring the pressure of his fingers. "Just tell him the truth."

"Which truth do you mean?"

To think, when he was very young he used to feel privileged to rub her feet because it was an honor reserved for him alone. L'Altro had not been worthy to touch Rosa Spina's naked foot, nor was he permitted access to her bed for naps. At naptime, Rosa Spina used to slip her hand inside Emanuele Mosè's shirt and lightly tickle his back to help him doze off. Drowsing, he would think, *She loves me, not him.* The big bed, wherever they lived, belonged to Rosa Spina and Emanuele Mosè. L'Altro always had to content himself with a small bed in another room. Not just for naps, but for nighttime sleep, too. This changed when the twins reached puberty. Emanuele Mosè pushed his mother away every time she tried to tickle him to sleep. He wanted to free himself from her touch and from her bed. He won, in the end, preferring to sleep apart from his mother, even together with his brother when necessary, when their house in any particular town afforded no more than a single cot for the boys to share. He had yet to divest himself, however, of his foot-rubbing duties. He wished he could.

"Tell him the true truth, of course." Rosa Spina's red lips formed a cherubic smile. "Tell the priest that the Lord called me into church when I was but a maiden. And there a voice announced that I was with child and was to call his name Emanuele Mosè—"

"'*In principio erat verbum*,'" Emanuele Mosè said with an irony lost on his mother. "'In the beginning was the Word.'"

"—and then you were born."

"'*Et verbum caro factum est et habitavit in nobis.*'" He knew she thought his words to be in earnest. Would she ever be aware of his doubts? "'And the Word was made flesh, and dwelt among us.'"

"Precisely," she said, opening her eyes. "Remind the priest that ever since then we have done nothing but follow the calling of the Lord, humbly performing whatever work He bids us do, even when your brother has followed us around like the shadow of evil incarnate."

Emanuele Mosè sighed. He wanted to speak with someone—honestly speak—but his mother's biblical-sounding words struck him as the opposite of genuine communication. For the millionth time in his life, looking at his mother in hopes of finding a human face, he hit up against her sacred mask, impenetrable as a fortress wall. Her holy façade, together with her girlish voice, made some part of her untouchable to him, leaving him wondering who she was in truth.

"How can you be sure," he said, voicing one of the infinite questions inside him, "that God announced my birth?"

"How can I not be sure? I was there."

"But maybe you were only thinking what you wanted to think."

"Never question who you are," she cooed. "Doubt comes from the Devil. It's your brother's way of thinking, not yours." Then she said, "Here." She pulled her right foot away and flexed her left foot just below his face. "Time for the other one."

He grasped this other warm foot in his hands and applied his thumbs to the sole. Emanuele Mosè knew that he was not giving his mother the enthusiastic complicity she craved, that sullenness was often all she found now when she looked to him for affection. It had been years, though, since he could respond to her touches and kisses with joy. He was a child no more. He did not want to disappoint her, but everyone, he told himself, grows up sooner or later. Had his mother left him a choice, he would be rubbing not hers but other, younger, feet. That was the problem, right there: When did his mother ever leave him a choice?

Emanuele Mosè said, "Why don't you get Signor Cappelli to massage you instead?"

"Don't be jealous," she laughed.

"I'm not. I'd be happy if he were here to do this in my place. Really."

"Little danger of that. No one will ever take your place, my son. You don't have to fear."

"He's not a bad man, Signor Cappelli."

"He's our guardian angel, and I make sure that he has no reason to complain about any of our activities in his house. The Lord helps me do whatever needs to be done."

"I would imagine," said Emanuele Mosè, "that by now he'll have fallen entirely in love with you."

She tittered, as if her son had flattered her. "You don't have to worry. Signor Cappelli, in love? It's not his love that we need." She arched, then scrunched, her foot. "And speaking of love," she said, "you don't think that girl could become a problem, do you?"

"Which girl?"

"You know who." Rosa Spina wiggled her toes. "The girl who thinks she has fallen in love with L'Altro."

Emanuele Mosè pressed his knuckle hard into a sore spot on her sole.

"Ayeee!" Rosa Spina said. "A little softer, please. That hurts."

"Sorry." Emanuele Mosè lightened the pressure of his knuckle. "Strange, but you sound like the jealous one."

"Jealous? Me?" She laughed, then arched her foot in response to his touch. "Oh, that's better," she said. "Yes. Like that. I only meant that we should all be careful about letting that girl get too close. Getting too close will only end in tears. The poor girl will learn that for herself. Your brother never has learned. But you see that, Emanuele Mosè, no?"

He said nothing.

"We mustn't get distracted in our service of the Lord," she persisted. "L'Altro has always allowed himself too many distractions. God expects sacrifice from each of us. You understand that better than your brother, don't you?"

Emanuele Mosè did not reply, but rubbed in silence.

"Enough said," she allowed. "And this evening, once you've finished with the people who come for prayer," she said, "you promise to go and see the priest?"

"Is there an alternative?"

"If you don't go, everyone in town will hear how he invited you but you were too scared to go."

"I might not say the right things."

"Don't be childish," she scolded, but her tone was more sisterly than motherly.

Emanuele Mosè sighed. "I'll improvise," he decided aloud. "I'll see what the priest asks me, and I'll think of the answers, there and then."

She rolled her ankle to unkink the muscles that lay beneath her smooth skin. Heated by the sheets and blankets that covered her body, her spicy perfume drifted through the air. "You're a good boy. The Lord will guide your tongue."

Marta talked. She talked about how diligent she was in never setting foot in the shop of "that Jew." She talked about how she had discovered L'Altro and Don Luigi in cahoots with the evil dwarf. She talked about her insomnia. She talked about the curse that, inexplicably, was still upon her. She talked and talked. Emanuele Mosè listened just enough to give the impression that he was concentrating compassionately on each of her words, but mostly he heard only a mouth making noise. This woman could drive a person mad, he thought. Marta was a cup that he wished the Lord would let pass from him. But his somber, unchanging face gave no indication of what he felt.

It was not a good day for Emanuele Mosè. He was nervous enough about his appointment with the priest without having to absorb the waves of anxiety that poured out from the woman with the violet hair. At least he did not have to face the flock that assembled for its collective meeting on Sunday evenings. He would not have had the energy to deal with an entire group in his present mood of antsy distraction. This being a Thursday evening, he had only to pray with his followers one by one.

He watched Marta's talking mouth. It's her selfishness that makes her so unlovable, he considered in the privacy of his thoughts. We all have problems, but God save us from people who are *too* aware of what's wrong in their lives. They end up treasuring their precious grief. They become obsessed until other things and other people disappear and their tiny world is full of nothing but Self.

She was talking about how she had stopped visiting the Jew but still, still she could not sleep. "You don't think"—she interrupted herself, for a new idea had come to her old head—"you don't think that it's your brother who put a curse on me as well?"

"L'Altro?" Emanuele Mosè was not displeased that she should mention this other. The more feverishly she feared L'Altro as a threat to her well-being, the more avidly she would look to Emanuele Mosè for protection. "My brother certainly is a deceiver. It hadn't occurred to me that he might go around cursing people, but now that you've said it—"

That was all it took. Her mouth running fast in renewed frenzy, Marta explored aloud the many potential manifestations of L'Altro's alleged ill will at work against her. Emanuele Mosè tried to absent himself from her gibbering. He could not wait to be done with the praying over her so that he could send her on her way. He wondered if priests ever felt the same when, locked in their booths by obedient duty, they had to sit through the rantings of parishioners whose sins, too boring to merit confession, held nothing that was intriguing or original.

Finalmente, he thought when Marta had left and he could see that the man who stood in front of him would be this evening's last prayer-seeker, for there was no one else waiting for his services. Get through this one, he told himself, and then we'll go and sort out the priest.

"Please be comfortable," said Emanuele Mosè, indicating the chair opposite his own. What could this man's problem be? he wondered. Reading people's problems was usually an easy trick, for people wore their problems like neon signs if you knew how to decode them. And once the problem was clear, then the solution was no mystery. He watched, and if he saw nail-biting or nervous tics, he would offer a prayer for tranquillity. When someone came and complained of constant tiredness, he would hold the face between his hands and tug down on the lower eyelids with his thumbs. If the eyelids had lost the rosiness of health, he would recognize the anemia, pray for the return of strength, and mention that an iron supplement or two might also be a good idea. He could cure headaches by massaging hands. Stomach pains, he'd recommend a bland diet and, of course, a prayer. He observed and people felt understood, healed. If the circumstances of his life had been different, he might have been a doctor.

The old man took off his hat, sat down, and cleared his throat. His face was thin as a skeleton, but the eyes were kindly.

"Your name?"

"Ah. My name." The man smiled. "Coniglio. Giuseppe Coniglio. Most people call me Beppe."

"Beppe." Emanuele Mosè nodded. He waited. The man's moist eyes stared back but the mouth did not speak. "And the reason you have come?" the young man prompted.

"The reason." Beppe Coniglio's head bobbed affirmatively, but words were slow to emerge. Had age befuddled his brain, leaving him nothing to say? Or was there too much that he wanted to express, so much that he did not know where to start? He swallowed, then said, "This is my first time."

"Yes. Your face is new to me."

First time, the old man said, that he had come to this house, yes, but also the first time that he had ever gone anywhere except to the church for prayer. And he would not even have come now if his situation had not been what it was. He had heard that Emanuele Mosè had cast out demons from that woman, Signora Genoveffa. "So I thought if this boy has the power to help poor Genoveffa, who knows? Maybe he can do something for me." His smile contained few teeth but much gentleness.

"You suspect that you have been possessed by a demon as well?" Emanuele Mosè hoped not. He hardly felt up to an exorcism.

Beppe Coniglio shook his head. He explained that his was a life of simplicity. He lived in the brick house next to the tracks where his job had been to operate the level crossing every time the train passed. Not much to it: flip the switch on the signal bells, lower the bar to block the road, wait for the train to go by, raise the bar, switch off the bells. He had been there for every train, every day and every night.

The railroad company gave him the house to live in so that he was always no farther from work than one step out the door. He had lived there with his wife. Children the Lord had not decided to give them. His wife died a long time ago. Then the railroad company automated the level crossing. His job ceased to exist, but he was allowed to keep the house. "That was my life, spoken in two words. Why would any demon want to waste its time on me?"

Emanuele Mosè realized with no small surprise that he liked the man. It was rare for him to like any of the prayer-seekers that sat before him. Beppe Coniglio, though, had a face he would have been happy to see every day. "If not a demon troubling you," Emanuele Mosè asked with affection, "then what?"

The lips, dry as onion skins, parted. A breath barely made itself heard. "I'm dying," said the man. "Doctor told me not to even hope to have a hope." He swallowed. "There's more tumor than meat on these bones. If you knew the energy it took to walk up these stairs. I don't think I can come again. Doctor tells me by Eastertime I'll be gone."

Emanuele Mosè felt the heat of life leave his limbs. He had expected to hear no words of this sort. The merciless irreversibility of the old man's destiny made the young man shiver. "Why have you come to me? What would you have me do?"

"Nothing, probably." He closed his eyes, then opened them again. "I'm here because I'm scared."

Emanuele Mosè folded his hands on the table. He lowered his eyes to a nick in the tabletop halfway between himself and the man. He appeared deep in contemplation when really all he was doing was avoiding the old man's eyes. He felt like the physician who, after a day of listening to the self-indulgent bellyaching of whining hypochondriacs, finds himself unable to do anything useful when confronted by authentic suffering. His own powerlessness was excruciating; worse still was the sadness he felt for the man.

"'Don't even hope for hope,'" Beppe Coniglio repeated. "Not an easy idea to digest. We're always hoping for something, no? And when I heard about you . . ." Beppe's eyes stared at the young hands, the palms of which were concealed inside the dark fingerless gloves. "They say that saints can do things even when there is no hope."

"Would the gentleman like a cup of tea?" Rosa Spina called from behind her cooking pots in the kitchen.

Emanuele Mosè's eyebrows raised in question.

"I don't have much appetite," said Beppe; then, "but the signora's offer is too kind to be ignored. Maybe a little cup, *sì.*"

"A little cup, yes," Emanuele Mosè called out on Beppe's behalf.

"Ready in a minute," said Rosa Spina.

"Signor Beppe," Emanuele Mosè said more softly, unfolding his hands and opening the palms as if to show that there was nothing there. "I have no magic. I only have my prayers. We could pray for a healing, if you wish, but I have to tell you the truth: As far as I know, I am not a saint. I wish I could promise a miracle. I can't."

The man chuckled. "You're no saint, and I'm no fool. You haven't disappointed me. I wasn't expecting a miracle from your hands."

"Then what do you want?"

Their conversation stopped for a moment because Rosa Spina brought the cup of tea. She asked how many spoons of sugar Beppe Coniglio desired, then stirred the sugar in. He took a sip though he did not want the tea. He wanted instead to show Rosa Spina that he was grateful for the trouble she took in making it. When she returned to the kitchen, he pushed the cup aside.

"I want you to help me with the fear," he went on. "I've never died before."

"Neither have I," said Emanuele Mosè. "Tell me something. Why didn't you go to speak with Don Luigi instead of with me?"

"Don Luigi is a good man," said Beppe Coniglio. "He's a friend. I have no problem with him. The only problem is that he's a priest. He would tell me not to worry because my soul will go to Heaven."

"I see. You're concerned about where your soul will go."

"Concerned about my soul? Not especially." Beppe Coniglio smiled. "I hope it will go to Heaven. I'm almost certain. What sins do you think I could commit when all my days were spent at the level crossing? But it's not Heaven I'm worried about. *È la morte.* It's death itself that scares me. You don't have to tell me where my soul will end up. But you've traveled a lot for a young man, I've heard. You've spoken with more people than I've ever met. You've seen a lot of life, and probably a lot of death. Please. Tell me something to make me less afraid."

Emanuele Mosè was silent, but silence, he knew, would not suffice as an answer. Words were required; he, for once, had none.

I deserve this, he thought. Lead people to believe that you have a gift to give and they will come and ask. What can you give when your cupboard is empty?

"The only thing that comes to mind," he said at last, "is that neither you nor I have died before, but we have a meticulously written account of someone who has." He went on to suggest that Beppe might find a step-by-step guide to dying in the various last words of Jesus. Not Jesus the Lord, but Jesus the man. A man who knew he was dying, just like Beppe himself. First Jesus asked God to forgive his executioners. Had Beppe attained the ability to forgive? Had he settled accounts with the people who had populated his life? And the next two sayings from the cross also had to do with forgiving and with putting earthly affairs in order. That was why Jesus promised the dying criminals that he would see them in Paradise that very afternoon, why he handed his mother over to his disciples to ensure that she would be cared for. In the fourth utterance, Emanuele Mosè was certain there would be something that Beppe could recognize only too well. Jesus cried out that he had been abandoned by God. He added, "Maybe that's what everyone who is dying feels."

Beppe listened quietly but intently, like a thirsty person drinking from a well.

Next Jesus said he thirsted, and that made sense because the body, until the last, refuses to let go of its needs. The living body, after all, loves life.

When enough life had left the body so that he could peer through the window of death, Jesus said, "It is finished." Emanuele Mosè understood from the reading he had done that the Hebrew word Jesus said was related to *shalom*, meaning peace. In peace, all is complete.

Nothing missing. In that state of peace, Jesus spoke his ultimate words, commending his soul to the hands of God.

After Emanuele Mosè had stopped, Beppe Coniglio reflected, then said, "*Mi piace.* I like what you said. I like your thoughts. *Grazie.*"

Emanuele Mosè apologized for not having more to offer. "I'm sorry if it sounds as if I'm sermonizing. I don't mean to give you some pretty little discourse. I hope you can hear that, though my words are insufficient, they come from my heart. Honestly, I don't know what to say in the face of your fear."

He paused, thought, then recommended that Beppe Coniglio do everything he could so that he, too, might move beyond the feeling of isolated abandonment and reach the peace of completion. "What will it take to make you secure that you will be putting your soul in God's hands? Will it take a blessing from the Church? Will it require the last rites?"

"Church blessed me on my way into the world, blessed my first communion and my marriage. Maybe it should bless me on my way out, too, no?"

In that case, Emanuele Mosè advised, when the time to die approached, Beppe should ensure that Don Luigi would come and give him the last rites. He surprised himself while he spoke. So many of his everyday energies were devoted to luring people away from the Church. When had he ever encouraged someone to seek help from a priest? This moment was special, however. He had no doubt that Beppe's interests were the only ones to be taken into account. The compassion Emanuele Mosè felt terrified him.

"I understand why you have not asked the priest for help yet," he explained. "The priest, as you say, would talk to you about the future of your soul, and for now your worries are still with the body. But a time will come, closer to the end—the same as it came for Jesus— when the body loses concern for itself and the moving on of the soul becomes the only thought. That, I suppose, is why the last rites exist. I can do nothing for you in that moment. You are a child of the Church and you will need no one but the priest. Do what is necessary for you. Have the priest give you your last rites."

Beppe Coniglio breathed out slowly and sat very still. Then he reached across the table and took the young man's hands in his own. He opened the hands and kissed each glove-covered palm. *"Grazie,"* he said.

At the door, Rosa Spina waited to see him out. Beppe Coniglio reached for his wallet, but Emanuele Mosè, seated still at the table, told him to put his money away.

"But I want to give your family something, to thank you all."

"He wants to express his gratitude," Rosa Spina said.

Forcefully Emanuele Mosè called to his mother and told her to accept not a cent from this man.

Beppe Coniglio nodded in Emanuele Mosè's direction. "Then good evening," he said. "I don't believe you'll see me again."

It had been a difficult day indeed, a draining day. *Scosso* was how Emanuele Mosè felt: shaken. Insecure. And now he had an appointment in the church up the road. Don Luigi, he knew, was waiting to topple him. If the priest had any idea how precarious I feel right now, Emanuele Mosè thought, he could save his strength. One good shove is all it would take to make me fall and crumble to dust.

"Dinner will be waiting when you get back," Rosa Spina told her son, helping him put on his coat. "I still think you should have let that man express his gratitude."

Emanuele Mosè closed the door and left without giving her a reply.

On the table before the statuettes, the postcard-sized saints, and the bleeding Jesus on the wall, Beppe Coniglio's cup of tea was starting to cool, full except for a single sip.

27

"Laying on of hands?" Don Luigi's eyes, blinking in agitation behind the thick lenses of his glasses, appeared huge. "Working miracles for the hopeless?" Impatient for answers, the big eyes scrutinized the young man's face. "Healing sheep?"

Emanuele Mosè, resenting that the discussion should be here on Don Luigi's home turf, sat beside the priest on the foremost pew of the echoing church. Several degrees colder than the fresh air outside, the dampness in here made Emanuele Mosè tighten the scarf around his neck. The smell of candle wax and incense prickled his nose. Avoiding the priest's gaze, he looked at the frescos on either side of the altar. Paradise, with its timeless joys, was painted on the wall to the right; Hell, with its ceaseless griefs, on the wall to the left. In the center an ancient crucifix held a wooden body nailed to a cross. Looking again at Don Luigi, he said, "The sheep was healed. Ask Renato Tizzoni. He never even comes to my house for prayer, but he'll tell you himself. The sheep was healed."

"And what about exorcism? Casting out demons now, are we? If you have plans to raise the dead," said Don Luigi, "let me know by all means and I'll ask Sculati to leave the cemetery gates open for you."

"Don't look surprised. The Bible is full of wondrous acts. It's all part of your faith, no?"

"The End of Days is part of my faith, too"—the priest smiled—"but I still feel relatively confident in making appointments, sometimes weeks in advance."

"Meaning?"

"Meaning that the extremes in religious faith—you know, possessions, demons, the Apocalypse—may well have their foundations in truth, and they certainly succeed in exciting the popular imagination. But most of our life is made of smaller stuff. We don't have to look to the extremes to find God's love. Real love is made manifest in the banal, in the everyday. You don't have to dazzle the world with special effects if your faith is sincere. Wouldn't you agree?"

"I impose nothing on anyone," said Emanuele Mosè. "I address the needs that people present to me. Nothing more. Nothing less."

"The Church exists to meet people's needs, but you don't seem to take the Church very seriously. You would do well, young man, to remember that the Church has been in Italy for two thousand years. Somewhat more established than your own brief ministry, wouldn't you say?" Don Luigi tightened his lips and exhaled loudly through his nose. "Would you care to tell me by what authority you perform such wondrous services for the people of this town?"

"Are you quoting the twenty-first chapter of Matthew to me?"

"No. I'm asking a direct question."

"*Bene.* By what authority." Concentrate on what you're saying, he told himself though he trembled inside, and your words will find their own strength. "Similarly I could ask by what authority Saint Catherine traveled from Siena to Avignon and asked the Pope to return to Italy. By what authority did Saint Francis decide to live in poverty among the leprous and the wretched of the earth?" Liking the sound of what he was saying, Emanuele Mosè started to convince even himself. "Can you tell me that the Church has ever been quick to acknowledge individuals who are motivated by a higher, more personal calling? Recognition may come occasionally, but only after the death of the person concerned, of course. No, the Church is slow to authorize, but ready always to accuse in its fear of heresy. Is that what you would like to happen to me, Don Luigi? Shall I be condemned like Savonarola for unorthodox doctrines? Would you have me hanged and burned in the piazza outside?"

"You have an uncommon sense of the dramatic, young man. I'll grant you that." Don Luigi had to smile. "But what would you ask me to believe? Are you a modern-day saint? Is that what you're saying?"

"I don't recall any saint to have declared himself or herself as such. To do so would be immodest and decidedly unsaintly."

Exasperated, the priest removed his glasses and rubbed his eyes. "Your talents are wasted in your line of work." He cleaned his glasses with his handkerchief. "Add a little bit of serious study to your ability to manipulate words, you could easily grow up to practice politics or law." He held his glasses in front of his mouth and fogged the lenses with humid breath. "You're a clever one, I admit. Too obvious it would be if you used the charlatan wizard's standard tricks. No tarot cards or crystal balls. You're too sophisticated for that. You sell something subtler. Prayer. Oldest magic there is. Magic I say, instead of faith, because genuine prayer grows from genuine belief, and it would take a lot of convincing to make me think you had any of that." He shifted his leg in its heavy cast. The movement made his bone ache. He winced.

Seeing the expression of pain, Emanuele Mosè smiled. "I can pray over your leg, if you like."

The priest shuddered, remembering his dream. "Thanks all the same, but I'm happy to let nature do its healing work." He put his glasses back on so that he could see the young man sharply. "One question for you," he said. "*Che vuoi?* What do you want? It is money that you're after, am I right?"

"I've never asked for a cent. If people give, they do so voluntarily, and they do so to express gratitude, to help further the work of God's servant."

"God's servant. You mean you?" Don Luigi laughed. "And your treatment of our Jewish friend, Signor Trieste. Il Piccino, as most people call him—" At the mention of Il Piccino, Emanuele Mosè closed his eyes as if in pain. "Have you acted as God's servant in your behavior toward him?" the priest insisted, his voice rising. "*Santo cielo!* The Church has done so much to atone for its history of anti-Semitism. The Pope himself has asked forgiveness for our intolerance in the past. Now you come along and try to bring back the Inquisition! Do you dare to tell me that you are working in the service of the Lord?"

"I didn't throw the rock that shattered his window."

"No? I can't prove that you did or did not. Even if you did not, you pushed the arm that did."

Emanuele Mosè lowered his head minutely and breathed out.

Was it Don Luigi's imagination, or did he hear a sigh of contrition escape the lips?

The little sound changed something in Don Luigi, for it revealed the possibility of vulnerability where the priest had expected to hit up against nothing but monolithic arrogance. Could it be that remorse—the first seed of salvation—might sprout hidden in that other heart?

Don Luigi was torn. He wanted to rebuke the smug-faced youth who clearly had already chosen the path of wickedness. But this creature, too, the priest told himself, is a sheep in need of healing. If I'm in any way capable of following the example of the Good Shepherd, then I must put aside my own pride and offer even this miscreant a gesture of brotherly love. Though the priest wanted to be granite hard, he knew that softness required a strength greater than that of any stone.

"My son," said Don Luigi gently, like a father reassuring a distraught child, "are you happy with your life?"

Emanuele Mosè had not foreseen a question of this sort. He had counted on sparring with the cleric, swapping verbal jabs, hopefully getting in a good body blow or two, and walking away, if all went as planned, without a bruise. Instead here was a solicitous question that showed concern for his well-being. He was astonished to discover not punitive fists but a pair of open arms. "My happiness," he said, "is irrelevant."

"Irrelevant? Who ever told you that? Why would you think such a thing?"

"As a servant of the Lord, I must not seek to—"

"Can we stop discussing your holy mission for just a moment? Can we give a little thought to you?"

A tremendous tiredness came over Emanuele Mosè. What had

exhausted him so? Was it the uneasy duty of rubbing his mother's feet? Was it the absolute sadness he felt before the inevitability of Beppe Coniglio's death? Or perhaps it was a desire he did not know he possessed: the wish to curl up and sleep, right there on the hard wooden pew, while this fatherly man might stroke his head and protect him for an instant after his lifetime of fatherlessness.

Without meaning to, he yawned, then felt embarrassed to have revealed the weariness within. "Excuse me," he said by force of good social manners, the verbal gesture as reflexive and involuntary as the yawn itself. He lifted a glove-covered hand to suppress yet another yawn.

"I remember," said Don Luigi, "what my mother used to say when I was a little boy. 'There's no such thing as a bad child,' she would say when I was doing my best to be bad. 'There are only tired children.'" The priest's eyes, seen through his thick glasses, lost their monstrousness and showed their humanity instead. "I would like to believe, though it's difficult, I admit, that you, young man, are nothing but a confused and very tired child."

Despite himself, Emanuele Mosè laughed without rancor.

Sensing that a door was opening and not closing, the priest said, "I would be willing to listen, if you would like to confess."

The response that came implied an inner world full of more torment than the priest would have imagined. "*Potessi,*" said Emanuele Mosè. "If only I could."

"You can," Don Luigi encouraged. "Simple. Let your mouth speak."

His mouth opened and, beginning its confession, said, "*Padre.*" The word lacerated Emanuele Mosè. When had he ever called another man Father? Stopping his mouth before it spoke again, the young man looked down at his hands encased in their fingerless gloves. "No," he said, as if he had no choice but to walk away with reluctance from a mystical opportunity that had appeared unexpectedly in his path. "I can't."

"Why not? What are you defending? Whom are you afraid of betraying?"

Silently the young man shook his head.

Don Luigi and Emanuele Mosè sat for many minutes in silence, a pair of opposites, intimate enemies, side by side, both catching their breath during the battle's lull, neither in a hurry to pick up his weapon once more.

In the end it was Don Luigi who broke the truce. "There's nothing I can say, is there, to persuade you to leave the people of this town untouched?"

"Not a thing."

"And you know that, were it in my power, I would have you and your family go away from Sant'Angelo D'Asso."

"It could be argued that God wants us here," Emanuele Mosè said, the self-protective tone returning to his voice. "How can you be so sure that we were not sent by God?"

"How can you prove to me that you were?"

It was clear: Nothing could move Emanuele Mosè to deviate from his course, and nothing could weaken Don Luigi's bond to his beloved Church.

"I don't know what to do about you," said Don Luigi. "But I'll tell you something. The one thing I will do is pray. I promise I will. I'll pray to God that He, in His infinite creativity, might find the way to convince you to change your life and reveal to you a new road."

Rocklike composure returned to Emanuele Mosè's face. "Then good luck in your prayers, priest. We'll see whose prayers find more favor in the ear of God. If indeed it is the Lord's desire to change my life, you'll have your wish." He stood up, a frescoed image of Heaven behind one shoulder and of Hell behind the other. "God's will be done." Emanuele Mosè turned to leave. "Oh," he added, "I do, however, have a favor to ask."

"I'm intrigued," said Don Luigi. "Ask."

"Look in on Beppe Coniglio," Emanuele Mosè said without smiling. "Please. And you might want to take the eucharist with you when you visit. He'll be needing the last rites before too long."

"Beppe Coniglio?" Don Luigi knew Beppe Coniglio well. He knew, too, of the man's failing health. "But what better subject for your services than a dying man?" the priest said. "And you tell me that I should administer the last rites. Thank you for telling me how to do my job. But what's wrong? Don't you intend to milk him for the little money he has? Or maybe you have a conscience after all."

"Beppe Coniglio is one of yours. He needs you, not me. Keep an eye on him, all right?"

The serious young man left the church as he had come in: without shaking the priest's hand. The opportunity ended. The door between the two men, like the heavy door of the church, banged shut.

28

The car sat by the side of a dirt road at the edge of an olive grove on a hill outside town. Olive trees, like tortured ghosts, raised twisted leafless branches to the moon. The air smelled of damp earth.

Petula had driven them there. She was always the driver. At first she had laughed when she discovered that L'Altro had no license. But how could he have one? she later reasoned. He had been in a prison cell at the age when most young people were in driving school classrooms.

Usually, when she and L'Altro escaped from their homes to spend a few secret hours together in the car, Petula could feel his body tremble at nothing more than the smooth sliding sensations of a kiss. When she could hear the breath escape his lips tremulously, she knew that to him she had the inebriating potency of some rare fruit with a slight and delicious aftertaste of melancholy, for she was precious to him and, she sensed, he was afraid she might not be there always.

Tonight, however, kissing had no ease. His mouth, touching hers, was tense.

One of us is holding back, Petula told herself, and tonight it isn't me.

If anything, she had exhausted her brain with too much thinking—about Daniele, about how downhearted Beniamino seemed—and she wanted to put aside worrying for now, to lose herself in a brief moment of release.

But L'Altro, she could tell, was distracted.

"What's wrong?" she asked him.

"Nothing." He stopped kissing her and sat back in his seat.

Then he made a request so singular that Petula did not know what to think. "Would you mind," he said, "taking off your shoes and socks?"

"My feet will get cold," she said.

"I'll keep them warm."

She asked why he wanted her barefoot, and his answer was surprisingly tender. He wanted, he explained, to pretend they were a real couple at liberty to explore each other entirely. He wanted to make believe they were in a comfortable, bright bedroom and not in a cold, moonlit car. He wanted to see more of her than he had seen before.

So she did as he had asked, then sat with her bare feet in his lap. He took her feet in his hands and rubbed them until they were warm.

He raised the foot he was massaging and admired it in the silver-blue moonlight. It was a strong foot, handsomely sculpted. He kissed the center of the sole. "There is beauty in every part of you, Petula," he said. "Unbelievable beauty. Do you know what Dostoevsky said? He said that Beauty will save the world. In the end, he was probably right."

He shook his head as if admitting a painful truth. She heard a sadness behind his words.

"Has Daniele ever massaged your feet?" he asked.

"Not that I can remember."

"Well, you could always ask him to."

"Tell me what's happening in your thoughts," she said. "Why would you talk about Daniele now?"

He closed his eyes, as if to savor the moment before saying magic words that might change everything beyond repair. "Our time together is sacred for me," he said, "but you have to do what you decide is right for you."

Petula breathed out loudly. "I know what the problem is. You were upset by the way Beniamino spoke about Daniele yesterday, weren't you? You should have seen how your face fell."

"Upset? It's natural for the boy to care about his father, no? Why should that make me upset? But maybe I was a little—how can I say this?—envious." He gave a light laugh. "Petula, you have to do what's right. Everything that I can offer you is in the present tense. Your past was with Daniele. I don't know how to make promises for the future."

"I've never asked you for a promise."

"True. You haven't."

"And I haven't asked you to be responsible for the future, mine or my son's. Maybe all that I need is what's in the present." She looked for signs on his moonlit face. He did not seem to be searching for a gentle excuse to separate himself from her. Instead he sounded genuinely grieved that he could not give her what he imagined she expected. "Stop feeling that you'll disappoint me," she said. "You haven't yet. If you do, I won't be shy. I'll let you know."

He kissed her ankle. "That's one of the things I like about you. You're sincere. Do you know the origins of the word?"

"L'Altro, please don't hide behind fancy discussions of etymology."

"In the marketplace of ancient Rome," he said, ignoring her request, "some unscrupulous merchants of earthenware vases used to rub wax on imperfect products to disguise the cracks. Honest vendors did the opposite. They put up a sign on their stalls: 'Sine Cera—Without Wax.' Maybe the jars weren't perfect, but at least the customers could see exactly what they were buying, cracks and all. You're sincere, Petula. The truth comes easily to you. You're not timid about the truth."

"Then tell me the truth now," she insisted. "I've never seen you this sad. Tell me what's pulling you down."

"Where should I start? I have more anchors than I can count." He started rubbing her feet again. "What's pulling me down? Here's one thing for you. My brother. It's true what they say, you know, about the telepathic kind of empathy we twins are supposed to feel with each other. You think I'm low, you should see my brother. A man came to him for prayers this evening. Beppe Coniglio."

"I know Beppe Coniglio. One of the kindest people on earth."

"That's the impression Emanuele Mosè got. Anyway, your friend Beppe is dying. He knows he's dying, and he's scared."

"*Mamma mia.*"

"He asked my brother to make him less scared. What the hell was Emanuele Mosè supposed to say? He tried to give a few comforting words, but in the deep part of his heart, he knows he can't do a thing. Not a thing."

"That's terrible. But why does it surprise me to hear that your brother has a heart?"

"I can see you're not a fan."

"What do you expect?" said Petula. "He tries to make everyone believe that one quick prayer from him and all problems disappear."

"They seem to swallow it," L'Altro said. "God knows why."

"And how about you? In the deep part of your heart, what do you believe in?"

L'Altro laughed. "Talk about big questions." He kissed her toe. "Seems out of place, too. I mean, you expected other things when you drove me here tonight. You didn't count on me sitting like a miserable idiot, rubbing your feet while launching into grand orations on what I believe."

"Quit thinking about what I expect. I like what your hands are doing to my feet, and if I didn't like hearing what you have in your head, I wouldn't have asked."

In the deep part of his own heart, L'Altro noticed the loveliness of their being together in a parked car beside a moonlit grove full of ghostlike trees. The window was open an inch or two to let in the soft breeze with its earth smells. Petula's perfume and the fragrance of her clean skin scented the night air. Outside the window the only sound was the call of an owl. L'Altro was tempted to cry. He was in the company of a beautiful young woman who reclined on the car seat as if it were a sofa of comfort. She was perhaps the only friend he had ever had. Peace passed between them. "I believe," he said, "that talking with you is a treat."

"Then talk. I mean, I hear people tell stories of exorcisms going on in your house, and I have no idea where you fit in. You can't believe in any of that, can you? Your family seems so *extreme.* I only want to understand you. God? The Devil? Curses? Casting out demons? What do *you* say?"

"I say . . . How can I put this? I say it's so much simpler than the difficult systems people try to construct. Forget the devils and the theatrics, is what I say. They're just for show. Or better yet, they're poetry, just like the Bible, or the word *God*. Beautiful poems that become lies when you stop reading them poetically."

He rolled down the window enough to put his hand out. He touched the moisture on the roof of the car, then held the hand close to Petula's face so that she could see waterdrops on his fingertips. "See? Here's God. The water in these drops. Without water, there's no life. Instead, there's life everywhere you look. The Great Ocean of Life created us smaller drops in Its own image. The soul inside me, the soul inside you, the soul inside Beppe Coniglio or inside the owl on that tree outside the car? Each of us, a drop of life." He rubbed the tips of his thumb and forefinger together, playing with the water. "What difference could it possibly make whether the drop keeps its identity after we die? The drop goes back to the Ocean. Who cares if it lives afterward as an iceberg, or a snowflake, or a speck of dew? Life goes back to Life. I don't see why things have to be more complicated than that. How can a drop not believe in the Ocean from which it came? The Ocean is Life and Love, the Love, as Dante said, that moves the sun and the other stars. I am in the Ocean and the Ocean is in me. We are of the same substance. We are *all* of the same substance." He held out a fingertip toward Petula. She smiled, touched the finger with her own, and felt the water on her skin. "Maybe that's what my brother should have told Beppe Coniglio," said L'Altro. "Maybe he should have wished him a pleasant trip back to the Ocean. Or then again, maybe not. Maybe the thought doesn't give the kind of reassurance that Beppe Coniglio wants to hear. In any case, that, more or less, is what I believe."

After silence, Petula said, "Thank you for telling me." After more silence, she added, "Know what I think? I think if you didn't wear the gel in your hair, your head would emanate rays as bright as the sun."

"You don't like my gel."

"I like your gel fine. What I'm saying is that I think Emanuele Mosè is the dark one and you're the brother of light."

"Myth says that Lucifer was the brightest angel before he fell from grace."

"I'm serious." She poked his chin with her toe.

"So am I."

"No, really. Haven't you ever thought that maybe your mother got it wrong? How can she be sure that you're the baby who came out second? I mean, think about your mother's story that a divine voice foretold the birth of a God-sent child. Let's assume that the story holds some little grain of truth."

"Always a dangerous assumption with any of my mother's stories."

She laughed. "Then I guess you don't believe it."

"With my mother, I never know what to believe. The way I see it, there are two kinds of people in the world."

"Yes, yes. You told me. The home-lovers and the wanderers?"

"No. Two different kinds this time. There are the mythmakers and the truthseekers. My mother is a mythmaker. Life doesn't satisfy her unless it's larger than life. Problem is, I think she believes her own mythical version of the facts. And I'd like nothing better than to know the facts for what they are, because I'm trying as hard as I can to be a truthseeker, which isn't an easy task with my mother around."

"Yes, but I almost start to believe your mother's story about the annunciation of a miraculous birth. But how can we tell that the name Emanuele Mosè wasn't meant to be yours, not your brother's? What if *you* were the firstborn? What if he were the dark shadow making you miserable all your life? Isn't it possible that, when you were both a day or two old, your mother got confused about who was who?"

He stopped massaging her feet. "I'm not sure I want to follow this thought," he said. "Am I supposed to like the idea that I don't know who I am?"

"Maybe you've suffered an injustice your whole life. Your mother has made you feel evil, but you're not. I can only see you as good. Your brother is so different from you that I can't help but—"

"My brother and I are opposite sides of the same coin. Our whole life, everyone has told us that we are as alike as two drops of water. And you know what people say. The identity of one twin usually ends up being absorbed by the identity of the other."

"Doesn't look that way to me," Petula said. "Don't you think it's time that you should be proud of yourself?"

"I think it's time," he said, lightly brushing her sole with his fingers, "to put words aside. Thanks for your kind words about me. I know you're trying to make me feel better. But it's enough now. *Basta.*" To distract her, he kissed her foot once more, this time giving her sole a playful lick.

L'Altro, she could see, was using sex to cut conversation short. "Tell me one thing," she insisted. "Why does your brother always wear those gloves? Some people say his hands have the stigmata. I want to know the truth. What is he hiding inside the gloves?"

"Can you keep a secret?" he asked.

"I can. *Sì.*"

"Good," he said. "So can I." He kissed her ankle, and moved up her leg. With his hands he untucked her shirt. He rolled toward her until his lips warmed her belly's bare skin.

She decided to give in to his evasion. "I see your sadness has left you," she said, kissing the top of his head.

"No, it's still there. But thanks to you, a certain joy has come to keep it company."

His agile hands explored inside her clothing, and she was gratified to feel a faint yet excited tremble in his touch.

"Madonna miracolosa!" Cappelli sighed, unable to believe his good luck. Too good to be true, he told himself. That amazing mouth of hers is kissing me *there*. And now she's opening her lips. *"Madonna benedetta e santissima!"* he gasped, his habitual blasphemy transformed into the most fervent and thankful of prayers. Blessed God, what a sensation! That mouth, with me, inside.

There was a special quality in the way Rosa Spina made love. She was gifted. Some people had cerebral intelligence, though that was not a trait that would have excited Cappelli very much. Others, including Cappelli himself, demonstrated an acute manual intelligence whenever some mechanical device happened into their hands and begged to be taken apart and repaired. There were so many kinds of intelligence in the world. Rosa Spina's particular endowment—or at least the one that enthralled him right now—pertained to the senses, an intelligence of the flesh. She knew how to make her perfume thrill the nose. She knew how to move. She was aware of the erotic potential of every part of her body, and she knew how to use that body to elicit pleasure from unexpected parts of his.

Cappelli, inside her mouth, felt his happiness to be complete. It lacked nothing, except perhaps the warm certainty that the same happiness would be there for him tomorrow and the day after that. He was like a man who, having tasted a succulent, mouth-thrilling, stomach-satisfying dish, knows that he would want to eat the same recipe daily, forever, and would never yearn for other food.

I want to tell her, he thought. I want to tell her that I want her with me until the day they plant me in the tomb.

The word-uttering part of his brain had switched off, however; the physical sensations were too intense. He closed his eyes, lay back, and let the delight ripple over him from down there where her mouth was busily consuming him as if he himself were some luscious morsel to be savored upon the tongue.

"Stop," he said suddenly, trying to push her lovely head away. "Better for you to stop what you're doing. If you continue like this, I'll—" He was reluctant to use the coarse language of sex. Somehow she made him want to be delicate. She made him yearn to be softer than the man he had always been. "I'll finish right away, if you don't stop. I'm too close."

"But that's fine," she said. She sniffed. "Why hold back?" She kissed him with soft lips. "Go ahead."

"No." He held her head between his hands to make her stop. "I want to be closer to you."

"Not necessary for you to be so kind. You're *too* kind," she said with a courtesy that left him almost lonely. "You can let go wherever you want. It's all right. Where do you want? Here?" She took him inside her mouth again.

"*Madonna incredibile!* No." He pulled her away once more, this time with greater strength.

She responded to his pull by slithering her body slowly upward along his. With her hands she cradled his penis between her breasts. "How about here?"

"No," Cappelli said.

She slid farther up, rubbing his penis into the softness of her belly. "Here?"

"No. I want to hug you as close as I can."

He guided her body and rolled over some until they lay on their sides, embracing tightly, face-to-face.

"Here is where I want," he said, nudging his pelvis into hers.

She parted her legs to let him in. Once inside, Cappelli, kissing her neck, face, mouth, could not hold back.

Had Cappelli been a musician, he could have spent a lifetime trying to compose a symphonic crescendo equal to the bliss that overwhelmed him. He was no artist, though. He was a simple man, relishing one of the most generous gifts that nature offered to animals of every sort. He was sure he was in love, but, adept in no artistic medium, he would never find a way to express the immensity of emotion that she skillfully made him feel.

"I'm happy to see you happy," Rosa Spina said after Cappelli's satiated body collapsed. She gave him a quick kiss on the side of his neck and waited for him to detach himself.

As he rolled away, cozy weariness drugged his limbs. "Happy, yes." Sleep would be no more than a minute away if he let himself fall into its easy gravity, yet he wanted to stay awake long enough at least to speak his mind. I'll ask her now, he thought. What better moment could there be?

Then he remembered what Renato had told him. Ask her, fine, Renato had counseled, but remember that the answer to a question can be either *sì* or *no*.

She wouldn't say *no* if he opened his mouth and asked her, would she? The worm of doubt began to nibble at him. The happiness of the moment, now that he thought about it, was one little detail away from full, but maybe that detail had to be reckoned with. He would have wanted to propose marriage after a mutual burst of mystical joy; the explosion of a minute ago had been his alone. He had never been one to concern himself with a woman's pleasure, but right now—no denying it—something was missing from the wholeness of the mood. Come to think of it, had he ever seen her lose control?

"Sorry that the pleasure is all for me," he said, speaking to the ceiling. "If I had waited a little longer, then who knows? Maybe you, too, could have—"

"But look what a kind man you are!" she said in her little-girl voice. "Really, you don't have to worry. It's fine this way. No need to make problems for yourself. I couldn't be more content. Now close your eyes and enjoy a good sleep." She kissed his eyelids. His eyelids could not remember the last time they had been kissed.

Yes, he was comforted by the maternal affection of the kisses, but he was less than convinced. Something in her words hinted that she had serviced him. He could pay a woman to service him, if being serviced was what he was after. With her he wanted instead to be sure that, in doing the things she did with him, she did them with all her heart. How much of her heart had she given him tonight?

Maybe Renato's right, Cappelli thought. I won't ask her tonight. I'll wait a little longer. I'll wait until I know for certain that her heart wants me, too.

Tiredness after the body's exertions overpowered in the end, and Cappelli fell asleep. The sleep that swallowed him was not sweet and deep. Confused and not entirely at peace, Cappelli dreamed of emptiness in his belly, hollow as hunger. Looking down in his dream, he saw that his body had been gutted like a wild boar after the hunt, rib cage splayed open, nothing left inside.

When Rosa Spina heard him grunt in his sleep, she got up, dressed, left Cappelli's apartment, and went downstairs to her own bed.

In her lavender-scented flannel sheets, Marta's skin started to sweat. Her nervous eyeballs twitched beneath wrinkled lids, beholding visions of people who had died during her life. She saw her parents. She heard again her husband's final breath. The air leaving his lips smelled of lavender like her sheets at first, then, as she fell further into her dream, the smell transformed, assuming the sweetness of carnations at a funeral Mass. Sweetening more, the odor became the stink of rotting bodies, and all around her she watched the decomposing flesh of the people she had loved become food for hungry worms. She lay inside the cemetery and listened to the decay of the dark enclosing walls.

Her heart hurt when she awoke. It beat too quickly to keep in rhythm with itself, skipping beats, then thrumming fast in a useless effort to pump sufficient blood. Pain paralyzed her limbs. "*Aiuto,*" she whispered. With her shutters, windows, and doors barred tight, there was only empty blackness to hear the weak call for help.

Then a presence entered to comfort her. Thankfully she received it, grateful that Emanuele Mosè had come in person and had not merely sent his likeness in a dream. She was awake, wasn't she? She couldn't tell for sure. The blackness of her room mirrored the bottomless blackness inside her skull, vast pain her only certainty. The pain was real, and so, thank God, seemed the pale luminosity of the young man with the saintly face. "Help me," she said to him.

Loving-kindness warm in his eyes, he bent over her and kissed the violet strands of hair which her chilly sweat made cling to her forehead. She trusted him. In return for her faith, he slowly slipped off the gloves that concealed his hands, and turned the palms to her eyes so that finally she could witness the truth. She saw the holes in the center of the hands. She wanted to kiss them, and suck into herself their healing strength. He held the hands before her face and, looking closer, she saw that the hole in each palm was a serpent's mouth, needle sharp fangs dripping poison, bifurcated tongue flickering to pick up her scent. One hand he pressed to her throat, the other to her breast. In unison the serpents bit deep. In her last moment of panic, she forced her eyes open and saw laughter in the young man's mouth.

Heart attack, would be the coroner's verdict. Sculati's shovel would be busy again with another grave to dig. The death knell would ring from the church tower once more, now that the population had sunk to one thousand, two hundred and eighty-four. Don Luigi, amid carnation wreaths, would celebrate another funeral in the presence of gray-haired churchgoers who had grown used to mourning. Marta Sorcini was dead.

29

Then spring, astonishing as a miracle. Yesterday fog had obfuscated everything. This morning the waking world smelled fresh, a new wind whisking over it. The first red and yellow wildflowers speckled the unbelievably green hills, clean air and sunshine everywhere, Easter only four weeks away.

The big windows of the bar up at the train station let in more light than the room seemed capable of containing. The radio murmured the news of the day. "A delegation of Vatican officials," said the announcer's voice, "has reached Calabria to investigate more reports of the miracles performed in a remote hilltop town. The alleged *santone* in question is a fifty-seven-year-old woman named Maria Pia. Claiming that the unschooled woman heals with her prayers, devoted followers arrive in throngs. They attribute curative properties to incense crystals that materialize spontaneously, according to eyewitnesses, on the skin above the woman's heart. Reserving further comment until a full examination has been conducted, a Vatican spokesman advises cautious skepticism with regard to the woman, whose miraculous powers have yet to be officially acknowledged by the Church. And on the political front today, union leaders threaten new strikes in response to the government's reluctance to . . ."

This news was nothing new in Italy, and no one in the bar was listening. Too much work to do. Too much conversation.

Working amid the mocha-scented steam of the espresso machine, Daniele made frothy cappuccini and coffees corrected with shots of liquor. Petula waited while Daniele placed the cups, one by one, on a tray.

When he could take his eyes off his work, Daniele watched Petula to see where her thoughts were. He caught her looking at L'Altro seated by the window at a table with Nuzzi, Renato, Cappelli, and Sculati the gravedigger. Daniele saw the quick private smile that Petula and L'Altro exchanged.

"You're sleeping with him," Daniele said quietly so that no one else in the bar could hear. "Aren't you?" He wanted to take the coffee cup he was filling and hurl it across the room at L'Altro's face.

Petula lost her smile. She lowered her eyes to the cups on the tray. She said, "If you say so." Daniele's question tore her in two, but she struggled not to show how close to tears she suddenly felt.

Daniele's gut went empty, as if all his organs had dissolved. He wanted a cigarette. He wanted to explode. Instead, saying nothing, he breathed slowly and forced himself to control the temper that had created his misery.

The construction workers rose from their usual table in the corner. Daniele interrupted his coffee making and went to the cash register to ring up their bill. "Some of us have got to get back to work," said Spillo, paying for the others. His injuries had healed for the most part. Still, in the back of his mind, there was one person he blamed for his fall. He steered clear of L'Altro, neither speaking to nor looking at him. Spillo pocketed his change, jerking his head and smiling at Petula. "Will you miss me while I'm gone?" he said.

"Of course," she answered. "But I'll try to bear the suffering with quiet dignity."

"You do that," he said, not entirely pleased to be mocked in the presence of his pack. "But we'll be here again tomorrow, so you won't have to suffer long."

"Don't hurry," Petula laughed.

When the door had closed behind the builders, Petula returned her attention to Daniele. He slapped slices of prosciutto onto bread, then held the sandwich with one hand and finished preparing the coffees with the other.

"Kind of early in the morning for lunch," said Petula.

"I've got a hunger like the end of the world." Daniele tore off a big bite. "Haven't you noticed?"

"Noticed what?"

"Got to do something to keep my mouth busy. I haven't touched a cigarette for two weeks."

"*Bravo!*" she said, relieved that he had let the subject of L'Altro drop. Maybe, she hoped, they could simply have a conversation that wasn't a fight. "You've never wanted to stop smoking before. Why now?"

He chewed and swallowed. "You don't smoke, do you?"

"What have I got to do with whether you smoke or not?"

"Only everything," he said as calmly as he could.

"Daniele, you don't have to do things to make me happy."

"Maybe I do," he said. "Maybe I should have a long time ago." He looked across to L'Altro. When their eyes met, L'Altro turned away. Daniele bit off more prosciutto. "Only problem is, without the cigarettes, I have a black hole in my stomach that doesn't get filled no matter how much I stuff in. They say the metabolism finds a new balance in a couple of months." He felt a lump in his throat to be talking with her about how he was trying to change. "In the meantime"—he hesitated; should he risk an intimate joke?—"I figure you'll still love me even if I get big around the belly for a little while, no?"

"Of course I will," she said. Then, hearing herself, she felt her heart beat quickly. Why had professing her love for Daniele been so effortless? Was it only an old reflex speaking, or had her instincts finally shaped themselves into words without her conscious mind getting in the way? Maybe she should say something to take back her words. But how could she take back the truth? She glanced at L'Altro by the window. Had he heard?

Daniele, ecstatic, relieved, wanted to wrap her in a hug and cry. But he was wise enough to say nothing more on the subject. Sometimes silence, he had learned, is the most effective answer. "*Pronti,*" he said. "Coffee's up." Why say anything to spoil what Petula had said? Besides, Daniele had a plan fully ready to be realized. He had been waiting only for a sign that the moment was right. Tonight, he thought as he watched Petula carry the tray to the table of men by the window. *Sì*, tonight. Why not?

Petula, carrying the tray and making sure not to let a drop spill, felt fragile and full of life. Ever since she and Beniamino had moved out of Daniele's house, she was exposed to the world as if she had lost her skin. Layers of habit had been stripped away, leaving her unaccustomedly vulnerable both to heartache and to pleasure. She had no vision of what her future might become, but she was grateful, somehow, to have woken up to the knowledge that it would be of her own choosing. Her senses tingled with possibility.

At the window table, L'Altro, ever keen to read the messages held in other people's faces, watched Daniele watching Petula. Let him dream, L'Altro thought. Let him desire her as much as he wants. In time he'll learn he can't have her back.

Renato watched his daughter and thought that she was still so young. A grown woman, yes, and the mother of a beautiful boy. Her life, though, had taken an unexpected and precipitous left-hand turn. Not a bad thing, on its own. Change, never easy, often led to better directions. But in searching for happiness, would she know where to look?

Cappelli's eyes were fixed on the tray. He watched the approaching cup of a little coffee and a lot of sambuca that he had ordered. Since when had he ever been a creature of doubt and insecurity? Since thoughts of a woman had come to set up home inside his head, he answered himself. Thank God the aniseed of sambuca was on its way to soothe his mouth, the alcohol to ease his brain.

Sculati the gravedigger was in top form. He had been sleeping wonderfully lately, now that the electric bell in the cemetery no longer clanged at all hours of the night. L'Altro had seen to setting right the timer which Nuzzi before him had rigged with his usual incompetence. Sculati would drink grappa abundantly at this liquid breakfast, and abundantly again at lunch and at dinner after that. Then, in his rooms above the chapel within the cemetery walls, he would snore his way through a night of slumber as profound as that of any of the cemetery's other residents. Dead neighbors were never troublemakers. Life was good.

Filling the other seat at the window table was Nuzzi, the glummest of the group. Signor Nuzzi. Nuzzi the Insipid. When people considered him, which was hardly ever, they thought of him as the electrician who did not know his way around a roll of wire. What more was there to say about the small, balding, nervous-eyed man who touched everything, even a coffee cup, with a slight shake in his fingertips as if the thing might be wired badly and, consequently, sting him with a few volts?

"*M'hanno fregato,*" Nuzzi said with a dejected voice when Petula had placed a cup before each man. "They screwed me."

"A cappuccino was what you ordered," Renato said. "And that's a cappuccino sitting there under your nose. Where's the problem?"

"Not today." Nuzzi shook his head. "It was yesterday that they screwed me."

"Why? What did they give you yesterday?"

"Not here at this bar. Up in Siena, when I went there yesterday to buy wire and some new sockets."

"They screwed you in a bar in Siena?"

"Not in a bar. Out in the parking lot at the gas station." Nuzzi searched for sympathy and solidarity in the faces around him. Confusion, instead, was all that he saw. "Maybe I didn't explain myself well," he said.

"I, for one," said Sculati, "haven't understood a word of what's been said. But this is nothing new, when Nuzzi's doing the talking."

Nuzzi sighed. He had started, so he could not stop. He would have to recount every shameful detail of the recent event.

"Remember how foggy it was yesterday?" he asked everyone. In the morning, fog thick as milk; in the late afternoon, thick as cream. He was on his way back from the wire store on the outskirts of the city of Siena, only an hour or so before dusk. He stopped at the gas station not because he needed fuel but because the bathroom was something he could not do without. "Problems lately with constipation, you know," he explained. And all day he had been feeling pains that he couldn't tell if they were only gas or maybe things were finally moving inside and the good moment had come for him to unblock the situation.

"Help me understand this," said Sculati, a big bearlike man who never had problems with his intestinal tract. "They screwed you at the gas station because you were constipated?"

"The constipation had nothing to do with why they screwed me."

"Then you couldn't have saved that part of the story for yourself? If you're blocked up or not, what difference does that make to us?"

"Because it explains why I stopped at the gas station when I didn't even need gas. I was driving past, and I knew I had the long road home ahead of me with not many other bathrooms along the way. Which is why I parked by the gas station and went inside the bathroom they have there out back. Fog was so dense you couldn't see the building from the car, and it was no farther than from where I'm sitting now to Daniele over there at the bar."

"So at this point you have to tell us," Cappelli said, not without genuine curiosity. "In the bathroom. Any luck?"

"In the bathroom," Nuzzi said, his face relaxing at the memory of the relief he must have experienced, "things went well. But not just well. *Meravigliosamente!* Smooth as oil."

"What a nice satisfaction," said Sculati with a trace of teasing in his tone.

L'Altro laughed.

"And they screwed you when?" Renato prompted, impatient for the story to refind its thread.

"*Ah, sì.* Screwed me." It was when he came out of the bathroom, he continued, that the trouble started. He was in high spirits, for, as any-one who had lived through the same thing was sure to know, the joy of emptiness inside intestines that had only recently been blocked too tight brought with it a giddy sensation of lightness and freedom, so Nuzzi was in no particular rush to get back in the car. Just then his in-terest was pricked by voices he heard in the fog. He followed the sound to the far end of the parking lot, and found himself entering a strange scene, surrounded by a wall of dirty white fog which was penetrated only by the noises of heavy traffic from the main road. A group of men were huddled around one man standing behind a small foldaway table. Intrigued, Nuzzi sidled into the small crowd until he was next to the man at the table. The man looked greasy and untrustworthy. A lowlife hoodlum you could recognize as such from a mile away. "And on the tabletop, this thug was playing a game, fast as a magician doing tricks." Three walnut shells were on the table, a single green pea beneath one of the shells.

"Tell me you didn't bet," said L'Altro. "Oldest con game there is."

"That wasn't what they locked you up for?" Daniele, listening from behind the bar, could not resist taking a shot. "Or was it?"

"Please." L'Altro favored Daniele with a brief look. "Give me more credit than that. I'd never resort to anything so common." He returned his eyes to the electrician. "Tell me you didn't bet on the pea, Signor Nuzzi. Tell me you didn't fall for it."

"What? Do I look like a fool?"

"You want an honest answer?" Sculati laughed.

"I did *not* bet," Nuzzi insisted. "I would never be that dim."

"I don't follow," said Sculati. "They screwed you, but you didn't bet?"

"If you listen I'll explain." Indeed everyone was listening eagerly. Few stories are as intriguing as those of how someone else got conned. "I did not bet, but the other people, yes. Especially the Germans."

"Germans?" Cappelli asked.

Germans. Before the table were four or five German men. Businessmen maybe, or tourists. Travelers in any case. They were throwing lots of money on the table. "Not just tens," said Nuzzi, "but twenties, fifties, hundreds were flying from their hands." They lost game after game. "They were swearing in that language of theirs," Nuzzi said. Most of the Italian men standing around just chuckled to see the Germans losing so much cash. "But not the fellow standing next to me," Nuzzi said. "He was an ordinary Italian, a workingman, just like me. Even looked like me. He wasn't laughing at all. In fact, he started to get upset."

It was to Nuzzi that the Man Like Nuzzi voiced his complaint. No wonder Italy has a bad reputation among the other countries, said the Man Like Nuzzi. Visitors come here and get worked over by people like this thug. No wonder the other countries think we're a nation of thieves. Somebody ought to do something to stop this kind of thing. Someone ought to call the police and get the walnut-shell operator arrested. He might as well be stealing money straight from the Germans' wallets, that's how much chance they have of winning. Look, said the Man Like Nuzzi. If you watch carefully, you can see that the pea isn't under any walnut shell at all. Soon as he's shown which shell it's under at the start of the game, he palms it and holds it hidden in his hand. Doesn't matter which shell the Germans pick. They'll always be wrong. See? There! He's palming it now!

Nuzzi was close enough to the thug that, tilting his head, he could see the sleight of hand. The Man Like Nuzzi was right. The pea was curled up in the thug's fingers. The shells were empty, all three.

Nuzzi was amazed. How could the Germans be so foolish as to be taken in by a game the trick to which was transparent enough for even Nuzzi to see?

Enough of this! said the Man Like Nuzzi, raising his voice. I'm going into the gas station and I'm calling the police to arrest this son of a whore.

He had spoken too loudly, for the Thug with the Walnut Shells gave him an angry glare. Fuck off, said the Thug, his hands not missing a motion in the game. Fuck off and let me do my job.

Fuck off my prick, answered the Man Like Nuzzi. You're stealing from hardworking people and someone's going to teach you a lesson.

And who would that be? asked the Thug.

Who? I'll tell you who. Us, said the Man Like Nuzzi. Me and my friend here. We're going to teach him, he said, nudging an elbow into Nuzzi's ribs. Aren't we?

Me? said Nuzzi. Listen, I'm just watching for a little minute then I'll go. I'm not betting, so I don't win and I don't lose. I don't want to get involved.

The Man Like Nuzzi appeared disappointed by Nuzzi's lack of moral fiber. Then I'll call the police on my own, the man persevered. This son of a whore has to be stopped.

At that very moment, Nuzzi and the Man Like Nuzzi noticed a big barn of a man who had moved in behind them. He wore a large woolen overcoat. He was clean-cut, a dapper gangster type. Strange thing was, his face was reminiscent of the face of Nuzzi's father. And his aftershave even smelled like the cologne Nuzzi's father used to put on.

"Your father?" Sculati interrupted. "But he's been in the cemetery for thirty years now, right next to old Lombardi who used to have the pastry shop. What's your father got to do with this?"

"Nothing," said Nuzzi. "I'm just saying that this man looked to me the way my father looked when he was getting on a bit and I was young. I'm telling you, this guy could have been my old man. And my old man was someone you didn't want to be on the wrong side of."

Why call the police? asked the Man Who Could Have Been Nuzzi's Father, smiling friendly as a shark. His accent was unmistakably from the South. He leaned against Nuzzi and the Man Like Nuzzi. His hands were in his overcoat pockets. There was no saying what he held in his fists. Why did they have to stick their noses in another person's game? Why should they come here and break another person's balls?

Because innocent people are being stolen from, the Man Like Nuzzi said, and Nuzzi started to think that silence would be wiser than words that might lead to them getting beaten up if not killed.

I told them to fuck off but they're still here bugging me, said the Thug with the Walnut Shells.

The Germans, not understanding a word, carried on playing.

The Man Who Could Have Been Nuzzi's Father seemed to be holding on to his patience just long enough to try a bloodless solution. Maybe they'll fuck off peacefully, he said, if you let them win.

Why not? shrugged the Thug with the Walnut Shells. We're pulling in an avalanche of money from the Germans, he said from the side of his mouth, his hands busying working the shells. Losing one little round won't hurt us any. We'll let them win, but they better promise to fuck off.

Win how much? the Man Like Nuzzi wanted to know, his principles apparently dispensable if the price was right.

Show us what you've got and we'll double it, said the Thug with the Walnut Shells.

I'm in, said the Man Like Nuzzi. He winked at Nuzzi. We've got these turds now, he gloated. They come here to cheat and now they see that we can bust up their scam. We win and they lose. You can't get better justice than that.

Do what you want, Nuzzi told him. I don't want to play. I don't want to lose.

Are you stupid, the Man Who Could Have Been Nuzzi's Father said in Nuzzi's ear, or simply slow to get the point? You can't lose. He'll double your money just to make you leave him in peace. Not every day a person finds an opportunity like this.

It was a rare occasion, Nuzzi began to think, and there would be a pleasing kind of justice to it after all. Nuzzi and the Man Like Nuzzi had been clever enough to unmask the trick and now the criminals would have to pay.

Watch me carefully, said the Thug with the Walnut Shells, and I'll let you see exactly where the pea is. Only for one game though, all right? You'll see where the pea is, you'll put your money on the table, you'll win, I'll double your money, then the two of you fuck off. Clear?

Vai! said the Man Like Nuzzi, laughing now because he was celebrating triumph already. Go ahead!

The Thug with the Walnut Shells shuffled the shells around the table. His hands slowed down for an instant, just long enough for Nuzzi to see with absolute clarity that the Thug slipped the pea under the shell right in front of Nuzzi.

Stop! shouted the Man Like Nuzzi. He reached forward and put his index finger on the shell that contained the pea. This is the shell we want, he told the Thug. Then he turned to Nuzzi and said, This one, no? You saw, too.

That's the one, Nuzzi had to agree. He did not trust the Thug with the Walnut Shells and he did not trust the man who could have been his father, but certainly he could not doubt his own eyes.

Then put your money on the table, said the Thug with the Walnut Shells. How much do you have?

"How much did you have?" Sculati asked Nuzzi.

"You have to understand," Nuzzi justified, "that I had been careful the entire time. I didn't even trust them not to pick my pocket, so I kept my wallet in my front pocket, close to my balls, with my hand on it the whole time."

"How much did you have?" Sculati asked again.

"I didn't have any money," Nuzzi said.

"Thank God for that!" said Renato.

"No money of my own, that is. But I did have money from the Public Works Department."

Renato moaned, wiping his eyes with his palms. "Don't tell me."

"You see, I had taken five hundred out of the little cash box we keep for small expenditures, and I had counted on spending every cent up at the wire store. But the wire store didn't have all the right supplies that I had ordered, so I ended up only spending three hundred and fifty. I had the change in my pocket."

"One hundred and fifty of the town's money!" Renato shook his head. He was a public servant himself. In his years of handling the Waterworks funds, he had always been scrupulous to avoid any transaction that might be interpreted as an unauthorized personal loan.

"But I thought it would work out well for the town and for me, don't you see? Doubling the money, the town would keep its one hundred and fifty, and there would be an extra one hundred and fifty for me."

"I need some anesthesia to get me through the end of your story," said Cappelli. He motioned to Petula, who, understanding his pouring gesture for *bottiglia*, brought over the sambuca liqueur that had flavored his coffee.

Pressed from behind by the Man Who Could Have Been Nuzzi's Father, Nuzzi kept his hand on his wallet in his front pocket close to his balls. If you don't show him your money, the Man Who Could Have Been Nuzzi's Father breathed in Nuzzi's ear, how do you expect him to double it?

No arguing with reason, Nuzzi figured. Very carefully he took the wallet from his pocket and showed the contents to the Thug with the Walnut Shells.

Put it on the table, said the Thug.

But why do I have to put it on the table? Nuzzi tried to protest.

The Germans, impatient for their game to continue, motioned for Nuzzi to hurry up and play.

The Thug with the Walnut Shells jerked his head in the direction of the Germans. Can't let them see me giving away money for free, can we? We have to make it look like you're playing same as them.

There was a logic to what the Thug said. With utmost reluctance, Nuzzi removed the three fifties from his wallet and placed them on the table beside the shell with the pea. The Germans, agreeing with Nuzzi's choice, put their money on top of his. Nuzzi started to think he might come away the winner after all.

The Man Like Nuzzi had remained motionless with his index finger pressing down hard on the shell. My turn now, he said. I want to take these sons of whores for everything they have. Here, he said, to Nuzzi. Put your finger here where mine is. I have to get my wallet, and I don't want anyone to touch this shell.

Concentrating hard, Nuzzi put his finger on the shell, never taking his eyes off his own cash sitting right there on the table.

The Man Like Nuzzi produced a fat wad of bills. Five hundred, he said. That means you bastards will have to pay me a thousand. A thousand for me and three hundred for my friend. Today we're sending you home broke.

Just remember you promised to fuck off after this game, said the Thug with the Walnut Shells. He tapped Nuzzi's finger. You can't win until you let go.

Victory assured, Nuzzi pulled his hand away.

The Thug turned over the shell and revealed that the pea was not there. I'm sorry, gentlemen, he said. You lose. With breathtaking rapidity, he pocketed all the money that had been on the table.

The Germans gave groans of disappointment.

What do you mean we lose? said Nuzzi. I wasn't even playing.

The Man Who Could Have Been Nuzzi's Father leaned against Nuzzi's shoulder and said, Your finger was on the walnut shell. Your money was on the table.

But I would never have been stupid enough to play, Nuzzi said. I never said I was willing to play.

The Thug with the Walnut Shells stared coldly in his eyes. You would have been willing enough to take my money if you had won. Then he turned his attention to the Germans, who were anxious to try their luck some more.

"Problem is," Nuzzi told the people sitting with him at the station bar, "he was right. I would have been happy to take his money. And he knew that from the start. He hooked me on my own greed."

"And the guy who looked like you?" asked Cappelli. "How did he take to saying good-bye to five hundred?"

"Seemed troubled at first, just like me. But then he said we had to be sporting about it and take it with philosophy. 'Philosophy my prick,' I told him, but there was no point arguing with him. He had lost more than I had, and he wasn't even that worked up."

"How about the Public Works' money?" said Renato.

"Went to the bank first thing this morning and took money out of my own account," Nuzzi said miserably. "I've already put the hundred and fifty back into the cash box. My wallet's lighter, but the town hasn't lost a cent."

"Didn't you get angry?" Cappelli asked. "I would have become a beast."

"Oh, I was angry, all right. And I started to raise my voice. But the Germans kept on playing and the man who could have been my father started leaning against me in a way that would have looked friendly if you had been watching from the outside. He was leaning, you know, and pushing me toward my car. Twice my size, he was. 'Keep your voice down,' he said, smiling wide the whole time. 'It's only a game. Sometimes you win, sometimes you lose.' I told him that wasn't our deal. I was supposed to double my money for leaving them in peace. But he didn't listen, he kept saying over and over, 'It's only a game.' 'Some shitty game,' I told him, but his face started to get dark all of a sudden when I was loud, so I figured maybe it was better not to make too much noise."

"Good thing you backed down," L'Altro said. "Cause too many problems for him, and he would have put you in the hospital. That's his job. I've met gorillas like him. You don't want to mess with them. And was that the end of it?"

"The end, I guess. As soon as I got in my car and shut the door, the man who could have been my father disappeared in the fog. I sat in the car for a minute or two and didn't know what to do. I thought about going in the gas station to call the police, but how long would the police take to turn up? It was already too late. More I thought about it, the angrier I got. And maybe I started to feel safe because now I had my car to protect me, so I made sure the windows were rolled up tight and I locked all the doors and I put the car in first gear and decided to drive back to the table. I don't think I would actually have run anybody over, but at least I could make them see how mad I was. Drove back over to that side of the parking lot, but the strange thing was I didn't see a soul. No one. I drove around in little circles, not a person in sight. Only the fog."

"No Germans?" said Daniele, who had been listening from the bar.

"Not one."

"They could have been part of the con," said L'Altro. "Maybe yes, maybe no. Hard to say."

"No table?" said Cappelli.

"Nothing."

"No man with the walnut shells?" said Sculati.

"Not even the green pea. It's my own fault, I suppose. I almost deserved it. Never bet on anything, never once in my life. But, as the Thug with the Walnut Shells said, I was willing enough to take money for free. How did they know what I wanted when I didn't even know it myself?"

"They have a nose for people's needs," said L'Altro. "And I'd imagine you couldn't find any sign of the man who looked like you."

"Not even him," Nuzzi sighed. "Which surprised me. I mean, he had been so set on ruining their game at the beginning. Then, when he lost, he hardly seemed to care. I can't make sense of it."

"It hasn't occurred to you," said Renato, "that he was one of the crooks?"

Nuzzi rubbed his balding head, befuddlement showing on his face. "You think so?"

"Not just part of the group," said L'Altro. "The man who looked like you was the most important figure in the whole game. He was the shill."

"The what?"

"The plant. Call it what you want. Without him to draw you in, you'd be a hundred and fifty richer. Think about it. If he hadn't been there, would you have got involved?"

Nuzzi considered. "If not for him, I would have seen a group of men gambling, and I would have kept my wallet in my pocket and let them carry on with their stupid game. If they wanted to lose their money, that was their problem. I never would have done anything more than watch."

"You see? And he got to you exactly the right way, by making you feel that you and he were on the same side."

The young man's words made Nuzzi sad. "To think, I was good and wary of everyone, but I put my trust in the one person who looked trustworthy but who was the last person I should have trusted. *Bel coglione che sono.* Makes an idiot of me."

L'Altro, about to speak, had the sensation that eyes were watching him. He looked across the room and saw Petula drying saucers behind the bar. She studied his face. He believed he saw more of an accusation than a question in her eyes. He looked away. "Human is all it makes you," L'Altro muttered. "Like every one of us here."

Petula put the dry saucer on the stack and took up another with the towel. She had listened to the story from start to finish. L'Altro's remarks at the end were the part that alarmed her the most. Everybody else in the bar accepted what L'Altro had to say as judicious remarks on Nuzzi's lapse in common sense. Petula, however, was anything but reassured. She felt as if, forgetting himself for a moment,

L'Altro had given away his own secret. Could it be that she was the only person to have heard a hinted confession? But confession of what crime? Why had they sent him to prison anyway? She had no answers, nothing but a disconcerting suspicion that she knew only the smallest part of L'Altro's truth.

She watched him drink the last drop of coffee from his cup. His eyes now, she thought, avoided hers.

"If you'll excuse me," he said to everyone at the table, "I've got to use the bathroom for a minute before we get back to work." He looked at Petula and asked, "Do I need a key to get into the bathroom here?"

"It's unlocked," she said. She pointed to a doorway at the end of the bar, regarding him as if he had done something wrong. "Through the storage room," she said. "The door against the back wall."

"Thanks."

In the bathroom, L'Altro washed his face with cold water. "Damn," he said to his reflection in the mirror. He had seen Petula's expression after he had spoken to the men about the workings of the con game. He could tell that his knowledge of the subject had perplexed her. Why hadn't he kept his mouth shut?

He dried his face on a piece of paper towel. Had he said too much only because he liked the men at the table and, pulled along by the conversation's flow, had wanted to console Nuzzi? Or was it something else? "Damn," the young man said again. His brother would have been more careful, less sentimental.

Returning through the storage room, L'Altro saw what he knew well was there. The wall safe between hanging hams. He stopped and stared at the safe, observing the numbers on the dial, the dull metal of the door, the curve of the handle.

"Well, look at this!" said Daniele.

L'Altro jumped. He had not heard Daniele come in.

"I come in here to get a bottle of vinegar," Daniele said as if genuinely amused, "and look who I find examining the safe."

"It's a beautiful antique," L'Altro said, pretending to be calm. "I couldn't help but notice."

"Certainly," Daniele said, leaning his shoulder against a shelf. "You were admiring its aesthetic qualities." He smiled. "I'm surprised you haven't opened it already. Haven't you convinced Petula to tell you the combination?"

"I haven't asked."

Daniele shook his head slowly. "You know the crazy part? I thought you were the good guy at first. I thought your brother was the slippery one. But you know what I think now? I think, with so many people dying around here lately, why don't you just go ahead and die, too?"

L'Altro squared his shoulders. "Are you threatening me?"

"And if I say yes? Will something terrible and mysterious happen to me? Will I fall off a ladder or choke on a piece of salami?" He laughed and, with a fingertip, traced a line in the dust on the edge of a shelf. "No, not threatening. I'm just wishing out loud."

L'Altro thought for a moment, then said, "You want me dead." He rubbed the back of his own neck. "I can understand why, I suppose. I take it that Petula has told you."

"She didn't have to. I have eyes that work." He picked up a bottle of vinegar from the shelf. "I'll tell you one thing, though. God help you if you hurt her."

"I'd say you've done a good job of that already," L'Altro said.

Daniele opened his mouth to speak, then chose in favor of self-restraint. If I fight with this guy, he thought, I lose even if I win. Petula, he knew, would think no good of him if he reasoned with his fists.

When Daniele spoke at last, he kept his voice steady. "I'm going to find out who you are. That's a promise."

"Why go looking for a mystery where there is none?"

"I don't know who you are," Daniele said. "But I know you're not who you seem to be."

L'Altro laughed. "Nuzzi's probably waiting for me. Talking with you is always a pleasure. We can continue another time." He walked past Daniele and left the storage room.

Back out in the bar, L'Altro saw that the men, on their way out, were patting Nuzzi on the back and telling him he should be more careful with the town's money in the future. Their tone was teasing, but not harsh.

"Come on," Nuzzi called to him. "I've taken care of your coffee. Next time it's your turn."

"See you soon," L'Altro said to Petula as he headed for the door to catch up with the others. She thought the smile on his lips looked tense. He seemed anxious to leave.

Watching him cross the room, a dark silhouette against a big window full of light, she wondered about the person in whom she had been placing her faith.

As the door swung back into place behind him, sunlight glinted off its glass in a flash, violently bright.

30

Sleepless, Petula looked at the clock: well past two in the morning. She would be a ruin tomorrow. She had to rise early and get Beniamino ready for school before going to work herself. But what could she do? You can't make yourself sleep, not when thoughts drone in your head like bees in a hive.

For her, love had always been a simple thing given to only one young man. Now two faces, two smiles, memories of two bodies, two tastes, two intimacies inhabited her thoughts. Each created in her its own kind of desire, each its own reason for doubt.

A new and unfamiliar power was at work in Petula despite, or perhaps because of, her unrest. She felt more of a woman, less of a child. Mature people had always appeared stable and uninteresting to her young eyes. Now she began to perceive the untidy inner worlds concealed by the masks that adults put on daily to make themselves presentable. Who would have guessed that grown-up life meant learning to exist while pulled in opposite directions? She was the rope in her own tug-of-war in deciding who she wanted to be, yet strangely, in being torn, she was becoming whole.

She could hear the soft in and out of Beniamino's breathing in the rollaway cot near her bed, breathing fundamental to her as her own. There at least was one love which felt like an answer and not like another question.

She rolled over under the blankets. Air in the room was perfumed by the shampoo she had used on Beniamino during his evening bath, the same chamomile shampoo her mother had used on her when she was a little girl. Her bed smelled of clean warm sheets. Everything around her smelled of childhood, of home. It was comforting to be here in this precious womb from the past.

But this was not where she wanted to stay forever. She longed for the bedroom of womanhood. Her own space, her own house, not the house of her parents. She missed the king-sized bed she had shared with Daniele. She missed the late-night luxury of nestling into a man's body, Daniele's body, and feeling his arms enfold her, even when he was more asleep than awake. And thinking of Daniele, she thought of L'Altro, and the smoothness of his skin when they were to-gether in the car.

A noise from outside. Petula turned her head on the pillow to hear better. Music at this hour? She listened. Had it been playing before and only now did her concentration focus on the sound, or had the music started only a second ago? And what was the melody? Too dis-tant to tell. Probably as far away as the road. Who would be listening to a radio this late? Had a couple of furtive lovers parked along the roadside in front of the house? Perhaps it was no melody at all: Lis-tening more attentively, Petula could make out only disjointed notes but no particular tune. If this had been summer, she would have thought of nocturnal birds. A nightingale? No. The notes were not nearly high enough. An owl? A loon? Her brain, addled by fatigue, played with the possibilities. But it's not a bird, she told herself, rous-ing from near sleep. I know that sound. The notes are held too long.

Then she recognized it. She had heard it a thousand times, every time she went to one of Daniele's band concerts, just before the band began its first piece. It was the drawl of wind instruments tuning up. Laboring dissonantly to reach an agreement as to pitch, the sound bent, tightening sharp, souring to flat, until achieving at last a single on-key note.

The noise stopped.

Petula heard the opening and closing of car doors, followed by footsteps that were anything but weightless on the gravel drive lead-ing to the house. Burglars, she thought for a moment, but what thieves would be stupid enough to tune instruments in their car before sneaking up to commit the theft?

The footsteps came nearer, halting immediately beneath her window. Silence then. Petula waited. A single instrument began to play. A tenor saxophone. Not used to hearing those notes coming out of a sax, Petula's mind struggled to place the tune. When the tenor saxophone had sung its theme, it was joined by a second saxophone, by a third, and by a fourth still, until four threads of music wove around one another, each smooth strand bright with a gentle beauty written centuries before to express love at its most sublime. The brass throats of the instruments spoke of the longing of the soul. Petula knew the piece.

"Am I dreaming," said Renato, waking in the bedroom across the corridor, "or is there a band playing outside?"

"What time is it?" Milena leaned on her elbow and looked at the phosphorescent numerals of the alarm clock. "It's after two. The alarm will ring in a few hours."

"What should I do?" whispered Renato, his body so close to hers, it shared the same pocket of warmth beneath the sheets. "Call the police?"

"Wonderful idea. Tell them to send out the Band Control Squad."

"Fine, but people can't go around giving concerts in front of houses in the middle of the night."

"It's not just people who are playing, Renato."

"You think it's Daniele?"

"If not Daniele, who? Charlie Parker?"

"I'll go and have a look."

Milena put an arm across his chest. "You'll stay right where you are. You think you're the one Daniele came to serenade?"

"*Mah,*" Renato grunted, unable to shake off the displeasure of having been stirred from a comfortable sleep. "If you ask me, I think it's a very strange approach."

"If you ask me, it's a prettier approach than I ever would have imagined. Shows a good dose of fantasy, no? *Bravo,* Daniele, I say. *Bravo.*"

"*Sì, bravo*, she says. I'm less convinced. I'm going to take a look."

"Don't you dare."

"And if I tell you that, now that I'm awake, I have to go and piss?"

She reached between his legs and grabbed him in her fist. "Cross your legs. Hold it inside. Piss in the bed if you have to. Just don't mess things up for Petula."

"You can be cruel when you put your mind to it," Renato laughed, trying to push her away, but she held on tight. "Good thing I like a woman with spirit. *Bene.* You win. You can let go now. I'll stay out of it." When Milena released his groin, Renato rolled onto his side. Milena put her arm around him, hugging him from behind. "Let's hope this isn't the first movement of a long symphony," said Renato. "Let's hope they stop playing some time before dawn."

"Babbo?" Beniamino mumbled in his sleep.

"Yes, it's your babbo," Petula said. "Why don't we go to the window? What do you say?"

Wrapping themselves in bathrobes, Petula and Beniamino opened the window and leaned out. The night air was surprisingly warm.

There, an arm's length below, stood a quartet of musicians, dimly visible in the light of the streetlamps on the road. They were saxophonists from the town band, all four. Daniele with his tenor sax stood in the middle of the group, the soprano, alto, and baritone forming a half-moon around him.

Petula wondered how Daniele had convinced these others. In daylight hours they were a carpenter, a farmer, and a bricklayer, not the sort of men given to artistic outbursts when the rest of the world was asleep. By the sound of it, they had been practicing for weeks, for they played their parts from memory and their harmonizing was not nearly as squeaky and fragmented as it was during most band performances. To the contrary. Graceful and persuasive, the music flowed.

The man who wrote the motet must have been a genius indeed. In this one short piece—two mere minutes of simple phrases—Palestrina expressed more piety and passion than lesser composers managed in a lifetime of notes.

But this was L'Altro's music. At first Petula felt odd hearing the notes come from Daniele. She wondered how he had known about her attachment to this piece, then remembered that she had played the tape once at the bar. Should she feel angered or touched that he had dared to turn L'Altro's music into his own? More than anything, she was amazed that Daniele had seen deeply enough into her to understand how much this music moved her. When had he ever put aside his feelings in deference to hers?

Having listened to the tape until she had learned the text by heart, Petula caught herself mouthing the words now while the instruments played. *"Sicut cervus desiderat ad fontes aquarum . . ."* Over and over the theme passed from one instrument to the next. "Like as the deer desireth the water brooks . . ." Each line replied to the call of the line before, *"Ita desiderat . . . Ita desiderat . . . desiderat . . . desiderat . . ."* and Petula heard the repetition. "So longeth . . . longeth . . ." She looked at Daniele, whose eyes watched her own. *". . . Anima mea . . ."* he played to her, the other instruments cushioning his phrase with similar phrases above and below. ". . . My soul . . . my soul . . ." She could not tell in the near darkness whether or not the spark of light on his cheek was a tear. *". . . Anima mea,"* echoed the baritone sax, creating a brief and melancholy shadow with its sudden shift to the minor key, as the other instruments blended for a conclusion on a single sentence of desire. *". . . Ita desiderat anima mea ad te, Deus,"* the cadence coalesced. ". . . So longeth my soul after Thee, O God."

The final chord held, Daniele signaled with the tip of his saxophone. and the musicians stopped. Beniamino clapped, elbows on the windowsill.

Never unhappy with applause, the three other musicians performed a bow. Daniele remained upright.

"Ciao, Beniamino," he called.

"Ciao, Babbo."

"You like the music?"

Beniamino nodded yes.

Daniele smiled at Petula. His voice not entirely steady, he said, "*Ciao*, Petula. I wanted to tell you something."

"What?"

"*Desiderat anima mea ad te.* My soul longs after you."

Many times in the past months Petula wondered how she would respond if Daniele were to ask to be together again. She had enacted different scenes in her mind. Sometimes they were scenes of anger, other times scenes of sadness, scenes of joy. In none of her imagined rehearsals had she expected a reaction like the one she felt, now that Daniele had come to her in the flesh. Rising within her were many emotions—anger, yes, but tenderness, too, and stubborn refusal, and the fear of being hurt, and love—simultaneous sentiments, each of overwhelming power.

She wiped tears from her eyes with the back of her hand. "How did you put this together?" she said, unable to stop her voice from shaking.

"The band conductor got me the sheet music for the piece you played on the tape deck at the bar. I studied the words and I guess I understood why it's so important to you."

More tears fell from Petula's eyes.

"I transcribed it for the four saxes myself," Daniele continued. "Copied the music by hand. Had to transpose everything to B-flat, which almost wore my brain out. Naturally I took the tenor part. Opening line was mine, didn't you hear? It's not every day a sax player from the band gets center stage."

"And the rest of you?" Speaking was difficult. Petula's feelings were too many, too mixed. "How did he coax you into this?"

"Wasn't easy," said the bricklayer with the baritone sax.

"We drove a hard bargain with this man of yours," said the carpenter with the soprano sax.

"Made him promise to give us free coffees for a month at the bar," said the farmer with the alto sax.

"With," added the burly bricklayer, "the occasional pastry to be thrown in on request."

Petula laughed, then something like a sob thickened in her throat.

"Why have you done this, Daniele?" she asked. "God, you've confused me. Tell me why."

"Why? Because I see you, Petula, and you, too, Beniamino, and I see the only things in the world that to me are—" He sighed. "Indispensable. No other way to say it. *Assolutamente indispensabili.* The two of you are water to me, and a person without water does nothing but die. I'm sorry for not seeing it earlier."

"He said he's sorry, Mamma," Beniamino said. "He said he's sorry. Can we go back home now?"

Not knowing what to say, Petula said, "It's not that easy."

"Why not?" Beniamino asked.

"Because it's not."

"Listen," the bricklayer interjected, "looks as if you two have things to talk about. Might be a good time—no?—to let us get back to our homes? My wife's already furious I'm staying out so late. She'll probably punish me by not speaking for a week, but I can't say that the idea displeases me very much. As for *their* sweeter halves"—he jerked his head in the direction of the farmer and the carpenter—"I bet they're busy in bed with other men."

Cries of protest were predictably swift. To silence them, Daniele said, "*Andate.* Thanks for your troubles. Go."

"Long walk back to town," said the carpenter.

"What long walk? Just up the road and over the bridge."

"*Sì,* but we'd have to get the saxophone cases out of the car, then we'd need to carry the heavy instruments all the way. You're young. People like us, though, we reach a certain age . . ."

"Fine." Daniele tossed the keys to the carpenter. "Take the car. I'll pick it up from you tomorrow. *Buonanotte.* Good night."

"Coffee for a month," said the farmer, leaving. "Don't forget."

"And a pastry or two," said the bricklayer.

"And maybe a drop of grappa," said the carpenter, "to make the coffee good."

"*Buonanotte,*" said Daniele.

"*Buonanotte,*" the three men called out.

"*Grazie,*" said Petula. "*Buonanotte.*"

"Buonanotte," Beniamino said.

When the men had gone, Petula patted Beniamino's head and said, "I want you to get back to bed."

"But Babbo's here."

"Exactly. He and I have to talk alone. That means without you. Go ahead." She put him in bed. "I'll be here at the window. You try to sleep."

Beniamino lay back on the pillow, his eyes wide open. He wanted to hear every word.

Petula returned to the window and leaned out toward Daniele, just below the ledge. "We have to talk," she whispered.

"I know," Daniele whispered back. He bent down toward a sack that he had placed on the ground near his feet. "I have something for you." From the bag he produced what appeared to be, in the faint light, a bunch of flowers. He reached up to pass the bouquet to Petula. "Made them myself."

"Made them?" She took the bouquet and rubbed the paper petals between her fingertips. "What are they?"

"Look," Daniele said.

"I can't see. It's too dark."

"Look hard," he whispered.

Tilting the flowers toward the distant streetlamp, Petula's eyes perceived the colors. The flowers were shiny, and no two colors were the same. "They're beautiful," she said softly.

"What did Babbo give you?" Beniamino called from his bed.

"Go to sleep," Petula answered.

"There's a promise in those flowers," Daniele whispered, leaning against a budless wisteria vine immediately under the window with his saxophone hanging from a strap around his neck. "Where did I find paper in so many different colors? you'll be asking yourself. Well, you wouldn't believe the fight the hardware store man put up when I told him I wanted to take all those little sample strips he keeps to show the different colors of paint. In the end, I had to promise that we'll buy lots and lots of paint from him soon, seeing as how we're about to redo the entire bar."

"But you don't want the bar to change."

"I *didn't* want. I was wrong. Ugly thing to admit, but I haven't known how to work with you. I've only known how to tell you what to do so that nothing in the bar would be different from the way it's always been. And that's why it's the same old run-down, depressing place. Every day when I go in there, all I want to do is leave."

"Then why haven't you done anything before?"

"Because I've still been working for my old man. It's as if all I'd have to do is change some little thing, order a different kind of paper napkin, and my father would come up from the ground or wherever the hell he is just to redecorate my face with punches the way he used to do. Whenever I get tempted to think I'm man enough to choose something new for the bar, I can hear my mother whimper, 'Don't upset your babbo. You know how angry he gets.' For seven years you and I have been employed by a pair of ghosts. Isn't it time we made the bar ours, not theirs?"

"Nice idea." Petula looked at the multicolored bouquet.

"I can't do it myself. It has to be something we create together. We have a wall safe full of cash. Whatever look you choose, I know it will be good. First thing we'll do, though, is go to the lawyer's office and change the title of ownership. I want you to be my equal partner."

Petula shook her head. "You should think this over first."

"Think it over? I've been doing so much thinking, I thought my brain would break. I want us to be partners." He looked up into her face. "And I want us to be husband and wife."

Petula never would have imagined that Daniele was capable of astonishing her. Her heart quickened, however, with nearly painful force. "You're asking me to *marry* you?"

"The word we've never mentioned. Strange, no? Between Beniamino and the bar, we never had time. I've never asked you, and you've never asked me. And I don't think anyone in your family dared ask us. Maybe everyone was afraid that if they pushed too hard, they'd make us split."

"We managed to split on our own."

"I'm asking you now, Petula. I know it's what I want, because I want you in every way that one person can want another." He stared at her. "And you? You have to decide for yourself whether you want me."

"*Sì,*" came the response, but it came from Beniamino's mouth as he squeezed in beside Petula at the window ledge.

"Beniamino, go to bed," Petula scolded.

"What's Mamma say?" Daniele asked.

"Mamma says yes," Beniamino answered.

"How about me?" said Petula. "Do I get to think for myself?"

"Babbo and Mamma are getting married," said Beniamino. "No?"

Petula kissed his forehead. "Babbo and Mamma love each other." Tears came to her again at hearing herself admit what she felt. "But Mamma needs a little time." She wiped her eyes. "I can't answer now for the rest of my life."

"*Giusto,*" said Daniele. "Your mamma's right, Beniamino. She needs time. And I think it's time for all of us to go to sleep tonight. Since you both left the house, I haven't slept straight through to morning. Not once. Do me a favor, Petula, to maybe give me some peace tonight. Can you tell me if I've got hope?"

"Go home and sleep," said Petula. "I'll see you at work."

"A little hope?"

"A little hope." Petula smiled. "*Sì.*"

Daniele blew a kiss to her and a kiss to their son. "*A domani.*"

Petula returned the gesture. "Until tomorrow. And thank you. Sleep well."

He walked away, then, upon reaching the road, turned back for a moment. "Did I do a bad thing, coming here tonight?" he called in a loud voice.

"Best thing you've done in years," Renato's voice answered from a different window.

Daniele heard the windows shut. He started toward town, hugging his saxophone to his chest.

A knock came at Petula's bedroom door. "Petula?" Milena said from the corridor. "*Permesso?*"

"Come in."

Milena entered. "You all right?"

"I'm fine." She was tucking the boy in to the rollaway cot.

"Would you do something for me, Beniamino?" Milena asked. "Go and say good night to your grandfather."

"Already have."

"Say it again. I want to talk to your mother."

His eyelids were heavy. "There's school tomorrow."

"We'll let you sleep an extra half hour in the morning. I'll take you to school myself and I'll tell the teacher it's my fault you're late."

The thought of thirty minutes more of sleep and thirty minutes less of school revived the boy. He climbed out of bed.

"Put your slippers on," said Milena. "A minute ago your grandfather said he had to go and make peepee. I think he wants you to take him to the bathroom."

"Nonno's not afraid of the dark," Beniamino laughed.

"Go. Just give me a minute with your mamma."

"Are Mamma and Babbo getting married?"

"Go," Milena said affectionately, steering the boy by the shoulders until he was out of the room. "Married?" she said to Petula when they were alone.

"Who would have thought?" Petula said. And she started to cry.

"Your father and I heard the music." Milena sat down on the bed beside her daughter. "I don't know what you said to each other afterward. But a concert in the middle of the night? And look. A bouquet of paper flowers? Sounds as if things are changing between the two of you. A good change maybe?"

"Daniele was unhappy before. Beniamino and I made him feel suffocated. I couldn't even give a name to the shadows he had inside. But, yes, something has changed." She wiped her eyes. "In me, too."

"And now he wants to get married." Milena's fingers brushed strands of hair away from her daughter's face. "Listen, Petula. I can only guess at the confusion inside your head. I don't really know what you've been doing with that other young man. With L'Altro. I haven't said anything. I've trusted you to do what's right for you."

"But *I* don't know what the right thing is. L'Altro's always saying not to worry about him. Says I should follow my instincts. Problem is, I have instincts ripping me in ten different directions."

"If nothing else, he's been a good friend for you. Who knows?" She spoke slowly, as if forcing herself to say words that were not easy for her. "Experiencing another man, seeing new parts of yourself, living a little beyond the life you've always lived, doesn't seem to have done you bad, no?"

Petula found an opening in a mother she had expected to be closed. She held out her arms, and Milena answered with a hug.

"My sweet girl. Listen to me, Petula. You have a lot to think about. While you're thinking, keep in mind that Daniele's not the ogre he thinks he is. I know he's been afraid of harming you and Beniamino the way he was harmed."

"Know what he told me once?" said Petula. "He said he couldn't handle seeing Beniamino's vulnerability. It reminded him too much of his own as a boy, only there was no one to put the brakes on his father."

"Listen, Petula. Do you think your father or I would let him near you if we thought he was dangerous to you or Beniamino? Daniele has enough brains and enough heart to stop him from becoming the monster his father was. It's no tragedy if he gets tired and impatient at times, like the rest of us humans. He should trust himself more." With her hand, Milena readjusted the way Petula's nightgown fell against her neck—a mother's unconscious movement to make things better for her girl. "Let me tell you a little thing," she said. "Choices aren't easy. Don't worry about what your father and I think, that's what I want to tell you. We're not just telling you to think what's best for Beniamino. You know us too well. We're not like that. I know for years your father couldn't stand the sight of Daniele, but your father's not made of stone. He softens when he needs to. And how can he blame Daniele for doing things that he's done himself? They're not that different from each other, you know. You don't think your father has had his times of doubt?" She paused. "You don't think I've had mine?"

"You always seem so sure of each other," said Petula, surprised, without pulling away from her mother's hug.

Milena sighed. "It doesn't mean I love your father less. In the end you listen inside yourself and you ask which speaks louder, the doubt or the love." She placed a kiss on Petula's forehead. "You'll make your own decision."

Petula listened and let herself be hugged. Since earliest memory, family myth—that great creator of caricature—had painted her as her father's daughter. Love had never lacked between her mother and herself, but the two females had often seemed like members of unlike species. Tonight Milena had allowed a glimpse of the doubt that was as much a part of her inner world as devotion and warmth. In laying bare her uncertainty, she revealed her strength. Petula had tripped upon the discovery that inside her mother's body lived a spirit that could have been her own. Now, for the first time, she saw in her mother a mirror of herself.

She pressed her ear to Milena's bosom until she could hear the beating of the heart within. One word was all she said. "Mamma." Then she added, *"Grazie."*

31

In town, doors were opened once more to let in fresh air. Pots of geraniums gave color to windowsills, and upper-story clotheslines bloomed with vivid laundry hung out to dry. The first swallows, migrating home from Africa, swooped acrobatically overhead while people did their business along the *corso* at dusk.

Petula was tormented by every kind of private tempest. The winds of spring, for all that they announced the coming of the beautiful season, brought little peace. March winds tested everything in Sant'-Angelo D'Asso, permitting only the deeply rooted to stay firm and not be swept off to someplace else. The winds made people restless, awakening in them longing, loss, desire, memories, nostalgia, the shiver of hope.

Petula struggled to hear the quiet voice of her own heart amid the rushing whirlwinds within. The decision before her seemed bigger than the windswept sky, because she was choosing not so much between two men as between two versions of herself. First decide, she pushed herself, then be resolute in your actions, and soon you will become your choice. Doubt may not disappear, but maybe a pinch of doubt is inevitable any time a man and a woman are together. Hadn't Milena confessed that her own marriage was not devoid of doubt?

Petula watched her parents, studying the way they moved at the sink in the bathroom while her father brushed his teeth when Milena wanted to wash her face. The two bodies negotiated worldlessly, bumped into each other, nudged, stepped aside to make room. This man and woman were not the single entity they had appeared for all of Petula's childhood. They were separate beings who had chosen, each selecting the other among a world of alternatives. Even now, after a lifetime together, they daily reaffirmed their choice, even when one turned on the hot water to wash the soap off her hands and the other preferred cold water to rinse the toothpaste off his toothbrush.

Listen inside, Milena had said, and you'll hear which voice speaks louder, doubt or love? Petula listened. In the end her choice was clear.

One breezy night she switched off the car in the olive grove that overlooked the town. L'Altro leaned over to kiss her, but she put a hand on his chest and pushed him away. "Let's get out," Petula said. "We have to talk."

Outside, they stood against the car. Streetlamps marked the shapes of the town across the valley.

"You don't have to talk," L'Altro said, sniffing the earth smells of the olive grove. "You push me away. Your voice has all the courtesy of a polite passenger on a train. You don't need to explain. I understand already."

"Stop playing mind reader for once." Petula's voice was sharp-edged. "Can't I speak to you without your interpreting my thoughts for me?"

"But it's clear already, no? Why waste words? You're going back to him. What else do you need to say?"

"You are my extraordinary friend," she said. "As a friend, you might be interested to hear what's going on in my mind."

L'Altro looked toward the ground and shook his head. "I've tied my own hands," he said. "I've only left myself one way to react. All our talks together about adventure-loving chimps and how they dread the inertia that homebodies crave, and about how you had to do what's right for you—" He laughed, working hard to maintain the dignity of his demeanor. "I said it myself, that I couldn't offer you a future. And you told me you weren't looking for the future, but you wanted to live a little in the present. Fine. You've lived. We had our nice moments in the present tense. Now you've decided to consign our time together to the past. I'd be contradicting everything I've ever told you if I tried to cling." Never in his life had L'Altro been more upset. The fear of losing Petula made everything inside him ache, but he did not want her to know. "What can I say? That I'm pleased for you and feel honored to remain your friend? All right. I've said it. And it's true. The last thing I've ever wanted to do is limit your freedom. I can't tie you down now." Hearing the self-sacrifice of his own words, L'Altro took pride in the honor and chivalry he was showing. He was sure Petula would appreciate these qualities, too.

Instead she groaned in frustration and said, "You and your pretty speeches. You're too good with words for your own good. I'd hoped we could talk about what we really feel. Never mind. Get in the car. I'll drive you home."

"Wait." He put his hand on her arm. "You want to know how I feel? Petrarch wrote a poem—"

"My God!" she said, exasperated. "You never tell me about you. I don't even know why they put you in prison. And when it's time to speak about yourself, you quote somebody else's words from six hundred years ago."

"Stop talking!" L'Altro shouted suddenly, losing hold of the selfless magnanimity that had comforted him a moment earlier.

Petula stopped. She had never before heard L'Altro scream.

"Listen to me!" he insisted. He breathed hard, steadying his quavering voice. "Petrarch, I was saying. A sonnet he wrote after his beloved Laura left him and married someone else. '*Zefiro Torna*—The Wind of Spring.'

> *Zephyr returns and brings the sunshine back*
> *and flowers and grass, his sweet companions,*
> *and warbling swallows, lamenting nightingales,*
> *and Spring, milk-white and scarlet.*

That's what Petrarch says in the first verse. That's what's happening now. Can't you see that?

> *Earth and water are filled with love,*

he says in the second verse,

> *and every animal renews its courtship.*

> *But for me, alas, the heaviest sighs*
> *return, drawn from the depths of my heart*
> *by the one who took its key with her to heaven.*

You want to know how I feel, Petula? How did Petrarch feel when he looked at the beautiful world and all the people around him but could not be with the woman he loved?

> *And birdsong, and the flowers of the field,*
> *and the sweet sincerity of lovely women*
> *are as a desert and pitiless wild beasts."*

When L'Altro finished, he realized that Petula was crying. He turned to her and wiped the tears from her cheek. "You're crying," he said. "That should show you where your real feelings are."

She stepped away, turning her back to him.

"You asked me what I feel," L'Altro said. "I told you. If the sadness in the poem makes you this distraught, you have to ask yourself why."

She cried more, but refused to speak.

"We've always told each other the truth, Petula," he said, talking to her back. He reached to put a hand on her shoulder, but she moved away. "Tell yourself the truth," he said. "And don't be afraid to listen."

"The truth is," she said without looking at him, "I'm not crying for you. The poem makes me think about how sad and alone Daniele must be."

"*Vaffanculo,*" L'Altro blurted out. "He's a bartender! You have too good a brain to waste on him."

"I see that *your* truth is coming out at last," said Petula, turning with anger in her eyes. "*'Desiderat anima mea,'*" she said to his face. "'My soul longeth.' Remember that? But my soul longs for him. How's that for truth?"

L'Altro stared at her in silence. Then, with no hope of winning her, he put on a smile. "If nothing else," he said, "I did a good job as catalyst. Clarified your feelings for you, didn't I?"

"Who ever said it was your job to play with my head?"

He did not answer. But groping for a little triumph, he said, "I thought I had found my *anima gemella* in you, the twin soul who wanted to wander with me. I thought you had the courage. Instead you're a provincial girl who's happy to settle for her childhood sweetheart. You disappoint me, Petula. You're not the person I thought you were."

Quickly she got in the car and started the engine. She rolled down the window a crack, just enough to speak through. "It's a beautiful night for a walk, Wanderer. Wander your own way home."

She drove away, leaving him in darkness on the hill.

32

Beniamino woke up early the day he and his mother would return to Daniele's apartment. "Hurry!" he said to Petula through breakfast. "I want to go home!"

Daniele came to pick them up after breakfast. Milena and Renato helped Petula with the move.

"It's not only the bar I want you to change," said Daniele when he turned the key to his front door, "but here, too. Do whatever you want to transform this house into *casa tua*. Make it yours. Make it ours."

Stepping in, Petula looked at the large windows and the high ceilings, and realized the place was far more full of light than the sad apartment it had become in her imagination. She hugged Daniele, kissed him, and said, "I'm glad to be back."

"Permesso," said Renato, pushing through the doorway, huffing with the weight of suitcases. "I think the stairs grew since the last time I was here."

"You've kept it nice and clean," said Milena, entering with a box in her arms.

"It wasn't so clean yesterday," Daniele laughed. "I stayed up half the night dusting and mopping. I wanted things to look their best," he said, kissing Petula again.

Beniamino ran up and down the corridor, beside himself with joy. He put his toys back in their place in his bedroom, his *real* bedroom.

——

Daniele held true to his promise of helping Petula change things. With energetic enthusiasm he shifted furniture upon request and threw out boxes of things that belonged to the past. He praised the way Petula got down to the task of redecorating and rearranging the apartment. With paint and cloth, with flowers and light, every space she touched started to become more lovely and livable than it had ever been before.

Petula found again in Daniele the vitality that had thrilled her when they had first fallen in love. Now that he had an unexpected second chance, he took care not to let small irritations spoil things that mattered more. Petula saw how hard he was trying. She disciplined herself, too, to concentrate all of her thoughts on him. L'Altro had left a hole in her heart. He never came to the station bar. If Petula saw him in town, she walked the other way.

On the subject of marriage, Daniele told her he wanted to be with her forever. He wanted Beniamino to have the full security that other children had in the durability of their parents' love. He wanted to make the commitment now that had frightened him in the past. Responsibility, he said, was no longer a burden.

"Let's take our time and see how things go" was Petula's answer at first. As the weeks passed, however, and she saw that Daniele could be trusted not to fall back into the bleakness that had marred his moods, she started to feel her own tensions ease. What can you say in the face of happiness? The thought of a ceremony to give their happiness a permanent shape began to feel like the natural next step. Why say no to what feels good?

"Of course I would be delighted to perform the rite," said Don Luigi when together Petula and Daniele appeared in his office. Nothing could be more gratifying for a man of God, he explained, than a couple's eagerness to make a sacrament of their love. Only shame was that more young people today didn't see things the same way.

Clearly, he said, they would have to wait until after Easter, for mar-
riages could not be held in the church during Lent. "You've waited
this long," he joked. "A few more weeks couldn't do any harm.
True?" Besides, weddings always take more planning than anyone
would hope, so the extra weeks of waiting would give them time to
organize the grand event.

A date was duly chosen: first Saturday of May.

The future bride and groom were sure of their intentions. Their
son thought his sweetest dream was coming true. Petula's parents
and grandparents found in the smile on their girl's face the brightest
omen they could ask for. Anxious to surround the young spouses
with nothing but positive thoughts, they threw themselves into wedding preparations, discussing flower arrangements, deciding who
would cook what for the feast. The feast! Where should they hold the
feast? Renato and Milena's garden, everyone agreed, for there could
be no more beautiful a spot.

Preferring a handmade to a store-bought dress, Petula asked Tita
Vezzosi if she would mind getting down to work with scissors and
needle. Maestro Baldesi offered the chairs from the band's rehearsal
room for the wedding banquet. And the band, he said, would be honored to provide music for free. Don Luigi told the couple they could
take as many tables as they wanted from the church's social hall. The
whole town of Sant'Angelo D'Asso joined in the family's mood of
prenuptial euphoria. A daughter of the town was marrying one of its
sons, and there's nothing like a springtime wedding to make everyone remember that life without romance might as well be death. Who
could do anything but be caught up by the love between two young
people? The tree of life showed its sweetest buds, ready to bloom.
Why look between the branches in search of a snake?

One evening Petula and Daniele were trying to get Beniamino into
bed. The boy's favorite television program had ended—a nature
show for children—but he was sure that, if his parents would let him
stay up only a little longer, the next would be even better than the one

he had just watched. "Come on," said Daniele. "I want to talk with your mamma. Time for you to go to bed."

"Talk about what?" Petula asked.

"I'll tell you when there aren't little ears listening. Come on, Beniamino. Bed."

Overexcited, the boy started running laps of the corridor, squirming away from his parents' grip every time they were about to catch him.

"That's enough," said Daniele. "Time to stop."

Beniamino giggled and said, "You don't boss my brain."

The challenge to Daniele's authority heated the blood in his face. If I had answered my old man that way, Daniele said to himself, he would have smashed me against the walls. Then he looked at his playful puppy of a son and saw another self, himself as a kid the way he would have wanted to be. He felt love, not rage. "What did you say?"

"You don't boss my brain," Beniamino giggled out again.

"You hear what he said?" Daniele turned to Petula.

"He said you don't boss his brain." She smiled, but waited to see how he would react.

"*Ometto!*" Daniele grabbed Beniamino in a hug and kissed the crown of his head. "Little man! I would never want to boss this brain. It's yours. But you and your brain both need to get some sleep."

Petula's smile broadened. This was a Daniele with whom she wanted to be one flesh. "You see?" she said to him.

"See what?"

"You're not your father."

Holding Beniamino still, Daniele leaned over and gave her a kiss. "When did you learn to read minds?"

She took the boy from Daniele. "Let's go and brush these teeth."

Beniamino brushed his teeth, put on his pyjamas, then ran more laps in the corridor. After much pleading, he got to watch television for ten more minutes. In the end, tiredness won. He fell asleep on the sofa.

Once they had carried Beniamino to his bed, Petula and Daniele sat at the kitchen table. "You wanted to tell me something," she said. "Tell."

Daniele looked around the kitchen. He needed a cigarette. Instead, he picked an apple from the fruit bowl to give his mouth something to do. "Bite?" he offered.

She bit the apple he held in his hand. "Good," she said.

He bit it himself. "Very good."

"Tell me," she said.

"Tomorrow," he said while chewing, "I'm taking a little trip. Only for the afternoon. I want you to look after the bar by yourself."

"Fine. But where are you going?"

He took another bite. "It's important to me. I'm not sure I want to tell you."

Holding him by the wrist, she pulled the apple toward her own mouth and bit. "I'm trying to remember the last time you took a trip. I can't think. Maybe never."

"Maybe never." He nodded. "It's about time I ventured out a little, wouldn't you say?"

"But you don't want to tell me where. Interesting." Feeling playful, she raised her eyebrows and said, "Should I be jealous?"

"I'm not the one with other interests."

Petula lost her playfulness. "Stop thinking about him," she said. "I told you. He's past."

"I can't stop thinking. That's the problem. I close my eyes at night and I see you together with him."

She took his wrist again, this time to pull it close and kiss his hand. "Try closing your eyes and feeling me next to you."

Responding, he put down the apple and pressed her hand to his lips. "I do feel you next to me. It's the best feeling in the world. You say he's in the past for you. Maybe he is. Maybe he isn't. But he's not past for me. I want to be free of him before you and I get married."

"And you think this trip will make you free," Petula said.

"That's the idea. If this doesn't, I don't know what will."

"So tell me where you're going. How can a trip make a person disappear?"

Daniele took a final bite from the apple. "Tell me something, Petula. Who *is* he?"

"I don't honestly know," she said. "I asked. He wouldn't tell me. But what difference does it make now?"

"It makes a big difference because part of you will always wonder, no?"

Brushing hair away from her eyes, Petula said nothing. But Daniele, she knew, was right.

"I can't live with that, Petula. You'll never get rid of him completely until you know what name to give him. I have to find out who he is. What he is." He got up and crossed the room to throw away the apple core. "I might as well tell you where I'm going tomorrow. I want there to be truth between us. You remember Alboretti? The chubby kid I used to sit next to at school?"

"He moved away years ago."

"He moved away because he got a job up at the prison in Volterra. The same prison your friend L'Altro used to call home."

"That's where you're going tomorrow? To the prison? I don't understand, Daniele. What do you hope to find?"

"Prison records are probably confidential. But Alboretti wasn't a bad guy. I figure if I pay him a visit, he'll tell me what I want to know."

"You want to know L'Altro's crime."

"Don't you? Maybe he hacked people to pieces with an ax."

"You'd like that," Petula said.

"*Sì*. It would make him terrible enough. You'd never think about him again. Neither would I. Or maybe he was an ordinary pickpocket or burglar. I wouldn't mind that either. It would prove he's just another punk."

"You don't have to prove anything to me," said Petula.

"But I need to know. I need to get him out of my head."

Petula rose from the table, crossed the kitchen, and hugged Daniele. "I don't want to live with a question mark hanging in the air either," she said.

"So I'm not the only one with L'Altro still stuck in the brain?"

The kiss Petula gave him held tenderness and sadness in equal measure. "No," she said. "You're not the only one." Strange, how close she felt to Daniele in the very act of admitting that her thoughts lingered on another man. There was intimacy in confession. Maybe Daniele really could help free her of the shadow that thoughts of L'Altro cast on her love for him. "Go to Volterra," she said. "My parents can look after Beniamino tomorrow evening. I'll take care of the bar."

Hugging her tight, Daniele wondered if any information could ever erase from his mind the picture of his Petula in the other man's arms.

33

The next morning, brisk energy animated Daniele as he worked side by side with Petula at the bar. He had a trip to take, a mission to fulfill. As soon as the office opened, he bought his ticket and asked Enzo the stationmaster for a printout of the train schedule. In between making coffees, pouring drinks, and handing clients their pastries, he pulled the schedule out of his back pocket and checked and rechecked the connections. The trip would take three hours, a ridiculous amount of time to get to a town hardly a hundred miles away. There were no direct trains to Volterra. He would have to change at Siena, then Empoli, then Livorno Central. Had he wanted to, he could have taken the car, cutting out half of the trains' absurdly circuitous north-west-southeast route, but why rush things? The idea of crisscrossing half of Tuscany by train turned the trip into an adventure. And after years of watching others board trains, Daniele could not wait to ride the rails. The farther the better. Besides, he would retrace the route that L'Altro had taken when, leaving prison, he had come to haunt Sant'Angelo D'Asso. Stalking the same path, Daniele might come closer to understanding his target.

He helped Petula make an extra supply of sandwiches for lunch. He apologized for leaving her to deal on her own with the one o'clock rush of hungry customers, but, as he told her with a mixture of fearful solemnity and undeniable thrill, "I've got the 12:54 to catch."

He boarded at 12:53 and waved at Petula from the train window, his jacket his only luggage.

"Northbound 12:54 now leaving from track number one," Enzo announced over the loudspeaker in his nasal voice. "*In partenza.* Track number one."

Daniele felt a surge of freedom and fear when the whistle blew and the train pulled out of the station. He was traveling light beneath a clear spring sky. He tapped his jacket pocket: Tucked next to his train ticket, a pencil and a blank piece of paper waited at the ready to record the information he would unearth in Volterra. He pulled the window open to let the breeze in. The air carried the smell of the diesel fuel from the engine. The rumbling of the metal wheels on the tracks grew loud as the train picked up speed. Suddenly, goose bumps of jittery agitation prickled on his skin when he thought about his destination: a prison. He laughed at his own tension, leaned his forehead against the window, and watched his town slip behind him and the familiar contours of his small world slide by.

The town of Volterra sat on a hilltop far higher than anything else around. Daniele caught a local bus to take him up to the town center from the low-lying station in Le Saline. Perched over the brink of a drop-off to the deep valley below, the prison rose, an austere fortified castle from the Middle Ages with guards patrolling the battlemented ramparts between the towers.

The afternoon was chilly. Approaching the visitors' entrance, Daniele pulled his jacket close to his body. Stepping inside the metal door, he thought what everyone thinks when entering a prison: Let's hope getting out is as easy as getting in.

Inside, Daniele walked a lengthy corridor that smelled of ammonia toward another metal door.

"Last name and first name of the prisoner you wish to see," said the guard at the door.

"No prisoner," Daniele said. Speaking was hard. The tension of prison walls thickened his throat. "I'm looking for a guard. We grew up together. Alboretti is his name."

"Pippo Alboretti?" the guard said, brightening at the mention of a colleague he evidently liked.

"Filippo Alboretti, *sì*," said Daniele. "Pippo, *sì.*"

"*Un momento*," said the guard. He picked up a telephone on the wall by the door. "Oh!" he said into the receiver. "Pippo anywhere in sight? Well, tell him to come to the visitors' entrance. He's got a guest named . . ." He raised his eyebrows in question.

"Mangiavacchi," Daniele said. "Daniele Mangiavacchi."

"Daniele Mangiavacchi," said the guard. He nodded into the telephone, said, *"Bene, grazie,"* and hung up. "He'll be right down," he told Daniele.

Waiting, Daniele looked around him at the stone walls painted industrial beige. Same color, he thought, that my parents chose for the bar. But that'll soon change.

A moment later Pippo Alboretti opened the metal door from the inside. "Look who's here!" Pippo said with the smile that Daniele remembered, a smile never far from a good-natured laugh. Pippo's former chubbiness had grown into full-blown obesity. His pink scalp shined through thinning hair. Same age as me, Daniele thought, but by the time he reaches thirty he'll be bald as a watermelon. "Come in!" Pippo said. "Come! Come!"

Like a host welcoming a guest to his home, he held the door while Daniele passed through, then escorted him along a series of fluorescent-lit corridors and corners, nodding to other guards who turned keys to open barred doors. "The town?" Pippo asked as they walked.

"Same as always."

"And you?"

"I've got a son," said Daniele. "Boy of six."

"Fantastico!" Pippo exclaimed. "My wife and I, we've got a little girl. Two years old. Another on the way. I didn't know you got married. Congratulations."

Daniele felt the musty air of the inner passageways clog his windpipe. He coughed. "Petula and I are getting married after Easter. Fifth of May."

"Petula Tizzoni? She still as pretty as ever?"

"Prettier."

"And with wedding preparations up to your neck, you come all this way just to pay me a friendly visit?"

"I was wondering if you could help me out," said Daniele.

"Come on in here," said Pippo, unlocking a small, windowless room that the guards used as a lounge. No one else was there. "Sit," he said, pointing to an ugly sofa covered in brown imitation leather. "Can I get you a coffee?"

Sitting, Daniele looked at the old coffeemaker encrusted with dribbling stains. "I'm fine. Thanks."

Pippo pulled up a metal chair beside Daniele, and said, "*Dimmi.* What can I do for you?"

Daniele began the explanation he had rehearsed on the train. "I wanted to find out about a prisoner. Innocenti. L'Altro Innocenti. I was hoping you could—"

"L'Altro." Pippo nodded.

"Then you remember him."

"Remember? I know just about everyone in here. And it's hard not to notice someone with a name like that. Can you imagine calling your kid *L'Altro*, the Other One? Sure I know him. L'Altro the *imbroglione*. But how do you know him?"

"*Imbroglione?*" Daniele had not expected answers to come this fast. "The swindler?"

"*Sì. Imbroglione,*" said Pippo. "*Truffatore.* Con artist. Charlatan."

"And that's what they locked him up for?" Daniele was triumphant. Then again, he thought, it makes perfect sense. Look at the way the family operates. One strategy or another, they get their hands on people's cash. Wait until I tell Petula. L'Altro lives on lies. It's hardly her fault that he tricked her. The man's a professional. She'll forget him in a hurry.

"Of course that's why they locked him up," said Pippo. "Sentenced for fraud. Screwed people out of their life's savings. I can't remember how many counts." Pippo's eyebrows came together as if he had not grasped an important detail. "The help you want me to give you has something to do with him?"

"I think you've already told me what I came here to find out," said Daniele, amazed by the ease of his mission's success.

"But you tell me something," said Pippo. "Don't you want to see him?"

"What are you talking about?"

"If you want, I'll ask the chief if you can have a visit."

"I don't know what you're saying," said Daniele. "L'Altro's out."

"Why don't you tell me what the hell *you're* talking about?" Pippo shook his head. "L'Altro's not out."

"You're kidding me, right?" Daniele gave an unconvinced half-smile, not understanding why Pippo would want to tease him this way. "L'Altro's in Sant'Angelo D'Asso."

"*Aspetta.*" Pippo stood up, his pleasant face turning serious, showing no sign that he was saying anything but the truth. "Hold everything. You stay here a little minute. Let me sort this out."

During the minutes of Pippo's absence, Daniele's fingernails tugged at the stitching on the ugly imitation leather sofa. His brain tried without luck to put its thoughts in order.

"Come and see," Pippo said, poking his head back in the door of the guards' lounge, motioning for Daniele to follow him. "Our man is just where he belongs."

"But I've served him at my own bar," said Daniele as he rose from the sofa.

"Daniele, a person can't be two places at once." Pippo smiled, holding the door. "Anyway, you can ask him for yourself. They're bringing him down to the visitors' room. I don't know who it is you think you've been serving at your bar, but you can clear things up face-to-face. *Andiamo.* He'll be there in a minute."

Daniele walked behind Pippo through more passageways, more doors, the labyrinth of stone not half as convoluted as the thoughts Daniele followed in search of something that he could understand.

Pippo showed him into an airless room with a table and two chairs in the middle and another door on the far side. "I'll let you two talk on your own when he gets here," Pippo said. "You need me, I'll be right outside." He locked Daniele in.

Daniele sat and stared at the other door. When it opened, in came a young man with a face identical to the face Daniele was sure he knew. How many twins, he asked himself, can one crazy family have?

34

At closing time that evening, Petula lowered to hip level the roll-down metal shutter over the bar's door. The radio played a Neapolitan ballad about the perfect beauty of a mother's love for her son. Petula overturned all the chairs, placed them on the tabletops, swept the floor, then went to work with the mop.

Remodeling here would wait until after the wedding, but Petula and Daniele together had already picked out the materials. Not long now, she sang to herself while she mopped, and never again would she see the chipping beige plaster, the dingy wooden skirting, the metal bar-top, the mud-colored linoleum on the floor. Looking around, she could envision the place as it would become soon. Fresh stucco on the walls tinted with broad swirling brushstrokes in a mixture of sunflower yellow and soft rose, and, for the surface of the bar, lovely slabs of travertine from Rapolano. The room would be sunset-hued. When sunlight flooded through the big windows, everything would glow. Though for now it existed only in her head, she already loved the new bar.

Today the long afternoon of working alone had tired her. Dowsing the mop in the bucket, Petula felt the weariness in her arms. Daniele had phoned early in the evening, saying only that she wouldn't believe what he had discovered in Volterra and that he would tell her everything when they were face-to-face. She heard the excitement in his voice and an eagerness spread over her at the thought that Daniele's news might help rid L'Altro from her mind once and for all. Whenever

L'Altro's face came to her thoughts, it laughed in disapproval. Provincial, he had called her that night in the olive grove, as if her decision to be with Daniele proved only her fear of throwing herself into adventurous life in the bigger world from which L'Altro had come. Would she ever lose her vision of L'Altro as the face of judgment and of temptation, a vision which he, like a sorcerer, had planted inside her head?

Splashing the wet mop back onto the floor, she glanced at the clock on the wall. Forty minutes now, and Daniele should return.

Just then, she heard a knock at the roll-down shutter. Turning, she saw a pair of legs in the lower part of the doorway where the shutter remained open. "*Chiuso*," she called. "Sorry, we're closed."

"Petula." She heard L'Altro's voice. "Open up. Please."

Her stomach knotted. Think of the devil. "You should leave me in peace," she said. Looking at the open space under the shutter, she noticed that his shoes were untied.

"Please, Petula." He had the broken voice of a person devastated by tragedy. "Open up. Please."

She leaned the mop against a table, went to the door, and lifted the shutter. L'Altro's face was pale. He blinked in his effort to show a presentable expression, but too much crying, she could see, had burned his eyes red. His hair, usually sleek and well ordered, was disheveled. For a moment she wondered if it was the other brother. But the young man standing here could not be Emanuele Mosè. The frantic eyes showed all of L'Altro's sensitivity, and none of the other twin's detached indifference. Most disconcerting were the hands, for they were covered by fingerless gloves. Why wear gloves, Petula wondered, on an evening as mild as this? Even on cold nights, L'Altro's hands had always been bare.

"Are you alone?" he asked.

"Daniele will be here soon," she said, thinking, *And he'll tell me who you really are.*

"Beniamino? I would be happy to see him again."

"He's safe with my parents," she said, glad that her son was out of reach of the young man with this strange, wild look. "What's wrong?" she asked, her voice a mixture of irritation and concern.

"Everything," he replied with the urgency of a madman.

The last time Petula had seen a person this destroyed by grief, it was Daniele the night his parents died. "Is your mother all right?" she asked.

"She's fine. *La mamma, sì.* She's fine."

"Something happened to your brother?"

L'Altro squeaked a high-pitched, nervous laugh. "My brother has nothing to do with it."

The question in Petula's head was too strong to resist. "You are L'Altro, no?"

"Yes, yes. Let's say yes."

Anger came to her fast. "Answer me straight," she shot back. How dare he come here and speak in riddles? "What's the problem?"

"I'm the problem." He breathed hard, struggling not to cry. His body seemed to go limp for a moment, as if tension had exhausted his strength. "I'm sorry for disturbing you. If you don't mind, I absolutely need to talk."

"And if I do mind? Anyway, I don't see why you'd want to talk with a provincial girl like me."

He closed his eyes. "I'm sorry for speaking to you that way. I was wrong." When he opened his eyes again, tears spilled over the lower lids.

Petula stared. L'Altro's sharp, word-loving mind had succumbed, she could see, to some huge, intense emotion. Had he lost his senses? Should she be afraid? But he looked sad above all, too sad to do her harm. "I don't want to talk in here," she said. "This is Daniele's bar. And mine. There's a bench outside. Wait there. I'll close up and be out in a minute."

When he turned away, she saw that he walked as if the feet inside his untied shoes caused him pain. She put the mop and bucket away in the storage room, checked that the safe was closed tight, switched off the radio and the lights, shut the front door, and pulled down and locked the rolling shutter, dreading to find out what L'Altro had come to tell her.

———

Outside, appearing calmer for the moment, L'Altro sat in the well-lit emptiness of the station platform, no other people in sight.

Petula sat down on the bench, leaving distance between her body and his. The crystalline atmosphere around them glowed in the white glare from the lampposts, the air scented with the wild fennel that grew in clumps along the tracks. "Seems a good setting for what I have to tell you," L'Altro said bleakly. "A train station. People arrive. People leave."

"When your mother and brother first turned up here," she said, "just about everyone suspected that they wouldn't bring anything good. We should have trusted that instinct."

"You're angry with me for saying angry things to you."

"Observant, aren't you? Words hurt."

"I tell you again, I'm sorry." He went silent, collecting himself, then said, "I'll never, never forget how beautiful you were that day my mother and I came into this bar. Frighteningly beautiful. I hardly dared look at you."

"Don't twist things around," Petula said. "You weren't there. You didn't come here until Christmas Eve. First time we saw each other was in the piazza."

"Petula," L'Altro started. He stopped, his eyes avoiding hers. "Dear Petula." Fresh tears came. He looked at the palms of his glove-covered hands. "Ever played a pinball game?" he said, his voice struggling to produce words that made sense. "Anything like that?"

Why, when saying one thing, did L'Altro always have to speak about another? Petula was in no mood to follow him through a further round of verbal hide-and-seek to catch his meaning. "When I was little, maybe. Does it matter?"

"You know what it says in flashing letters at the end?"

"Something in English. So what?"

"*Game over,* is what it says. Means your time is finished. Can't play anymore." He held out his hands. "That's what happened to me.

Clearer than flashing lights. *Game over.* That's what it says here on my hands. On my feet, too."

"L'Altro, I'm tired. You say you have to talk. Fine. Tell me straight. What happened?"

"Who sent me the message?" he said, ignoring her. "Was it God, do you think? Not the God I've always imagined. But now, who can say?"

She moaned, exasperated. "Care to tell me what the hell you're talking about?"

"Petula. I saw you for the first time here at the bar when my mother and I got off the train."

"Listen, L'Altro. Do me a favor. Don't tell me I didn't see what I know I saw. That was Emanuele Mosè, not you."

"*Sì,*" said the young man. "That was me."

Petula recoiled physically, as if discovering suddenly that she was sitting beside a viper. She stared at the face, unable to discern which twin it was. "Then I'm not sure I want to talk with you like this." She shifted farther away on the bench and told him she would feel more comfortable speaking with L'Altro.

"Petula, it's me." He slid closer to her.

"Who are you?" she said, starting to panic. "I don't understand."

"You can if you try. The truth couldn't be simpler."

"Then explain, damn it!"

"Isn't it evident?" He coughed as if confession hurt his throat, already raw from crying. "How can you not see?" His voice rose. It seemed incredible to her how, in his anguish, the young man changed moods from one second to the next. "Is a little hair gel all it takes? A pair of gloves, different clothes, different posture, a different way of modulating the voice? My God! Is fooling people as easy as that? It's *me,* Petula," he urged, his voice turning high-pitched. Then he fell silent. "Relax," he said with sudden softness. "It's me. The Emanuele Mosè who got off the train and came through the door of the bar, the brother, L'Altro, who walked up the street on Christmas Eve, we're the same. Can't you see? There's only one of us. I've been telling you in a thousand ways since we met. Is a thing A or not-A? It's neither. It's both."

"L'Altro?"

"That's me."

"You can't be Emanuele Mosè."

"I can," he said. "I am."

Petula had fallen into a distorted world where people were the opposite of who they appeared to be. This has to be a dream, she told herself. If I try hard, I can wake up.

"Think," he said, appearing a lunatic in her eyes. "The first time you saw L'Altro, where was Emanuele Mosè?"

"In the house," she remembered. "He went to bed early. He said he had to pray."

"The garden shed in Signor Cappelli's yard," Emanuele Mosè explained, "the shed just below the bathroom window. If that shed hadn't been there, I would have had a hell of a jump to reach the ground."

Petula's equilibrium lurched off center. She felt the wooden bench beneath her turn to stretchy rubber and she watched the solid pillars of the station platform warp. Her woozy head became top-heavy. Had she ever seen the twins together, not just on Christmas Eve but at any time? "But Signor Cappelli," she said. "I thought he spent time with you all."

"Never both twins at once." A little excuse about the other brother's absence was enough to convince Cappelli. An honest person himself, Cappelli did not look for deceitfulness in others. "That's what makes him trust too much," Emanuele Mosè said.

"You're a monster," Petula said, starting to stand up. She wanted to run away. "A monster with two heads."

"Don't say that!" Emanuele Mosè grabbed her wrist and pulled her back to the bench. "Please," he begged, his eyes leaking tears like the eyes of a child. "You're the only woman I've ever loved." He clung to her wrist while he sobbed.

Hearing the word *love* come from his lips made Petula queasy. Forcefully she yanked her wrist away. When he touches me, she thought, I wish I could change my skin.

"You're the only one," he said again. "The first. I want no one else."

"Who *are* you?" she said, disgusted, shocked. "I don't even know your name."

Emanuele Mosè's words assumed the singsong of a nursery rhyme as, weeping, he recited the only story he had ever been told of his own identity. "When Mamma was a maiden, younger than you or I," he sniffled, "a voice told her to enter the church, and there the voice announced that she would give birth to a boychild—"

"Not this again," Petula said. "You've told me this before." Her tolerance of the tale of miraculous conception had run out. She wanted truth. "Then you really are the scary brother," said Petula, "and the L'Altro I thought I knew was just a lie. Is that what you're saying?"

"I'm not so scary," Emanuele Mosè said, wiping his eyes on the back of his gloves, "if you look past the mask."

"Is there anything real behind the mask?" she said. "Or is there just another mask?"

"There's the face you've kissed."

His words, she knew, meant to touch her sentiments, but she was too horrified to be moved. "And L'Altro?" she said. "He's just an illusion you created, isn't it?"

"He's real enough, but you've never met him," said Emanuele Mosè. "Still in Volterra. Still in jail."

Then this is what Daniele found out, she thought, what he'll tell me as soon as he gets back. The twins who had come to town were one person. The other twin did exist but was still locked up. Why the Innocenti family should manipulate reality so thoroughly, she had no idea. And the strange part was that Petula felt sad, as if she *missed* L'Altro. She could not help wishing that the Emanuele Mosè who sat beside her would go away and that the L'Altro she had made love with would come to comfort her. But reason told her that the L'Altro whom she had cared about was none other than the distraught young man on the bench with her now. However hard she tried, she could not hold both notions of L'Altro in her head at once.

Not daring to look Petula in the eye, Emanuele Mosè told her of his brother's guilt as a con man who took people's money without losing a second's sleep. "I love him, of course. But he was born with-out a conscience. Maybe it's not his fault. What hope did he have? Mamma has spent our lifetime wishing he hadn't been born."

"So *he* is the deceiver and you're not," said Petula. "Is that what you expect me to believe?"

"How can I point a finger at him without pointing it at myself? If he's a criminal, then what am I?" The answer caught Petula off guard. Since when was Emanuele Mosè prepared to accuse himself? What did self-recrimination mean when it came from the mouth of a person who until now had done everything to seem a saint?

"You're no better than your brother in prison," said Petula. "You do whatever it takes just to get a little cash."

Emanuele Mosè raised his eyes and watched a pair of bats that swooped in the light of the lampposts. "People have always wanted to donate in return for being healed. Sometimes a lot."

"Donate!" Petula echoed in disbelief. "You're not seriously telling me there's any truth to your act as the great mystic healer, are you?"

"We've never asked for a cent. That much is true."

"No," Petula said, "you just make them think they'll be cursed for eternity unless they empty out their bank accounts into your pockets."

"The decision to give or not is theirs," Emanuele Mosè said with-out looking at Petula. His crying had stopped. He spoke dispassion-ately for the moment, discussing his life as if analyzing another person's past. People paid, he said, for what they believed they were getting, as Rosa Spina always pointed out. When they locked up L'Altro, Rosa Spina decided it was time to leave the town they were in. They moved from one to another, but no place welcomed them. "Then Mamma looked at the map," Emanuele Mosè said, "and picked this part of Tuscany."

Petula laughed dryly. "Aren't we blessed?"

Emanuele Mosè's shoulders slumped. An inner compulsion pushed him to speak, to purge himself and make everything plain. He breathed in deeply, mustering strength. Then he began to recount, his voice faltering while he spoke.

Rosa Spina had not at first pinpointed Sant'Angelo D'Asso as their destination, he said, but even before they got off the train, they heard other passengers from here talk about nothing but all the bad luck in town. Rosa Spina whispered to him that the Lord had led them to the right place, because where there's bad luck, people will be in need of prayer.

Petula listened. By listening, she hoped, she would make herself free.

As to why he had to pretend to play the part of L'Altro as well as himself, that, naturally, was Rosa Spina's idea. "Only Mamma could be that imaginative," he said. The reason for presenting the town with two brothers and not just one was the same principle that underlay the walnut shell game to which Nuzzi had fallen victim. If the thug with the shells had been standing there working the players on his own, poor Nuzzi never would have got involved. What roped him in was the shill, the other man in the crowd who played the role of the outraged victim. "People join in the game when there are sides to be taken, don't you see?"

He spoke a flood of words. Like a reluctant magician who had been forced to perform against his will, he could not wait now to unveil his own tricks.

As long as he could remember, he said, his family had offered just that: clear sides. And until L'Altro's arrest, one son had fit neatly into each role, with Emanuele Mosè as the good son and L'Altro the bad. People who needed prayers aligned themselves with Emanuele Mosè. Others preferred the rebel, the freethinker. "L'Altro," he said, looking at Petula, "has always been more popular among the young."

Petula recognized L'Altro's style in the way Emanuele Mosè spoke now. For a moment she had the impression that she was back in L'Altro's company. The theory behind his discourse, clearly of crucial importance to him, interested her not at all. Only the concrete reality struck her, the fact that she had been fooled. Guiltily, Petula lowered her eyes. "I fell for it," she said.

"You didn't fall for anything," said Emanuele Mosè. "I love you for real."

"*Per favore!*" she said with sarcasm. "And who is it who says he loves me? Which role," she asked, "is really you?"

"Both," Emanuele Mosè said. "You discover new sides of yourself when you pretend to be someone else." How he sounded like L'Altro when he spoke! "I learned what it means to fall in love."

"*Vaffanculo,*" she said, "whoever you are. You can't trick me anymore."

"I'm not tricking you. I want you to know the truth."

"You've got some nerve talking about the truth," Petula laughed. "We Tuscans have a saying, you know. 'The truth is like a fart in water—it always rises to the surface.'"

"The truth is," Emanuele Mosè went on, "L'Altro is locked away in prison, but Mamma didn't want to change the setup of the game. When we got here, Mamma gave the old plan a new twist." With Emanuele Mosè playing L'Altro as well as himself, the town would divide. Needy older ladies on one side would come to pray with Emanuele Mosè. Signora Marta, people like that. The donations would come in like a flood. On the other side, the more sensible people of the town would give L'Altro a job. A regular salary never hurt. And the saner-minded crowd would admire the efforts of the ex-convict to make a decent life for his family while his mother and brother seemed more absorbed in magic spells. "You have to give Mamma credit," said Emanuele Mosè. "It worked." Rosa Spina had found a way to tap into almost everyone in town, not only the superstitious who sought to pray their problems away. Money from the steady job, more money from the prayer meetings, donations stacking up, there certainly was no shortage of cash.

Petula looked at the young man. How had the town been so gullible? How, she wondered, had she?

"Of course, there was another reason, too, for me to play both parts." Emanuele Mosè sniffed. "The reason was your fault."

"My fault?" said Petula.

"Yours and Daniele's. When we got off the train and sat in your bar, we heard the two of you arguing. Mamma paid particular attention to the part about the money in the wall safe."

"What does the safe have to do with anything?"

"Mamma figured if I"—he looked down, as if in shame—"got

close to you, Petula, you might tell me the combination. Or at least be
tempted to take money and donate some. Mamma said the safe was
full of banknotes that the Lord needed for His good work." He raised
his eyes to hers. "But you should have seen the way you looked at
Emanuele Mosè. Mamma noticed. No one fools her intuitions. She
could read on your face that the saintly son"—he smiled sadly—
"repelled you. Attraction or repulsion, no? Mamma could see the repulsion you felt for me as me. So she decided right there at the bar. A visit
from L'Altro, she figured, would have better success."

"All because of the damned wall safe!" Petula said. "But you never
even asked me about the safe."

"I couldn't bring myself to use you," he said.

"How noble," Petula said without sympathy. "Poor you. You must
have exhausted yourself with so many jobs to do."

"Tiring, yes," he admitted. His work as L'Altro in the mornings
with Nuzzi, then afternoons and evenings as himself with the prayer
groups—

"And nighttimes," she said angrily, "there were your visits with
me. Poor lamb, was that the hardest part?"

"That was different. That was love." A teardrop glistened in the
corner of his eye.

She laughed. "I don't believe a word. You're nothing but a family
of snakes. Cold-blooded as snakes. Your mother made me your *as-
signment*. Can't you see how disgusting that is?"

"I gave you my virginity." Emanuele Mosè looked in her eyes, trying to reach the part of her that had loved him, too. "Mamma certainly
didn't tell me to do that." For an instant, she saw again the vulnerable
open heart that had attracted her to him. The family plans, he said,
had never taken his romantic life into account, which was fine, he supposed, "Because I never had one until now. When I met you I didn't
know how to—how can I say this?—make an approach. I'm not the
one with experience. My brother is.

"So I started to imagine," Emanuele Mosè continued, "what L'Altro
would tell me if I asked him for advice. 'Express yourself,' is what he
would have said. 'Stop being so shy. Find a way to show her what you

feel.'" He had a tape that his brother sent him from prison, music L'Altro had first heard on Radio Madonna. L'Altro loved the music. Having learned to love it as well, Emanuele Mosè made a copy of the tape and gave it to Petula. "I figured the song could tell you what I didn't know how to say."

Petula thought of the tape of Palestrina. She thought of Daniele's transformation of the piece into his own music. In her head she heard the words of the text. *Desiderat anima mea a te.* My soul longs for you. "This is madness," she said. She scratched her head hard as if her scalp itched, trying to claw away her thoughts. "I don't trust anything you say. How can I trust a person who is twisted enough to split himself in half?"

"But I told you. The idea wasn't mine," he said. "Ever since L'Altro and I were tiny, Mamma has choreographed everything."

"Your mother must be the most evil creature on earth."

"She's family." Emanuele Mosè laughed sadly. "And Mamma is beyond good and evil. What she believes in is above opposites."

"There's something she believes in?"

"Furbizia," said Emanuele Mosè. "Good old Italian value, no? Cunning. She could have taught Macchiavelli a trick or two. 'You may be good or bad,' is her approach to people. 'You may be richer than I am. You may have more intelligence. But I have cunning on my side, so I will be victorious.'"

"Victorious, no. Heartless, yes," said Petula. "I should turn you both in to the police right now."

"Try it"—his face went stony—"and we'll be gone before the police have time to hear a word of what you intend to say. We're good at disappearing. Even better than Nuzzi's playmates in the fog."

"Doesn't it bother you, though? Or are you heartless, too?"

"Look at me, Petula. Do I look like a person at peace with his own heart?" His eyes, in fact, were the most tortured image of despair that Petula had ever seen. "You think I'm happy about the money that Mamma collected from Marta, to name only one? Thousands, she gave us."

"And wasn't it lucky for you," said Petula, "that Signora Marta died before she had the chance to change her mind? But your other benefactors are still alive. You could give the money back, you know."

Emanuele Mosè had to laugh. "Wouldn't that be nice? Good triumphs in the end and everyone learns their lesson. Is that what you expect?" He smiled. "Don't hold your breath. The money is always in Mamma's hands, not mine. Mamma never gives back. In my little way, however, I try to mitigate. Beppe Coniglio. Mamma was black with anger when I told him to put his money away. And I gave him back to the priest, you know."

"Gave him back, you say." Petula was aghast. "You talk about people like chess pieces. How about Il Piccino? You almost ruined the man."

"I *like* Il Piccino," he said, seeming sincere while he spoke, "but Mamma said it was necessary. Best issue for dividing people that history has to offer: Are you for or against the Jews? Take a side. There's nothing as precious as an enemy to make people rally around the Good Cause."

"You broke his window, didn't you?" she said, her voice rising. "You threw the rock."

"That's one thing I did not do."

"No? Then who did?"

"Your guess is as good as mine. Just shows, though, how little it takes for hatred to explode. And I get no joy from thinking that Il Piccino has suffered because of me."

"You forgive yourself too easily," she said. "You hit Il Piccino with one hand and soothed him with the other."

A new expression showed on his face as he swore he had tried to set things right. If Petula hadn't learned caution regarding this young man, she would have taken this to be the bare face of repentance. "The people who came for prayer sessions this evening, I told them that I was wrong. I told them Il Piccino had never cursed a single soul. I said they should tell everyone to give him their business again."

"An overdue act of kindness makes bad things pure? I don't think so."

"Was I bad for you?"

Anger told Petula to say yes. Listening to a different part of herself, looking at Emanuele Mosè, she spoke the truth. "Not entirely bad. No."

Emanuele Mosè smiled in gratitude for her reply. "I have to believe I did some good, Petula. And didn't I heal your father's sheep?"

He gave a rueful laugh and pulled a curlicue of thick, sharp wire from his pocket, holding it up in the bright lights of the station platform. "My new good luck charm," he said, going on to explain that at first he had no idea what to do for the sheep. He thought he'd have a look anyway to see if a little prayer might work. So he prayed, holding the sheep's head in his hands, and this wire pricked his finger. It was lodged in the soft spot at the base of the sheep's skull, just at the top of the spinal cord. With his fingernails he picked the wire out. He didn't know how it got there. Quarta must have rubbed herself against some fencepost or something. "No wonder she felt better when I took it out. Hallelujah!" he called out too loudly, seeming mad in Petula's eyes. "I smeared some mud on the spot so no one would see the speck of blood. Hosanna! Not quite the miracle that Jesus performed in the Bible, but it had a certain flair."

"Why God would want to put a miracle in your hands," said Petula, "I have no idea."

"And I even less."

"How about Mauro Giannetti?" she wanted to know. "Everyone says he died because of a curse."

"People die every day."

"And Spillo's little accident on his ladder?"

"Where's your sense of the poetic?" Emanuele Mosè said, looking away as if modestly. "Can't we leave one little mystery unexplained?"

Again, in his tone, she recognized a touch of L'Altro's sense of irony, and she could not help feeling relieved to find something recognizable in this person. Her vision of the twins began to come together, like individual rivulets of water running into each other, becoming one. The young man sitting beside her was not the rebellious ex-convict she had known; neither was he the aloof saint. Both selves had been an act, both contained elements of an identity that had not yet come to life.

"So what's your scam tonight?" Petula said. "Why did you come here to tell me the truth? Why the change of heart?"

He raised his glove-covered hands and, with a broken voice, said, "Here's the reason."

35

At the same moment, a glove-covered hand knocked on Cappelli's door.

Every living being, even one as simpleminded as a hen, can learn in time to associate an elaborate reaction with a stimulus, be it a color, a smell, a noise. Feed a hen from the same paper bag of grain every day and in not too long the hen will thrill to the rustling sound the bag makes as it is opened. "Good things are coming," thinks the hen, in whatever way it is that hens think. "I've heard the bag; food must be on its way."

So it was with Cappelli, an animal with intellectual capabilities decidedly more evolved than those of a hen. He had learned to associate the wondrous emotion of joy with the basic sound of a knock on his door at night. Repeated experience had taught him that the knock was the opening chord to a great symphony of indescribable pleasure. When there was a knock, soon there would be love.

He had bathed and shaved this evening and had just put on fresh clothes when he heard the sound. In its clean underwear, his penis gave a small electric twitch. Cappelli, aroused by the knock, was already awash in rolling waves of expectant joy. *"Avanti!"* he called out, tucking his shirt in over his belly because he wanted to appear well groomed and enticing. "Come!"

Rosa Spina stepped in. She had on the same gypsy-style clothes she had been wearing when Cappelli had first seen her at the train station: high-laced boots, cleavage-revealing dress with flowing skirt,

velvet shawl over her shoulders, fur collar at her neck, hands deco-
rated in the black lace of fingerless gloves. She held in her arms a
large box. Peering over the edge of the container, the hen's bright eye
watched Cappelli. The bird was wary, never having seen these upstairs rooms before.

"*Buonasera*, Signora Rosa Spina," Cappelli said.

"*Buonasera*, Signor Cappelli. Am I disturbing you?"

"You couldn't disturb me if you tried. Your little visits are always
a pleasure. Come. Sit."

"Thank you." Placing the box on the table, she accepted the chair
that, gallantly, he held for her. "I can't stay long, but I wanted a quick
word." Her cheeks were bright with the excited blood that pumped
beneath her skin. God had sent a miracle. Not since the annunciation
of Emanuele Mosè's birth had Rosa Spina received such a direct sign.

"What's the hurry?" Cappelli asked. "I see you're all dressed up.
Going somewhere?"

"I wanted to thank you for the infinite kindness you have shown
my sons and me. *Ostrega,* what a generous person you are!" She could
not wait to leave. "You've made us so happy here."

"If this is a happy place for you, then that makes me happy, too. In
truth, I'm the one who should be thanking you if anybody is to be
thanked. Thank you for your thanks, but really there's no need.
What's to thank?"

"I wanted to say good-bye." Her elaborate lips opened to show a
beautiful smile. Staying in this town had become impossible. That
was what the miracle told her, though she could say nothing about
this, of course, to Cappelli. Time for a big city again, she knew. Time
to cast a broader net to reach more souls than any small town could
provide.

"You're leaving?" Cappelli's neck tightened. "What does that
mean?"

With delicate feminine fingertips she touched his large fleshy
hand. "I'll never be able to repay your hospitality. I can only pray that
the Lord will find a way to reward you for your goodness." Excitement made her heart flutter with every breath.

"Rewards from the Lord aren't what interest me, thanks just the same. Leaving, you say? And when are you coming back?"

She did not answer with words. With her eyes smiling into his, she slowly shook her head.

"Why leave?" Cappelli insisted. "Did anything happen to you or the boys? Did somebody do something bad to you? Tell me who it was and I'll make them more than sorry. People are funny sometimes in a town like this. They say things without thinking. They don't mean to cause offense. Who was it? Tell me and we'll set them straight."

"Nothing like that," she said with a light laugh.

"Was it me?" Cappelli said, his face quick to show his shame. He would not have been surprised if she accused him of some accidental wrongdoing. He was, he knew, a *rozzo*. One of life's uncouth. He had been astonished that a woman of her worldly refinement should find pleasure in his company. It seemed probable to him that in his ill-mannered crudeness he had unknowingly done her some disservice. A word from her mouth, and he would prove how ready he was to atone.

She took his hand and pressed it to her lips. "You've been an angel." She shook her head. "Our leaving has nothing to do with any person's blame. The call that bids us leave is not human." Her ecstatic eyes seemed to ask why he was slow to understand. "It's the voice of God."

"God spoke to you? Here, in my house? Why would He do that?"

What fondness there was in her face! She smiled as if Cappelli, simple soul that he was, could not make sense of a concept that any child could grasp. "The voice of God doesn't always speak in words. But it illuminates the path, and when it does, you have no choice but to follow."

"And this path would be one that leads away from here?" Cappelli could remember no similar pain in his life.

"*Sì.*" She nodded.

"And where will this path take you to?"

"That, we won't know until our journey has begun. God asks us to take the first step ourselves. For the later steps, He'll be with us as our guide."

"*Certo,*" Cappelli said, understanding not a thing. "Of course.

But—" Why did words never come to him when he needed them most? "That is, *cioè*, I mean to say, and I think you understand this, too, that between you and me, there was, no, there *is* a certain . . ." He put a hand to his chest to demonstrate he was talking about the heart.

"But naturally!" she said, her voice as fresh as that of a little girl. "That won't change ever. There will always be a special Signor Cappelli–shaped place in the profoundest part of my heart."

"*Sì*, but why only have a Signor Cappelli–shaped place when you can have all of Signor Cappelli himself?"

"You are such a dear person," she laughed. "I knew from the beginning that we perceived things in the same manner. We are both travelers on the long road of life, and it was our divinely appointed destiny to walk a portion side by side. You have been a marvelous companion for this brief stretch. A comfort. A friend. A passionate lover—"

He interrupted the flow of her words with a sentence that left his throat before he had time to close his mouth. "*Mi vuoi sposare*, Signora Rosa Spina?"

"Marry?" she said, surprised.

"Yes. Do you want to marry me?" he repeated, hardly believing that he had heard himself say what he had just said.

A great breath left her bosom, but the smile stayed on her lips. Her eyes looked into his, and Cappelli was frightened by what he saw. In her eyes there was strength, passion, coldness, vulnerability, comfort, maternal protectiveness, child-devouring hunger.

When she spoke at last, she said in her girlish voice, "You are a good man, Signor Cappelli. Were it up to me, I might even be tempted to entertain a thought or two of keeping you to myself forever. But certainly it would be wrong to ever dream of locking a free man like you in the cage of marriage. Be reassured. And now the call has come from the Lord, so I must put aside what might have been my weak and womanly temptations. I know that you have seen things this way from the start, that our days together—our nights—would not be numberless, and could never last beyond this little piece of road. This is how you've seen things, no?"

What could he say? Her smile, her voice, her imperturbable eyes placed her beyond his reach. Her perfumed body sat with him still, but a nameless part of her had left. On its voyage already. Far away. The mysterious intimate thing inside of her that he had held, that he wanted to cling to forever, was here no more. He wanted to howl like an abandoned baby. He knew he must make himself behave like a man instead. "Absolutely," he said, betrayed by his own mouth. How could it speak words that were so untrue? "Of course," he said, "a woman like you" (seeing her as a princess) "and a man like me" (seeing himself as an old and ugly dog). "Of course. Me, married?" He forced a laugh. "Not in this lifetime, *Madonna porca!*"

He called the Blessed Mother a sow on purpose. Since spending time with this woman, he had grown ashamed of his own unthinking habit of punctuating every phrase with an imprecation against the Holy Virgin. At work it was one thing, or in the company of men at a bar. But he had cleaned up his speech whenever Rosa Spina was around. Now, however, he meant to swear. In defiance, he wanted to prove to her and to himself that he was capable of being once again the person he had been before.

Hearing the blasphemy, Cappelli did not feel like the same person he had always been. The words sounded ugly, even to him. He waited for rebuke. None came, and Cappelli was sure that her silence proved that she no longer cared.

"You're certain you have to go?" he said.

"I'm sure."

"When?"

"I've packed our things. One of my sons seems to have stepped out for a moment. But he should be back soon. We're taking the late train."

"I can help you with your bags."

"No need. We travel light. What we have, my sons can carry. I will ask you, though, to take care of this pretty hen. She's grown used to living in human company. I know you'll give her a good home."

Cappelli looked at the hen in the box. The hen said, *"Clo-clo-clo?"*

"You can't leave," Cappelli said, unable to hide his desperation. "You never even called me by my name."

"I asked you once but you wouldn't tell me."

Cappelli stared at the floor. And then his words came out of him as if he were a spigot. "Your apartment downstairs used to be my grandmother's. I told you that, no? She would call me by my name when I was a kid. Parents, too, I guess. Once they all died, everyone else called me Cappelli. Just as well. My first name is too old-fashioned. If people in town knew what it was, they'd only make fun. My boss, Renato, knows. He has to sign my paycheck. But he keeps quiet about it. Other people wouldn't be so nice. Mothers and fathers don't give this name to their sons anymore, not if they love them."

She smiled. "What's your name?"

Cappelli eyed the hen, then his own calloused hands, pink from his bath. "Giacinto," he confessed.

"Hyacinth?" she said.

"*Sì.* Hyacinth," he said, mortified. "Not an easy name for a man to have."

"Giacinto Cappelli." She lifted her lace-gloved hand and caressed his cheek. "A beautiful, beautiful name."

"Too beautiful for my tastes."

"No more beautiful than the soul to whom it belongs. There's no reason for anyone to make fun. Whenever I think of you, which will be very often, I'll think of who you really are. *Mio carissimo* Giacinto. The dearest man I've ever known."

She raised her lovely face, waiting until he pressed his mouth to her cushiony lips. Kissing her, he put a hand on her miraculous breast, finding it impossible to believe that she was going away, that he would never touch her again. He had seen it in a thousand old films: the condemned prisoner being led to the firing squad, the gallows, the ax. How does the wretch do it? he had always wondered. How can you take a step when you know your legs will walk no more? How can you breathe when, in an instant, your lungs will become eternally airless? Now Cappelli knew. You concentrate, was the answer. Concentrate with excruciating attention.

As if witnessing his own death, Cappelli concentrated on the delicate flavor of Rosa Spina's mouth, the feel of her breast, soft and fragrant as warm bread. He watched her closed eyelids as she, too, appeared to concentrate on the kiss.

She pulled away and patted his face. He was glad he had shaved. His face had become soft for her. Soon enough his bristles would return. "*Addio,* Giacinto. You've been an oasis of calm for me. May God bless you." Lightly she kissed his mouth.

"Not *addio,*" he said, his mind racing to find something that might make her stay. "Please. *Aspetta,*" he said, and he held her by the wrist wrapped in its *coroncina* of rosary beads. "Wait. What if you're wrong? What if it wasn't really the voice of God that spoke to you?"

"But it was."

"What if it wasn't? What if it was an illusion?"

"It's no illusion, dear Giacinto. I've never been more certain. But even if it were, I would follow the voice all the same." Her face was luminous in Cappelli's eyes. "Everyone needs illusions," she said, "no?"

He cleared his throat and let go of her wrist. "I don't understand the voices and things like that. I don't know why they'd call you away. But you ever hear a voice from God saying that He's changed His mind, you know where to find me. I'm not going anywhere. Door's always open. You can come back."

A final kiss from her lipsticked lips, and she left.

Cappelli stared at the door while he listened to her footsteps go down the stairs. He did not understand what she meant about illusions, but that was no surprise. Only rarely had he understood any word coming from her lovely mouth.

Cappelli turned and looked around him, at the walls, at the light over the table, at the sink, at the bed. Everything around him was well scrubbed and orderly, thanks to her. Furniture wax and glass polish scented the air. He would rehire Carla the cleaning lady to give him a hand around the place, but he knew his house would lose the beauty it had acquired under Rosa Spina's care.

"*Accidenti a me,*" he said aloud, hating himself for how much he hurt, hating the person he had been before he knew her. "Damn me."

She had made him feel young, and graceful, and clean. Even as he stood, he sensed an achy tiredness in his knees and in his back. Inside his trousers, his penis was lifeless: poor limp conduit, relegated once again to only its less lofty use. He did not want to return to his old self. He was not the same person as before.

Why, he wished he understood, had he bothered to love when there was no one to receive what he was prepared to give? Cappelli did not know whether he believed in God or not. It was not a question that had ever required his thought. In this moment, aware of his loneliness for the first time, he was almost tempted to pray that some benevolent force in the universe might send him someone. Her. Someone. Soon.

He sniffed the shirtsleeve of the hand that had touched her breast. He could still smell the spice of her perfume.

"Damn me," he said, walking toward the table with painful knees. He sat down and stroked the pretty, shiny feathers of the hen in the box.

Its glassy eye reciprocating the stare of the gray-haired man, the hen said, "*Clo-clo-clo?*"

36

Lifting his palms, Emanuele Mosè said to Petula, "It happened this evening right before people came for their prayers. It took all my strength not to run away at once."

"What's the story with the gloves?" Petula nearly shouted. "Do you expect me to tremble? *Basta!* Show me your damned hands."

The fever of emotion seized him once more as he pulled off the black woolen gloves. His hands, like those of a boxer, were wrapped to the wrist in white gauze.

"You tried to kill yourself," said Petula, imagining how much the cutting of flesh must hurt.

Tears falling again, he said, "Worse."

With the finger of one he raised the gauze bandages to show the pad of cotton pressed to the palm. "There was this flow coming out," he said. His body began to tremble.

Petula's stomach turned when she saw the cotton wet with fresh red blood.

"I ran to the bathroom and washed and washed." He cried while he spoke. "The blood kept coming." His voice sounded half exalted in mystical trance, half ravaged by terror. "My hands," he said. "And my feet." With shaking fingertips, he lifted the cotton pad. In the center of each palm a hole gaped, large as the irises of the stricken eyes that searched Petula's face for a reassuring sign.

"*Madonna*," said Petula, too stunned to formulate a more complete thought. "The stigmata?" she said, incredulous. "Is this some sick trick?"

His desperate eyes wide, Emanuele Mosè said, "It's no trick. I wish it were."

"Let me see," Petula insisted, unable to resist grasping the young man by the wrists. She lifted the bandages and examined the palms. The holes were deep enough to reveal the muscles inside. "You did this to yourself?" Petula asked, releasing him. "You're crazy enough."

"But not brave enough," Emanuele Mosè said. "I didn't do this."

There had to be an explanation, she thought. "Then you did it with your mind."

"You tell me," said Emanuele Mosè. "How hard would a person have to concentrate to make his hands and feet bleed?" They both stared at the hands, perforated like the hands nailed to the cross inside the church.

Never had Petula given any credence to newspaper or radio stories about supposedly God-sent signs. And from what L'Altro had told her of his philosophy, she knew that manifestations of this sort were equally foreign to his thoughts. But neither she nor he could deny the tangible reality of the blood on his hands. Whatever the meaning of the wounds, she found herself feeling concern for the person who had been so close to her heart.

Petula touched his wrists again to steady him, but he shook beyond control. She had always believed L'Altro to be extraordinary. Not L'Altro, she reminded herself. Emanuele Mosè. She thought she had known him, only to learn that he was not the person he seemed. Now gruesome marks of blood had come to him, as if to designate him as a singular child of destiny indeed. She saw a different Emanuele Mosè from the grim, priestly pose. No longer repulsive, but human and afraid. Maybe she knew nothing of his character. Was he a criminal or a saint? And he, humbled by the signs on his hands, appeared to know even less of himself.

Emanuele Mosè looked around the station. It was a photograph of stillness: black windless sky, cold white light from the lampposts, gray hardness of the platform, parallel lines of the train tracks converging toward the fennel-fragrant darkness far away. The only motion was the swirling flight of moths and bats. Emanuele Mosè said, "Come with me. Please. The last train leaves here at midnight. Mamma and I will be on it. Come with us. Don't marry Daniele. Marry me."

"You can't be serious," she said. "I don't even know who you are."

"You know me better than anyone does. A name is not what counts."

"You're a stranger to me. What am I supposed to believe? And what is this?" She gestured to his hands. "Tell me who you are."

He opened his mouth to speak, but the tears running down his cheeks made words difficult. "I don't know." He shook his head. "Mamma says a miracle has come to us again," he wept, delirious with misery. "Says God wants us to go to a big city. More people there. More souls to pray for. More donations. She's singing her own Magnificat. Blessed is she among women, she's always said. And with this blood, I start to wonder. What if this really is a sign from God?"

Petula said nothing.

"Why would God do this to me?" Emanuele Mosè cried. Watching his convulsive sobs, Petula thought of the way Beniamino cried when a nightmare cornered him into pure fear. "Is this punishment or reward? Is God giving me a healing tool or crucifying me for my sins? What does it mean? In God's eyes, am I good or am I bad?" He opened his mouth, panting like an animal in pain. "And in your eyes, Petula? Good or bad?"

She thought, then said, "Bad." She said, "Good." She said, "You are neither. You are both."

"Cruel!" he spat. "How can you throw my words at me like that?"

"Isn't that your truth?"

"I don't have a truth anymore." He shook his head dizzily. "I have a head full of thoughts, and I can't tell which are mine and which aren't. Don Luigi prayed that God would change me." He held his hands toward Petula. "Maybe that's *exactly* what He's doing. But is this change a blessing or a curse?" Blood dripped down his wrists.

"What's this supposed to mean?" she insisted. "I want you to tell me the truth."

"The truth is I don't know the truth."

The young man's confused suffering, she saw, was authentic. "You're scared," she said with new gentleness in her voice. Despite her horror, Petula felt compassion at seeing another person break.

"I'm terrified." Then he added, "But not only." He breathed heavily, noticing every sensation. "Dazed. Dead, I feel. Part of me is dying." Shaking in the night air, he sensed his own naked fragility, like a snake that freshly lost its skin, or a still-wet chick finally free of the egg. "I feel new," he said. Blood dripped onto his clothes. "Cleansed."

Petula sat silently and watched him cry. He appeared so young in her eyes. Beautiful and young. A life that had yet to find its shape. A potential killer, an embryonic saint. "I'll tell you who you are," she said, with unexpected and motherly warmth in her voice. "You're Pinocchio, like the book they read to Beniamino at school. You're a little boy made of wood and you haven't done enough yet to make yourself real. The holes in your hands have always been there, even if you couldn't see them. They're for tying you with string." She took a paper tissue from her pocket and wiped the blood from his wrists. "I know how your mind works. You'd love to see yourself as a tragic marionette worked by the hand of God. And you're clever enough with words to convince even yourself that Jesus was no different. You'd love to put you and Jesus on the same level, as if Jesus and you were an equal pair of God's toys. But don't flatter yourself. God gets little chance to play with you while your mother is keeping you all to herself. Your mother's puppet is who you are, her shell game." She threw the tissue away in a garbage can near the bench. "*Sì*, you're a walnut shell for now, and you'll always be empty as long as your mother is running the game." She tucked the bandages back over his wounds and patted them as a mother would soothe a child's injury.

Her words had stopped his tears. He was a reader of people; now this young woman had read him. He felt loved and less alone. "I need you," he said. "You're my salvation. Save me, Petula. Please. If you come with me, we can leave my mother. You, Beniamino, and me."

Let you near Beniamino? Petula thought. Never again. "Daniele is a good father," she said.

"A son needs a mother more than a father," said Emanuele Mosè.

"Really? Look where your mother got you."

"We can start out together. Leave the money here in the safe—"

"Magnanimous," sighed Petula. *"Grazie tante."*

"Money never mattered to me," Emanuele Mosè went on. "We can do anything, Petula, wherever you choose. The world is big."

She looked at the man she had loved and her heart was calm. "But I've made my decision," she said serenely. "Daniele and Beniamino are my home. I'm not like you. I know my life. You have to go and invent yours."

He pulled away and sat desolately against the bench. "I've lost you," he said in wonderment. "I'm not used to losing." For all he had talked in the past of the change-loving wanderer's spirit, he had found the person he wanted to be with forever, but never would she be his. He stared at Petula, here beside him on the wooden bench, unspeakably beautiful in his eyes, infinitely out of reach.

"Promise me you'll leave us in peace," she said softly. "Be compassionate, not cunning. Never come here again. Never telephone. Never come looking for me. In exchange you'll have an ally in life. One person who wants the best for you, even from a distance." She smiled. "That's my promise to you. It's not much, but it's not so little either."

"This is unbearable, Petula. You're saying good-bye."

She lifted her hand to his tear-streaked cheek. He rested his head against her palm, as if it were the only pillow that might offer him rest.

"'The foxes have holes,'" he quoted, closing his eyes and savoring the touch of her hand, "'and the birds of the air have nests; but the Son of man hath not where to lay his head.'"

"You and your mother have bags to pack," she said with just the hint of a challenge to him in her voice. "She'll be waiting for you." She pulled her hand away and said, "Go."

Emanuele Mosè put the gloves back on over his bandages. He looked into the darkness across the tracks and, trying to find again his usual princely composure, inhaled a deep lungful of fennel-scented air, then slowly breathed out. Gathering strength to walk away, he stood up and looked at Petula's face as if to memorize every detail.

"Addio," she said with a smile. "Whoever you are."

He started to go away, but stopped, turned, and opened his mouth to speak. Thinking better of it, he closed his lips, leaving no final comment, only an unspoken word.

She watched the young man's back as he walked along the platform. Black-winged bats swooped and angel-like moths fluttered in the white light of the lamps high above his head.

Petula sat alone on the bench for many minutes.

Suddenly, though alone in the station, she said aloud, "I found the solution." Something had reminded her of the riddle L'Altro—or Emanuele Mosè pretending to be L'Altro—had asked in the bar: two twins sitting at a fork in the road through the desert. One twin tells only the truth, the other only lies, though you can't be sure which twin is which. With a single question to a single twin to find out the road to the oasis and avoid the road to death, what would you ask?

I know the answer, Petula thought now. I would speak to either twin and ask him, "Which road would your brother recommend?" and then I would take the other road. You'll never know which brother is the liar and which the lover of truth, but that doesn't matter. Listen to either, listen to them both, and go the opposite way. That's all that counts if you want to stay alive.

A white dot of light appeared in the darkness up the tracks, the train too distant to be heard. Then, as the nearing headlight grew brighter, the sound came. Over the crackling loudspeaker, Enzo's nasal voice announced the arrival.

The southbound train braked to a stop, let out a single passenger at the far end of the platform, waited to make sure that there were no passengers to board, then blew its whistle and rumbled away.

Petula recognized the figure running toward her in the lamplight, the welcome form of Daniele's body as familiar to her as her own.

Epilogue

The first Saturday in May, early morning rain bathed Sant'Angelo D'Asso. Drops fell from the low-lying clouds, then splashed against the stones of the roads and buildings, each pearl of water brief, like the lives of the people who inhabited the town. Water, in the end, is stronger than rock. Single drops flow together, softening stony corners before soaking back into the earth.

The rain that veiled the dawn now was benign, different from the harsh deluges that had plagued the town last autumn. This springtime rain destroyed no harvest but pumped the valley full of life. And people waking today no longer paid attention to notions of bad luck. *Sfortuna* had passed, already forgotten, as natural as the change of seasons. Who needed miracle workers? The Innocenti family had gone. Almost everyone in Sant'Angelo D'Asso was eager for memory of them to fade. Death and trouble, forever cyclical, were sure to reappear. But why worry, when once again a fresh spring had exploded into bloom?

By the end of breakfast, a comfortable sun pushed away the rain. Generously watered, the green hillsides glowed with red swaths of poppies and purple flecks of violets. Hyacinths ringed the budding cherry, peach, and plum trees, every vigorous blossom a petaled proof of the earth's effort to bear a thousand kinds of fruit. The sky sparkled, pristine blue.

This morning, people in town were pleased it had rained. *"Sposa bagnata, sposa fortunata,"* the old motto maintained. A rained-on bride

is a fortunate bride. On a wedding day, everybody knew, a cloud-
burst promises good luck, not bad.

The town roiled with activity. So much to be done, and at the last
minute! Renato set up the tables in the garden as soon as the rain
stopped. Il Piccino, his unshaken monotheism intact, worked busily
in the church, placing a booklet on every seat. He had connections in
the printing business. The booklets to be used during the ceremony
were his gift to the couple, along with the printed invitations.

Don Luigi, off crutches now, readied his vestments in the sacristy.
Only three days ago, he had been obliged to perform yet another funeral: Beppe Coniglio's. The priest, heedful of Emanuele Mosè's advice to keep an eye on the dying man, had gone to give the last rites.
No sooner had Beppe swallowed the Host than his soul, qualmless,
disappeared from his body, leaving it as inanimate as clay. Anxious to
put death behind him, Don Luigi was glad for today's wedding. Too
many townspeople had died this past winter. Better the bright bou-
quets of marriage than the sad carnations of death.

Members of the band, entrusted with music for the ceremony, took
instruments out of their cases. Maestro Baldesi set up the music
stands in neat order, not displeased by the band's performance of the
Verdi medley at the recent Easter concert.

Also in church, Maria Severina grunted orders. She and Tonino
were paying for the flowers. Maria Severina insisted on double-
checking the floral arrangements in person, for she did not trust the
florist not to sneak in a wilted flower or two in the hopes of passing it
off as fresh.

Tonino organized the cars to take immediate family to the church.
Yesterday evening Cappelli had helped wash the car that would
carry the bride. Proud of Petula, he willingly participated in the preparations. But Rosa Spina's absence pained him still, and he could not
believe he had come so close to marriage himself. Now that he had
glimpsed that possibility, he wondered if there would ever be a day
when he could celebrate as groom.

Daniele had surprised Petula by insisting on last night's sleeping
arrangements. Weddings bring out the superstitious side of the

unlikeliest people. He would take care of Beniamino, he promised. He would get the boy washed and dressed in his first real suit. Petula was to spend her last night as a single woman in the bedroom of her parents' house and that was that. Daniele wanted to do nothing to risk a curse.

Beniamino was thrilled with his role as ring bearer. At this very moment, Renato and Tonino went off to pick him up.

Liberated from their stall, the four sheep showed off their shampooed fleece. During the feast in Renato and Milena's garden, the four sheep would wander among the guests. Folk wisdom held that sheep at a wedding meant good fortune. A pretty red ribbon adorned Lola's neck.

Just beneath Petula's open window, the flowers of the old wisteria vine gave off inebriating perfume. In came the sound of wedding bells—rigged by Nuzzi—from the center of town across the river.

Following the line of Petula's spine upward from the waist, Tita Vezzosi took care not to force the crisp fabric of the gown as she worked the silk-covered buttons into their eyelets one by one. The dress Petula wore was like the woman who had sewn it: unpretentious, yet radiant with simple grace.

Hairpins between her lips, Milena, overwhelmed by her daughter's beauty, worked orange blossoms into Petula's hair.

Petula had always imagined brides to be frantic females in the midst of nerve-wracking flurry, but there was nothing frenzied in what Petula felt this Saturday morning in May.

Finishing their work, the women stood back and admired. "Petulina," said Milena, kissing her on the cheek, holding back tears. Then, with her thumb, she rubbed away the lipstick smear.

Outside, the car pulled in fast and crunched on the gravel of the drive. Beniamino honked the horn.

Renato, finely dressed himself, felt emotion thicken in his throat when he came in to the bedroom and saw his daughter. "My little girl," he said, hugging her gently so as not to spoil her perfection. Daniele was waiting in church, he said. Everyone was standing in the piazza. Time to go, he told her. "Oh. The postman said these are all for you." He handed her a stack of greeting cards and telegrams from distant relatives.

The address on one plain envelope showed handwriting that Petula recognized at once. She had seen it before on the "Sicut Cervus" tape.

Telling Renato, Milena, and Tita she would be down shortly, she asked them to give her a moment. When they left her alone in the bedroom, Petula opened the envelope and read.

Emanuele Mosè had written to her on the kind of brown paper you buy bread in. His letter explained how he had left his mother at the train station in Bologna, to make her way and cast her own spells without him.

> You asked me who I am. If you'll permit me a bit of self-aggrandizement, I'll answer with the words that God spoke (yes, I can hear you smiling) when Moses asked Him to state His identity: "I will be what I will be." I'm no closer to understanding the signs of blood on my hands, but something pushes me on to search for a sense of who I might become.

She read, too, his warning about his brother, who had been intrigued by Daniele's visit, intrigued by Petula.

> While Mamma and I were in your town, I wrote letters to L'Altro. I told him about the most important thing in my life, which is, of course, you. He says you seem like the kind of woman he has waited a lifetime to meet.
>
> He is more dangerous than I am. Naturally, it would be up to you to decide if you like him or not.

Emanuele Mosè vowed to respect her wishes and leave her in peace, but he could not promise her that L'Altro would stay away from Sant'Angelo upon his release.

> Be careful. I will never be the person stepping off the train. If you see my face again, it will be L'Altro's, not mine.

Above the signature, Emanuele Mosè swore his love for her.

With a pang, Petula wrapped the letter in a handkerchief and put it in her drawer, in an old box where she kept treasured souvenirs from her girlhood. Not everything was meant for Daniele's eyes.

She looked at herself in the mirror on the wall, the only human presences in the room a woman and her reflection, two maidens draped in immaculate white.

Her heart quickening, she shook her head and shoulders as if shaking off the past, lifted the skirts of her wedding dress, and left the bedroom of her childhood.

Beyond the threshold outside, the bright air of spring vibrated with the clangor of church bells. In the piazza, the people of Sant' Angelo D'Asso awaited their newest bride.